Fragment From a Lost Diary
and Other Stories

FRAGMENT
FROM A LOST DIARY
and Other Stories

Women of Asia, Africa, and Latin America

EDITED BY
NAOMI KATZ AND NANCY MILTON

PANTHEON BOOKS
A Division of Random House, New York

Library of Congress Cataloging in Publication Data
Katz, Naomi, 1931–   comp.
    Fragment from a Lost Diary and Other Stories.
    1. Short stories, English—Translations from foreign literature. 2. Women—
Fiction.
    I.   Milton, Nancy, 1929–   joint comp.
    II. Title.
PZ1.K178Fr3   [PN6071.W7]   808.83′1   73-7014
ISBN 0-394-48475-4

Myrtha Afelia Chabran translated "Times Gone By" and
"Cotton Candy" for this edition.

"Benediction," "Ah Ao," and "Fragment from a
Lost Diary" are from *Living China*,
edited by Edgar Snow (London: George
G. Harrap & Co., 1936).

Manufactured in the United States of America
by Haddon Craftsmen, Scranton, Pennsylvania

FIRST EDITION

ACKNOWLEDGMENTS

The following material is reprinted by permission of the publishers.

Cambridge University Press: "Recitation of the Bride," from *Yoruba Poetry* by Ulli Beier. Copyright © 1970 by Cambridge University Press.

David Higham Associates, Ltd.: "The Truly Married Woman" by Abioseh Nicol.

East African Publishing House: "Mrs. Plum," from *In Corner B* by Ezekiel Mphahlele. Copyright © 1967 by Ezekiel Mphahlele. "A Woman's Life" by Marjorie J. Mbilinyi, from *Ghala—East Africa Journal,* January 1972. Copyright © 1972 by East Africa Cultural Trust. Excerpts from *Song of Lawino* by Okot p'Bitek, and from *Song of Ocol* by Okot p'Bitek. Copyright © 1970 by Okot p'Bitek.

Harper & Row, Publishers, Inc. and William Morris Agency, Inc., on behalf of the author: "Who Cares?" from *Gifts of Passage* by Santha Rama Rau. Copyright © 1958 by Vasanthi Rama Rau Bowers.

Liveright Publishing Corp.: "Woman" by Fu Hsuan, translated by Arthur Waley, from *Lotus and Chrysanthemum,* edited by Joseph Lewis French. Copyright 1927 by Boni & Liveright, Inc.

Richard Rive: "Resurrection," from *Modern African Prose* edited by Richard Rive. Published by Seven Seas Publishers. Used by permission of the author.

Stanford University Press: "Wedding Dance" by Amador T. Daguio, from *Stanford Short Stories 1953* edited by Wallace Stegner and Richard Scowcroft. Copyright 1953 by the Board of Trustees of the Leland Stanford Junior University.

Charles E. Tuttle Co., Inc.: "Order of the White Paulownia" by Tokuda Shūsei, from *Modern Japanese Stories: An Anthology* edited by Ivan Morris.

The Regents of the University of California: Poem from *The Bamboo Grove* edited by R. Rutt, University of California Press, 1971.

Yale University Southeast Asia Studies: "On the Outskirts of the City" by Rosman Sutiasumarga and "Inem" by Pramoedya Ananta Toer, from *Six Indonesian Short Stories* by Rufus S. Hendon, 1968.

To the Women of Vietnam

Mother-in-law, don't fume in the kitchen
    and swear at your daughter-in-law.
Did you get her in payment of a debt?
    Or did you buy her with cash?
    Father-in-law, tough as a rank shoot
    from a rotten chestnut stump,
    Mother-in-law, skinny and wrinkled
    as cow dung dried in the sun,
    Sister-in-law, sharp as a gimlet poking
    through the side of a three-year-old basket,
    your son has bloody feces
    and is like weeds in a field of wheat,
    a miserable yellow cucumber flower.
How can you criticize a daughter-in-law
    who's like a morning glory
    blooming in loamy soil?

                    —Anonymous, Korea

CONTENTS

PART III

INTRODUCTION

THE USEFULNESS or delight of an anthology lies finally in the extent to which stories speak for themselves. We believe that these speak strongly and well. They cover a range of experience and response which, although not comprehensive, reflects some of the realities of women's lives in Asia, Africa, and Latin America. This book was originally conceived as a collection of short stories representative of twentieth-century Third World literature. However, in the process of gathering stories from Asia, Africa, and Latin America, we found a substantial number of particularly interesting ones centered on the lives and problems of women. It was then clear that this would be one of the book's central themes, but in time, we decided instead to put together an anthology entirely devoted to stories about women. No doubt this decision was influenced in part by our own interest as women in the stories we found and in part by the current American concern with the role of women. We share this concern. However, this book does not duplicate what is being done in America, but rather attempts to bring an additional perspective to the question.

Women have figured very slightly in the recorded history of the world but not so slightly in its literature. Although the historian finds them largely absent from the power politics of the centuries, the novelist, poet, or short story writer cannot portray the life of a people without them. Consequently, although we find no definitive portrayal in literature of "the woman" of any society, we find there a richer recording of women's lives than in any other written source. That this recording, like others, has been done largely by men might be considered a weakness of fiction as a means of capturing something of the experience of women. However, having decided upon a collection of fictional accounts reflecting some of the realities of non-Western cultures, we worked with what in fact exists. We found some striking stories by women writers and others by men. We chose them on the basis of what seemed to us to be their aesthetic merit, not for their ability to fit smoothly into categories.

We agree, as Third World spokesmen have been asserting in recent years, that the primary cultural definitions must come from the "inside." These stories shed light on various problems women face in different cultures, and we have tried to organize the collection around core themes, examined in a variety of ways—psychologically, culturally, and artistically.

The stories we have chosen come not from the area of folklore, but from the repertoire of professional writers. In some cases, they are the writings of authors well-known in both their own countries and beyond; in other cases, of writers quite unknown in the West except to specialists in a particular national literature. These writers are separated from their people by all of the factors that tend to separate the intellectuals of any country from the mass culture. Nevertheless, the stories were written largely for the people of the writers' own countries, not for those outside. Many of the writers were educated in Western or Westernized universities and no doubt their perceptions and style have been influenced in the process. However, this factor is one of the realities of Asia, Africa, and Latin America in this century. At the same time, many of the same writers have lived their lives immersed in the struggle of their people for liberation—Ezekiel Mphalele, exiled finally from the struggle in South Africa, Lu Hsun, leader of the radical Chinese literary movement during the tumultuous 1920s and '30s, Nguyen Sang, writing virtually anonymously from the long revolution in Vietnam, are but a few. The writers, like their characters, thus tend to reflect much of the significant experience of their area of the world during this century. This experience includes increasing national consciousness and cultural awareness, the exploitation and influence of the West, and the break with the old traditions often followed by a re-examination and rejection of the new. The women of their stories live out many of these conflicts, intensified and complicated by their particular oppression as women. A theme central to the latter two sections of the book is that of the changing environment and the unfamiliar problems posed for women in a new, nontraditional social context. In a setting of changing reality, the woman herself changes and the many levels of perception or awareness are reflected in the stories selected.

All of the women in the book confront their situations as women; not all do so successfully or even with a consciousness of what that situation is. Like all of us, they are caught within the confines of their particular culture, history, and class and have a greater or lesser comprehension of themselves and their situation. The fact that the stories represent such a range of problems and solutions, such a diversity of cultures—different both from each other and from our own—adds yet another dimension to our understanding of the liberation of women.

The division of the collection into three sections is necessarily a fluid one, for stories from such a wide variety of countries, classes, and cultural traditions are not neatly placed within tight thematic structures. Life, after all, does not fit into the categories of its organizers. Within the first section, however, there is an inherent consistency both in the general situations within which the women find themselves and in their limited capacity to alter them. Most of the problems are centered around marriage, usually the central factor in the lives of women in the traditional societies represented. The arranged marriage is the central theme of several stories, and in the Korean "The Memorial Service on the Mountain" and the Indonesian "Inem," it is a tragedy compounded by being the arranged marriage of a child bride, the familiar companion to poverty in many peasant societies. Poverty is an integral element of most of the stories in the opening section of the book. The Chinese "Ah Ao" speaks poignantly of the ancient and ubiquitous sexual double standard and of the brutality with which it smites the daughters of the poor. Lu Hsun's "Benediction" is a monument to Chinese women helpless under the crushing weight of traditional village life. The Philippine "Wedding Dance" presents the other side of the coin—the woman, happily married and in love with her husband, but after too many years still childless and thus doomed. And from Cuba comes "Times Gone By," the story of a slave woman, now old and mated by claim of ownership to her master, and still torn by conflicting loyalties of sex, race, and class.

The women of the first section might be seen as the tragic figures of the book, for despite their efforts to cope with the tremendous injustices of their lives, their possibilities are very limited. Some of them engage in acts of courageous desperation—suicide, burnings, and flight—but these amount finally to heroic gestures, intensely personal, intensely painful, for little else is possible. They are the victims of family and social structure, of poverty and the mercilessness of custom; representative of the uncountable sacrifices to the historical position of women.

Although Part II also contains a number of stories that take place within the context of marriage, alternatives now are not only possible and perceived as such, but are themselves frequently a source of conflict. The alternatives are often very personal ones, offering perhaps only the possibility of moving and maneuvering about somewhat more comfortably within the same old confines. The West African "The Truly Married Woman" presents a lighthearted and charming solution within the domestic context. Yet more often, the new opportunities provide little comfort. While the Japanese woman of "Order of the White Paulownia," is aware of alternatives to her grim marriage, she is unable to act upon them.

Women must still cope with their particular problems as women, but they now do so in a variety of new situations. For some women, the changes pose a threat. The need to deal with a rapidly, drastically changing world challenges the women in the East African "Song of Ocol" and "Song of Lawino" and the Chinese "Fragment from a Lost Diary." Lawino finds security in the old ways and warns her husband, "Don't uproot the pumpkin." But the young Chinese student of the 1920s attempts a revolutionary solution, only to find in her pregnancy an age-old obstacle to continued action. Within the stories in Part II, one finds an interesting variety of attitudes among both men and women in the conflict between the old and the new. The new ways transform the experience of childbirth in both the African "The Message" and the Indonesian "On the Outskirts of the City," but in the latter, it is the husband's middle-class nativism and his insistence on the maintenance of tradition in his poverty which place his wife in conflict and sends her back to village and midwife for the birth of her third child.

In her sophisticated presentation, Santha Rama Rau portrays a modern professional woman of India, perhaps the author herself. Having moved out of the traditional female household position, not entirely without misgivings, she observes the continued security of the old marriage patterns. The price for independence is not exacted painlessly. The Cuban writer Dora Alonso in "Cotton Candy" speaks with brilliant artistry of another kind of woman alone—the "old maid"—and of another side of the old prohibitions, the fierce horror of sexuality and its strange delayed blooming in the old virgin.

Part III of the collection finds women in a new relationship to society, and as a consequence, in a changed relationship to men. The importance of the male/female relationship remains, to be sure, but because of their increased involvement in the larger society, women bring to it new perceptions and a sharpened awareness. Men are no longer *the* determining factor in the lives of the women portrayed. The locus of the oppression shifts from its traditional center in marriage and the family, and the stories presented here are more concerned with women in relation to the problems of the larger society. Even in Marjorie Mbilinyi's "A Woman's Life," in which a woman who has achieved professional respect independent of her husband's position is still subjected to his violent authority, there is an acute awareness of these external realities. It is, in fact, the contradiction between the woman's new independence and her old dependence that makes the story. And it is her husband's ambivalent relationship to his new social role that is at least partially responsible for his oppressive male chauvinism.

It is hardly coincidental that a number of the stories in this section are from South Africa, where problems of race and caste discrimination overwhelm problems of sex, although the combined oppression produces its own peculiar cruelty. The contrast between Mrs. Plum and her black servant Karabo is far greater than their similarity as women, and in spite of Mrs. Plum's liberal intent to dilute the differences, the distance of class and racial oppression cannot but distort and finally submerge her patronizing "good intentions." For all her self-assurance, her well cut clothes, her obvious middle-class security, the mother in "Coffee for the Road," driving her children to Cape Town, is victimized not by sex or even by class, but by the irrationality of color prejudice. And Mavis, the black daughter of "Resurrection," screams her hatred for the same oppression at the funeral of her mother, a woman doubly victimized into bending to the system that has caused her to treat her light-skinned children so differently from her dark daughter.

The possibilities for women today inevitably include revolution, and for the young Vietnamese liaison guide of "The Ivory Comb," her problems as a woman are incidental to the larger struggle she has chosen. The problems posed are those of the entire society.

Underlying some of the earlier stories is the assumption that a marriage made through choice would be the best answer to a woman's problems. However, new social developments bring not only different problems, but an awakened consciousness, and the new solutions are in no way so simple. The cause of the problems no longer seems so clearly defined. Even when it maintains the old force, as in "A Woman's Life," the role of the male as the direct oppressor has lost some of its former simplicity. Mama Thecla's daughter asks questions to which neither mother nor daughter has the answer, but they are questions which could not have been asked in a more traditional social context. Thus women in more "modern" conditions not only inherit many of the vestiges of the ancient and powerful restrictions upon their sex, but now confront the social, economic, and political questions of the larger society.

The women of the earlier part of the collection are to a large degree helpless victims of a social order and family structure which offer no possibility of a way out. For the women of the later stories, there are alternatives, but they are alternatives which bring with them new choices containing their own conflicts. So while this anthology opens with a presentation of some of the most painful problems facing women, it closes with some of the most difficult questions.

N. K.
N. M.

April, 1973

PART I

WOMAN

How sad it is to be a woman!
Nothing on earth is held so cheap.
Boys stand leaning at the door
Like Gods fallen out of Heaven.
Their hearts brave the Four Oceans,
The Wind and dust of a thousand miles.
No one is glad when a girl is born:
By *her* the family sets no store.
When she grows up, she hides in her room
Afraid to look a man in the face.
No one cries when she leaves her home—
Sudden as clouds when the rain stops.
She bows her head and composes her face,
Her teeth are pressed on her red lips:
She bows and kneels countless times.
She must humble herself even to the servants.
His love is distant as the stars in Heaven,
Yet the sunflower bends toward the sun.
Their hearts more sundered than water and fire—
A hundred evils are heaped upon her.
Her face will follow the years' changes:
Her lord will find new pleasures.
They that were once like substance and shadow
Are now as far as Hu from Ch'in.*
Yet Hu and Ch'in shall sooner meet
Than they whose parting is like Ts'an and Ch'en.†
                              —*Fu Hsüan, China*

* Two lands.   † Two stars.

BENEDICTION

Lu Hsun

THE END of the year according to the lunar calendar is, after all, the right time for a year to end. A strange almost-new-year sort of atmosphere seems to overlay everything; pale gray clouds at evening, against which flash the hot little flames of firecrackers giving a thunderous boost to the kitchen god's* ascent into heaven. As one draws into it the scene grows noisier, and scattered on the air is the sting of gunpowder.

On such a night I return to Lo Ching—my home town as I call it, but in reality I have no home there at all. I stay with Lo Shih Lao-yeh, a relative one generation older than myself, a fellow who ought to be called "Fourth Uncle," according to the Chinese family way of reckoning. He is a *chien-sheng,*† and talks all the time about the old virtues and the old ethics.

I find him not much changed; a little aged of course, but still without a whisker. We exchange salutations. After the "How are you?" he tells me I've grown fat. With that done, he at once commences a tirade against the "new party." But I know that to him the phrase still means poor Kang Yu-wei,‡ and not the Renaissance, of which he probably has not even heard. We have at any rate nothing in common, and before long I am left alone in the study.

---

* The kitchen god is supposed to report at this time to the Heavenly Emperor about the conduct of the family during the past year. He returns to earth after seven days.

† An honorary degree which is purchased.

‡ A scholar who led the attempted reform movement under the Emperor Kuang Hsu, toward the end of the Manchu dynasty. The movement was suppressed by the Empress Dowager.

The next day I get up very late, and after lunching go out to call on some relatives and friends. The day after is the same, and the day after that. None of them has changed much, each is a little older, and everywhere they are busily preparing for New Year prayers-of-blessing. It is a great thing in Lo Ching: everyone exerts himself to show reverence, exhausts himself in performing rites, and falls down before the god of benediction to ask favors for the year ahead. There is much chicken-killing, geese-slaughtering, and pork-buying; women go around with their arms raw and red from soaking in hot water preparing such fowl. When they are thoroughly cooked they are placed on the altar, with chopsticks punched into them at all angles, and offered up as sacrifices at the sixth watch. Incense sticks and red candles are lighted, and the men (no women allowed) make obeisance and piously invite the blessing-spirits to eat away. And after this, of course, the firecrackers.

Every year it is that way, and the same in every home—except those of the miserable poor who cannot buy either sacrifices or candles or firecrackers—and this year is like any other. The sky is dark and gloomy, and in the afternoon snow falls—flakes like plum blossoms darting and dancing across a screen of smoke and bustle, and making everything more confused. By the time I return home the roof tiles are already washed white, and inside my room seems brighter. The reflection from the snow also touches up the large crimson character, LONGEVITY, which hangs on a board against the wall. It is said to be the work of the legendary Chen Tuan Lao-tso. One of the scrolls has fallen down and is rolled up loosely and lying on the long table, but the other still admonishes me: "Understand deeply the reason of things, be moderate, and be gentle in heart and manner." On the desk under the window are incomplete volumes of the *K'ang Hsi Dictionary*, a set of *Recent Thoughts*, with collected commentaries, and the *Four Books*. How depressing!

I decide to return tomorrow, at the very latest, to the city.

The incident with Hsiang-lin Sao also has very much disturbed me. This afternoon I went to the eastern end of the town to visit a friend, and while returning I encountered her at the edge of the canal. The look in her staring eyes showed clearly enough that she was coming after me, so I waited. Although other folk I used to know in Lo Ching have apparently changed little, Hsiang-lin Sao was no longer the same. Her hair was all white, her face was alarmingly lean, hollow, and burnt a dark yellow. She looked completely exhausted, not at all like a woman not yet forty, but like a wooden thing with an expression of tragic sadness carved into it. Only the movement of her lusterless eyes showed that she still lived. In one hand she carried a bamboo basket: inside it was an empty broken bowl; and she held herself up by leaning on a bamboo pole. She had apparently become a beggar.

I stood waiting to be asked for money.

"So—you've come back?"

"Yes."

"That's good—and very timely. Tell me, you are a scholar, a man who has seen the world, a man of knowledge and experience" —her faded eyes very faintly glowed—"tell me, I just want to ask you one thing."

I could not, in ten thousand tries, have guessed what she would ask. I waited, shocked and puzzled, saying nothing.

She moved nearer, lowered her voice, and spoke with great secrecy and earnestness. "It is this: after a person dies is there indeed such a thing as the *soul*?"

Involuntarily I shuddered. Her eyes stuck into me like thorns. Here was a fine thing! I felt more embarrassed than a schoolboy given a surprise examination, with the teacher standing right beside him. Whether there was such a thing as the soul had never bothered me, and I had speculated little about it. How could I reply? In that brief moment I remembered that many people in Lo Ching believed in some kind of spirits, and probably she did too. Perhaps I should just say it was rather doubtful—but no, it was better to let her go on hoping. Why should I burden a person obviously on the "last road" with even more pain? Better for her sake to say yes.

"Perhaps," I stammered. "Yes, I suppose there is."

"Then there is also a *hell*?"

"Ah—hell?" She had trapped me, and I could only continue placatingly, "Hell? Well, to be logical, I dare say there ought to be. But, then again—there may not be. What does it matter?"

"Then in this hell do all the deceased members of a family come together again, face to face?"

"Hmm? Seeing face to face, eh?" I felt like a fool. Whatever knowledge I possessed, whatever mental dexterity, was utterly useless; here I had been confounded by three simple questions. I made up my mind to extricate myself from the mess, and wanted to repudiate everything I had said. But somehow I could not do so in the gaze of her intensely earnest and tragic eyes.

"That is to say . . . in fact, I cannot definitely say. Whether there is a soul or not in the end I am in no position to deny or affirm."

With that she did not persist, and, taking advantage of her silence, I strode away with long steps and hastened back to Fourth Uncle's home, feeling very depressed. I could not help thinking that perhaps my replies would have an evil effect on her. No doubt her loneliness and distress had become all the more unbearable at this time when everyone else seemed to be praying for benediction—but perhaps there was something else on her mind. Perhaps something that had recently happened to her. If so, then my answers might be responsible . . . for what? I soon laughed about the whole thing, and at my absurd habit of exaggerating the importance of casual happenings. Educators unquestionably would pronounce me mentally unbalanced. Hadn't I, after all, made it clear that all I could say was "Cannot definitely say"? Even should all my replies be refuted, even if something happened to the woman, it could in no way concern me.

"Cannot definitely say" is a very convenient phrase. Bold and reckless youths often venture so far as to offer a positive opinion on critical questions for others, but responsible people, like officials and doctors, have to choose their words carefully, for if events belie their opinion then it becomes a serious affair. It is much more advisable to say, "Cannot definitely say"; obviously it solves everything. This encounter with the woman beggar impresses upon me the importance of that practice, for even in such cases the deepest wisdom lies in ambiguity.

Nevertheless, I continue to feel troubled, and when the night is gone I wake up with the incident still on my mind. It is like an unlucky presentiment of a movement of fate. Outside the day is still gloomy, with flurrying snow, and in the dull study my uneasiness gradually increases. Certainly I must go back to the city tomorrow . . . To be sure, there is still unsampled the celebrated pure-cooked fish-fins at Fu Shing Lou—excellent eating and very cheap at only a dollar a big salver. Has the price increased by now? Although many of my boyhood friends have melted away like clouds in the sky, there must remain, at least, the incomparable fish-fins of Lo Ching, and these I must eat, even though I eat alone . . . All the same, I am returning tomorrow . . .

Because I have so often seen things happen exactly as I predicted—but hoped against, and tried to believe improbable—I am not unprepared for this occasion to provide no exception. Toward evening some of the family gather in an inner room, and from fragments of their talk I gather they are discussing some event with no little annoyance. Presently all the voices cease except one, that of Fourth Uncle, who thunders out above the thud of his own pacing feet: "Not a day earlier nor a day later, but just at this season she decides upon it. From this alone we can see that she belongs to a species utterly devoid of human sense!"

My curiosity is soon followed by a vague discomfort, as if these words have some special meaning for me. I go out and look into the room, but everyone has vanished. Suppressing my increasing impatience, I wait till the servant comes to fill my teapot with hot water. Not until then am I able to confirm my suspicions.

"Who was it Fourth Uncle was blowing up about a while ago?"

"Could it after all have been any other than Hsiang-lin Sao?" he replies in the brief and positive manner of our language.

"What has happened to her?" I demand in an anxious voice.

"Aged."*

"Dead?" My heart twinges and seems to jump back; my face burns. But he doesn't notice my emotion at all, doesn't even lift his head, so that I control myself to the end of further questioning.

"When did she die then?"

---

* Since the word "die" and its synonyms are forbidden at this season, "aged" is commonly used to describe death. Ordinarily Chinese refer to the dead as "not here," or "outside."

"When? Last night—or possibly today. I cannot definitely say."

"What did she die of?"

"What did she die of? Could it indeed be anything else than that she has been strangled to death by poverty?" His words are absolutely colorless, and without even looking at me he goes out.

My terror at first is great, but I reason that this is a thing which was bound to happen very soon, and it is merely an accident that I even know about it. I further reassure my conscience by recalling my noncommital "Cannot definitely say," and the servant's report that it was simply a case of "strangled to death by poverty." Still, now and then I feel a prick of guilt—I don't know exactly why—and when I sit down beside the dignified old Fourth Uncle I am continually thinking of opening a discussion about Hsiang-lin Sao. But how to do it? He still lives in a world of religious interdicts, and at this time of year these are like an impenetrable forest. You cannot, of course, mention anything connected with death, illness, crime, and so on, unless it is absolutely imperative. Even then such references must be disguised in a queer riddle-language in order not to offend the hovering ancestral spirits. I torture my brain to remember the necessary formula, but, alas, I cannot recall the right phrases, and at length have to give it up.

Fourth Uncle throughout the meal wears an austere look on his face. At last I suspect that he regards me also as "belonging to a species utterly devoid of human sense," since "neither a day earlier, nor a day later, but just at this season" I have put in an appearance. To loosen his heart and save him further anxiety I tell him that I have determined to return tomorrow. He doesn't urge me to stay very enthusiastically, and I conclude that my surmise was correct. And thus in a cheerless mood I finish my meal.

The short day is ended, the curtain of snow dropping over it earlier than usual even in this month, and the black night falls like a shroud over the whole town. People still busy themselves under the lamplight, but just beyond my window there is the quiet of death. Snow lies like a down mattress over the earth, and the still falling flakes make a faint suh-suh sound that adds to the intense loneliness and the unbearable melancholy. Sitting alone under the yellow rays of the rape-oil lamp, my mind goes back again to that blown-out flicker, Hsiang-lin Sao.

This woman, who once stood among us in this house, thrown now, like an old toy discarded by a child, onto the dust heap. For those who find the world amusing, the kind for whom she is created, no doubt if they think about her at all it is simply to wonder why the devil she should so long have had the effrontery to continue to exist. Well, she has obliged them by disappearing at last, swept away thoroughly by Wu Chang,* and a very tidy job. I don't know whether there is such a thing as the soul that lives on after death, but it would be a great improvement if people like Hsiang-lin Sao were never born, would it not? Then nobody would be troubled, neither the despised nor those who despise them.

Listening to the suh-suh of the leafy autumnal snow I go on musing, and gradually find some comfort in my reflections. It is like putting together an intricate puzzle, but in the end the incidents of her life fit together into a single whole.

Hsiang-lin Sao was not a native of Lo Ching. She arrived in early winter one year with Old Woman Wei, who bargained in the labor of others. Fourth Uncle had decided to change the servant, and Hsiang-lin Sao was Old Woman Wei's candidate for the job.

She wore a white scarf wrapped around her head, a blue jacket, a pale green .vest, and a black skirt. She was perhaps twenty-six or twenty-seven, still quite young and rather pretty, with ruddy cheeks and a bronzed face. Old Woman Wei said that she was a neighbor of her mother's. Her husband had died, she explained, and so she had to seek work outside.

Fourth Uncle wrinkled up his brow, and his wife, looking at him, knew what he meant. He didn't like hiring a widow. But Fourth Aunt scrutinized her carefully, noting that her hands and feet looked strong and capable, and that she had honest, direct eyes. She impressed her as a woman who would be content with her lot, and not likely to complain about hard work; and so in

* A sheriff-spirit who "sweeps up" the soul at the last breath of life.

spite of her husband's wrinkled brow Fourth Aunt agreed to give her a trial. For three days she worked as if leisure of any kind bored her; she proved very energetic and as strong as a man. Fourth Aunt then definitely hired her, the wage being five hundred cash per month.

Everybody called her simply Hsiang-lin Sao, without asking her surname. Old Woman Wei was, however, a native of Wei Chia Shan (Wei Family Mountain), and since she claimed that Hsiang-lin Sao came from that village no doubt her surname also was Wei. Like most mountaineers, she talked little, and only answered others' questions in monosyllables, and so it took more than ten days to pry out of her the bare facts that there was still a severe mother-in-law in her home; that her young brother-in-law cut wood for a living; that she had lost her husband, ten years her junior, in the previous spring; and that he also had lived by cutting firewood. This was about all people could get out of her.

Day followed day, and Hsiang-lin Sao's work was just as regular. She never slackened up, she never complained about the food, she never seemed to tire. People agreed that Old Lord Lo Shih had found a worthy worker, quick and diligent, more so in fact than a man. Even at New Year she did all the sweeping, dusting, washing, and other household duties, besides preparing geese and chickens and all the sacrifices, without any other help. She seemed to thrive on it. Her skin became whiter, and she fattened a little.

One day when New Year had just passed she came hurrying up from the canal, where she had been washing rice. She was much agitated. She said she had seen, on the opposite bank, a man who looked very much like her late husband's first cousin, and she was afraid he had come to take her away. Fourth Aunt was alarmed and suspicious. Why should he be coming for her? Asked for details, Hsiang-lin Sao could give none. Fourth Uncle, when he heard the story, wrinkled his brow and announced, "This is very bad. It looks as though she has run away, instead of being ordered."

And, as it turned out, he was correct. She was a runaway widow.

Some ten days later, when everybody was gradually forgetting the incident, Old Woman Wei suddenly appeared, accompanied by a woman who, she claimed, was Tsiang-lin Sao's mother-in-law. The latter seemed not at all like a tongue-bound mountaineer, but knew how to talk, and after a few words of courtesy got to the subject of her business at once. She said she had come to take her daughter-in-law back home. It was spring, there was much to be done at home, and in the house at present were none but the very old and the very young. Hsiang-lin Sao was needed.

"Since it is her own mother-in-law who requests it, how can we deny the justice of it?" said Fourth Uncle.

Hsiang-lin Sao's wage, therefore was figured out. It was discovered that altogether one thousand seven hundred and fifty cash were due. She had let the sum accumulate with her master, not taking out even a single cash for use. Without any more words, this amount was handed over to the mother-in-law, although Hsiang-lin Sao was not present. The woman also took Hsiang-lin Sao's clothes, thanked Fourth Uncle, and left. It was then past noon . . .

"Ai-ya! The rice? Didn't Hsiang-lin Sao go out to scour the rice?"

Fourth Aunt, some time later, cried out this question in a startled way. She had forgotten all about Hsiang-lin Sao until her hunger reminded her of rice, and the rice reminded her of the former servant.

Everybody scattered and began searching for the rice basket. Fourth Aunt herself went first to the kitchen, next to the front hall, and then into the bedroom, but she didn't see a trace of the object of her search. Fourth Uncle wandered outside, but he saw nothing of it either till he came near the canal. There, upright on the bank, with a cabbage near by, lay the missing basket.

Apparently not until then had anyone thought to inquire in what manner Hsiang-lin Sao had departed with her mother-in-law. Now eyewitnesses appeared who reported that early in the morning a boat, with a white canopy, anchored in the canal, and lay there idly for some time. The awning hid the occupants, and no one knew who was in it. Presently Hsiang-lin Sao came to the bank, and just as she was about to kneel down for water two men quickly jumped out, grabbed her, and forcibly put her inside the boat. They seemed to be mountain people, but they certainly took her against her will; she cried and shouted for help several times. Afterward she was hushed up, evidently with some kind of gag. Nothing more happened until the arrival of two women, one of whom was Old Woman Wei. Nobody saw very clearly what had happened to Hsiang-lin Sao, but those who peered in declared that she seemed to have been bound and thrown on the deck of the cabin.

"Outrageous!" exclaimed Fourth Uncle. On reflection, however, he simply ended impotently, "But after all . . ."

Fourth Aunt herself had to prepare the food that day, and her son Ah Niu made the fire.

In the afternoon Old Woman Wei reappeared.

"Outrageous!" Fourth Uncle greeted her.

"What is this? How wonderful! You have honored us once more with your presence!" Fourth Aunt, washing dishes, angrily shouted at the old bargain-maker. "You yourself recommend her to us, then you come with companions to abduct her from the household. This affair is a veritable volcanic eruption. How do you suppose it will look to outsiders? Are you playing a joke at our expense, or what is it?"

"Ai-ya! Ai-ya! I have surely been fooled and tricked. I came here to explain to you. Now how was I to know she was a rebel? She came to me, begged me to get her work, and I took her for genuine. Who would have known that she was doing it behind her mother-in-law's back, without in fact even asking for permission? I'm unable to look in your face, my lord and lady. It's all my fault, the fault of a careless old fool. I can't look you in the face . . . Fortunately, your home is generous and forgiving, and will not punish insignificant people like myself too strictly, eh? And next time the person I recommend must be doubly good to make up for this sin—"

"But . . ." interjected Fourth Uncle, who, however, could get no farther.

And so the affair of Hsiang-lin Sao came to an end, and indeed she herself would have been entirely forgotten were it not that Fourth Aunt had such difficulty with subsequent servants. They were too lazy, or they were gluttonous, or in extreme cases they were both lazy and gluttonous, and in truth were totally unde-

sirable, "from the extreme left to the extreme right." In her
distress, Fourth Aunt always mentioned the exemplary Hsiang-lin
Sao. "I wonder how she is living?" she would say, inwardly wishing that some misfortune would oblige her to return to work. By
the time the next New Year rolled round, however, she had given
up hope of ever seeing her again.

Toward the end of the holidays Old Woman Wei called one
day to *k'ou-t'ou** and offer felicitations. She had already drunk
herself into semi-intoxication, and was in a garrulous mood. She
explained that because of a visit to her mother's home in Wei
Village, where she had stayed for several days, she was late this
year in paying her courtesy calls. During the course of the conversation their talk naturally touched upon Hsiang-lin Sao.

"She?" the old woman cried shrilly and with alcoholic enthusiasm. "There's a lucky woman! You know, when her mother-in-
law came after her here she had at that time already been
promised to a certain Hu Lao-liu, of Hu Village. After staying in
her home only a few days she was loaded again into the Flowery
Sedan Chair and borne away!"

"Ai-ya, what a mother!" Fourth Aunt exclaimed.

"Ai-ya, my lady! You speak from behind a lofty door.† We
mountaineers, of the small-doored families, for us what does it
matter? You see, she had a young brother-in-law, and he had to
be married. If Hsiang-lin Sao was not married off first, where
would the family get money enough for the brother-in-law's
presents to his betrothed? So you understand the mother-in-law
is by no means a stupid woman, but keen and calculating. Moreover, she married the daughter-in-law to an inner mountain
dweller. Why? Don't you see? Marrying her to a local man, she
would have got only a small betrothal gift, but, since few women
want to marry deep into the mountains, the price is higher. Hence
the husband actually paid eighty thousand cash for Hsiang-lin
Sao! Now the son of the family has also been married, and he
gave his bride presents costing but five thousand cash. After

---

* The prostration made at this time in wishing greetings.

† That is, an upper-class family. It is not against the mother-in-law's
tyranny that Fourth Aunt protests, but her lack of virtue in remarrying her
widowed daughter-in-law.

deducting the cost of the wedding there still remained over ten thousand cash profit. Is she clever or not? Good figuring, eh?"

"And Hsiang-lin Sao—she obeyed all right?"

"Well, it wasn't a question of obedience with her. Anybody in such a situation has to make a protest, of course. They simply tie her up, lift her into the Flowery Sedan Chair, bear her away to the groom's home, forcibly put the Flowery Hat on her head, forcibly make her *k'ou-t'ou* in the ancestral hall, forcibly lock her up with the man—and the thing is done."

"Ai-ya!"

"But Hsiang-lin Sao was unusually rebellious. I heard people say that she made a terrific struggle. In fact, it was said that she was different from most women, probably because she had worked in your home—the home of a scholar. My lady, I have seen much in these years. Among widows who remarry I have seen the kind who cry and shout. I have seen those who threaten suicide. There is in addition the kind who, after being taken to the groom's home, refuse to make the *k'ou-t'ou* to Heaven and Earth, and even go so far as to smash the Flowery Candles used to light the bridal chamber! But Hsiang-lin Sao was like none of those demonstrators.

"From the beginning she fought like a tigress. She screamed and she cursed, and by the time she reached Hu Village her throat was so raw that she had almost lost her voice. She had to be dragged out of the sedan chair. It took two men to get her into the ancestral hall, and still she would not *k'ou-t'ou*. Only for one moment they carelessly loosened their grip on her, and, ai-ya! by Buddha's name! she knocked her head with a sound whack on the incense altar, and cut a deep gash from which blood spurted out thickly! They used two handfuls of incense ash on the wound, and bound it up with two thicknesses of red cloth, and still it bled. Actually, she struggled till the very last, when they locked her with her husband in the bridal room, and even then she cursed! This was indeed a *protest*. Ai-ya, it really was!"

She shook her gnarled head, bent her gaze on the floor, and was silent.

"How was it afterward?"

"They say she did not get up the first day, nor the second."

"Afterward?"

"After that? Oh, she finally got up. At the end of the year she bore him a child, a boy. While I was at my mother's home I saw some people who had returned from Hu Village, and they said they had seen her. Mother and son were both fat. Above their heads was fortunately no mother-in-law. Her husband, it seems, is strong and a good worker. He owns his own house. Ai-ya, she is a lucky one indeed."

From that time on Fourth Aunt gave up any thought of Hsiang-lin Sao's excellent work, or at any rate she ceased to mention her name.

In the autumn, two years after Old Woman Wei had brought news of Hsiang-lin Sao's extraordinary good luck, our old servant stood once more in person before the hall of Fourth Uncle's home. On the table she laid a round chestnut-shaped basket and a small bedding-roll. She still wore a white scarf on her head, a black skirt, a blue jacket, and moon-white vest. Her complexion was about the same, except that her cheeks had lost all their color. Traces of tears lay at the corners of her eyes, from which all the old brightness and luster seemed washed away. Moreover, with her once more appeared Old Woman Wei, wearing on her face an expression of commiseration. She babbled to Fourth Aunt, "So it is truly said, Heaven holds many an unpredictable wind and cloud. Her husband was a strong and healthy man. Who would have guessed that at a green age he would be cut down by fever? He had actually recovered from the illness, but ate a bowl of cold rice, and it attacked him again. Fortunately she had the son. By cutting wood, plucking tea leaves, raising silkworms—and she is skilled at each of these jobs—she could make a living. Could anyone have predicted that the child himself would be carried off by a wolf? A fact! By a wolf!

"It was already late spring, long after the time when anyone fears wolves. Who could have anticipated this one's boldness? Ai-ya! And now she is left with only her own bare body. Her late husband's elder brother-in-law took possession of the house and everything in it, and he drove her out without a cash. She is, in fact, in the 'no-road no-destination' predicament, and can but return to beg you to take her in once more. She no longer has any connections (such as a mother-in-law) whatever. Knowing you want to change servants, I brought her along. Since she already knows your ways, it's certain she'll be more satisfactory than a raw hand."

"I was truly stupid, truly," said Hsiang-lin Sao in a piteous voice, and lifting up her faded eyes for a moment. "I only knew that when the snow lies on the mountains the wild animals will sometimes venture into the valleys and will even come into the villages in search of food. I did not know that they could be so fierce long after the coming of spring. I got up early one morning, took a small basket of beans, and told little Ah Mao to sit in the doorway and string the beans. He was very bright, and he was obedient. He always listened to every word, and this morning he did so, and I left him in the doorway. I myself went behind the house to chop kindling and scour rice. I had just put the rice in the boiler and was ready to cook the beans, so I called to Ah Mao. He didn't answer. I went round to the door, but there was no Ah Mao; only beans scattered on the ground. He never wandered to play, but I hurried to every door to ask for him. Nobody had seen him. I was terror-stricken! I begged people to help me hunt for him. All the morning and into the afternoon we moved back and forth, looking into every corner. Finally we found one of his little shoes hanging on a thorn bush. From that moment everyone said that he had been seized by a wolf, but I would not believe it. After a little while, going farther into the mountains, we . . . found . . . him. Lying in a grassy lair was his body, with the five organs missing.* But the bean basket was still tightly clutched in his little hand." Here she broke down, and could only make incoherent sounds, unable to string a sentence together.

Fourth Aunt had at first hesitated, but after hearing this story her eyes reddened, and she instantly told the widow to take her things to the servants' quarters. Old Woman Wei sighed with relief, as if she had just put down a heavy bundle. Hsiang-lin Sao

* Completely eviscerated.

quieted somewhat, and without waiting for a second invitation she took her bedding-roll into the familiar room.

Thus she once more became a worker in Lo Ching, and everybody still called her Hsiang-lin Sao, after her first husband.

But she was no longer the same woman. After a few days her mistress and master noticed that she was heavy of hand and foot, that she was listless at her work, that her memory was bad, and all day there never crossed the shadow of a smile over her corpselike face. One could tell by Fourth Aunt's tone of voice that she was already dissatisfied, and with Fourth Uncle it was the same. He had, as usual, wrinkled his brow in disapproval when she had first arrived, but since they had been having endless difficulties with servants he had raised no serious objection to rehiring Hsiang-lin Sao. Now, however, he informed Fourth Aunt that, though the woman's case seemed indeed very lamentable, and it was permissible because of that to give her work, still she was obviously out of tune with Heaven and Earth. She must not, therefore, be allowed to pollute precious vessels with her soiled hands, and, especially on ceremonial occasions, Fourth Aunt herself must prepare all food. Otherwise the ancestral spirits would be offended and, likely as not, refuse to touch a crumb.

These ancestral sacrifices were, in fact, the most important affairs in Fourth Uncle's home, for he still rigidly adhered to the old beliefs. Formerly they had been busy times for Hsiang-lin Sao also, and so the next time the altar was placed in the center of the hall and covered with a fine cloth she began to arrange the wine cups and bowls and chopsticks on it exactly as before.

"Hsiang-lin Sao," Fourth Aunt cried, rushing in, "never mind that. I'll fix the things."

Puzzled, she withdrew and proceeded to take out the candlesticks.

"Never mind that, either. I'll get the candlesticks," Fourth Aunt said again.

Hsiang-lin Sao walked about several times in a rather dazed manner, and ended up by finding nothing to do, for Fourth Aunt was always ahead of her. She went away suspiciously. She found the only use they had for her that day was to sit in the kitchen and keep the fire burning.

People in Lo Ching continued to call her Hsiang-lin Sao, but there was a different tone in their voices. They still talked with her, but smiled in a cool way, and with faint contempt. She did not seem to notice, or perhaps did not care. She only stared beyond them, and talked always about the thing that day and night clung to her mind.

"I was truly stupid, truly," she would repeat. "I only knew that when the snow lies on the mountains the wild animals will sometimes venture into the valleys and will even come into the villages in search of food. I did not know that they could be so fierce long after the coming of spring . . ."

Retelling her story in the same words, she would end up sobbing and striking her breast.

Everyone who heard it was moved, and even the sneering men, listening, would loosen their smiles and go off in depressed spirits. The women not only forgot all their contempt for her, but at the moment forgave her entirely for her black sins—remarrying and causing the death not only of a second husband but also of his child—and in many cases ended by joining with her in weeping at the end of the tragic narrative. She talked of nothing else, only this incident which had become the central fact of her life, and she told it again and again.

Before long, however, the entire population of Lo Ching had heard her story not once but several times, and the most generous old women, even the Buddha-chanters, could not muster up a tear when she spoke of it. Nearly everybody in the town could recite the story word for word, and it bored them excessively to hear it repeated.

"I was truly stupid, truly," she would begin.

"Yes, you only knew that when the snow lies on the mountains the wild animals will sometimes venture into the valleys and will even come into the villages in search of food . . ." Her audience would recite the next lines, cruelly cutting her short, and walk away.

With her mouth hanging open, Hsiang-lin Sao would stand stupefied for a while, stare as if seeing someone for the first time, and then drag away slowly as if weary of her continued existence. But her obsession gave her no rest, and she ingenuously tried to interest others in it by indirect approaches. Seeing a bean, a small

basket, or other people's children, she would innocently lead up
to the tragedy of Ah Mao. Looking at a child three or four years
old, for instance, she would say, "If Ah Mao were still here, he
would be just about that size."

Frightened by the wild light in Hsiang-lin Sao's eyes, the children signaled for a retreat by pulling on their mother's skirts.
She would therefore soon find herself alone again, and falter off
until the next time. Pretty soon everyone understood these tactics
too, and made fun of her. When they saw her staring morosely
at an infant they would look at her mockingly.

"Hsiang-lin Sao, if your Ah Mao were still here, wouldn't he
be just about that big?"

Probably she had not suspected that her misery had long since
ceased to afford any vicarious enjoyment for anyone, and that the
whole episode had now become loathsome to her former sym-
pathizers, but the meaning of this kind of mockery pierced her
armor of preoccupation at last, and she understood. She glanced
at the jester, but did not utter a word of response.

Lo Ching never loses its enthusiasm for the celebration of
New Year. Promptly after the twentieth of the Twelfth Moon
the festivities begin.

Next year at this time Fourth Uncle hired an extra male worker,
and in addition a certain Liu Ma, to prepare the chickens and
geese. This Liu Ma was a "good woman," a Buddhist vegetarian
who really kept her vow not to kill living creatures. Hsiang-lin
Sao, whose hands were polluted, could only feed the fire and sit
watching Liu Ma working over the sacred vessels. Outside a fine
snow was matting the earth.

"Ai-ya, I was truly stupid," sighed Hsiang-lin Sao, staring
despondently at the sky.

"Hsiang-lin Sao, you are back on the same trail!" Liu Ma
interrupted, with some exasperation. "Listen to me, is it true you
got the scar by knocking your forehead against the altar in protest?"

"U-huh."

"I ask you this: If you hated it that much, how was it that later
on you actually submitted?"

"I?"

"Ah, you! It seems to me you must have been half-willing, otherwise—"

"Ha, ha! You don't understand how great were his muscles."

"No, I don't. I don't believe that strength such as your own was not enough to resist him. It is clear to me that you must have been ready for it yourself."

"Ah—*you*! I'd like to see you try it yourself, and see how long you could struggle."

Liu Ma's old face crinkled into a laugh, so that it looked like a polished walnut. Her dry eyes rested on Hsiang-lin Sao's scar for a moment, and then sought out her eyes. She spoke again.

"You are really not very clever. One more effort that time really to kill yourself would have been better for you. As it is, you lived with your second man less than two years, and that is all you got for your great crime. Just think about it: when you go into the next world you will be held in dispute between the spirits of your two husbands. How can the matter be settled? Only one way: Yen Lu-t'a, the Emperor of Hell, can do nothing else but saw you in half and divide you equally between the two men. That, I think, is a fact."

An expression of mingled fear and astonishment crept over Hsiang-lin Sao's face. This was something she had not considered before, had never even heard of in her mountain village.

"My advice is that you'd better make amends before it is too late. Go to the Tu-ti Temple and contribute money for a threshold. This threshold, stepped on by a thousand, stepped over by ten thousand,* can suffer for you and perhaps atone for the crime. Thus you may avoid suffering after death."

Hsiang-lin Sao did not say a word, but felt intolerably crushed with pain. Next day dark shadows encircled her eyes. Right after breakfast she went off to the Tu-ti Temple to beg the priest to let her buy a new threshold. He stubbornly refused at first, and only when she released a flood of tears would he consider it. Then, unwillingly, he admitted that it might be arranged for twelve thousand cash.

---

* It is believed that the stone threshold acts as a kind of proxy body for the sinner, and every step on it is a blow subtracted from the total punishment awaiting him in Hell.

She had long since stopped talking with the villagers, who shunned her and the tiresome narrative of Ah Mao's death, but news soon spread that there was a development in her case. Many people came now and inquisitively referred to the scar on her forehead.

"Hsiang-lin Sao, I ask you this: Why was it that you submitted to the man?"

"Regrettable, regrettable," sighed another, "that the knock was not deep enough."

She understood well enough the mockery and irony of their words, and she did not reply. She simply continued to perform her duties in silence. Near the end of her next year's service she drew the money due to her from Fourth Aunt, exchanged it for twelve silver dollars, and asked permission to visit in the west end of the town. Before the next meal she returned, much altered. Her face no longer seemed troubled, her eyes held some life in them for the first time in months, and she was in a cheerful mood. She told Fourth Aunt that she had bought a threshold for the temple.

During the Coming-of-Winter Festival she worked tirelessly, and on the day of making sacrifices she was simply bursting with energy. Fourth Aunt brought out the holy utensils, and Ah Niu carried the altar to the center of the room. Hsiang-lin Sao promptly went over to bring out the wine cups and chopsticks.

"Never mind," Fourth Aunt cried out. "Don't touch them."

She withdrew her hand as if it had been burned, her face turned ashen, and she did not move, but stood as if transfixed. She remained standing there, in fact, until Fourth Uncle came in to light the offertory incense, and ordered her away.

From that day she declined rapidly. It was not merely a physical impoverishment that ensued, but the spark of life in her was dimmed almost to extinction. She became extremely nervous, and developed a morbid fear of darkness or the sight of anyone, even her master or mistress. She became altogether as timid and frightened as a little mouse that has wandered from its hole to blink for a moment in the glaring light of day. In half a year her hair lost all its color. Her memory became so clouded that she sometimes forgot even to scour the rice.

"What has got into her? How has she become like that? It's better not to have her around," Fourth Aunt began saying in her presence.

But "become like that" she had, and there did not seem to be any possibility of improving her. They talked of sending her away, or of returning her to the care of Old Woman Wei. Nothing came of it while I was still in Lo Ching, but the plan was soon afterward carried out. Whether Old Woman Wei actually took charge of her for a while after she left Fourth Uncle's home or whether she at once became a beggar I never learned.

I am awakened by giant firecrackers, and see yellow tongues of flame, and then immediately afterward hear the sharp pipi-papao of exploding gunpowder. It is near the fifth hour, and time for the prayers and blessings. Still only drowsily aware of the world, I hear far away the steady explosive notes, one after another, and then more rapidly and thickly, until the whole sky is echoing, and the whirling snowflakes, eddying out of little white balls themselves like something shot from above, hover everywhere. Within the compass of the medley of sound and gentle storm I feel somehow a nostalgic contentment, and all the brooding of the dead day and the early night is forgotten in the stir around me, lost in the air of expectancy that pervades these homes about to receive benediction. What a satisfaction it is to understand that the Holy Spirits of Heaven and Earth, having bountifully inhaled their fill of the offertory meat and wine and incense, now limp about drunkenly in the wide air. In such a mood they are certain to dispense boundless prosperity on the good people of Lo Ching!

China

THE MEMORIAL SERVICE
ON THE MOUNTAIN

Czoe Zông-Hûi

"Oh! How it hurts!" Zzogan could no longer stand the terrible pain that was eating out her insides and almost suffocating her. She jerked open her eyes, pushed off her husband, who pressed on her breast as heavy as a big rock, and rushed forward from her bed completely unconscious of what she was doing—striking, pushing, and shaking whatever she came across. Time and time again she struck, pushed, and shook the door, until her fists were as painful as if she had been beating them against iron. The door would not move. The pains spread from her fists through her whole body, and she stopped and sat down for a while staring at her fists.

The door became a wall before her breast, stretching so far that she could not see the ends of it, however she might try, and so high that with her head twisted straight back she could not see the top of it. She dropped her head again, and murmured, "Where am I?"

She suddenly felt herself coming to her senses, turned a little, and felt her husband stretched out in front of her, like a statue at a mile post. But it was not the terrible room where her husband had lain so ponderously. Around her the pale faces of her companions in distress, sleeping under their cotton quilts, peered out at her. The dream was over, and as she looked around, she wiped the cold sweat from her forehead and breathed out a long sigh.

She took a step or two backward and regarded the hard concrete wall, dark now at night, against which she had been beating with all her strength, and the dim electric light, like a light in a distant village, as it hung in the center of the high ceiling and glared down on the long, high wall. She lowered her gaze to the heavy-looking door which was kept closed day and night, the small, square watch-hole for the guards nearby, the large, shining toilet pot in the corner, and the rest of the grim scene. When she was sure that it was not that terrible room, but the comfortable jail, she breathed out a long sigh of relief. "It was only a dream after all!" Zzogan murmured, and slipped back under the quilt, from which she had just jumped out. It was midnight, and her friends were still sleeping like corpses. She could only hear the noise of the guards opening and shutting the stove doors, way beyond the high wall, borne in on the wildly singing wind.

She covered her head completely with the quilt for a while, as if to shut out the terrible figure of her husband, which she could never forget even in her sleep, and curled up like a snail. After the guards' footsteps had passed by once or twice, she stretched herself out, and, putting her two cold feet onto the breast of the friend who lay opposite, she fell quietly asleep, as if she were quite happy.

She used to think of the fortresslike red-brick walls, the dark, high wall within the heavy iron gate, and the constant watches of the guards—the whole jail with its concrete walls and massive doors—not as a prison of pain and sorrow, but as a sure defense against the outside world.

She was brought to the jail three months ago on an evening in late autumn, and had at first trembled like a frightened rabbit every time the guards' footsteps were heard approaching down the corridor. She refused to relieve herself for so long that she had once released all that she was holding back in her bed, and for this she was ill-treated by a guard. But as time went on, she made friends in the jail and learned the rules and regulations. First, one of the matrons, a widow herself with a daughter of fourteen, took pity on her. Then the worst young woman prisoner became very kind to her. And on the whole she came to enjoy the life of the prison, except for an occasional beating from a guard or criticism from one of the prisoners who had been there longer.

On her twentieth day in jail, the judge sentenced her to six years' imprisonment.

Her matron friend said sympathetically, "My poor dear! But you will be going home when you are nineteen."

But Zzogan surprised her by answering, "I want to stay here a long, long time."

This was true. She would be happy to stay there for a very long time. Before she was sentenced, some had said to the guards that one so young could not have done anything serious, and that she would probably be released at once under a suspended sentence; others thought that she would get a year or two—perhaps three at the most. But when the worst young woman prisoner said that she had got six years for the same crime at the same age, and that Zzogan would get the same, Zzogan prayed that she would be proved right. Least of all did she want to be released at once under a suspended sentence.

She felt that if she returned immediately there would be the shame of her acts, which would still be in people's minds, and, what was worse, she would have to go back again to that hateful house of her husband's, unless her parents could return to the bridegroom the unhulled rice and barley which they had received as the price of the match.

So she wished to stay in jail for many years—years in which her parents could have good harvest. Then she could go back to the house in Kûnmaûl—The Big Village—where her dear father and mother and younger brothers and sisters lived.

On the morning of the tenth day after the unhulled rice and barley had been delivered to her house, Zzogan had left her parents' home in a palanquin. On the day before the wedding, the expected attendance of the bridegroom at the bride's house was abruptly canceled, and a palanquin was called for the bride instead. Mr. Yi, the bride's father, had said that it was poverty alone which had caused him to have the bride carried out of his house while the dusk of dawn was still on the village, and before Mr. and Mrs. Yun could be there, as if she were a cat straying from home. This was what he had told the villagers, his wife, and even Zzogan, that he was too poor to receive the bridegroom, but this was not the truth. It was something that Mr. Yun had told him a few days before as he was on his way home from the market, where he had gone to buy things in preparation for his daughter's wedding.

Mr. Yun had called to him as he was hurrying home late in the afternoon with his bag on his shoulder, full of dried pollack, eggs, and many sweets and fruits besides.

"Hey! Mr. Yi! I've something to tell you."

"What is it?"

Mr. Yun seemed to be in some difficulty, as he said with much hesitation, "As the proverb says, The true crystal may have some dirt in it, and, er, heh, er, I am sorry but he . . ."

"Mr. Yun, what are you trying to say?"

"Mr. Yi, you won't blame me, since I did not mean to cheat you. The bridegroom, though lacking some quality, may still take good care of his wife, may he not?"

Mr. Yi, who had been walking ahead, stopped and turned back to Mr. Yun, who had been following right behind him. Mr. Yun stopped too on seeing the changed color of Mr. Yi's face and said in a lower tone, "I'm speaking of the bridegroom. His health was affected by the cursed measles."

At these words, Mr. Yi felt as if he had been struck by thunder roaring from the skies, and he was unable to go a step further. Mr. Yun continued, "I would not take an incapable man myself, so I was very careful from the beginning, and went to his house and saw him. Everything seemed to be all right, except for his one eye . . . As I said before, he is very diligent indeed, and honest. He farms not only his own field, but others as well. He gets on well with the other villagers, and they think highly of him. I should have told you about this earlier, but . . ."

As Mr. Yun was saying this he had to walk more and more slowly to stay beside Mr. Yi, who had been striding ahead so happily a moment before. Now as he looked on Mr. Yi's paled face, he faltered, and mumbled into silence.

Mr. Yi kept silent, his hollowed eyes full of tears. It was plain to see what a blow this had been to him. Mr. Yun, trying to help him a little, repeated the words that he had used when he first began to act as go-between in the match. "It's better for her than starving at home. She can be well-off and make it easier for her parents and brothers to live at home, can't she?"

Mr. Yi plodded on in silence, only occasionally opening his mouth unconsciously to swallow his tears. He thought first of canceling the wedding, but this would be very difficult, since he would have to return the rice and barley which had been delivered to his house, and some of which had already been used, partly for his own family's food, and partly to repay debts that he had owed—at least half of the five sôm of unhulled rice and ten sôm of barley. He simply could not repay this, and even if he could, he could not cause Mr. Yun to lose face by canceling the arrangements he had made. Mr. Yun was his closest and best friend and he knew that he had made the arrangement only for the sake of Mr. Yi's family. If it had been anyone else, he had excuse enough to cancel the whole thing. It was for his daughter Zzogan's sake that he grieved most, and he felt that he might be guilty before God for having sold her in this way.

Only two days after Mr. Yun had completed the arrangements, the rice and barley were delivered from the bridegroom's house in Bangzu-ggol on two oxen. His fellow villagers had come to his house and told him enviously that now he had no need to worry until the next barley harvest, and Mr. Yi had almost cried with relief as he sat in front of his house, smoking dried pumpkin leaves and gazing at the dark mountains. Now, having learned of the bridegroom's disability in this sudden way, he felt as if his whole world had gone black. But when Mr. Yun turned to him again, concerned at the way his steps were faltering, he straightened up his neck like a wild goose and answered, "Don't worry about it, Mr. Yun! He may be one-eyed, but he can still run things all right, can't he?"

His voice was so indistinct and trembling that he could not believe that it was his own, but Mr. Yun, relieved to hear him speak in this cheerful way after his long silence, said with a laugh, "Quite right! I'm glad to see you looking at it in that way."

Mr. Yi responded with a pretended laugh, out of feeling for Mr. Yun, and regretted having caused him even a moment's anxiety. They had been the closest of friends, almost like brothers, for forty years, seeing each other through all difficulties.

They were of the same age and had always led very much the same sort of life. When Mr. Yi was eleven both his parents had

died of influenza. Later he had been employed by the Kûndêmun-
zib or Big Gate House as a cowherd. At that time Mr. Yun was
living with his parents, who were also employed at the House,
in a happier position than Mr. Yi. Mr. Yi's childhood name was
Czun-Dûg, and Mr. Yun's Ûl-Ssoe; they were friends in their
quarrels, at their ball games, and as they tended the cows, until
they were thirteen. Then in the spring of their fourteenth year,
Ûl-Ssoe's father took sick and died suddenly. His mother lived
on in poverty with her children for about half a year, before
running away one night while Ûl-Ssoe was sleeping. Ûl-Ssoe
missed his mother very much, and his sadness made Czun-Dûg
sad too. They lived together in the same room where Ûl-Ssoe had
lived happily with his parents.

When they grew up, they were promoted from cowherds to
farm workers, and worked honestly in that position until they
were over thirty, when Ûl-Ssoe married the daughter of a man
who worked at the next house and moved out of the place he
shared with Czun-Dûg. The autumn after his marriage he acted
as a go-between and arranged a marriage for his friend too, and
Czun-Dûg also moved into a new house nearby.

They rented a field belonging to the Big Gate House and
farmed it as servants of that house. Gradually, as they lived in
the comfortable atmosphere of their own homes with their wives,
the unhappiness of their former lives passed away like winter's
snow melting in the spring sunshine. First a son was born to
Ûl-Ssoe, and then, in the following year, a daughter, as charming
as a cotton flower, to Czun-Dûg. The two men seemed never to
tire of work, and though they had no land of their own to till
and no cattle of their own to tend, they would pile up in their
gardens huge harvests of barley, soybeans, red beans, and rice.

They were now much better off, their children were growing up to be fine and healthy, and the pair seemed as happy as if
they had thrown off the bonds of farm workers, so that their fellow villagers began to refer to them with titles of more respect.
Everybody called Ûl-Ssoe Mr. Yun, and Czun-Dûg Mr. Yi, though
no one knew who had first conferred these titles upon them. For
some years after their change of life style, they continued to pros-

per, but as the years passed by, things began to change. Like most small farmers, they found that their duties were beginning to overwhelm them. Soon they fell into debt and their grain was seized in the fields when they were unable to pay. They had never known such a catastrophe before. The harvest for which they had given their blood and sweat had to be turned immediately over to their creditors instead of being reaped by those who had planted it. Then, in the years that followed, drought and floods often spoiled their annual crops and reduced them to poverty. Their happy home lives gradually became a misery. But though all else changed, the friendship between the two men never changed. Even when they were reduced to keeping themselves alive on the roots of grasses and the bark of trees, forgetting completely the days when they had had rice to eat, they used to meet every day to help each other and to discuss their day-to-day problems.

It was this regular friendship which led to Mr. Yun's arranging Zzogan's wedding.

Mr. Yun was as poor as Mr. Yi, but he could not bear to see the faces of his friend's family so swelled up and a sickly yellow like rotten fruit with maggots in it, the result of constipation caused by eating stodgy cakes after days of fasting. So he came to the conclusion that the only way in which they could improve their lot was to get Zzogan married, and he remembered what his wife's elder sister had told him about an honest, diligent, and quite well-off man who lived in her village of Bangzu-ggol, who had never been accepted in marriage because he was one-eyed. One day, early in the morning, he had gone over to Bangzu-ggol, seen the prospective bridegroom, and arranged for him to marry Zzogan, at a price of five sôm of unhulled rice, and ten sôm of barley.

He told Mr. Yi about it, and Mr. and Mrs. Yi agreed reluctantly that if they did not get their child married they might die of hunger together.

"In olden times a girl of fourteen could give birth to a baby! She's better off there than starving at home, and by doing this she can save her parents and brothers. You can keep your family for some time on five bags of rice and ten bags of barley, can't you?"

So he succeeded in persuading Mr. and Mrs. Yi. They were

obliged to accept his word gratefully, without checking up for themselves on the bridegroom's house, and when the rice and barley were delivered the next day, they accepted them.

Since this was the way things had been arranged, how could Mr. Yi possibly cancel his daughter's marriage or complain of the arrangement, even though he had first heard of the bridegroom's disability as he and Mr. Yun were walking back from the market? So he thought the thing over and over and decided that it would be better for him to take Zzogan to the bridegroom's house for the wedding, regardless of what might happen afterward, than to wait for him to attend at the bride's house, only to be laughed at by others and cause disappointment to Zzogan and his wife. The day before the marriage, Mr. Yi sent word to the bridegroom's house that he could not afford to receive his son-in-law in his house, and, as the journey was too long to be done there and back in one day, he would rather have a palanquin sent for the bride early on the day of the wedding than have the bridegroom attend at the bride's house. Even so, Mr. Yi did not feel easy in his mind, and he spent the whole day vacantly smoking dried pumpkin leaves. Late in the evening, when the guests had gone home, and his wife was preparing the big dining table for the bridegroom and pulling out the downy hairs of Zzogan's forehead with a cotton thread by making her kneel down, he went over to his wife and said, as if it were a matter of course, "I have told the bridegroom not to attend here."

This surprised his wife very much; she stopped what she was doing, and asked, "Why on earth did you do that?"

Mr. Yi had not expected his wife to be so shocked by his news, and he stammered out his excuse about his house not being good enough to receive the bridegroom.

"What will people say?" His wife clucked her tongue in dismay.

"What can people say, since it was our poverty which forced this arrangement upon us?"

"Well, that will be a funny wedding, without a bridegroom!"

"Don't worry too much about it! Now, the palanquin will be here early in the morning, so you had better be getting Zzogan ready."

"I don't like this at all. Why can't we do the same as others do? The house may be small, but the bridegroom's party can go back on the same day, so why not . . ."

"Don't make such a fuss about it, woman!" Mr. Yi interrupted, angered by this continued discussion of the marriage rather than by his wife's complaining voice.

The rough tone her husband had used hurt Mrs. Yi, and this on top of the sadness which had been growing in her as the day of her daughter's wedding approached made her burst out crying like a child. Zzogan, kneeling down in front of her mother, wept with her. Mr. Yi wanted to take them both in his arms and weep with them to relieve his feelings, but he went out of the room without a word.

After he had left, Mrs. Yi caressed her daughter, trying to soothe her, "There now, don't cry! If the bridegroom had to attend here first, it would be very late before the wedding was over, and our house is disgracefully small, isn't it? Don't cry now, or your eyes will be a terrible sight tomorrow. In the olden days, the bride was always carried to the bridegroom's house for the marriage, and he never came to fetch her."

But Zzogan went on crying, as if she had not heard her mother's words. She was not crying because she hated the thought of a wedding without a bridegroom. Ever since the rice and barley had been delivered, a sadness which she could not explain had filled her heart. Often she had slipped away behind the house to cry her heart out. She was still crying now.

Her mother did not understand what Zzogan was feeling and still thought that her daughter was sad because the bridegroom had not come to their house for the wedding. She had managed to stop her weeping, but she said to the villagers who came to visit her after the palanquin had slipped out early in the morning with her husband following behind, "It is dreadful that our cursed poverty would not allow me to prepare things here for her as others do, and it breaks my heart to think that she may be weeping all the way because she has not been called for by her husband!" If her mother was feeling so bad, what about her father who was walking slowly behind the palanquin, dread-ing the moment when the dreadful truth about her husband was revealed to her?

As the sunlight reached down into the valleys, the palanquin passed by the fields of Kûnmaûl and the hill of Zarumog and climbed up to the pass of Bugzzog. Now that the autumn harvest was in, there was no one about in the fields, and only the noisy cries of the magpies could be heard among the dark compost heaps, built up like houses. The palanquin bearers were breathing heavily and sweating as they toiled up the hill. Mr. Yi was gasping for breath too as he tried to keep the pace of the young bearers and also to support the back of the palanquin, with the sharp stones of the road tearing at his feet and his sweat-soaked shirt clinging to his back. Anxious too about his daughter, who might be feeling dizzy inside the palanquin, he gasped out, "Zzogan, are you feeling all right?"

His voice sounded very sad; but what could have happened to her that she did not answer?

"Zzogan, are you sure you're not feeling dizzy?" he asked again. But Zzogan still kept silent, and there was nothing to be heard but his gasping breath. He thought that her not replying meant that she was weeping, and when he thought that he heard her sobbing, he felt like sitting down by the roadside himself and crying. He had a pain in his heart and noises in his ears; the earth seemed to shake under him, and he would have fallen to the ground if he had not clung onto the palanquin. His hollowed eyes were full of tears. He wanted to speak to his daughter again, but he just kept on walking, fearful that his voice might tremble if he spoke. As he walked along, he was full of regret that he had not been able to cancel the match on hearing from Mr. Yun that the bridegroom was one-eyed. As soon as the palanquin was over the pass and the village of Bangzu-ggol appeared, he wiped away his sweat and tears and spoke to his daughter, since she might want to relieve herself, and, in any case, he wanted to caress her once more before they reached the bridegroom's house.

"Zzogan, do you want to get out for anything?"

His daughter did not reply, and so he went up to the palanquin and, putting his head inside, he asked her, as though he were speaking to a baby, "My dear child, don't you need to wee-wee?"

But still Zzogan did not answer. The bearers themselves, on hearing what Mr. Yi said, felt the call of nature, and, realizing that the bride would probably be feeling the same, put down the palanquin and cleared off. Mr. Yi, glad of the opportunity presented by their absence, quickly opened the door of the palanquin and shouted as loudly as he could, "Zzogan!"

His daughter, whom he expected to find weeping, was sleeping soundly.

At first he was terribly surprised and worried that she had been crying so much that she had lost her senses. He was relieved when she opened her dry eyes, as the autumn wind rushed in through the open door of the palanquin.

"Zzogan, have you been sleeping?"

Zzogan nodded with a smile in reply. She had fallen asleep as soon as she had got into the palanquin, since she had not slept for several nights before, and now she felt refreshed and managed to put on a smile when she saw her father's face, red with tears.

Mr. Yi was relieved to find that his daughter was all right, and his voice altered as he said, "My child, we are getting near. Are you sure that you don't want to relieve yourself?"

Zzogan indicated by turning her head that she did not wish to.

"You won't be able to go to the toilet in the house for a whole day, you know."

"I know, father."

Zzogan was still in good spirits as she answered this, and Mr. Yi was glad to find his daughter, whom he had thought still a child, behaving so happily, as if she knew all she had to know, even smiling instead of weeping, and he asked her with some surprise, "How do you know it all so well?"

"My mother told me!"

"And did your mother tell you everything else as well?"

Zzogan nodded. Mr. Yi, who had imagined that his wife had done nothing but weep before sending her daughter off to the bridegroom's, was glad to discover that she had taken care to instruct her fully, and even more glad to know that his daughter could remember what her mother had told her. And now he asked her in a low voice, "Are you happy at being married?"

He had wanted to ask her before, but had not been able to bring himself to do it because he did not expect her to answer. Zzogan tried to answer with a smile, but suddenly her eyelids felt warm and her nose sour, so she dropped her head quickly. Mr. Yi's happiness turned to gloom again. He recalled the case a few months earlier of the bride of the house of the cement maker. The bride came from Zinan and committed suicide by hanging herself on a pine tree on the hill behind the village on the terrible dark night of the third day of her marriage to the eldest son of the house, a cripple, because she found him horrible and hated him. Her mother had visited the house after the tragedy and lamented, as she held her daughter, whose tongue hung out and whose eyes had turned completely over and showed white.

"I made my daughter die because of our poverty!"

Mr. Yi could see the scene as if on a lantern slide; he felt his backbone go rigid, and a frost fall over his body. It looked as if the same sort of thing would soon be happening to him too. He felt dizzy, and his long, drawn-out shadow, swinging in front of him, seemed to be like a goblin haunting him and his daughter as they went on; he could only keep walking by holding on to the palanquin with his eyes closed.

The bearers brought them to the bridegroom's house at noon, as the shadows under their feet were reduced to their smallest size. The bridegroom's house was fairly crowded. Zzogan passed the rest of the day as though in a dream, playing the unfamiliar part of a bride as her mother had instructed her. Meanwhile, she did not forget to find out what her bridegroom looked like, and she often dropped her head and took a side glance at him.

She had first imagined that her bridegroom would look like the bridegroom of the Big Gate House, a short man with a round, clever face, usually smiling, who wore a thin blue robe and black shoes. She had not had that idea when she first saw that bridegroom, but only since the evening of the day when the rice and barley had been delivered from the bridegroom's house, while she had been feeling so sad, lonely, terrified, and fearful.

When the rest of the day had passed, those guests who were attending in the bride's room went home, saying that the bride must be tired. After a while, her bridegroom entered the room, opening the door carelessly. He was not at all the sort of bridegroom Zzogan had imagined, but a giant of about nine feet, with a broad chest and a wide face in which she was struck at once by one dark, hollowed eye, and a horrible big mouth like a tiger's. She was especially frightened at the abrupt way he tried to take off her clothes without a word. She wanted to be excused, but he grasped her tightly in his strong hands, as if he had caught a baby sparrow, and slipped off her clothes; gasping, he blew out the dim lamp, in the farther corner of the room and got under the quilt alone. Zzogan was unable to move at all, like a rat in front of a cat, and stood trembling in the darkness, half out of her mind. She passed the whole night in this state of paralysis and only came to her senses when the light of dawn began to show in the window. The bridegroom was most surprised at this.

As if she had been awakened from a dream, Zzogan opened her eyes suddenly and looked around. When she found her husband lying beside her, she kicked off the quilt and leaped out of bed. She tried to put on her clothes, but her waist and hips felt as if they did not belong to her, and she could not move them; she cried out in horror.

She thought she might be dead. The bridegroom was awakened from his sound sleep by her cries and her hurried dressing. He realized that something was wrong by her cries and her way of dressing, and he tried to caress his bride in many ways. The more he touched her, the more horrified she was; her eyes opened wide, as if she were trying to keep off a terrible, awful snake, and she turned her face aside.

It was quite natural that she should feel so since she had not yet even reached the age of puberty, and of course she was trembling, horrified by the sudden contact with a man. Never before had she had such an experience. Her mother, worried about her tender age, had instructed her about everything, right up to the time when she got into the palanquin, but she had never told her about the accident that would happen to her at night in the bridal chamber. Everyone knew that such things were not proper subject for discussion, so Zzogan's mother could not tell her about this, though she told her about everything else.

The bridegroom did not know what to do when he saw the frightened eyes of his bride, and he really felt a little ashamed of himself, as he said rather scoldingly, "There's no need to cry, is there?"

At the same time, he repented deeply his behavior during the night because she seemed so horrified by it. He had had no desire at all to do such a thing before he had met her.

He had realized the handicap under which he suffered by being one-eyed and had been ashamed of the way all arrangements for his marriage had failed because of this. So before he entered the bride's room that night, when he had an opportunity to do so without being noticed by the others, he had cleaned out the dirty liquid and waxes from his deformed eye. And as he went about the house, he felt a little nervous, as if he were embarking on a new adventure. He intended only to cover himself with the quilt as quickly as possible when he entered her room, and fall immediately into a sound sleep. But he must have been enchanted by the pretty little girl, like a cotton flower, and the awakened passion of a man of thirty years finally exploded.

"I'll not do it again! Please don't cry!"

But however hard he might try, he could not stop her crying. So, having said what he could, he left her alone in the room, for he was feeling nervous, uneasy, and weary.

When the husband left the room, some people looked in, opening the door a little. Then a young woman brought in a basin of water and asked Zzogan to wash her face. When it was placed in front of her, she bent her head over it and applied water with both hands because she did not want others to look at her weeping face. If she had been at home, she would have wept her heart out, but here, among strangers, she swilled her tears away in the basin, opening her eyes wide or splashing water on her closed lids, trying hard to stop her tears. More tears could have flowed, but she could not allow herself to weep to her heart's content.

Before her tears had stopped, the breakfast was served. After repeatedly wiping away her tears by pretending to wash her face, she reluctantly sat at the dining table. But the salted fish, pork, baked pollack, bean sprouts, and the rest of the meal were tasteless, and the cooked rice seemed as hard as grains of sand. She laid aside her spoon after eating only a little, but the young woman who had brought in the basin of water put it back into her hand, and asked her to eat with her, which might help her appetite. Zzogan was obliged to hold the spoon, but she had no appetite at all; the table appeared dimly through her tears, and the sound of spoons seemed far away as in a dream.

The young woman was at a loss as to how to console her. Introducing herself as the bridegroom's sister, she explained that it was natural for the bride to weep at first, but she would soon get used to it and forget her parents' home. The young woman prattled on, even praising the bridegroom, but soon the smiles on her face were replaced by grimaces, as if she were displeased by Zzogan's unwillingness to listen to her advice, and she complained, "Come on, now, no more weeping, please!"

But what effect could the complaints of her husband's sister have on Zzogan? Tears were still dropping from her eyes as she held her spoon in her hand when she heard someone say, "The bride's father has left!"

Though other sounds did not reach her ears, these words came to Zzogan like an arrow. She threw away the spoon, opened the door abruptly, and left the room. But when she rushed outside the gate into the wide street, those who had seen him off were coming back, and her father had already passed the farmed fields and had reached the sloping path of Mount Gûmbong. Zzogan, held by the arms by the young woman, who had chased after her, and by others, stamped hard on the ground, and shouted, "Father, let me go with you, let me go with you!"

Her voice sounded tragic, as if her throat would break and her breast choke. Her sorrowful words may or may not have reached her father's ears, but his white figure soon disappeared behind the other side of the hill. When her father's back had gone out of her sight, she felt stranded under the sky, and the world went dark about her.

"What's the matter with you? You should be ashamed!"

The young woman tried to soothe her, but her ears were deaf.

She did not care about the whispering voices of the villagers, old and young, and as she was being taken back to the house, she kept weeping still, looking at the mountain path.

From that day on, that mountain path was a source of sadness to her. Right up to the evening when the memorial service was held on the mountain, by which time she had but a vague memory of what had happened, the path of the mountain remained in a corner of her mind as a reminder of her sorrow.

The memorial service on the mountain was held on the fourth night after her marriage. Every year without fail after the harvest was gathered in, the rents delivered, and all the other formalities carried out, all thirty families of this small village of Bangzu-ggol used to hold the annual memorial service on Mount Sem-ggol. Even though they might be holding their stomachs because of their hunger at the time, for the sake of their future happiness, they would make the full preparations for the service to the God of the Mountain, and all the villagers, men and women, young and old, would have to stay at home for a number of days before the service took place. All, whether farm renters or landowners, as tough as tigers toward the farm renters, would solemnly stay at home together to ensure their prosperity. And on the actual day of the service, everyone would put on new clothes, as if it were a big festival, and hold the service in a most pious manner. They usually took turns with the various offerings each year: some, for instance, would make cakes, others offer cooked rice; some houses would be responsible for the fruits, while others fried fish. So each was kept busy with its allotted share for the year.

This year, Zzogan's husband had to offer a pig to the God of the Mountain, and after lunch, Zzogan climbed up and down the mountain with her husband's sister several times, gasping for breath, to take water to the big kettle which her husband had taken onto the mountain in the morning.

The mountain valley, Sem-ggol, was surrounded by hills, which hid it like screens, and from here it was impossible to see the houses of the village or the mountain path where her father had crossed over. Zzogan, with the help of her husband's sister, filled the big cowherd's kettle with six jars of water, and, looking around vacantly, she said, pointing to a mountain in the west, "I wish I could climb that mountain!"

Whenever in the five days since her marriage she had seen the mountain path over which her father had passed, she had thought that she could go back to her parents' house. Now, in the deep mountain valley, from which she could not locate the path, she looked at all the mountains around, and, believing she saw the path on one of the mountains to the west, she thought, "If I cross that mountain, I shall get back home!"

Her husband's sister, who was four years older than she, felt that she should agree when Zzogan spoke to her, though she knew that on that particular day she should prepare the supper earlier than usual. She answered, "You may if you like!"

Usually a husband's sister, a sister-in-law, was not kind to her brother's wife, but this one was sympathetic.

Her husband was different, but her mother-in-law also took care of Zzogan as if she had been her own sister, quite unlike the usual mother-in-law. They were a very good-natured family and did their best to get her to be more interested in the house. If Zzogan had liked her husband the good-natured mother and sister-in-law might have been jealous or disliked her, but in fact, as things were, they took very good care of her. Since the first night of her marriage, Zzogan had not gone into her husband's room, but had tried to sleep in the stable or on the stack of barley straw. Her mother-in-law had never complained of this but had given Zzogan advice and ordered her own daughter to do the sewing, kitchen work, and so on, instead of her daughter-in-law.

This was quite natural on the mother-in-law's part because she had been widowed at forty years of age and since then had had a great affection for her son and daughter, who, she hoped, would be made happy with a nice daughter-in-law and a good son-in-law. But her son had not married until he was over thirty, and her daughter-in-law wept every day in great sorrow. She was ashamed of this and, moreover, felt more pity for her son than she had before he was married, and for her daughter too, who had grown old, losing the chance of a good marriage because of her brother. At the same time, Zzogan's sister-in-law would have felt very sorry for her mother and brother if Zzogan had run away or returned to her parents' house and not come back, and the rumors might affect any marriage which she might arrange for herself later.

But Zzogan could not understand how they felt and was rather displeased by their kindness.

No sooner did she hear the answer of her sister-in-law, "You may if you like!" than she ran as if she were jumping or flying up the mountain in the direction that she had fixed in her mind, and was soon halfway to the top. Her figure grew smaller and smaller.

Then her sister-in-law, who was doing her best to follow her, gasping for breath and stretching out her neck in her eagerness, shouted, "Sister! Let's go together!"

Zzogan did not look back at all, shuddering with fright and feeling sick, as on seeing a snake, at hearing her sister-in-law's voice, and she ran fast, clenching her fists tighter. She was able to reach the top much sooner than her sister-in-law, but then the dream that she had had in the valley was broken to pieces. She had expected, on reaching the top, to be able to see the big village of tangerines where her dear father, mother, and brothers lived, but there was no village to be seen, only many mountain slopes like the one on which she was standing, swimming in her tears. The wind was blowing through the pine trees. The mountain sparrows were twittering. She might have wandered on, crying, over all the mountain slopes trying to find the village of Kûn-maûl, if her sister-in-law had not followed her. But she was obliged to take her advice and come down again by the same road as she had gone up. When she got back to her husband's house, her mother-in-law had already prepared the supper, and her husband, who many times had looked out along the valley of Sem-ggol, was glad to see her coming back. With the rope which he had been preparing for carrying the pig up to the memorial service on the mountain in his hand, he crawled in and out of the kitchen like a child. He could have guessed whether or not Zzogan liked him, but he concentrated all the sight in his one eye on her lovely face and body—he wished to stroke her, to speak to her, or to embrace her as tightly as possible. How different were their feelings toward each other!

In this mood, her husband went on ahead up the mountain after supper, carrying the pig and firewood on his back, and Zzogan, her mother-in-law, and sister-in-law followed with a big wooden box to put the pig in, a gourd bowl, a pottery bowl to be filled with its blood, a sharp knife, and a chopping board.

At the site of the service on the mountain, the elder of the village, old Mr. Czambong, was erecting the altar with some young men. They were sweeping around the big pogi tree and preparing the torch-lights of firewood on both sides of the altar. Zzogan, standing near her husband, who was boiling the water for the pig-killing, kept looking at those young men as they walked about under the altar tree, to see if any of them were one-eyed. But all of them had eyes in the right places; they were not so tall, their faces were not so broad, and they were not so old. She compared these men with her husband, whose face shone like copper in the light of the bright-burning firewood, with which he had been busy along with the others. The young men seemed to be creatures of Heaven, and her husband looked to her like some horrible devil of a fairy tale.

While Zzogan was thinking this, the evening became gradually dark, and the villagers, from the old men to the young children, gathered at the site of the memorial service on the mountain. Those who were responsible for the cakes, the cooked rice, the fried food, the fruits, and so on were there too.

The torch-lights, which were set up on either side of the service site, waved their flames, red like animals' tongues, and on the ground a bonfire of firewood was burning. The cakes, cooked rice, pollack, fried food, and fruits were offered to the altar by the hands of old Czozi. Now, when the pig was killed, the service would begin. The pig was to be killed after the other offerings had been made, surrounded by the people in a solemn quiet, because it was the ancient custom of the village that the dying shriek of the pig should be heard by the God of the Mountain.

As was planned, Zzogan's husband, squatting over the shrieking pig, which had been tied down with ropes and placed a little to one side, grasped its head tightly in his hand, and, stepping on its four kicking legs, plunged the sharp, shining knife into its neck, so that its dark crimson blood flowed out like a torrent.

The pig shrieked loudly enough to make the mountain tremble. When its blood had filled the pottery jar, its limbs went stiff and it died. The people were standing in a strained, solemn attitude, watching the last moments of the pig. Only Zzogan was horrified by the dreadful scene, trembling and dragging herself backward.

When she saw the blood flow, Zzogan was suddenly reminded of her dreadful experience on the first night of her marriage. The scene, as her husband sat on the pig, plunged the sharp knife into its neck to make the blood flow, and gasped for breath as the pig kicked and wriggled under his hip, which was moving up and down, almost made her suffocate. Zzogan imagined that one day she too might be killed like the pig, her blood spurting forth. The experience of her first night of marriage had not been repeated because since then she had slept at night on the barley straw or in the stable or beside her mother-in-law. But it seemed a terrible thing to her, and she broke out in a sweat at the thought of living in the same house as her husband.

At last Zzogan made up her mind to leave that horrible husband, however dreadful the night might be. So when the torches and bonfire were burning a fine, bright red and everyone was standing in a most pious mood in front of the altar, which shone in the red flames, she stole out of the crowd, unnoticed by anyone, and went to the entrance of Sem-ggol.

It was a starry night, and the wind was chilly. Night in the village, without the light of the torches and the bonfire, was very dreadful, and the unlit houses seemed to be crawling toward her like fierce animals, but she reached the gate of her husband's house without stopping. The dogs barked noisily. This frightened her, and she opened the gate and quietly entered the kitchen. When the poker got in her way, or the soybean hulls cracked under her feet, she felt her breast go cold and drew back. But she went on looking for something in the darkness, groping with her hands. She heard the special sounds of the gourd bowls, tin bowls, and crockery bowls as she touched them. Then at last she recognized the sound of the thing she was looking for, and she grasped it. She was not glad, but rather she felt her flesh creep.

She rushed out of the kitchen. The stars were still bright in the sky, and the wind was chilly so late at night. The dogs stopped barking. She brought several bundles of barley straw into her husband's room, and set a match to them. They began to burn well. She felt quite satisfied when the burning straws burned the dreadful room up to about a skirt's width, but when the flames stretched to the ceiling, the material of which it was made began to burn with a crackling sound, and she grew frightened and rushed out to the yard, shouting and jumping about here and there. The dogs of the village came up in a pack and barked with her.

The flames soon burned through the ceiling and stretched out onto the roof. Black smoke, ashes, red flames, the sounds of burning, the noise of the house falling down—all these made her shout the louder and start crying too. She had wanted to see the hateful house burned up, so that she might leave there for her parents' house by the same mountain path over which her father had gone. But now she was threatened by the furious flames which were stretching toward the sky, and she finally fell down on the wide road, out of her senses, before the fire had finished burning.

After Zzogan swooned, more of the village burned. Then the villagers came down from the mountain.

Her mother-in-law, her sister-in-law, and the other villagers— those whose houses had been burned—rushed in and scolded her violently, shouting indignantly, as if they wished to kill her. Only Zzogan's husband tried to revive her before trying to put out the fire.

The following day, Zzogan was arrested and tied up with a long rope by a policeman, in the midst of the villagers, and was pulled off behind the policeman's bicycle. Her husband followed the couple rubbing his hands, begging the policeman to forgive her, as Zzogan treaded on, trembling with frightened eyes, dry because of her fear.

Korea

INEM

Pramoedya Ananta Toer

INEM WAS one of the girls I knew. She was eight years old—two years older than me. She was no different from the others. And if there was a difference, it was that she was one of the prettier little girls in our neighborhood. People liked to look at her. She was polite, unspoiled, deft, and hard-working—qualities which quickly spread her fame even into other neighborhoods as a girl who would make a good daughter-in-law.

And once when she was heating water in the kitchen, she said to me, "Gus* Muk, I'm going to be married."

"You're fooling!" I said.

"No, the proposal came a week ago. Mama and Papa and all the relatives have accepted the proposal."

"What fun to be a bride!" I exclaimed happily.

"Yes, it'll be fun, I know it will! They'll buy me all sorts of nice clothes. I'll be dressed up in a bride's outfit, with flowers in my hair, and they'll make me up with powder and mascara. Oh, I'll like that!"

And it was true. One afternoon her mother called on mine. At that time Inem was living with us as a servant. Her daily tasks were to help with the cooking and to watch over me and my younger brothers and sisters as we played.

Inem's mother made a living by doing batik work. That was what the women in our neighborhood did when they were not working in the rice fields. Some put batik designs on sarongs, while others worked on head cloths. The poorer ones preferred

---

* A title of respect which Inem, as a servant, uses toward the son of the family for whom she works.

to do head cloths; since it did not take so long to finish a head cloth, they received payment for it sooner. And Inem's mother supported her family by putting batik designs on head cloths. She got the cloth and the wax from her employer, the Idjo Store. For every two head cloths that she finished, she was paid one and a half cents. On the average, a woman could do eight to eleven head cloths a day.

Inem's father kept gamecocks. All he did, day after day, was to wager his bird in cockfights. If he lost, the victor would take his cock. And in addition he would have to pay two and a half rupiahs, or at the very least seventy-five cents. When he was not gambling on cockfights, he would play cards with his neighbors for a cent a hand.

Sometimes Inem's father would be away from home for a month or half a month, wandering around on foot. His return would signify that he was bringing home some money.

Mother once told me that Inem's father's main occupation had been robbing people in the teak forest between our town, Blora, and the coastal town of Rembang. I was then in the first grade, and heard many stories of robbers, bandits, thieves, and murderers. As a result of those stories and what Mother told me, I came to be terrified of Inem's father.

Everybody knew that Inem's father was a criminal, but no one could prove it and no one dared complain to the police. Consequently he was never arrested by the police. Furthermore, almost all of Inem's mother's relatives were policemen. There was even one with the rank of agent first class. Inem's father himself had once been a policeman but had been discharged for taking bribes.

Mother also told me that in the old days Inem's father had been an important criminal. As a way of countering an outbreak of crime that was getting out of hand, the Netherlands Indies government had appointed him a policeman, so that he could round up his former associates. He never robbed any more after that, but in our area he continued to be a focus of suspicion.

When Inem's mother called on my mother, Inem was heating water in the kitchen. I tagged along after Inem's mother. The visitor, Mother, and I sat on a low, red couch.

"Ma'am," said Inem's mother, "I've come to ask for Inem to come back home."

"Why do you want Inem back? Isn't it better for her to be here? You don't have any of her expenses, and here she can learn how to cook."

"Yes, ma'am, but I plan for her to get married after the coming harvest."

"What?" exclaimed Mother, startled. "She's going to be married?"

"Yes, ma'am. She's old enough to be married now—she's eight years old," said Inem's mother.

At this my mother laughed. And her visitor was surprised to see Mother laugh.

"Why, a girl of eight is still a child!" said Mother.

"We're not upper-class people, ma'am. I think she's already a year too old. You know Asih? She married her daughter when she was two years younger than mine."

Mother tried to dissuade the woman. But Inem's mother had another argument. Finally the visitor spoke again: "I feel lucky that someone wants her. If we let a proposal go by this time, maybe there will never be another one. And how humiliating it would be to have a daughter turn into an old maid! And it just might be that if she gets married she'll be able to help out with the household expenses."

Mother did not reply. Then she looked at me and said; "Go get the betel set and the spittoon."

So I went to fetch the box of betel-chewing ingredients and the brass spittoon.

"And what does your husband say?"

"Oh, he agrees. What's more, Markaban is the son of a well-to-do man—his only child. Markaban has already begun to help his father trade cattle in Rembang, Tjepu, Medang, Pati, Ngawen, and also here in Blora," said Inem's mother.

This information seemed to cheer Mother up, although I could not understand why. Then she called Inem, who was at work in the kitchen. Inem came in. And Mother asked, "Inem, do you want to get married?"

Inem bowed her head. She was very respectful toward Mother.

I never once heard her oppose her. Indeed, it is rare to find people who are powerless opposing anything that others say to them.

I saw then that Inem was beaming. She often looked like that; give her something that pleased her even a little and she would beam. But she was not accustomed to saying "thank you." In the society of the simple people of our neighborhood, the words "thank you" were still unfamiliar. It was only through the glow radiating from their faces that gratitude found expression.

"Yes, ma'am," said Inem so softly as to be almost inaudible.

Then Inem's mother and mine chewed some betel. Mother herself did not like to chew betel all the time. She did it only when she had a woman visitor. Every few moments she would spit into the brass spittoon.

When Inem had gone back to the kitchen Mother said, "It's not right to make children marry."

These words surprised Inem's mother. But she did not say anything nor did her eyes show any interest.

"I was eighteen when I got married," said Mother.

Inem's mother's surprise vanished. She was no longer surprised now, but she still did not say anything.

"It's not right to make children marry," repeated Mother.

And Inem's mother was surprised again.

"Their children will be stunted."

Inem's mother's surprise vanished once more.

"Yes, ma'am." Then she said placidly, "My mother was also eight when she got married."

Mother paid no attention and continued, "Not only will they be stunted, but their health will be affected too."

"Yes, ma'am, but ours is a long-lived family. My mother is still alive, though she's over fifty-nine. And my grandmother is still alive too. I think she must be seventy-four. She's still vigorous and strong enough to pound corn in the mortar."

Still ignoring her, Mother went on, "Especially if the husband is also a child."

"Yes, ma'am, but Markaban is seventeen."

"Seventeen! My husband was thirty when he married me."

Inem's mother was silent. She never stopped shifting the wad of tobacco leaves that was stuck between her lips. One moment she would move the tobacco to the right, a moment later to the left, and the next moment she would roll it up and scrub her coal-black teeth with it.

Now Mother had no more arguments with which to oppose her visitor's intention. She said, "Well, if you've made up your mind to marry Inem off, I only hope that she gets a good husband who can take care of her. And I hope she gets someone who is compatible."

Inem's mother left, still shifting the tobacco about in her mouth.

"I hope nothing bad happens to that child."

"Why would anything bad happen to her?" I asked.

"Never mind, Muk, it's nothing." Then Mother changed the subject. "If the situation of their family improves, we won't lose any more of our chickens."

"Is somebody stealing our chickens, Mama?" I asked.

"No, Muk, never mind," Mother said slowly. "Such a little child! Only eight years old. What a pity it is. But they need money. And the only way to get it is to marry off their daughter."

Then Mother went to the garden behind the house to get some string beans for supper.

Fifteen days after this visit, Inem's mother came again to fetch her daughter. She seemed greatly pleased that Inem made no objection to being taken away. And when Inem was about to leave our house, never to be a member of our family again, she spoke to me in the kitchen doorway, "Well, good bye, Gus Muk. I'm going home, Gus Muk," she said very softly.

She always spoke softly. Speaking softly was one of the customary ways of showing politeness in our small-town society. She went off as joyfully as a child who expects to be given a new blouse.

From that moment, Inem no longer lived in our house. I felt very deeply the loss of my constant companion. From that moment also, it was no longer Inem who took me to the bathing cubicle at night to wash my feet before going to bed, but my adoptive older sister.

Sometimes I felt an intense longing to see Inem. Not infrequently, when I had got into bed, I would recall the moment when her mother drew her by the hand and the two of them left our house. Inem's house was in back of ours, separated only by a wooden fence.

She had been gone a month. I often went to her house to play with her, and Mother always got angry when she found out that I had been there. She would always say, "What can you learn at Inem's house that's of any use?"

And I would never reply. Mother always had a good reason for scolding me. Everything she said built a thick wall that was impenetrable to excuses. Therefore my best course was to be silent. And as the clinching argument in her lecture, she was almost certain to repeat the sentences that she uttered so often: "What's the point to your playing with her? Aren't there lots of other children you can ask to play with you? What's more, she's a woman who's going to be married soon."

But I kept on sneaking over to her house anyway. It is really surprising sometimes how a prohibition seems to exist solely in order to be violated. And when I disobeyed I felt that what I did was pleasurable. For children such as I at that time—oh, how many prohibitions and restrictions were heaped on our heads! Yes, it was as though the whole world was watching us, bent on forbidding whatever we did and whatever we wanted. Inevitably we children felt that this world was really intended only for adults.

Then the day of the wedding arrived.

For five days before the ceremony, Inem's family was busy in the kitchen, cooking food and preparing various delicacies. This made me visit her house all the more frequently.

The day before the wedding, Inem was dressed in all her finery. Mother sent me there with five kilos of rice and twenty-five cents as a neighborly contribution. And that afternoon we children crowded around and stared at her in admiration. The hair over her forehead and temples and her eyebrows had been carefully trimmed with a razor and thickened with mascara. Her little bun of hair had been built up with a switch and adorned with the paper flowers with springs for stalks that we call *sunduk mentul.* Her clothes were made of satin. Her sarong was an expensive one made in Solo. These things had all been rented from a Chinaman in the Chinese quarter near the town square. The gold rings and bracelets were all rented too.

The house was decorated with constructions of banyan leaves and young coconut fronds. On each wall there were crossed tricolor flags encircled by palm leaves. All the house pillars were similarly decorated with tricolor bunting.

Mother herself went and helped with the preparations. But not for long. Mother rarely did this sort of thing except for her closest neighbors. She stayed less than an hour. And it was then too that the things sent by Inem's husband-to-be arrived: a load of cakes and candies, a male goat, a quantity of rice, a packet of salt, a sack of husked coconuts, and half a sack of granulated sugar.

It was just after the harvest. Rice was cheap. And when rice was cheap all other foodstuffs were cheap too. That was why the period after the harvest was a favorite time for celebrations. And for that reason Inem's family had found it impossible to contract for a puppet performance. The puppet masters had already been engaged by other families in various neighborhoods. The puppet theater was the most popular form of entertainment in our area. In our town there were three types of puppet performance: the *wajang purwa* or shadow play, which recounted stories from the *Mahabharata* and the *Ramayana,* as well as other stories similar in theme; the *wajang krutjil,* in which wooden puppets in human shape acted out stories of Arabia, Persia, India, and China, as well as tales of Madjapahit times; and the *wajang golek,* which employed wooden dolls. But this last was not very popular.

Because there were no puppet masters available, Inem's family engaged a troupe of dancing girls. At first this created a dispute. Inem's relatives on her mother's side were religious scholars and teachers. But Inem's father would not back down. The dance troupe came, with its *gamelan* orchestra, and put on a *tajuban.*

Usually, in our area, a *tajuban* was attended by the men who wanted to dance with the girls and by little children who only wanted to watch—little children whose knowledge of sexual matters did not go beyond kissing. The grown boys did not like to watch; it embarrassed them. This was even more the case with the women—none of them attended at all. And a *tajuban* in our area—in order to inflame sexual passions—was always accompanied by alcoholic beverages: arrack, beer, whisky, or gin.

The *tajuban* lasted for two days and nights. We children took great delight in the spectacle of men and women dancing and kissing one another and every now and then clinking their glasses and drinking liquor as they danced and shouted, "*Huse!*"

And though Mother forbade me to watch, I went anyway on the sly.

"Why do you insist on going where those wicked people are? Look at your religious teacher: he doesn't go to watch, even though he is Inem's father's brother-in-law. You must have noticed that yourself."

Our religious teacher also had a house in back of ours, to the right of Inem's house. Subsequently the teacher's failure to attend became a topic that was sure to enliven a conversation. From it there arose two remarks that itched on the tip of everyone's tongue: that the teacher was certainly a pious man, and that Inem's father was undoubtedly a reprobate.

Mother reinforced her scolding with words that I did not understand at the time: "Do you know something? They are people who have no respect for women," she said in a piercing voice.

And when the bridegroom came to be formally presented to the bride, Inem, who had been sitting on the nuptial seat, was led forth. The bridegroom had reached the veranda. Inem squatted and made obeisance to her future husband, and then washed his feet with flower water from a brass pot. Then the couple were tied together and conducted side by side to the nuptial seat. At that time the onlookers could be heard saying, "One child becomes two. One child becomes two. One child becomes two."

And the women who were watching beamed as though they were to be the recipients of the happiness to come.

At that very moment I noticed that Inem was crying so much that her make-up was spoiled, and tears were trickling down her pretty face. At home I asked Mother, "Why was the bride crying, Mama?"

"When a bride cries, it's because she is thinking of her long-departed ancestors. Their spirits also attend the ceremony. And they are happy that their descendant has been safely married," replied Mother.

I never gave any thought to those words of hers. Later I found out why Inem had been crying. She had to urinate, but was afraid to tell anyone.

The celebration ended uneventfully. There were no more guests coming with contributions. The house resumed its everyday appearance, and by the time the moneylenders came to collect, Inem's father had left Blora. After the wedding, Inem's mother and Inem herself went on doing batik work—day and night. And if someone went to their house at three o'clock in the morning, he would be likely to find them still working. Puffs of smoke would be rising between them from the crucible in which the wax was melted. In addition to that, quarreling was often heard in that house.

And once, when I was sleeping with Mother in her bed, a loud scream awakened me: "I won't! I won't!"

It was still night then. The screams were repeated again and again, accompanied by the sound of blows and pounding on a door. I knew that the screams came from Inem's mouth. I recognized her voice.

"Mama, why is Inem screaming?" I asked.

"They're fighting. I hope nothing bad happens to that little girl," she said. But she gave no explanation.

"Why would anything bad happen to her, mama?" I asked insistently.

Mother did not reply to my question. And then, when the screaming and shouting were over, we went back to sleep. Such screams were almost sure to be heard every night. Screams and screams. And every time I heard them, I would ask my mother about them. Mother would never give a satisfactory answer. Sometimes she merely sighed, "What a pity, such a little child!"

One day Inem came to our house. She went straight in to find my mother. Her face was pale and bloodless. Before saying anything, she set the tone of the occasion by crying—crying in a respectful way.

"Why are you crying, Inem? Have you been fighting again?" Mother asked.

"Ma'am," said Inem between her sobs, "I hope that you will be willing to take me back here as before."

"But you're married, aren't you, Inem?"

And Inem cried some more. Through her tears she said, "I can't stand it, ma'am."

"Why, Inem? Don't you like your husband?" asked Mother.

"Ma'am, please take pity on me. Every night all he wants to do is wrestle, ma'am."

"Can't you say to him, 'Please, dear, don't be like that'?"

"I'm afraid, ma'am. I'm afraid of him. He's so big. And when he wrestles he squeezes me so hard that I can't breathe. You'll take me back, won't you, ma'am?" she pleaded.

"If you didn't have a husband, Inem, of course I'd take you back. But you have a husband . . ."

And Inem cried again when she heard what Mother said. "Ma'am, I don't want to have a husband."

"You may not want to, but the fact is that you do, Inem. Maybe eventually your husband will change for the better, and the two of you will be able to live happily. You wanted to get married, didn't you?" said Mother.

"Yes, ma'am . . . but, but . . . "

"Inem, regardless of anything else, a woman must serve her husband faithfully. If you aren't a good wife to your husband, your ancestors will curse you," said Mother.

Inem began crying harder. And because of her crying she was unable to say anything.

"Now, Inem, promise me that you will always prepare your husband's meals. When you have an idle moment, you should pray to God to keep him safe. You must promise to wash his clothes, and you must massage him when he is tired from his work. You must rub his back vigorously when he catches cold."

Inem still made no reply. Only her tears continued to fall.

"Well now, you go home, and from this moment on be a good wife to him. No matter whether he is good or bad, you must serve him faithfully, because after all he *is* your husband."

Inem, who was sitting on the floor, did not stir.

"Get up and go home to your husband. You . . . if you just up and quit your husband the consequences will not be good for you, either now or in the future," Mother added.

"Yes, ma'am," Inem said submissively. Slowly she rose and walked home.

"How sad, she's so little," said Mother.

"Mama, does daddy ever wrestle you?" I asked.

Mother looked searchingly into my eyes. Then her scrutiny relaxed. She smiled. "No," she said. "Your father is the best person in the whole world, Muk."

Then Mother went to the kitchen to get the hoe, and she worked in the garden with me.

A year passed imperceptibly. On a certain occasion Inem came again. In the course of a year she had grown much bigger. It was quite apparent that she was mature, although only nine years old. As usual, she went directly to where Mother was and sat on the floor with her head bowed. She said, "Ma'am, now I don't have a husband any more."

"What?"

"Now I don't have a husband any more."

"You're divorced?" asked Mother.

"Yes, ma'am."

"Why did you separate from him?"

She did not reply.

"Did you fail to be a good wife to him?"

"I think I was always a good wife to him, ma'am."

"Did you massage him when he came home tired from work?" asked Mother probingly.

"Yes, ma'am, I did everything you advised me to."

"Well then, why did you separate?"

"Ma'am, he often beat me."

"Beat you? He beat a little child like you?"

"I did everything I could to be a good wife, ma'am. And when he beat me and I was in pain—was that part of being a good wife, ma'am?" she asked, in genuine perplexity.

Mother was silent. Her eyes scrutinized Inem. "He beat you," Mother whispered then.

"Yes, ma'am—he beat me just the way Mama and Papa do."

"Maybe you failed in some way after all in your duty to him. A husband would never have the heart to beat a wife who was really and truly a good wife to him."

Inem did not reply. She changed the subject: "Would you be willing to take me back, ma'am?"

There was no hesitation in Mother's reply. She said firmly, "Inem, you're a divorced woman now. There are lots of grown boys here. It wouldn't look right to people, would it?"

"But they wouldn't beat me," said the divorcee.

"No. That isn't what I mean. It just doesn't look right for a divorced woman as young as you to be in a place where there are lots of men."

"Is that because there's something wrong with me, ma'am?"

"No, Inem, it's a question of propriety."

"Propriety, ma'am? It's for the sake of propriety that I can't stay here?"

"Yes, that's the way it is, Inem."

The divorcee did not say anything more. She remained sitting on the floor, and seemed to have no intention of leaving the place where she was sitting. Mother went up to her and patted her shoulder consolingly. "Now, Inem . . . the best thing is for you to help your parents earn a living. I really regret that I can't take you back here."

Two tears formed in the corners of the little woman's eyes. She got up. Listlessly she moved her feet, leaving our house to return to her parents' house. And from then on she was seldom seen outside her house.

And thereafter, the nine-year-old divorcee since she was nothing but a burden to her family—could be beaten by anyone who wanted to: her mother, her brothers, her uncles, her neighbors, her aunts. Yet Inem never again came to our house.

Her screams of pain were often heard. When she moaned, I covered my ears with my hands. And Mother continued to uphold the respectability of her home.

Indonesia

THE GREEN CHRYSANTHEMUM

AN SU-GIL

"AN AIRPLANE! An airplane! It's just like a dragonfly, isn't it?"

Under the clear, high dome of the sky, over the clearcut line of the distant peaks, an airplane appeared with a loud roar of engines. Bunyi paused in her corn harvesting and dropped her hands to her side. With a happy expression on her face, as if she were a child seeing an airplane for the first time, she cried in a clear voice, "So it is!"

Her mother-in-law looked up in the same direction as Bunyi. The dragonfly shape of the airplane soon grew larger and it came flying over the willows on the river bank.

"How fast it is! It must have our soldiers in it. Oh, it's too dazzling!"

Bunyi shaded her eyes with one hand and, stretching the other upward, waved and looked up at the airplane, as it flew above her head, its wings glistening in the sunshine.

"If we were in it, we would get to Seoul in no time at all, wouldn't we?" said her mother-in-law, who was always longing to go to Seoul, as she looked up at the airplane. The thought struck Bunyi that she would like to fly around in the clear, cloudless, vast, and lofty sky in an airplane with Mr. Yi, who had urged her to run away with him when they had met a few nights before.

The airplane vanished, and the sky and the field once more became quiet; all that could be heard was the unceasing sound of Bunyi and her mother-in-law gathering corn.

"What are they doing in Seoul? Surely we should hear today," said her mother-in-law, imagining that the airplane must have reached Seoul by this time. But Bunyi answered in a tone of annoyance, "Mother, are you still thinking of Seoul?"

"Why not? What else is there?"

"Haven't we escaped from Seoul? What's the use of brooding on it all the time?"

Her mother-in-law was silent.

"I like this place very much. They talk about caged birds being released. That's me. I really hate Seoul very much." So Bunyi said, but she meant that what she really disliked was not Seoul but her husband's family there.

"Thin bones grow big even when they quarrel with one another. Don't you miss them? It happens that they are your relations. There's nothing that you can do about that, is there?"

Her mother-in-law answered thus because she realized that Bunyi was not referring to the place. When they had started farming here in the country, she had seen Bunyi become gay and lively, and she remembered her own past life. She felt sympathy for Bunyi, who had spent her youth confined within the Ilgag Gate in Seoul.

"I heard that they were going to move tomorrow. But if we don't hear today, perhaps they won't come just yet. Anyhow they have sold their house in Seoul, and I expect that they will come here sooner or later."

"If they come here, won't it be just the same as being in Seoul, Mother? Do you like the idea of their coming here, or do you like it better with only us two farming here?"

Bunyi had come to this family when she was eight years old and had been brought up to be the daughter-in-law. Thus the relationship between her and her mother-in-law was not the usual one. The son, too, had been adopted, and had been brought from the country when he was five years old. So the son and daughter-in-law had both grown up in the same house. But the mother-in-law was naturally fonder of her daughter-in-law, who was strong and healthy, than she was of her foster son, who was a eunuch and had a peculiar character. She thought of Bunyi as her real daughter, and Bunyi thought of her as her real mother and felt very affectionate toward her.

"It won't be the same as in Seoul. In the first place we can go

out and work in the fields as often as we wish. Isn't that
emancipation, the word that's so popular nowadays?"

"Emancipation? But if grandfather comes here from Seoul
and sits inside curled up like a cat, holding forth interminably
and tapping with his pipe, how will we be any better off than we
were inside the Ilgag Gate in Seoul? The old man's not going
to die just yet, is he?"

Bunyi knew that her mother-in-law shared her dislike of her
grandfather, and so she could speak her mind without restraint,
but the last sentence of her complaint seemed to be aimed at her
own husband rather than at her grandfather.

"Nonsense!" Her mother-in-law rebuked her to maintain
her own dignity as her elder and even glared at her, but she
quite realized what Bunyi meant.

Her husband was a most peculiar character. His body smelled
foul, and he used to eat onions and garlic to strengthen his
energies and thoughtlessly breathed the strong smell out of his
mouth. He used to bite and scratch Bunyi every night with hands
and legs as thin as the whitened bones of a skeleton. When
Bunyi thought of this husband of hers and that he would come
up here and treat her in the same way, her feelings of gaiety
turned at once to gloom.

Bunyi was the daughter of a peasant. Her father had
seven children. As a tenant farmer he made scarcely enough to
live on, and in the end was obliged to sell Bunyi to a former
palace eunuch in Seoul, one Gim Dong-Zi, to be his granddaughter-in-law. Then he left for North Gando in Manchuria.
Bunyi was eight years old, and did not realize that Gim Dong-Zi
was a eunuch. She did not even know what a eunuch was. She was
just unhappy and sad to leave her parents and to be parted from
her younger brother and sisters. At first she refused to go, and
her mother wept, but the water had already run out of the over-
turned pot. Bunyi and her mother had barely time enough to
embrace and shed tears, and then she was led away to the residence of Gim Dong-Zi in Seoul, followed by his tenants, and was
confined within the Great Gate of his house.

When Bunyi came to live with the eunuch he was living

in a mansion of fifty gan in Waryomg-dong. The house was built on rather a small scale on a special plan, as the houses of eunuchs used to be. It had many gates, the Outer Great Gate, the Inner Great Gate, the Ilgag Gate, the Inner-Middle Gate and the Innermost Gate; the women's quarters were in the innermost place of all within all these gates.

As was usual in the house of a eunuch in the old days, no other male was allowed to come into the house and even the mother of a girl sold to such a house to become the daughter-in-law was not allowed to pass the Ilgag Gate. And when once a girl had passed inside the Ilgag Gate, she was obliged to stay within for the rest of her life, as if she were confined to prison.

Under the strict watch of Mr. and Mrs. Gim Dong-Zi, Bunyi was not allowed to go even one foot outside this Ilgag Gate. She spent every day inside and grew in the affection of her mother-in-law. When the eunuch bridegroom reached the age of nine years and Bunyi was twelve, a betrothal ceremony was held for them. One night in the inner room within the firmly locked Ilgag Gate, where not even a kitten could attend, the tragic marriage had taken place.

Though as yet an awareness of sex had not yet stirred in Bunyi, she seemed dissatisfied with her husband from the time they got into bed on their wedding night. As she grew older, her feelings of hate and contempt for him gradually grew stronger and she became unhappy and frustrated. Moreover, as she grew more mature physically, she could not but feel her impulses more and more pent up because she could not freely go into the outside world as she wished, and she could not find any pleasure in life without doing so. Of course, as he grew up, her husband, the eunuch Bag, tried to treat his wife more considerately. But she felt as great an aversion to her husband's coming close to her as if he had been a snake. Sometimes in the darkened room she kicked his scraggy chest roughly. Sometimes she twisted his skinny arms and cast them from her violently. And she often sighed and wept bitterly at her unhappy lot. Sometimes she felt pity for the miserable wretch who was her husband as he lay pale and panting, having fallen or been knocked down.

Perhaps his parents had been driven by poverty to sell him for a small sum of money, or perhaps they had sent him to the then wealthy home of Gim Dong-Zi, so that he could live in luxury, despite his miserable state—he did not know how he had become the old eunuch's foster son. At all events, he too was a fatally accursed eunuch. He had come to this house at the age of five. When he had finished his primary schooling, he had gone to a high school just like other boys, but his fellow pupils used to despise and mock him, shouting, "Eunuch, eunuch!" so that he became a laughingstock. He was as weak in character as in physique. He went all the way through the primary school while he was still a child, but he could not endure the high school. He left school when he was in the third year class, and then in his disappointment he usually stayed confined to the house. The only person he could love and trust with his heart was his wife, Bunyi. But she was a vigorous woman, while he was an incapable man, so that there lay a great barrier between them which he found utterly unsurmountable. He could not but bemoan his unhappy fate and sympathize with his wife. He tormented her because of his feelings of inadequacy toward a healthy woman. As this caused her nothing but pain, she used to kick him and twist his arms.

At first Bunyi had tried to understand her husband's feelings and had felt sorry for him. But as the days passed he gave himself up more and more to unpleasant practices and caused his wife ever greater pain, so that he alienated her sympathy and understanding and she came to feel only hatred and horror toward him. When he vexed her and she became angry, she not only kicked him and twisted his arms, but also pinched him and squeezed his neck as he lay prostrate. As time passed he became quite accustomed to his wife's ill-treatment, and was amused by her attacks. He would go out of his way to irritate her so that he could enjoy her assaults upon him. Bunyi did not like his purposely annoying her. She hated him with the horror she felt for a snake that would still drag itself along though cut in two.

So as well as the wide sky beyond the Ilgag Gate, Bunyi longed for a vigorous man—a man strong in mind and body, a man who could carry her on his back across high mountains and who would beat her when she erred and would afterward make things up with her again.

When she came to the village, Bunyi found such a man in the person of one of Bag's employees, Yi. She got to know Yi and felt all the more that her husband was a worthless and hateful person. She used to go and meet Yi secretly. When she heard the news that her grandfather-in-law and husband were going to come down from Seoul to live there she became gloomy and dispirited.

Dense clouds of steam billowed out of a Japanese-style kettle which stood on the stove made of a petrol tin with holes in it. An appetizing smell of boiling corn filled the air. Bunyi tossed a handful of the husks and awns of corn on the fire and stood up. She asked her mother-in-law to look after the fire and went out to the well, carrying a water jar on her head.

The well was situated near Yi's field. It might almost have been arranged to let her meet Yi privately that the well was dug in that place. Almost every time she went there, she could see Yi working in his field. Of course she could not speak to him near the well, for she was afraid someone might see them. But when she saw the sturdy and vigorous Yi squatting there like a great rock as he tore out weeds by the roots she felt really happy. Because of this, although the well was rather a long way from the house and she had to cross a small hill to get to it, she always went gladly to fetch water.

This time, however, she could not see Yi. She thought that perhaps he had gone down to the rice-field. So she had to go home again, dragging disappointed steps over the hill with the water jar on her head.

"I've just heard they are coming tomorrow," said her mother-in-law, ladling the boiled corn from the kettle to a bowl.

"Oh, they are really coming?"

Bunyi stood a few minutes in a daze with her water jar on her head and seemed to have forgotten all about it, under the shock of this bitter disappointment and surprise.

"Ri has been to Seoul, and he just dropped in with the news."

"Oh, whatever shall I do?"

Her mother-in-law took no notice and went on ladling out the boiled corn, but Bunyi was greatly worried.

The eighth eunuch ancestor of her grandfather-in-law had held a title of the highest honor, "Right Honorable Gentleman of Happiness and Goodness, Second Rank, Second Grade." He had acquired great wealth by arranging official appointments, such as county magistrate, for those who aspired to them. All this wealth had been dissipated by his adopted son and grandson, who were eunuchs too and lived in idleness, having no particular duties. By the time it came to Bunyi's grandfather, all that remained were the farmland at Yongin, which produced a couple of hundred sôg, and a large residence with an area of eighty gan in Gahwoe-Dong.

The eunuch Gim stood in high favor with King Sun-Zong and lived in luxury on the fortune he had inherited from his predecessors, not only in the old days but also after the system of palace eunuchs had been abolished. He held the same honorable title Dong-Zi, that had been bestowed on his eighth predecessor, he was known as Gim Dong-Zi, and was as influential as a fairly rich man. But as the years passed by his fortune gradually dwindled, primarily because of his adopted son, though the eunuch Czoe, the husband of Bunyi's mother-in-law was a man of some importance. He persuaded his father, who was proud of the honorable title bestowed on his eighth predecessor and who used to sit in an attitude of arrogant dignity, to agree to his mortgaging the farmland at Yongin. Then he set up in business. He opened a big dried fish shop in the market place at Dong Dê Mun, the Eastern Great Gate, and soon became well known among traders in such commodities. He had branches in the ports of Inezôn, Wônsan, Pohang, and Busan which kept him busy. But in the end he failed. He fell ill with nephritis and was confined to bed, and when his business failed completely he died. Gim Dong-Zi ignored the bank's demands on the grounds that his son's venture was no concern of his, but in the end he had to sell more than half the mortgaged land to settle the debt.

When Gim's son died and he lost more than half his land he was forced to effect economies in his household. The house of eighty gan in Gahwee-Dong where the family had lived for generations he exchanged for one of fifty gan. And now the eunuch Yun, whom he had adopted to be his grandson and the husband of Bunyi, stole money and ran away. This was immediately after the Sino-Japanese hostilities in Manchuria, and he ran off to Manchuria with the money. A widespread search was undertaken, and after a month he was caught and brought back home, but he had spent all the money. He was sent back to his parents, and the eunuch Bag, the present husband of Bunyi, was adopted in his place. It was now that Bunyi was brought to the house. Gim's was not a large family, but they spent money freely, just like eating dried persimmons one by one, and lived in idleness. They had to pay notes and taxes to the government, and their living expenses mounted daily. Their fortune decreased considerably after Bag was sent to high school. The house of fifty gan in Waryong-Dong was sold and they moved to one of thirty gan in Gye-Dong. Then they lived on the profit they had made by selling the house and on the income from their land. But when the Second World War began the government collected all agricultural produce, and the household of Gim Dong-Zi was seriously threatened. They sold half of the land that was left, and then the next year half of the remainder, but even so he could not support his family properly. After the Liberation he had a short breathing space, but new regulations were brought in whereby the tenant took seventy percent of the produce of a farm and the landlord thirty percent. On top of this came inflation, so that he found it impossible to support his family. Bunyi's husband found a post in the administration, enlarged in the postwar Liberation period, but it was only on a very low grade, and his salary was not high. And so they were obliged to leave the house of thirty gan in Gye-Dong and move to a thatched house of only ten gan.

In this way Gim Dong-Zi, now more than seventy years of age, who had proudly borne an honorable title, at last lost the final shreds of his former dignity and was reduced to the status of a common eunuch in plain clothes. He became a garrulous old man who plagued his daughter-in-law and his granddaughter-in-law with talk, squatting like a cat in his room.

But he could not live by talking and keeping watch on his

family, and so he sent his women-folk to Yongin, parting from
them with tears and sighs. He meant them to work the farm
themselves. About this time the new government was planning
a new agricultural system whereby landlords might keep their
land if they worked it themselves. It was for this reason that he
sent the women of his family to the country. He appealed to
his tenants to let him have some of his land back, and the
previous spring Bunyi and her mother-in-law had started farming there. Gim Dong-Zi felt uneasy about sending only the
women on their own, but his grandson still had his post. Moreover in the country a eunuch would only be something of a
curiosity, whereas in Seoul there would still be some people who
would respect his title. Furthermore he had now fallen to the
level of a beggar, and he feared that he might be a laughingstock
as well as a curiosity. In times gone by he had owned much land
in the village, and was well known to the villagers. He feared
that if he went and lived there he would feel a sense of shame,
so he tried to remain in Seoul as long as possible. But when the
government reduced its staff and threw his grandson out of a
job, it became impossible for him to stay in Seoul. Therefore
he now sold his house in Seoul and decided to move to the
country permanently.

The moon was high in the sky and the fields were
silvered in its light, but all was dark in the shadows of a cleft
in the hillside made by a landslide. Concealed by the darkness
Bunyi and Yi sat talking side by side.
"Can you come away with me tomorrow?"
"Let me think."
"Is there anything not settled?"
"I don't mean that, but . . . ."
"What then?"
" . . . . . ."
Yi clasped Bunyi tightly in his strong arms. Bunyi buried
her face in his breast which made her think of a rocky cliff, and
at the smell of his sweat she tingled with excitement that trans-
ported her to the heights of ecstacy.
Yi now expected to get a job in Pazu from old Bag's uncle
who was in need of men to work for him. The next day was

market day and a propitious day for his journey, so it was arranged that he should start the following morning. Yi did not want to leave old Bag, of whom he was very fond, but his uncle, who often came to the house, seemed to be a good man and persuaded Yi to accept his offer of employment. He even offered to find him a wife. And this was why he was so anxious to find out what Bunyi wanted, for he could be married without difficulty in his new place.

"If I go there, he may start talking about my marriage, and you haven't made up your mind yet. That's what's troubling me, can't you see?"

"You can get yourself a wife there, if you like."

Bunyi was much displeased to hear him talk of marrying someone else, and she pushed herself away from him and sat down. She still could not make up her mind to leave with him the next morning. She was worried about what might happen to her mother-in-law if she were not there.

The eunuch Czoe, her mother-in-law's husband, was quite different from Gim Dong-Zi and was fond of his wife, and sympathized with her in her misfortune at becoming the wife of a man like himself. He used to ponder on ways to make his wife as happy as lay in his power. He often went to the country and used to bring her back seaweed and fruits in season. At the supper table he would tell her all the experiences of his day one after the other. Moreover he was generous toward his wife's family. He gave her parents a sum of money and bought a house for them without the knowledge of Gim Dong-Zi. He put up capital, too, for her brother to open a dried fish shop in Yang-Zu. In such ways he made it possible for his wife to endure her wearisome life within the Ilgag Gate, for her family benefited by it. But after his death, life was not so easy for her parents, and though she gained a certain relief from becoming a widow, it became almost unbearable for her to think about them. She tried to forget all these things, lavishing her love on Bunyi, until she reached the age of sixty-three, having preserved her chastity through all these years. If she had lost her daughter-in-law, she would have put an end to her life.

Bunyi understood the depth of her mother-in-law's affection, and she felt obliged to hesitate in the face of Yi's urgent demands. But he did not feel the same delicacy in the matter and pressed her for an answer.

"Are you coming with me in the morning?"

Bunyi was silent.

"Since we will be leaving this place for good and not coming back again, we won't have to run away at night. Old Dong-Zi will come down from Seoul when we are gone . . . Let us go courageously in the daytime."

"You sound like an ignorant fellow, you know."

"What? Ignorant? He's just a eunuch and a beggar. Are you still so afraid of old Dong-Zi? He's still got a stronger influence over you than anyone else, hasn't he?"

"That will be enough!" snapped Bunyi and glared at him. But Yi's foolhardy yet self-reliant nature exercised too powerful an attraction on her, and she gave in and forgot her mother-in-law's affection.

They sat in silence for a few moments. Then, with a serious expression on his face, Yi began, "Well, they expect me to go in the morning. I shall leave as arranged, and then you can follow me at night. There is a cold-noodle restaurant in the town by the street of the cattle market. Go there and ask for Zang-Swoe, and they will tell you where I am. Do you understand? I will wait for you."

The corn Bunyi ate for lunch gave her indigestion, and she had pains in her stomach. Her parting from Yi had given her heartache on top of her stomach-ache. She went to the toilet for a while and then went back to the house.

"Where have you been?" her mother-in-law asked her when she opened the door. She had apparently been waiting for her.

"To the toilet, Mother," she replied, as she came into the room. Her mother-in-law did not like her to go outside at night. She had gone to bed early, but these days she seemed to keep an eye on Bunyi's going out of doors at night.

"It's a bad habit to get into, going to the toilet at night, I say," said her mother-in-law. She seemed to mean that going to the toilet was not a good excuse.

"I think I've got indigestion from the corn I had for lunch,

Mother. I've still got a sharp pain in my stomach," Bunyi replied. By the faint moonlight that came in through the window her mother-in-law saw her clutching her stomach and she said with a worried look, "Let me see. Is it very painful?" She came over to Bunyi and stroked her stomach with her hand.

Bunyi remembered that before she had come to live with Gim Dong-Zi her own mother had soothed her by rubbing the painful place whenever she had fallen down or had a stomach-ache as a child. Her mother used to say, "I have a magic hand. The magic hand will make you better." So suddenly Bunyi missed her own family, of whom she had had no news since they went to North Gando in Manchuria. In her heart she was deeply appreciative of her mother-in-law's love for her, which was no less than that of her own mother.

"I'm all right, Mother," she said. As her mother-in-law rubbed her body both her stomach-ache and her uneasiness of heart grew less. When after a few moments her mother-in-law left her and went back to bed, her worries returned, and she could not sleep. Which was it to be? Her mother-in-law or Yi? She found herself at the crossroads where she must choose one or the other of those she loved. She tossed this way and that in bed and sighed.

"Have you still got a pain in your stomach?" her mother-in-law asked. She too seemed to be unable to sleep, late as it was, so long as Bunyi was in pain.

"No, Mother," she replied.

"Then why can't you sleep?"

"I don't know."

"You don't know?" said her mother-in-law and got out of bed. "You are worried about something, aren't you?"

"What would I be worried about?"

Her mother-in-law spat out of the window, and the moonlight stole silently into the room.

"How bright the moon is!"

"It's the seventeenth, isn't it, Mother?"

"I have often felt very lonesome, looking at the moon on an autumn night."

"You have too, Mother?"

Her mother-in-law closed the window without answering.

"Mother, what would you do if I were not with you?" asked Bunyi. She was not going to miss this chance now that her mother-in-law had become very sentimental. She wanted to pour out all the secrets of her aching heart. Her mother-in-law was astonished, and said, "What do you mean? Not with me?" And she came nearer. Her mother-in-law's firm attitude rather shook Bunyi's resolve, and she felt too ashamed to disclose her intimate relationship with Yi.

"I just meant . . ." she began and then shut her mouth tight. But Bunyi's recent behavior had made her mother-in-law suspicious, and there were rumors going around. So she would not let the matter drop.

"What did you want to say to me?"

Bunyi did not reply.

"You won't try to deceive me, will you?"

Still Bunyi would not reply.

"Is it true that you meet Yi often?"

Bunyi was silent.

Her mother-in-law grew impatient at Bunyi's refusal to answer, as if she were a Buddha made of stone. For a few moments neither spoke. Then her mother-in-law began, "I know everything. I've heard some strange rumors too. After your confinement behind the Ilgag Gate, it was rather to be expected that the freedom of this place should give you an idea like that. But what right have you or I to expect happiness in life? How could it come about that you were sold to this house unless you had been fated to a truly evil future? One cannot escape from one's fate, I tell you. I can understand what you intended to do and what you had in your mind. You might as well try to toss aside the Ilgag Gate and roam freely in the world. They say that the greatest pleasure is that of a man and a woman, and so you must wonder how precious youth can be cast aside to no purpose. Yes, you will long for a happy married life, to find the most suitable man and to give birth to sons and daughters. But the world does not shape itself to suit our desires, does it? Do you think that if we throw over the Ilgag Gate there will be any who will welcome us with pleasure? You may find someone who will accept you, but he may mean to take you for his passing pleasure only. How can we trust the men of this world? There may be some man who will love you wholeheartedly for the moment, but how can you be sure of his everlasting devotion? There are so many young women in the world that to love a eunuch's wife can be no more than a passing whim, I tell you. Look here, it was fated that we should not be happy. How can you be sure he will not cast you aside some day? You lived so long within the Ilgag Gate, gazing up at a narrow strip of sky, how can you know all about life? And yet you now want to embark upon a wild adventure, don't you? Bear in mind that the man who is pursuing you now may one day let you down. Will you be better off then than you were within the Ilgag Gate? The Ilgag Gate is not what it was. We can now come out and work by ourselves in the open fields like this. Isn't this 'liberation'? And your grandfather and your husband may not treat us so badly now, since the great misfortune has befallen them of having to come and live in a thatched house in the country . . . So you and I had better not have such wild ideas. We were fated to be unhappy, weren't we? We must rely on each other. I shall love you like daughter or, in a way, as my husband. Then you can rely on me as you would on our own mother as well as your mother-in-law. And when I die, you may arrange my funeral with your own hands, and you will observe the customary rites with all sincerity . . . "

Her mother-in-law sighed deeply and went on, "If you leave me, on whom can I rely, how shall I live?"

Then she blew her nose on the band of her skirt. Bunyi felt her eyelids hot with tears as she listened to her gentle and sorrowful words, so full of sincerity. Her tears fell fast, and her pillow was wet. In this way Bunyi suffered the whole night long. Her mother-in-law, Yi, the eunuch Bag, Gim Dong-Zi, the Ilgag Gate, the village in Pazu, the girl who might become the wife of Yi— they all passed confusedly through her brain, and she worked herself almost into a frenzy.

The next morning dawned bright and clear, a beautiful autumn day just like the previous one. Bunyi got up early as usual. She seemed quite calm and collected and betrayed no sign

of the agonies she had suffered during the night. She went and
fetched water, cooked the breakfast, and went out for a while
into the fields as usual with a towel wrapped round her head.
Then she came back to the house and rolled up the mat in the
inner room. She sprinkled water on the floor and swept up all
the dust. She beat the mat with a stick and put it back in its place.
She wiped the wooden floor with a cloth. Then she swept every
corner of the garden and put rows of stones around the flower
beds to make them neat. She mended the holes in the kitchen floor
neatly with mud.

Her mother-in-law was relieved to see her work so well. She
thought that she must have taken her advice of the night before
to heart and settled down. This idea made her feel grateful to
Bunyi, and at the same time she felt sorry for her.

After lunch a boy called Dolswoe, who lived in the next village,
called at the house on his way back from an errand to the fishmonger. He had with him a parcel, tied with straw string, containing two salted mackerel and four dried pollack. They were to be
offered at a service in the evening. He reported that he had met
Gim Dong-Zi and the eunuch Bag resting near Yun Zang-I's
shop in the fish market. They had a horse and cart loaded with
all their furniture. Gim Dong-Zi asked the boy to tell his family
that he would soon be there and that he wished them to come out
to meet him.

"He said his leather bag was very heavy," the boy went on. "I
offered to carry it for him, but he said it was not the sort of thing
for me to carry. It must have had something very important in it,
I should say. If they started soon after I left them they should be
near the Pear Village by now, however slowly they might be walking. So you had better hurry off to meet them, or he will take it
out on me afterward."

The boy was the son of one of Gim Dong-Zi's tenants and knew
all about Gim, for he used to come down from Seoul and complain
imperiously about the harvest. When he had delivered his message, he went on home.

Bunyi's mother-in-law would have liked to send Bunyi, but she
went herself instead because Gim Dong-Zi would have reproached
her if she had sent the young woman to meet them alone. So she

said to Bunyi, "I will go and meet them, and you stay here." She tidied her clothes and went out.

Less than an hour later Gim Dong-Zi, his adopted grandson the eunuch Bag, and Bunyi's mother-in-law came into the house. The garden was swept so clean that not the slightest trace of footsteps was to be seen. The hoes, rakes, and sickles were stacked in the place set aside for them. There was not a speck of dust on the wooden floor, so clean had it been wiped. The garden and the house stood silent. But there was no sign of Bunyi either in the garden or in the house. "Where has Bunyi gone?" Gim Dong-Zi screeched furiously, in a voice like a cat's. Her mother-in-law was greatly taken aback. The eunuch Bag crept stealthily to the back garden to find Bunyi, whom he had missed so much. "Ah!" he cried in great alarm when he got there and looked at the peach tree. "Bunyi's hanged herself!"

The flowers under the hedge were a fresh and vivid red, bathed in the bright sunshine of the autumn afternoon.

Korea

AH AO

SUN HSI-CHEN

THROUGHOUT THE DAY, from early dawn, Ah Ao had remained hidden under a bed in the small, dark room, her head bent, her body still, scarcely daring to breathe . . .

At the foot of the Purple-red Mountain, down which spilled a dense growth of fragrant pines and other trees, a small stream ran into the open corn fields, and beside it stood a row of seven houses, most of them old and dilapidated. This place was known as Tao Village. None of the inhabitants, however was named Tao. In four of the seven houses lived the family Chen, the house on the western end was a family temple reserved for the spirits, and in the center of the row stood a comparatively new and handsome residence (some eighteen years old) which was owned by Chin the Rich.

It was in the seventh house, poorest of all, consisting of five little rooms, where the Wang family dwelt, that Ah Ao lay hidden. Half of this house was in fact mortgaged to Chin the Rich, who, two years before, when old Wang died, had lent his widow forty thousand cash to pay for the funeral feast and obsequies. Consequently she now lived with her son, Small One Brother, and her daughter, Ah Ao, in only the nether part of the little hut, which did not belong to Chin the Rich. In the room next to the kitchen—or, rather, in one corner of the kitchen itself, for the bed was separated from it only by a few thin planks—Ah Ao, in secret dread, trembled and stifled her lungs all day. Some millstones and empty bamboo baskets leaned against the wall of the kitchen, which was just now very noisy. There were four square wooden tables, with long benches arranged on each side, and these, with their occupants, completely choked up the little room. Altogether one could count more than thirty men, including not only the male population of Tao Village, but also guests from the neighboring villages of Yu and Red Wall. They sat drinking and feasting in an exuberant mood. Most of them wore blue or white cotton shirts and trousers, and were in their bare feet. However, Chin the Rich, Wu the Merchant, who could read and write, and the Hairy-headed Village Elder, respected for his age, wore long gowns made of linen. Only on rare occasions did these long-gown men visit such a lowly establishment, and it was plain that they were now quite aware of the extraordinary dignity their appearance lent to the feast.

The food seemed simple enough, with but four big bowls of meat, fish, turnips, and soup spread on each table. But they were refilled again and again, and each time emptied almost as soon as replenished. Besides, later on, the women of the village would have to be fed. Everybody gorged, helping himself to great hunks of meat and full bowls of wine, without any pretense of etiquette; their presence at the feast was not in the interest of good will, but a punitive measure against the mother of a shameless daughter. Never mind the financial burden to Widow Wang! It was the way of justice.

The fact was that only by mortgaging the other half of her house had the unhappy woman managed to get together the money to finance this strange banquet. A sentimental person might have observed that what the guests clipped between the blades of chopsticks was actually Widow Wang's flesh and blood, for the feast meant utter ruin to her. By this sacrifice, however, she was saving the life of her daughter, who was, no one could deny it, guilty of that crime. Now, although a crime of such a nature necessarily requires two to commit it, the unwritten but powerful law of Chinese custom nevertheless made her alone responsible, and gave any villager the right to attack, insult, abuse, or kill her, as he saw fit. By what other means, then, could the child's life be saved than through this, an expensive banquet in honor of the offended villagers, and especially to win mercy from Chin the Rich, Wu the Merchant, and the Hairy-headed Village Elder? Even though it meant her own death in the end, still the widow would have gone through with it.

Two days before, in the afternoon, she had sent her son to

Chin. He had bowed, begged mercy, and requested the loan of thirty thousand cash, pledging the rest of the Wang house as security. Then with this money the boy had, again at his mother's instruction, gone on to the market, where he bought thirty pounds of meat, more than twenty pounds of fish, fully a bushel of turnips, and some other ingredients of the feast. Since early in the morning of the previous day Widow Wang had busied herself with cleaning and preparing this food, making rice wine, and attending to other duties, so that she not once had a moment to rest.

With the arrival of the guests she had become even busier. All alone, she worked ceaselessly, serving everybody, keeping all the bowls filled with food, pouring forth the warm wine, which was like emptying the vessels of her own body, but all the same managing to smile and give the appearance of enjoying her duties immensely.

"Brother Lucky Root," shouted one coarse fellow, "don't hesitate! This isn't an occasion for ceremony, but a free feed. See, you don't have to give anything in return, so eat up! Fill yourself to the brim!"

"You are quite right," agreed Lucky Root. "Why be slow about it, eh? Let's eat, for such opportunities as this are rare indeed . . . As a matter of fact, this girl, now, Ah Ao; shameless, but still rather good-looking. How many girls around compare with her? Actually—"

"The more girls like Ah Ao the more free feasts," yelled a third. "Personally I hope we'll have others—"

"Ai-ya, Old Fa! Always boasting. You, the hungry devil with women! But don't forget the facts in this case: the girl right under your nose chooses instead a fellow from a neighboring village, not you!"

"Old Fa, ha, ha!"

"Ho! What an . . . Old Fa!"

The Widow Wang did not appear to understand these remarks, but bent her attention on the tasks of service, and on maintaining the smile on her face. She did not once frown. But Ah Ao heard, and trembled, and crawled still farther toward the wall. She did not know whether the feeling she experienced was humiliation, or terror, or indignation, or merely a heavy sadness, but something like a great stone seemed to be crushing her down, and her heart burned as though pierced by a shaft of red-hot iron. A few days ago she had boldly resigned herself to whatever fate might bring, but now she wanted only to crawl, crawl, crawl.

The Hairy-headed Elder at last came to the issue. "To be precise," he began slowly, "this is perhaps after all not so serious a matter. It is natural for a grown girl to want marriage, isn't it so? But to make love . . . to a young man . . . in secret, you know, and without anybody's knowledge . . . without the usual formalities . . . who can excuse it?"

"Exactly!" exclaimed Wu the Merchant. "Widow Wang, this is something that can only come to a mother as punishment for her own sins in the past. Such a daughter, just consider, is not only a disgrace to your own family name, but to the whole Tao Village as well. You very well know that according to age-old custom this crime merits nothing less than death. Recall, now, the case of the Chao girl—it happened three or four years ago in Stone Gate Village—who was beaten to death for the very same offense. Do you remember, she was buried without even a coffin? Nobody could call it cruelty, but only justice, for she had violated the laws of right conduct. Moreover, the worst of it is that even after their death such girls continue to dishonor the good name of the community. Ending life does not end their sin . . . No, indeed, and, as everyone knows, death doesn't begin to make up for it!"

"What you have just said is undeniably true. Death doesn't cover up the crime at all. But, on the other hand, it's not altogether the girl's fault . . . The mother is to blame also: a certain laxness, a waning of discipline. Again, in this case it may be that the mother was not herself very virtuous in some previous incarnation . . . Widow Wang, let me advise you to take care. In this life you had better be more strict."

The Village Elder was the donor of this speech, which oddly did not seem to anger the widow, but on the contrary encouraged her to speak. She moved forward timidly, her hands pulling nervously on the edge of her worn dress. She spoke, in a very low voice, and smiled painfully. "Yes . . . Honored Elder . . . that is correct. If she did wrong it was really my fault. I don't know what unpardonable sin I have behind me in some previous existence, but it must be as you say. And this terrible crime of my daughter, you're quite right, death would only be the punishment deserved. Still—" she broke suddenly into tears. "But I can't speak, I haven't the face to say—only I ask—*mercy!* Spare her life at least!"

This was a bold demand, an extraordinary request indeed, and were it not that the villagers were at that moment eating her food she would never have escaped their ridicule. They believed in enforcing justice and morality to the letter, and ordinarily would stand no nonsense. Yet it seemed generally understood that because they had appeared, and had eaten, and had enjoyed themselves, and some of them had even come on their own invitation, they would not be altogether adamant. But their decision rested upon the opinions voiced by Chin the Rich, Wu the Merchant, and the Hairy-headed Elder. Everybody remained silent until Chin finally gave the verdict.

"Wu has, I agree, spoken very wisely, and very much to the point. 'Death doesn't begin to cover up the crime.' Precisely! Then, perhaps, or so it seems to me, little is to be gained by taking her life now. The guilt has been admitted, and the Widow Wang, asking mercy, has begged us also to give 'face' to her late husband. She wants us to spare her daughter's life and, everything considered, that is perhaps possible. But at the same time we cannot permit such an altogether immoral woman to continue to stain the village's good name. She must leave at once!"

The Elder shared this view. "What is done is done. Though she is totally without honor, still it's no use, now, to kill her . . . Better, as you say, expel her—move her out immediately!"

These two having rendered a judgment, the rest of the guests, who considered themselves a kind of jury, reined in their tongues. The decision was unanimously approved. The pale, weary face of Widow Wang broke out suddenly into a genuine smile, she bowed low to the three wise men, and obsequiously thanked the members of the self-appointed jury. Back in the darkness the hidden Ah Ao heard, and yet curiously she did not feel happy at all at this reprieve. She understood well enough that life had been miraculously restored to her, but while the prospect of death had been terrifying she was after all too young to have a deep fear of it, whereas to be banished from the village, to leave and never again to see her mother, to bid farewell to her brother, to plunge into an unknown, uncertain future—that was something which she knew to be worse than death. Grief shook her body, seemed to break, to shatter it, so that it was no longer whole, but a heap of something that mysteriously still trembled with life.

It happened two months before, in early April, on a day filled with an ineffable softness, and unbearable languor and gladness that made men dreamy-eyed, drowsy, and as if drunk with some wonderful wine.

Ah Ao, on her way home in the afternoon from nearby Yu Village, thought that she had never known such a glorious day. There was a new warmth in her body, a strange vigor in her as if she had just begun to live. The fields bordering the road were transformed from a withered yellow into a lush new green, the trees were coming to life, and in their budding limbs birds had appeared and were joyously chattering. The whole world, as far as she could see, was young, fresh, growing, awakened, expectant. She felt in harmony with all that she saw, and expectant too. Of what? She did not know, but somehow she found herself walking more slowly. Her face burned as from some inner fire, and she became all at once conscious of her body, vibrant and warm against the fabric of her garments.

"Ah Ao!" a voice called from somewhere.

Surprised and a little afraid, she stopped, looked around, peered over the fields into the clustered pines and through the rocky pass, but saw no one. Above her head a pair of eagles circled. She blushed, rubbed her burning face, and walked on.

"Ah Ao!" someone cried again, this time much nearer. She stopped, more puzzled, but saw no one, and started to go on, when once more she heard the same voice, now quite close, speak out, "Ah Ao, it's me."

Turning around quickly she saw, protruding from the bushes and greenery, a head. Then slowly a young man in a long linen gown gave her a full-length view of himself, including his handsome red-buttoned cap. He was perhaps twenty years old, not a bad-looking fellow, and he wore a pleased look on his face.

Ah Ao recognized him. He was the son of Li, a shop-owner in the neighboring village. His name, she knew, was Ah Hsian.

"Ai-ya! So it's you," said Ah Ao. "You frightened me almost to death. Where did you come from?"

Nevertheless, she seemed not altogether dissatisfied that he had appeared.

"I?" he demanded. "I? I just happened to be coming from town, saw you in the distance, and hid myself to have some fun with you."

"You impudent rascal!" she shouted gaily, raising her hand as if to slap him. "Frightening a person to death!"

"I apologize, Ah Ao, with all my heart. The truth is I have something very important to tell you."

"For example?"

But the youth suddenly became weak or timid. He kept murmuring "I . . . I . . . I—" Then he seized her hand.

"What is this?" Ah Ao started back quickly, but for some reason her legs refused to move. Her body quivered, as from some shock, and again she felt her flesh tingle under her cotton garments. All the strength seemed to run out of her. He put his arms around her, pulled her toward him, and then led her into the forest. She could not summon up any resistance, her mind did not seem to work as usual, she was hardly conscious that they moved at all; and she did not utter a sound. She only knew that within she felt intolerably buoyant and enlarged.

They sat down under the leafy arm of a tree, her head resting on his shoulder. Her eyes closed and she breathed rapidly. She felt his hand close softly over her breast, over her beating heart. His lips touched hers, and suddenly she felt a bodily glow that she had never known before.

"Caw—w—w!"

A magpie, wheeling overhead, startled her, and for a moment recalled to her that the world existed. She trembled.

"Ah Hsian! No, no! Don't, please! Mother will beat me to death!"

"Don't! You must not worry. Trust me, believe in me. Everything will be wonderful, like this always . . ."

His voice shook too, and some strange vibrancy of it, some summons she had never heard, and which would not be denied, completely overpowered her. He caressed her arms, her face, her throat. She ceased to resist.

"What is the matter with you, Ah Ao?" Widow Wang asked her daughter when, very much agitated, she returned home late that afternoon. "Fever?" She touched her forehead, which was covered with a short fringe of hair. "Have you caught a cold?"

"Nothing at all. I . . . I simply don't feel very well," Ah Ao murmured, half to herself. She went to the bed and lay down, and for a long time she did not stir. She knew very well the risks, the danger, the fate opening up ahead of her, but just as well she knew that she would meet Ah Hsian again, whenever he asked, yes, even tomorrow!

She expected something dreadful to happen; she prepared herself for it. In the future, after each interval with him, she waited dully for the exposure of their crime, and each time was rather surprised when no one came to denounce her. Nevertheless, she resigned herself to ultimate discovery, but found comfort in the thought that her lover would come to her defense, take the punishment as pronounced. She imagined herself, in his moment of disgrace, going proudly to his side, sharing whatever fate imposed upon him. And what she constantly feared did happen at last, but its consequences were nothing like what she had romantically foreseen. It was just three days before the Widow Wang offered the villagers such a splendid banquet.

Behind Purple-red Mountain there was a small hill, the name of which had long been forgotten. Halfway up its flank, nearly buried in the foliage, was a temple to the mountain god, but few visited it, and hardly anyone passed over the hill at all, with the exception of somebody now and then using a short cut to Stone Gate Village. The surrounding forests were owned by one of the great landlords; few ventured to trespass through the leafy lanes. The place was pervaded by a ghostly stillness, but it was gentle shelter for young lovers.

On this day Lao Teh, the Spotted Face, a woodcutter, had crept stealthily into the forest to steal wood. He had gathered a load and was prepared to leave just as the setting sun splashed ruddily against the wall behind the mountain temple. The sight invited him, and, lifting the burden from his shoulder, he sat down on the threshold of the enclosure, sighed, lighted his pipe, and leisurely gazed at the sky.

But was that not a sound? Thrusting the pipe into his belt he seized his ax, and stood ready to combat with any wild animal that might rush forth. He waited for several minutes, tense and excited. He thought of running away, but reconsidered, remembering that an offensive is the best defensive. Picking up a stone as big as a goose egg, he threw it with all his strength into the thickest part of the forest.

To his astonishment it was not a wild beast but a man that burst from the trees. He did not stop or even look in Lao Teh's direction, but vanished like a devil. Lao Teh nevertheless saw enough of him to recognize Ah Hsian. Somewhat perplexed, he advanced toward the spot whence he had emerged.

Then in a moment he came upon Ah Ao, languidly spread out, with her dress loosened, her dark hair starred with bits of green leaves, and altogether wearing a look of abandon. The spectacle somehow aroused in Lao Teh, the Spotted Face, an intense fury, and he shook with his extreme indignation. He stared with wide open eyes, and then he bent down and severely struck her.

"Ha! Ah Ao! The devil! You've done a fine thing!" She did not speak, but lifted up eyes that implored, and eloquently begged pity. "Scandalous and shameless one! To come here in secret and lie with him!" He viciously slapped her again.

Later on, this scene, and the subsequent abuse flung upon her by the infuriated Lao Teh, remained rather obscure in Ah Ao's mind. She could not remember how, under his guidance, she returned home in disgrace, nor how news of her love spread throughout the village in a few minutes. Only afterward all the eyes she looked into were full of wrath: cold-gleaming eyes of hate. Even her mother gazed at her with anger and bitterness, yet deeper, deep down in those eyes, was a look of poignant sadness that troubled her heart. But the blows of bamboo sticks, the beatings that came in rapid succession, the curses hurled at her, not one of these caused her any pain, nor any shame, nor even the least regret.

She had expected all this, and now it had come. It was no accident, but had all along been in the certainty of fate, and she was prepared for everything that happened. The single unforeseen development that dismayed and depressed her was that her lover suffered none of the consequences, and did not appear to be in the least interested in her any longer.

The three days had gone by as an incident in a dream, and now the verdict of the wise men had been pronounced. Not to die. It was true that she felt some relief at this decision; yet she was far from happy. Her body felt old, heavy, infinitely weary, and her spirit was completely crushed—crushed not by anything that had been said of her or done to her, not even by the bitter sadness of her mother's eyes, but by the singularly irresponsible and cowardly conduct of her lover.

Even before the men guests had finished sipping the last of their wine the women began to come for their share, and during all this time Ah Ao continued to press closely against the wall, hovering in her hiding place, hungry and shivering, not because it was cold, not because she felt any longer the fear of death, but from some nameless malady that had seized her inmost being. The women ate no more lightly than their men-folk. It was late at night when the last of them finished, and one by one began to return home. Like the men they dropped cynical, sardonic remarks meant to stab mother and daughter cruelly, as they ate, with enormous appetites, the food heaped before them.

The air seemed charged with heightened drama when Mrs. Li, the mother of Ah Hsian, unexpectedly appeared at the feast. She had come, it was soon apparent, not to apologize for the part her son had taken in the affair, but on the contrary to curse the Widow Wang for permitting her daughter to induce him to commit adultery. She began her vituperations even before she entered the house. The widow, seeing her fat body waddling along at a distance, went forth to meet her with a sinking heart. Mrs. Li propelled herself across the stone bridge arched over the mountain stream, and rushed toward the Wangs' door. Then, seeing the unhappy mother, she drew back a few feet, pointed fixedly at her, and began to revile her in a loud voice: "Miserable woman!

Where there is such a daughter, there is such a mother also! And you have the face to come out to meet me? Really? My son is pure, chaste, good; he has made the genuflection before the image of Confucius; he has understood well the teachings of the great sage. Yet you, shameless mother, and immoral daughter attempt to seduce and ruin him! I am resolved to die with you this instant!"

And, saying this, she did indeed rush toward the Widow Wang and appeared to be determined to dash her brains out against her. Other women guests grouped round them, forming a little circle (not without experiencing an inner satisfaction at the scene), and comforted and soothed the wrath of the offended Mrs. Li. In fact, the fat woman so far forgot her original intention that she permitted them to lead her into the house. She even partook heartily of the feast, and in the end contented herself with muttering now and then, "She abused my son, seduced him . . . From now on he will be unable to raise his head above others."

When the last guest had gone the old widow stepped slowly into the little dark enclosure, carrying an oil lamp in her hand. She called to Ah Ao to come out and eat. Ah Ao gradually dragged herself forth, but the whole day of hiding, lying cramped in such confinement, had so wearied her that she now had scarcely strength enough to stand erect. A moment ago she had thought she was famished, but now she could not swallow a morsel.

Midnight. Widow Wang was not yet in bed. She moved about in the little room, picking up articles from here and there, busily arranging them in the baggage which Ah Ao must take with her when she left at tomorrow's dawn. Finally she fastened the bag securely, and then at once opened it again, adding two more pairs of stockings. She stood silent for a moment, thinking; then from an old broken cupboard she pulled out a linen skirt, and that seemed to complete the traveler's wardrobe.

Spring nights are brief, and in a very short time the cocks began to crow. The widow awoke her son and daughter, lighted a lantern, gave them their morning food, and then accompanied Ah Ao to the barrow which stood beside the door.

"Understand, daughter, it's not I who wants to desert you— you have spoiled yourself—"

But the stooped figure shook with sudden tears. She seemed

to brace herself against the air, and continued, managing to smile very gently, "Just be careful, Ah Ao. From now on stand firmly on your own feet, and I shall have no more cause for worry. As for me, daughter, well, just think that I am dead, no longer in this world. If we can't meet here again, then perhaps after death . . . anyway, let's hope . . ."

She sat beside Ah Ao on the barrow pushed by her son until they reached the great oak, at the main road, half a mile from her home. She alighted there, bid a last farewell to her daughter, and stood watching the receding lantern till, like the last flutter of life in a great void of death, its dim spark crept into utter darkness.

China

WEDDING DANCE

AMADOR DAGUIO

AWIYAO REACHED for the upper horizontal log which served as the edge of the head-high threshold. Clinging to the log, he lifted himself with one bound that carried him across to the narrow door. He slid back the cover, stepped inside, then pushed the cover back in place. After some moments during which he seemed to wait, he talked to the listening darkness.

"I'm sorry this had to be done. I am really sorry. But neither of us can help it."

The sound of the *gangsas* beat through the walls of the dark house, like muffled roars of falling waters. The woman who had moved with a start when the sliding door opened had been hearing the *gangsas* for she did not know how long. The sudden rush of rich sounds when the door opened was like a sharp gush of fire in her. She gave no sign that she heard Awiyao, but continued to sit unmoving in the darkness.

But Awiyao knew that she had heard him and his heart pitied her. He crawled on all fours to the middle of the room; he knew exactly where the stove was. With bare fingers he stirred the covered smoldering embers, and blew into them. When the coals began to glow, Awiyao put pieces of pine on them, then full round logs as big as his arms. The room brightened.

"Why don't you go out," he said, "and join the dancing women?" He felt a pang inside him, because what he said was really not the right thing to say and because the woman did not stir. "You should join the dancers," he said, "as if—as if nothing has happened." He looked at the woman huddled in a corner of the room, leaning against the wall. The stove fire played with strange moving shadows and lights upon her face. She was partly sullen, but her sullenness was not because of anger or hate.

"Go out—go out and dance. If you really don't hate me for this separation, go out and dance. One of the men will see you dance well; he will like your dancing; he will marry you. Who knows but that with him you will be luckier than you were with me."

"I don't want any man," she said sharply. "I don't want any other man."

He felt relieved that at least she talked. "You know very well that I don't want any other woman, either. You know that, don't you? Lumnay, you know it, don't you?"

She did not answer him.

"You know it, Lumnay, don't you?" he repeated.·

"Yes, I know," she said weakly.

"It is not my fault," he said, feeling relieved. "You cannot blame me; I have been a good husband to you."

"Neither can you blame me," she said. She seemed about to cry.

"No, you have been very good to me. You have been a good wife. I have nothing to say against you." He set some of the burning wood in place. "It's only that a man must have a child. Seven harvests is just too long to wait. Yes, we have waited too long. We should have another chance before it is too late for both of us."

This time the woman stirred, stretched her right leg out, and bent her left leg in. She wound the blanket more snugly around herself.

"You know that I have done my best," she said. "I have prayed to Kabunyan much. I have sacrificed many chickens in my prayers."

"Yes, I know."

"You remember how angry you were once when you came home from your work in the field because I butchered one of our pigs without your permission? I did it to appease Kabunyan because, like you, I wanted to have a child. But what could I do?"

"Kabunyan does not see fit for us to have a child," he said. He stirred the fire. The sparks rose through the crackles of the flames. The smoke and soot went up to the ceiling.

Lumnay looked down and unconsciously started to pull at the rattan that kept the split bamboo flooring in place. She tugged at the rattan flooring. Each time she did this the split bamboo went up and came down with a slight rattle. The gongs of the dancers clamorously called in her ears through the walls.

Awiyao went to the corner where Lumnay sat, paused before her, looked at her bronzed and sturdy face, then turned to where the jars of water stood piled one on top of the other. Awiyao took a coconut cup and dipped it in the top jar and drank. Lumnay had filled the jars from the mountain creek early that evening.

"I came home," he said, "because I did not find you among the dancers. Of course, I am not forcing you to come, if you don't want to join my wedding ceremony. I came to tell you that Madulimay, although I am marrying her, can never become as good as you are. She is not as strong in planting beans, nor as fast in cleaning water jars, nor as good at keeping a house clean. You are one of the best wives in the whole village."

"That has not done me any good, has it?" she said. She looked at him lovingly. She almost seemed to smile.

He put the coconut cup aside on the floor and came closer to her. He held her face between his hands, and looked longingly at her beauty. But her eyes looked away. Never again would he hold her face. The next day she would not be his any more. She would go back to her parents. He let go of her face, and she bent to the floor again and looked at her fingers as they tugged softly at the split bamboo floor.

"This house is yours," he said, "I built it for you. Make it your own, live in it as long as you wish. I will build another house for Madulimay."

"I have no need for a house," she said slowly. "I'll go to my own house. My parents are old. They will need help in the planting of the beans, in the pounding of the rice."

"I will give you the field that I dug out of the mountain during the first year of our marriage," he said. "You know I did it for you. You helped me to make it for the two of us."

"I have no use for any field," she said.

He looked at her, then turned away, and became silent. They were silent for a time.

"Go back to the dance," she said finally. "It is not right for you to be here. They will wonder where you are, and Madulimay will not feel good. Go back to the dance."

"I would feel better if you would come, and dance—for the last time. The *gangsas* are playing."

"You know that I cannot."

"Lumnay," he said tenderly. "Lumnay, if I did this it is because of my need for a child. You know that life is not worth living without a child. The men have mocked me behind my back. You know that."

"I know it," she said. "I will pray that Kabunyan will bless you and Madulimay."

She bit her lips now, then shook her head wildly, and sobbed.

She thought of the seven harvests that had passed, the high hopes they had in the beginning of their new life, the day he took her away from her parents across the roaring river, on the other side of the mountain, the trip up the trail which they had to climb, the steep canyon which they had to cross. The waters boiled in her mind in foams of white and jade and roaring silver; the waters rolled and growled, resounded in thunderous echoes through the walls of the stiff cliffs; they were far away now but loud still and receding. The waters violently smashed down from somewhere on the tops of the other ranges, and they had looked carefully at the buttresses of rocks they had to step on—a slip would have meant death.

They both drank of the water, then rested on the other bank before they made the final climb to the other side of the mountain.

She looked at his face with the fire playing upon his features—hard and strong, and kind. He had a sense of lightness in his way of saying things, which often made her and the village people laugh. How proud she had been of his humor. His muscles were taut and firm, bronze and compact in their hold upon his skull—how frank his bright eyes were. She looked at his body, which carved out of the mountains five fields for her: his wide and supple torso heaved as if a slab of shining lumber were heaving; his arms and legs flowed down in fluent muscles—he was strong and for that she had lost him.

She flung herself upon his knees and clung to them. "Awiyao,

Awiyao, my husband," she cried. "I did everything to have a
child," she said passionately in a hoarse whisper. "Look at me,"
she cried. "Look at my body. Then it was full of promise. It
could dance; it could work fast in the fields; it could climb the
mountains fast. Even now it is firm, full. But, Awiyao, Kabunyan
never blessed me. Awiyao, Kabunyan is cruel to me. Awiyao, I
am useless. I must die."

"It will not be right to die," he said, gathering her in his arms.
Her whole warm naked breast quivered against his own; she
clung now to his neck, and her head lay upon his right shoulder:
her hair flowed down in cascades of gleaming darkness.

"I don't care about the fields," she said. "I don't care about
the house. I don't care for anything but you. I'll have no other
man."

"Then you'll always be fruitless."

"I'll go back to my father. I'll die."

"Then you hate me," he said. "If you die it means you hate
me. You do not want me to have a child. You do not want my
name to live on in our tribe."

She was silent.

"If I do not try a second time," he explained, "it means I'll
die. Nobody will get the fields I have carved out of the mountains; nobody will come after me."

"If you fail—if you fail this second time—" she said thought-
fully. Then her voice was a shudder. "No—no, I don't want you
to fail."

"If I fail," he said, "I'll come back to you. Then both of us
will die together. Both of us will vanish from the life of our
tribe."

The gongs thundered through the walls of their house, sonorous
and far away.

"I'll keep my beads," she said. "Awiyao, let me keep my beads,"
she half-whispered.

"You will keep the beads. They come from far-off times. My
grandmother said they came from way up north, from the slant-
eyed people across the sea. You keep them, Lumnay. They are
worth twenty fields."

"I'll keep them because they stand for the love you have for
me," she said. "I love you. I love you and have nothing to give."

She took herself away from him, for a voice was calling to him from outside. "Awiyao! Awiyao! Oh Awiyao! They are looking for you at the dance!"

"I am not in a hurry."

"The elders will scold you. You had better go."

"Not until you tell me that it is all right with you."

"It is all right with me."

He clasped her hands. "I do this for the sake of the tribe," he said.

"I know," she said.

He went to the door.

"Awiyao!"

He stopped as if suddenly hit by a spear. In pain he turned to her. Her face was agony. It pained him to leave. She had been wonderful to him. What was it that made a man wish for a child? What was it in life, in the work in the fields, in the planting and harvest, in the silence of the night, in the communings with husband and wife, in the whole life of the tribe itself that made man wish for the laughter and speech of a child? Suppose he changed his mind? Why did the unwritten law demand, anyway, that a man, to be a man, must have a child to come after him? And if he was fruitless—but he loved Lumnay. It was like taking away half of his life to leave her like this.

"Awiyao," she said, and her eyes seemed to smile in the light. "The beads!"

He turned back and walked to the farthest corner of their room, to the trunk where they kept their worldly possessions— his battle-ax and his spear points, her betel nut box and her beads. He dug out from the darkness the beads which had been given to him by his grandmother to give to Lumnay on the day of his marriage. He went to her, lifted her head, put the beads on, and tied them in place. The white and jade and deep orange obsidians shone in the firelight. She suddenly clung to him, clung to his neck, as if she would never let him go.

"Awiyao! Awiyao, it is hard!" She gasped, and she closed her eyes and buried her face in his neck.

The call for him from the outside repeated; her grip loosened, and he hurried out into the night.

Lumnay sat for some time in the darkness. Then she went to

the door and opened it. The moonlight struck her face; the moon-light spilled itself upon the whole village.

She could hear the throbbing of the *gangsas* coming to her through the caverns of the other houses. She knew that all the houses were empty; that the whole tribe was at the dance. Only she was absent. And yet was she not the best dancer of the village? Did she not have the most lightness and grace? Could she not, alone among all the women, dance like a bird tripping for grains on the ground, beautifully timed to the beat of the *gangsas?* Did not the men praise her supple body, and the women envy the way she stretched her hands like the wings of the mountain eagle now and then as she danced? How long ago did she dance at her own wedding? Tonight, all the women who counted, who once danced in her honor, were dancing now in honor of another whose only claim was that perhaps she could give her husband a child.

"It is not right. It is not right!" she cried. "How does she know? How can anybody know? It is not right," she said.

Suddenly she found courage. She would go to the dance. She would go to the chief of the village, to the elders, to tell them it was not right. Awiyao was hers; nobody could take him away from her. Let her be the first woman to complain, to denounce the unwritten rule that a man may take another woman. She would break the dancing of the men and women. She would tell Awiyao to come back to her. He surely would relent. Was not their love as strong as the river?

She made for the other side of the village where the dancing was. There was a flaming glow over the whole place; a great bonfire was burning. The *gangsas* clamored more loudly now, and it seemed they were calling to her. She was near at last. She could see the dancers clearly now. The men leaped lightly with their *gangsas* as they circled the dancing women decked in feast gar-ments and beads, tripping on the ground like graceful birds, following their men. Her heart warmed to the flaming call of the dance; strange heat in her blood welled up, and she started to run.

But the flaming brightness of the bonfire commanded her to stop. Did anybody see her approach? She stopped. What if somebody had seen her coming? The flames of the bonfire leaped in countless sparks which spread and rose like yellow points and died out in the night. The blaze reached out to her like a spreading radiance. She did not have the courage to break into the wedding feast.

Lumnay walked away from the dancing ground, away from the village. She thought of the new clearing of beans which Awiyao and she had started to make only four moons before. She followed the trail above the village.

When she came to the mountain stream she crossed it carefully. Nobody held her hands, and the stream water was very cold. The trail went up again, and she was in the moonlight shadows among the trees and shrubs. Slowly she climbed the mountain.

When Lumnay reached the clearing, she could see from where she stood the blazing bonfire at the edge of the village, where the dancing was. She could hear the far-off clamor of the gongs, still rich in their sonorousness, echoing from mountain to mountain. The sound did not mock her; they seemed to call to her from far; speak to her in the language of unspeaking love. She felt the pull of their clamor, almost a feeling that they were telling her their gratitude for her sacrifice. Her heartbeat began to sound to her like many *gangsas*.

Lumnay thought of Awiyao as the Awiyao she had known long ago—a strong, muscular boy carrying his heavy loads of fuel logs down the mountains to his home. She had met him one day as she was on her way to fill her clay jars with water. He had stopped at the spring to drink and rest, and she had made him drink the cool mountain water from her coconut shell. After that it did not take him long to decide to throw his spear on the stairs of her father's house in token of his desire to marry her.

The mountain clearing was cold in the freezing moonlight. The wind began to sough and stir the leaves of the bean plants. Lumnay looked for a big rock on which to sit down. The bean plants now surrounded her, and she was lost among them.

A few more weeks, a few more months, a few more harvests —what did it matter? She would be holding the bean flowers, soft in texture, silken almost, but moist where the dew got into them, silver to look at, silver on the light blue, blooming whiteness, when the morning comes. The stretching of the bean pods full length from the hearts of the wilting petals would go on.

Lumnay's fingers moved a long, long time among the growing bean pods.

The Philippines

TIMES GONE BY

Dora Alonso

THROUGH THE NARROW DOORS of the barracks, the figures of the blacks enter and leave. The shadow, the color of the man, and the kind of living, all are the same: black in one hundred tones, either so light as to be cinnamon flesh or as dark as black coffee, it carries the sign of subjection.

Barracks for blacks! When torn down, the sun filling the gloomy dwellings where men moaned under the power of man, in each stone of their walls that tumbled to the ground, there was a history of pain.

In the hour of dusk the flames sing amid a cracking of wood that burns under the huge caldrons where the food is prepared. The bubbling of the boiling food on the trivets also suggests a contented rhythm, promising a warm mouthful to those who wait patiently. Old Cirilo carefully hovers over the food, calculating its boiling point. With a long wooden spoon he digs into the golden mass of flour, which fills deep vats, and later, he goes up to the other pot, attending to the vegetables which, in the water, become soft, releasing a variety of peels.

At night the muted murmur of unusual conversations seems to tingle the backbone of the barracks. The bonfire, stirred up, gently illumines the blackness of the night and of the quarters of the sleepless slaves.

For several days a disquieting piece of news is discussed, robbing them of their interest in sleep. The soul of each slave is haunted by the sense of hope and fear. Carlos Manuel de Céspedes is the name of the white man who has kindled the voice of a bell, and ardent and red the echo of the bronze has scattered and run until it reached the oppressed. And Liberato, the runaway slave, in the language of mountains and of river waters, by force of the beauty of his words of freedom, came from far, slicing days and nights to take the news to his brothers at the San Lucas sugar plantation. For that reason every plantation worker, from the octogenarian mandinga, absorbed and sad, to the rebellious creole serf, senses a nebulous birth of hope within his chest, ready and dazzled.

With a nervous step, a figure with full and rustling skirts approaches the light of the fire: it's a black woman; the golden hoops of her earrings shine, balancing on her ears; the scarlet scarf covering her head looks like a scarf of blood. She walks until she reaches the first group of huddled figures; they surround her with eagerness, and the woman speaks in a low voice, with a tone of authority. "My son will not come tonight or tomorrow. Taita Julián has to wait."

Taita Julián, an old man, woolly haired and short bodied, though still strong, argues, "And if he doesn't come?"

The woman answers, "He always comes. Liberato does not deceive."

A young and powerful voice urges, "María Caridá, you delay the time because the whip respects you. For you there are no whippings, shackles, or blows."

"Shut up, Felipe, she knows."

But to this there is a clear response: "Let him talk; his blood boils like my son's. I can do no more. Don Crisanto, the overseer, is very cunning. Yesterday he said to the master, "As long as the news doesn't reach those dogs, everything will be all right. Afterward we'll have to whip them a lot so that they won't get excited by the Demajagua uprising."

Silence seems to descend, palpably, behind the woman's words. And once more, her rustling skirt is bathed in light before it's lost in the night.

San Lucas belongs to Don Jerónimo Fernández. With one of the best work crews in the zone, with fields of magnificent soil sealed in by canefields, with a sugar mill where a sugar boiler smells and the furnaces blaze, constantly swallowing the remains of the sugar cane and the bundles of wood brought by naked and dark arms—it is a rich property, kept and exploited by its owner.

A beautiful specimen of a man, Don Jerónimo. A Spaniard, old, with marked features sheltered by his broad-rimmed hat, always erect on his bright leggings, he proudly contemplates the turbulent work, caressed and enveloped by the light of midday.

His the carts that go forward, heavy, creaking, filled to the very top; his the oxen that pull them, slowly, head down, wide snout distilling threads of slaver which the sun transforms into crystal. And also the sugar mill and the fields that extend to the boundaries, enclosing the dusty sugar plantation, the earth, and about three hundred human lives in a ring of juicy greens. Dark ants carrying riches to the storerooms of the master.

At times like now, when his eye embraces the lively spectacle of the scene, he feels in his body, broad and long, the stirring of a boundless joy, causing his body and soul to expand.

He closes his fist, resting it on the handle of the short, tough whip; his strong body stands even more erect, and his eye inquires avidly for something, somebody on whom to unleash what he is holding inside.

The figure of the overseer stands out clearly in the shimmering of the midday sun, the short machete on his belt, a rough jacket: a rider on a pacing creole horse. A broad smile from the big man and the rein is shortened, the beast is still, and the submissive employee awaits recognition for his greeting. "Good afternoon, Don Jerónimo, beautiful work; the sugar harvest is good."

"Very good. But it's a little late. The gangs have to be hurried."

Wanting to flatter, he answers, "I had noticed it already. I was going over there to frighten those lazy bums with the stocks."

"Good idea. This is no time to let them slack off. Go."

When the hooves raise a cloud of red dust and beast and rider begin to recede under the solar heat, the pleasant emotion felt by the master of San Lucas has not vanished. Perhaps it is lust looking for an object, an object balanced on the small waist of a dark woman who goes across the plantation with a bundle of sugar cane on her head, in charming equilibrium.

The Spaniard's eyes catch the young female, and he goes toward her, elastic step, possessive gesture. He knows that before him everything is respectful and silent.

Following the woman into the sugar mill, surrounded by the noise of the machines, he smiles contemptuously at the image he supposes to be dangerous and demented: the image of the Cuban liberator of blacks, about whom the priest from Paredes had spoken a few days before when he came on his white mule, cassock pulled up around his waist, carrying an open umbrella like a dome protecting the shiny pate, to enjoy an abundant meal and good chocolate.

"No," he tells himself firmly, "San Lucas will not tolerate rebellions or contagions. As you have well said in your sermons, Father José, God made blacks different for a reason." "And we must obey God."

Days followed days, creating impatience in those who suffer hunger for freedom, and maturing the decision of those undecided. In vain Taita Julián, using his job as ox-driver as an excuse, meets the rose of dawn, laden with the thorns of the rooster chants, very close to the compact mountains, to the unknown, tangled paths extending far away, which always brought the runaway slave. Only once did Liberato come. Taita Julián would tell his brothers to wait for the big waters. They would know why when the time came. In the meantime, silence.

Life goes on, buried in pain for those who wait; swollen with haughtiness and arrogance for those who fear.

The master's house, surrounded by gardens, seems colder and more suspicious with its shutters half-shut, like a sideways glance, guessing treason.

The sonorous wave of the advancing revolution jumps the paths of resistance, throwing burning flames wherever there are fields made ready by the drought of injustice.

And injustice is a lacerating drought wherever slaves live dying.

San Lucas, so inaccessible and distant, has been the stage for unexpected visits and bustle. The tricorns of the Civil Guard, in their blue uniforms, visit the place frequently. Nervous dialogues are threaded, boasts and warnings are heard.

Cabs stop by the fence of the master's house. From them issue personages wearing jackets and large cravats, or fitted military coats with golden epaulets. Enemies of disorder, and friends of Don Jerónimo Fernández.

After dinner, while enjoying the delicious sweetness of the liqueurs, or drawing in the aromatic smoke of their cigars; or at midafternoon, on the large porticos, sheltered by flowering trellises, sipping slowly the delight of cold lemonades and tasty tamarind refreshments served by diligent dark hands, they speak unreservedly about the events of the island.

"Believe me, Governor," says the Spaniard, "I'm afraid there is more noise than substance. A madman and a handful of blacks, what can they do against Spain?"

The answer comes slowly, held back by prudence: "The government can do a lot, that's true; but the creoles seem ready to fight, and they want a free Cuba."

The master replies, jokingly, "And the slaves a free life, similar things, though Utopian. An army is ill-served if it depends in part on men who obey only instinct, or blows. Freedom, my friend, does not go well with skins the color of coal."

The reverend, who now always comes in a carriage, and accompanied, for fear of the rebels, nods his head, while he drinks another delicious refreshment; and then while he carefully deposits the empty glass on the silver tray, "It's true. These are things of the Devil. But, for all that, there isn't a day or a place where blacks don't rebel. I fear for your gang of slaves."

He intercepts his fear quickly, "Don't be afraid, Father. As long as I govern them with a hard hand, my blacks will be mine, like the oxen are mine, and the cane and the sugar that the cane produces, since I bought them as I bought the oxen and the land: with good money. There's no higher right than might, and I am mighty."

Then the military authority intervenes, "Anyway, it's good to be prepared. I am doing my duty warning you confidentially that this matter is not as simple as we have to make it appear. This place is isolated and it's mountainous, the rebels could hide out well. From there to a black uprising is just a step."

"Don't worry, Commander; my dogs know how to bring back the runaways. I'm afraid that the republic of the bellringer of Demajagua will not be made by my slaves. On my plantation a surprise attack coincides only with the freedom of the lash."

The Clergy, the Military, and the Civil Power take their leave; but they leave behind two bulldogs: fear and punishment.

The clamps do not loosen their teeth in their job of oppressing defenseless flesh.

Neither do the shackles rest from their lacerating noise from sunup to sunup. Nor does the cat-o'-nine-tails rest from the sweaty and muscular shoulders.

But the waters are coming nearer. The lagoons shine like mirrors; and the heron's wings trace their signature on the crystal of the blue space. Flowery May dresses up like a bride.

Then comes June. And then July . . .

How the thunderstorm roared with the fire lashes of the lightning tearing the blackness of the night! Crouching, the slaves twist and turn under their cots, and the murmur of the men and the woes of the women interrupt the clangor of the storm and the tireless rolling of the rain. And occasionally the cries of a frightened child who seeks refuge next to the body of his sleeping mother.

Outside, water; water, and the rolling of thunder; the rain hits the wornout rooftops; it hits the sparcely thatched roofs of the barracks with an endless noise, burrowing and maddening. It's been like that for three days.

"The demons have been crowned, Don Jerónimo," assured the steward. "The tubs of heaven must be overflowing. At least, there's no flood yet in sight."

"We can't quit watching; the river is very swollen. At the first sign we'll find shelter, as always, in Vega Alta. The cattle are already taken care of."

"And the blacks. I heard that you unshackled the punished ones and released the ones in the clinic; but Taita Julián can hardly move. The overseer really overdid himself this time."

"He'll get over it; perhaps now he'll learn that its not healthy to talk back in my sugar mill. It will be a good warning to the rest."

That happened yesterday afternoon. Today it's still raining, and the river grows with symptoms of swelling. It looks like a gorged snake with swellings on its rounded back, destroying itself in the canyons, biting the ravine.

The scouts sent by the white man every three hours to observe the distant current brought back an exact impression: "Master, the river is full, but it's not overflowing. There is no flood."

Night fell. The plantation went to sleep. Everything seemed peaceful except the liquid tongues, and the light that watches weakly from the lantern at the gate of the master's house. At intervals lights blink and a deafening thunder rolls, its echo prolonged in the soaked shell of the darkness.

Protected by the mosquito netting over the wide four-poster bed, Don Jerónimo rests. Somebody is hovering in the darkness, and slow steps like an elf's can be heard. The old man rises, saying loudly, "Will you get the hell out, and go to sleep?"

There is no answer; the noise stops and he turns, giving himself up to sleep.

But María Caridá is watching. The hook of the order caught her by the servile neck, under the webbing· of the transparent chandelier next to the monumental carved wood sideboard laden with fine china and crystal. Groping she takes off her shoes; looks through a shutter which she carefully opens. She is watching. What? The rain, the sky, the deep and gloomy night. Because she knows . . .

Many years ago—when she was young—she knew the heat of the master, mixed with her own heat. A fiery female, well formed, capable of taking into the circles of her skirt the sensuous spirits of all the local males, she left her laughing youth in the La Luisa coffee plantation in the violet covered mountains. While balancing on her graceful head the basket full of fresh grains collected from the very fruitful breast of the plantation, she would go to the huge drying sheds in which the silk-skinned fruit were chosen; or entering gracefully under the wide roof which covered the mill where the horses moving the great wheels turned in a despairing circle, she would always feel the looks of the overseers piercing her round and hard breasts and her pronounced and promising hips.

The ebony young man who, rope in hand, incited the beasts to run in circles, showed his symmetrical row of teeth to greet her, "Good morning, beautiful."

It was at that time that the overseer and the runaway slave

"Candela" fought with machetes. Only she knew the reason, but her mouth was kept shut by her fear of the whipping post.

Candela left her a son, Liberato.

A son who grew up away from the maternal arms, because by right of human sale she became the property of Don Jerónimo Fernández, who took her to his sugar cane lands. The new master, while he possessed her opulent and beautiful body, was always disdainful of the fruit born previously to the slave, not allowing him to grow up under the same roof as his mother, relegating him to the huts and the barracks, to the common life of humble people. The young woman, destined to domestic service in the master's house, had to resign herself to love from afar, in quick encounters, that piece of her flesh, which disgusted her master, until the shoot grew, and an adolescent, learned to shake submission by flight, as his brave father always had.

The master of San Lucas never married, and—once Doña Juanita, her master's aunt, died—she never needed to return to the murmuring corners in the tree groves, or the thick weeds, in order to give herself. She stayed in the house as cook and mistress, and she even enjoyed the birth of a cub who awakened a new joy in her life; but the child perhaps not prepared by his father's blood for the somber tones of tyranny, died a few hours after birth, wounding her weeping and humble soul.

María Caridá got old. María Caridá is no good any more. Her body broke down like the collapse of forked poles which could no longer bear the weight of an entire life dedicated to obedience, without a single pillar of rebellion to hold up the structure. She aged on the outside, and the desire of the flesh died out; but inside, rooted in her chest, was the deep and loyal attachment to the father of the vanished cub. He, however, kept himself in shape much longer. Perhaps the complete control of lives and fields helped him to remain erect for a longer time. He changed women; he enjoyed them right there, as he had enjoyed her. But she did not mind. She reduced her burnt out appetite to an even more pronounced humility, perhaps asking forgiveness for being a useless piece of furniture. Yesterday's light, she adjusted to being today's ashes, receiving in her breast the fiery reflections of the women enjoyed by Don Jerónimo.

Besides his brutal indifference, the bloody sneers, the cowardly blows, her affection without dignity swept submissively the last ashes which might be troublesome some day. Sweeping her own self from the life of the other, María Caridá.

Since she lived in the main house, close to the stove, taking care of the starched clothes, the golden hoops, the old silk head scarves, she would sometimes speak in commanding tones to the other blacks; and they, knowing she had lived in the Master's house for so many years, would lower their heads as a sign of obedience. Also because they always found her willing to offer her shrunken influence to mitigate a too inhuman punishment.

The son always found ways to see her. He was the condensation of María Caridá's love. And a day came when the runaway slave, during one of their furtive meetings, talked to her of freedom. Of freedom for the blacks, and rescue of the land; that land that was only good for wearing them out in their lifetime, and for receiving them in the disintegrating embrace.

Surely it was her son's dream, nothing more than a dream, but Liberato's vehement plea so touched her tender soul that, unable to say no, possessed also of the desire to let loose the living stuff of the slave's sorrow, she spoke to the blacks; first with fear, then decisively. Later, with childish pride, amazed for the first time at finding a personal, willful desire.

Like the cutting edge of lightning the new and avid faith spread to the poor flock. Silent and blind, the mole in a thousand ways was burrowing the path from dark to light. Céspedes called all sufferers without a country to the struggle, to lead them to conquer a new country, which would receive them without the stigma of race. In San Lucas the call was heard.

The time for flight and uprising had come. Nature, that great book, will help the struggle with her careful plan. There, in the intricate entrails of the far away mountains, they would found the fortress, and later on most of the men would join the insurrectionist ranks. That is why María Caridá watches, counting the hours.

The serf feels that her will is weakening, cracking at the moment of supreme decision. She does not even have the full voice of her son to hold onto and thus save herself. She feels fear; with her throat knotted by anguish, her fists tight, she rolls herself into a ball, her head on her unhappy breast. A warm wave floods her eyes, inducing her to feel affection and attachment to her surroundings, but they are tentacles born of her servitude.

A soft whistle makes her sit up quickly and, on opening the shutter, she is received by a damp, cold kiss.

They whisper from outside: "María Caridá."

Her whisper answers: "Refugio, did Liberato come?"

"And he took the people to the mountains, seeing that he was delayed. His white friends are waiting there. Come on, I came to get you."

She shakes her head energetically, and they urge her, "The river is coming like crazy, they won't catch up with us. We will be free, María Caridá."

The shutter is closed in mute response. The woman clutches the wood and remains still, as if fused to the wall, for a long time, hours perhaps. Her intuition receives the warning among the docile rumors of the ceaseless rain.

Each torn tree, dancing in the downpour, seems to shout its frightening message from its ghostlike boughs: "María Caridá: the water is coming."

And the big green frogs croaked, thunderstruck and happy, "The water . . . the water . . ."

Although the snake makes no noise, the black woman feels it coming, its eyes filled with tremulous fire, elastic and silent.

She paces barefoot through the house, stopping sometimes before the little light that trembles under a silver crucifix.

Faraway, in the darkness, voices are heard. And suddenly an alarm bell loosens its tongue. The bell of infamy and mourning at the San Lucas sugar mill.

Stumbling, she goes through the rooms, and grabs the sleeping old man, yelling in his ear, "My master, the flood . . ."

Half-awake, struggling with his sleep, he wakes, and furious, faces her. "What's going on; why this racket?"

She repeats her own fear, "The river, my master, is coming like a rabid dog."

He hears that, and the ring of the alarm bell. He dresses

with effort, and without looking back, he goes out. Not María Caridá.

First she locks the house, "her house," door by door, with an unconscious love for what seems to be a little bit hers. When she goes out, she feels seized by the enemy, which envelops her.

The bloody torches shine, and the lanterns project, in the liquid savannah, marvelous whitecaps which spread like luminous blood. Agitated silhouettes disappear in mad abandon. A voice is heard over noises: "This way, Don Jerónimo. The blacks have fled, killing the watchmen and the bloodhounds. We have to reach Vega Alta, or we will all drown. Here is your horse."

The slavewoman recognizes the voice of the steward. She is still too far away; her clumsy legs weigh her down, and with terror she sees the bloody lights take the road to salvation.

"My master, my master."

She feels a strong splash next to her body. The reins, the rider, and an authoritarian voice: "Who goes there?"

The horse has stopped, rebellious, shaking its bit, obedient to the firm hand of the Spaniard; and the water runs and curses between the noble legs, pushing.

She feels safe and cries out, "It's me, María Caridá."

All the fury of the master of San Lucas is discharged on this last serf.

His heels, shod with sharp spurs, dig into the nervous flanks of the horse, and it gives a jump and goes forward. The black woman hooks her tenacious hands onto the bridle, onto the horseman's leg. She receives a blow on the face and a curse, while with savage imperiousness he shouts: "Damn you, don't you want to let go? Let go, I tell you, María Caridá."

María Caridá, the water biting her body, her shadowed face bathed in shadow, opens her hands with fear and respect greater than death, and she mumbles stunned, letting the water pull her and sink her, "Yes sir, my master . . ."

In the night of the century, the bells rang for man's sorrow. Only one called to the mass of his freedom.

Cuba

PART II

My mother dressed me
in clothes so rich
I could confuse a god.
I am like a beggarwoman
turned into a king's daughter.
They wanted to lead me to my husband's house
like a sheep to the market.
But my mother said, I should be escorted
like a free born child.
Let everybody thank my mother:
she did not allow me to borrow dresses
from those who would abuse me later.
And you, my friend Ilajue,
you my best friend:
This sudden marriage has spoiled
many things for us.
We have been abusing people together,
we have been scorning together and laughing,
good things and bad, we never did them alone.
They say that marriage brings happiness
greater than any known before.
But were they thinking of you?
And you my parents:
when you don't see the river
will you forget the waves?
When you don't see the thunder
will you forget the rain?
When you don't see me any more—
will you forget me?
Is it not you who decide
when a child is old enough to have a quiver?
Is it not you who decide
when a child is old enough to have an arrow?

It was you who decided
that I was old enough
to move into another house.
Don't leave me alone in that place.
What I am proposing to do
you have done it yourselves with success.
Then let me succeed also. . . .

No one shall succeed in tying me.
Don't underrate the Oyoyo soup
because it is black.
It is a sweet soup.
Don't underrate me
because I am black
because I was born by a man
who is known by two hundred people
And today
fortune descends on my head.
The melon seed soup only offends the hungry man
who was not invited to the feast.
The smell of fried bananas only offends the hungry man
who was not invited to the feast.
I who have come to this world
with ripe breasts
I have offended my younger sisters.
Whom shall I turn to in this new house?
In the strange corridors I never walked?
In the strange doors I never entered?
Whom can I turn to in this strange house?
Some of them may say:
"See a loose girl coming."
Let them talk today—
for tomorrow they shall be silenced.
Today is a glorious day.

Traditional poem (excerpt), Yoruba

THE TRULY MARRIED WOMAN

ABIOSEH NICOL

AJAYI STIRRED for a while and then sat up and looked at the cheap alarm clock on the chair by his bedside. It was 6:15, and light outside already; the African town was slowly waking to life. The night watchmen roused from sleep by the angry crowing of cockerels were officiously banging the locks of stores and houses to assure themselves and their employers, if nearby, of their efficiency. Village women were tramping through the streets to the market place with their wares, arguing and gossiping.

Ajayi sipped his cup of morning tea. It was as he liked it, weak and sugary, without milk. With an effort of will, he got up and walked to the window, and standing there he took six deep breaths. This done daily, he firmly believed, would prevent tuberculosis. He walked through his ramshackle compound to an outhouse and took a quick bath, pouring the water over his head from a tin cup with which he scooped it from a bucket.

By then Ayo had laid out his breakfast. Ayo was his wife. Not really a wife, he would explain to close friends, but a mistress. A good one. She had borne him three children and was now three months gone with another. They had been together for twelve years. She was a patient, handsome woman, very dark with very white teeth and open, sincere eyes. Her hair was always carefully braided. When she first came to him—to the exasperation of her parents—he had fully intended to marry her as soon as she showed satisfactory evidence of fertility, but he had never quite got around to it. In the first year or so she would report to him in great detail the splendor of the marriage celebrations

of her friends, looking at him with hopeful eyes. He would close
the matter with a tirade on the sinfulness of ostentation. She
gave up after some time. Her father never spoke to her again
after she had left home. Her mother visited her secretly and
attended the baptismal ceremonies of all her children. The church
charged extra for illegitimate children as a deterrent; two dollars
instead of fifty cents. Apart from this, there was no other great
objection. Occasionally, two or three times a year, the pastor
would preach violently against adultery, polygamy, and unmarried
couples living together. Ajayi and Ayo were good church people
and attended regularly, but sat in different pews. After such
occasions, their friends would sympathize with them and other
couples in similar positions. There would be a little grumbling
and the male members of the congregation would say that the
trouble with the church was that it did not stick to its business of
preaching the Gospel, but meddled in people's private lives.
Ajayi would indignantly absent himself from church for a few
weeks, but would go back eventually because he liked singing
hymns and because he knew secretly that the pastor was right.

Ayo was a good mistress. Her father was convinced she could
have married a high-school teacher at least, or a pharmacist, but
instead she had attached herself to a junior government clerk.
But Ayo loved Ajayi, and was happy in her own slow, private
way. She cooked his meals and bore him children. In what spare
time she had she either did a little petty trading, visited friends,
or gossiped with Omo, the woman next door.

With his towel around his waist, Ajayi strode back to the
bedroom, dried himself, and dressed quickly but carefully in his
pink tussah suit. He got down the new bottle of patent medicine
which one of his friends who worked in a drugstore had recom-
mended to him. Ajayi believed that to keep healthy, a man must
regularly take a dose of some medicine. He read the label of this
one. It listed about twenty diseased conditions of widely differing
pathology which the contents of the bottle were reputed to cure
if the patient persevered in its daily intake. Ajayi underlined in
his own mind at least six from which he believed he either
suffered or was on the threshold of suffering: dizziness, muscle
pain, impotence, fever, jaundice, and paralytic tremors. Intelli-

gence and courage caused him to skip the obviously female maladies and others such as nervous debility or bladder pains. It said on the label too that a teaspoonful should be taken three times a day. But since he only remembered to take it in the morning and in any case believed in shock treatment, he took a swig and two large gulps. The medicine was bitter and astringent. He grimaced but was satisfied. It was obviously a good and strong medicine or else it would not have been so bitter.

He went in to breakfast. He soon finished his maize porridge, fried beans, and cocoa. He then severely flogged his eldest son, a ten-year-old boy, for wetting his sleeping-mat last night. Ayo came in after the boy had fled screaming to the backyard.

"Ajayi, you flog that boy too much," she said. "He should stop wetting the floor; he is a big boy," he replied. "In any case, no one is going to instruct me on how to bring up my son." "He is mine too," Ayo said. She seldom opposed him unless she felt strongly about something. "He has not stopped wetting, although you beat him every time he does it. In fact, he is doing it more and more now. Perhaps if you stopped whipping him he might get better." "Did I whip him to begin doing it?" Ajayi asked. "No." "Well, how will stopping whipping him stop him from doing it?" Ajayi asked triumphantly. "Nevertheless," Ayo said, "our own countrywoman Bimbola, who has just come back from England and America studying nursing, told us in a women's group meeting that it was wrong to punish children for such things." "All right, I'll see," he said, reaching for his sun helmet.

All that day at the office he thought about this and other matters. So Ayo had been attending women's meetings. Well, what do you know. She would be running for the town council next. The sly woman. Always looking so quiet and meek and then quoting modern theories from overseas doctors at him. He smiled with pride. Indeed Ayo was an asset. Perhaps it was wrong to beat the boy. He decided he would not do so again.

Toward closing time the chief clerk sent for him. Wondering what mistake he had made that day, or on what mission he was to be sent, he hurried along to the front office. There were three white men sitting on chairs by the chief clerk, who was an aging African dressed with severe respectability. On seeing them,

Ajayi's heart started thudding. The police, he thought; heavens, what have I done?

"Mr. Ajayi, these gentlemen have inquired for you," the chief clerk said formally. "Pleased to meet you, Mr. Ajayi," the tallest said, with a smile. "We represent the World Gospel Crusading Alliance from Minnesota. My name is Jonathan Olsen." Ajayi shook hands and the other two were introduced.

"You expressed an interest in our work a year ago and we have not forgotten. We are on our way to India and we thought we would look you up personally."

It transpired that the three Crusaders were en route and that their ship had stopped for refueling off the African port for a few hours. The chief clerk looked at Ajayi with new respect. Ajayi tried desperately to remember any connection with W.G.C.A. (as Olsen by then had proceeded to call it) while he made conversation with them a little haltingly. Then suddenly he remembered. Some time ago he had got hold of a magazine from his subtenant who worked at the United States Information Service. He had cut a coupon from it and mailed it to W.G.C.A. asking for information, but really hoping that they would send illustrated Bibles free which he might give away or sell. He hoped for at least large reproductions of religious paintings which, suitably framed, would decorate his parlor or which he might paste up on his bedroom wall. But nothing had come of it and he had forgotten. Now here was W.G.C.A. as large as life. Three lives. Instantly and recklessly he invited all three and the chief clerk to come to his house for a cold drink. They all agreed.

"Mine is a humble abode," he warned them. "No abode is humble that is illumined by Christian love," Olsen replied. "His is illumined all right, I can assure you," the chief clerk remarked drily.

Olsen suggested a taxi, but Ajayi neatly blocked that by saying the roads were bad. He had hurriedly whispered to a fellow clerk to rush home on a bicycle and tell Ayo he was coming in half an hour with white men and that she should clean up and get fruit drinks. Ayo was puzzled by the message as she firmly imagined all white men drank only whisky and iced beer. But the messenger had said that there was a mixture of friendliness and piety in the visitors' mien, which made him suspect that they might be missionaries. Another confirmatory point was that they were walking instead of coming by car. That cleared up the anomaly in Ayo's mind and she set to work at once. Oju, now recovered from his morning disgrace, was dispatched with a basket on his head to buy soft drinks. Ayo whisked off the wall all their commercial calendars with suggestive pictures. She propped up family photographs which had fallen face downward on the table. She removed the Wild West novels and romance magazines from the parlor and put instead an old copy of Bunyan's *Pilgrim's Progress* and a prayerbook which she believed would add culture and religious force to the decorations. She remembered the wine glasses and the beer advertising table mats in time and put those under the sofa. She just had time to change to her Sunday frock and borrow a wedding ring from her neighbor when Ajayi and the guests arrived. The chief clerk was rather surprised at the changes in the room—which he had visited before—and in Ayo's dress and ring. But he concealed his feelings. Ayo was introduced and made a little conversation in English. This pleased Ajayi a great deal. The children too had been changed into Sunday suits, their faces washed and hair brushed. Olsen was delighted and insisted on taking photographs for the Crusade journal. Ayo served drinks and then modestly retired, leaving the men to discuss serious matters. Olsen by then was talking earnestly of the imminence of Christ's Second Coming and offering Ajayi ordination into deaconship.

The visit passed off well and soon the missionaries left to catch their boat. Ajayi had been saved from holy orders by the chief clerk's timely explanation that it was strictly against government regulations for civil servants to indulge in non-official organizations. To help Ajayi out of his quandary, he had gone even further and said that violation might result in a fine or imprisonment. "Talk about colonial oppression," the youngest of the missionaries had said, gloomily.

The next day Ajayi called at the chief clerk's office with a carefully wrapped bottle of beer as a present for his help generally on the occasion. They discussed happily the friendliness and interest the white men had shown.

This incident and Ayo's protest against flagellation as a remedy for enuresis made Ajayi very thoughtful for a week. He decided to marry Ayo. Another consideration which added weight to the thought was the snapshot Olsen took for his magazine. In some peculiar way Ajayi felt that he and Ayo should marry, since millions of Americans would see their picture—Olsen had assured him of this—as "one saved and happy African family." He announced his intention of marrying her to Ayo one evening, after a particularly good meal and a satisfactory bout of belching. Ayo at once became extremely solicitous and got up and looked at him with some anxiety. Was he ill? she asked. Was there anything wrong at the office? Had anyone insulted him? No, he answered, there was nothing wrong with his wanting to get married, was there? Or had she anyone else in mind? Ayo laughed. "As you wish," she said. "Let's get married, but do not say I forced you into it."

They discussed the wedding that night. Ajayi wanted to have a white wedding with veil and orange blossoms. But Ayo with regret decided it would not be quite right. They agreed on gray. Ayo particularly wanted a corset to strap down her obvious bulge. Ajayi gave way gallantly to this feminine whim, chucking her under the chin and saying, "You women with your vanity!" But he was firm about no honeymoon. He said he could not afford the expense and that one bed was as good as another. Ayo gave way on that. They agreed, however, on a church wedding and that their children could act as bridal pages to keep the cost of clothes within the family.

That evening Ajayi, inflamed by the idea and arrangements for the wedding, pulled Ayo excitedly to him as they lay in bed. "No," said Ayo, shyly, pushing him back gently, "you mustn't. Wait until after the marriage." "Why?" said Ajayi, rather surprised, but obedient. "Because it will not somehow be right," Ayo replied seriously and determinedly.

Ayo's father unbent somewhat when he heard of the proposed marriage. He insisted, however, that Ayo move herself and all her possessions back to his house. The children were sent to Ayo's married sister. Most of Ajayi's family were in favor of the union, except his sister, who, moved by the threat implicit in Ayo's improved social position, advised Ajayi to see a soothsayer first. As Ayo had got wind of this through friends she met at market on Saturday, she saw the soothsayer first and fixed things. When Ajayi and his sister called at night to see him, he consulted the oracles and pronounced future happiness, avoiding the sister's eye. The latter had restrained herself from scratching the old man's face and accepted defeat.

The only other flaw in a felicitous situation was Ayo's neighbor Omo, who on urgent occasions at short notice had always loaned Ayo her wedding ring. She had suddenly turned cold. Especially after Ayo had shown her the wedding presents Ajayi intended to give her. The neighbor had handled the flimsy nylon articles with a mixture of envy and rage.

"Do you mean you are going to wear these?" she asked. "Yes," Ayo replied simply. "But, my sister," she protested, "you will catch cold with these. Suppose you had an accident and all those doctors lifted your clothes in hospital. They will see everything through these." "I never have accidents," Ayo answered, and added, "Ajayi says all the 'Ollywood cinema women wear these. It says so there. Look—'Trademark Hollywood.' " "These are disgraceful; they hide nothing. It is extremely fast of you to wear them," the jealous girl said, furiously, pushing them back over the fence to Ayo.

"Why should I want to hide anything from my husband when we are married?" Ayo said triumphantly, moving back to her own kitchen and feeling safe for the future from the patronizing way the wedding ring had always been lent her.

The arrangements had to be made swiftly, since time and the corset ribs were both against them. Ajayi's domestic routine was also sorely tried, especially his morning cup of tea which he badly missed. He borrowed heavily from a moneylender to pay the dowry, for the music, dancing, and feasting, and for dresses of the same pattern, which Ayo and her female relations would wear after the ceremony on the wedding day.

The engagement took place quietly, Ajayi's uncle and other relations taking a Bible and a ring to Ayo's father and asking for her hand in marriage, the day before the wedding. They took with them two small girls carrying on their heads large hollow gourds. These contained articles like pins, farthings, fruit, kola nuts, and cloth, which were symbolic gifts to the bride from the bridegroom, so that she might be precluded in future marital disputes from saying, "Not a pin or a farthing has the black-guard given me since we got married."

On arriving at Ayo's father's house, the small procession first passed it as if uncertain, then returned to it. This gave warning to the occupants. Ajayi's uncle then knocked several times. Voices from within shouted back and ordered him to name himself, his ancestry, and his mission. He did this. Argument and some abuse followed on both sides. After his family credentials had been seriously examined, questioned, doubted, and disparaged, Ajayi's uncle started wheedling and cajoling. This went on for about half an hour to the enjoyment and mock trepidation of Ajayi's rela-tions. He himself had remained at home, waiting. Finally, Ayo's father opened the door. Honor was satisfied and it was now sup-posed to be clearly evident to Ajayi's relations, in case it had not been before, that they were entering a family and household which was distinguished, difficult, and jealous of their distinction.

"What is your mission here?" Ayo's father then asked sternly. Ajayi's uncle answered humbly:

> "We have come to pluck a red, red rose
> That in your beautiful garden grows.
> Which never has been plucked before,
> So lovelier than any other."

"Will you be able to nurture our lovely rose well?" another of Ayo's male relations asked?

Ajayi's family party replied:

> "So well shall we nurture your rose
> 'Twill bring forth many others."

They were finally admitted; drinks were served and prayers offered. The gifts were accepted and others given in exchange. Conversation went on for about thirty minutes on every con-ceivable subject but the one at hand. All through this, Ayo and her sisters and some young female relations were kept hidden in an adjoining bedroom. Finally with some delicacy, Ajayi's uncle broached the subject after Ayo's father had given him an opening by asking what, apart from the honor of being entertained by himself and his family, did Ajayi's relations seek. They had heard, the latter replied, that in this very household there was a maiden chaste, beautiful, and obedient, known to all by the name of Ayo. This maiden they sought as wife for their kinsman Ajayi. Ayo's father opened the bedroom door and brought forth Ayo's sister. Was this the one? he asked, testing them. They examined her. No it was not this one they replied, this one was too short to be Ayo. Then a cousin was brought out. Was this she? No, this one is too fat, the applicants said. About ten women in all were brought out. But none was the correct one. Each was too short or too fat or too fair, as the case was, to suit the description of the maiden they sought. At this point, Ajayi's uncle slapped his thigh, as if to show that his doubts were confirmed. Turning to his party, he stated that it was a good thing they had insisted on seeing for themselves the bride demanded, or else the wrong woman would have been foisted on them. They agreed, nodding. All right, all right, Ayo's father had replied, there was no cause for impatience. He wanted to be sure they knew whom they wanted. Standing on guard at the bedroom door, he turned his back to the assembly, and with tears in his eyes beckoned to Ayo sitting on the bed inside. He kissed her lightly on the forehead to forgive the past years. Then he led her forth and turned fiercely to the audience. Was this then the girl they wanted? he asked them sternly.

"This *is* the very one," Ajayi's uncle replied with joy. "Hip, hip, hooray," everybody shouted, encircling Ayo and waving white handkerchiefs over her head. The musicians struck their guitars instantly; someone beat an empty wine bottle rhythmically with a corkscrew; after a few preliminary trills the flutes rose high in melody; all danced around Ayo. And as she stood in the center, a woman in her mid-thirties, her hair slightly streaked with gray, undergoing a ceremony of honor she had often witnessed and long put outside her fate and remembering the classic description of chastity, obedience, and beauty, she wept with joy and the unborn child stirred within her for the first time.

The next morning she was bathed by an old and respected female member of her family and her mother helped her to dress. Her father gave her away in the marriage service at the church.

It was a quiet wedding with only sixty guests or so. Ajayi looked stiff in dinner jacket with boutonniere, an ensemble which he wore only on special occasions. Afterward they went to Ayo's family home for the wedding luncheon. At the door they were met by another of Ayo's numerous elderly aunts, who held a glass of water to their lips for them to sip in turn, Ajayi first. The guests were all gathered outside behind the couple. The aunt made a conveniently long speech until all the guests had assembled. She warned Ayo not to be too friendly with other women as they would inevitably steal her husband; that they should live peaceably and not let the sun go down on a quarrel between them. Turning to Ajayi, she told him with a twinkle in her eye that a wife could be quite as exciting as a mistress, and also not to use physical violence against their daughter, his wife.

After this they entered and the Western part of the ceremony took place. The wedding cake (which Ayo had made) was cut and speeches made. Then Ajayi departed to his own family home where other celebrations went on. Later he changed into a lounge suit and called for Ayo. There was weeping in Ayo's household as if she were setting off on a long journey. Her mother in saying good-bye, remarked between tears, that although she would not have the honor the next morning of showing the world evidence of Ayo's virginity, yet in the true feminine powers of procreation none except the blind and deaf could say Ayo had lacked zeal.

They called on various relations on both sides of the family and at last they were home. Ayo seemed different in Ajayi's eyes. He had never really looked at her carefully before. Now he observed her head held erectly and gracefully through years of balancing loads on it in childhood; her statuesque neck with its three natural horizontal ridges—to him, signs of beauty; her handsome shoulders. He clasped her with a new tenderness.

The next morning, as the alarm clock went off, he stirred and reached for his morning cup of tea. It was not there. He sprang up and looked. Nothing. He listened for Ayo's footsteps outside in the kitchen. Nothing. He turned to look beside him. Ayo was there and her bare ebony back was heaving gently. She must be ill, he thought; all that excitement yesterday.

"Ayo, Ayo," he cried, "are you ill?" She turned around slowly

still lying down and faced him. She tweaked her toes luxuriously
under the cotton coverlet and patted her breast slowly. There was
a terrible calm about her. "No, Ajayi," she replied, "are you?"
she asked him. "Are your legs paralyzed?" she continued. "No,"
he said. He was puzzled and alarmed, thinking that her mind
had become unhinged under the strain.

"Ajayi, my husband," she said, "for twelve years I have got up
every morning at five to make tea for you and breakfast. Now I
am a truly married woman and you must treat me with a little
more respect. You are now a husband and not a lover. Get up
and make yourself a cup of tea."

Sierra Leone

THE MESSAGE

Ama Ata Aidoo

"Look here my sister, it should not be said but they say they opened her up."

"They opened her up?"

"Yes, opened her up."

"And the baby removed?"

"Yes, baby removed."

"I say! . . ."

"They do not say, my sister."

"Have you heard it?"

"What?"

"This and this and this . . ."

"A–a–ah! that is it . . ."

"Meewuo!"

"They don't say meewuo . . ."

"And how is she?"

"Am I not here with you? Do I know the highway which leads to Cape Coast?"

"Hmm . . ."

"And anyway how can she live? How is it like even giving birth with a stomach which is whole . . . eh? . . . eh? . . . I am asking you. And if you are always standing on the brink of death who go to war with your stomach whole, then how would she do whose stomach is open to the winds?"

"Oh, poo, pity . . ."

"I say . . ."

—O, sometimes leave me alone, leave me alone . . . I thought now I would have peace, just a little peace.

"And I say, where is the little bundle I made? . . . Here, come to my back. You and I are going to Cape Coast today."

—Cape Coast! how long ago it is when I went there . . . You have pursued me all my life. What is it that I alone have done, that even now that I have grown very old you still pursue me? None of the three marriages I entered into worked for me . . . But even that did not matter. If I had only got my little ones . . . but no. Would they allow them to grow up? How many were they? I have even forgotten but certainly more than ten . . . they snatched them up one by one, sleeping, playing, in the stream— the farm . . . They wheeled around me day by day like kites . . . until, now I must make a journey to Cape Coast, which I have not seen for thirty years, because they have slit my little one up. She has eaten the knife, my child; oh I must not think about it. Did they cut her navel up too? I remember, it did not heal quickly at all, when her cord was cut and since a scar is a scar . . . perhaps it hurt her. Oh, my child . . .

—I only hope they will give me her body . . .

"My little bundle, come. You and I are going to Cape Coast today."

—I am taking one of her own cloths with me just in case. These people on the coast do not know how to do a thing and I am not going to have anybody mishandling my child's body. I hope they give it to me. Horrible things I have heard done to people's bodies. Cutting them up and using them for teaching others . . . Even murderers still have decent burials . . .

I see Mensima coming . . . And there is Nkama too . . . and Adwoa Meenu . . . Now they are coming to . . . "poo pity me" . . . witches, witches, witches . . . they have picked mine up while theirs prosper around them, children, grandchildren, and great-grandchildren, theirs shoot up like mushrooms . . .

"Esi, we have heard of your misfortune . . ."

"That our little lady's womb has been opened up . . ."

"And her baby removed . . ."

"Thank you very much."

"Has she lived through it?"

"I do not know."

"Esi, bring her here, back home whatever happens."

"Yoo, thank you. But get your things ready. If the government's people allow it, I shall bring her home."

"And have you got ready your things?"

"Yes . . . No."

—I cannot even think straight. It feels so noisy in my head . . . Oh my little child . . . I mean the things which were ready for me. There is the coffin which is in Kwame Hofo's room. Then there is a whole twelve-piece of silk loincloth. Esi deserves something better for she lived on the coast all the time but the flour is already in the sand . . . I am wasting time . . . And so I am going . . .

"Yes, to Cape Coast . . . No, I do not know anyone there now but do you think no one would show me the way to this big hospital . . . if I ask around? . . . Hmmmm . . . it's me has ended up like this. I was thinking that everything is all right now . . . Yoo. And thank you too. Shut the door for me when you are leaving. You may stay too long out if you wait for me, so go home and be about your business. I will let you know when I bring her in."

"Maami Otua, where are you going?"

"My daughter, I am going to Cape Coast."

"And what is our old mother going to do with such swift steps? Is it serious?"

"My daughter, it is very serious."

"Mother, may God go with you."

"Yoo, my daughter."

"Eno, and what calls at this hour of the day?"

"They want me at Cape Coast."

"Does my friend want to go and see how much Oguaa has changed since we went there to meet the new Wesleyan chairman, twenty years ago?"

"My sister do you think I have knees to go parading on the streets of Cape Coast?"

"Is it heavy?"

"Yes, very heavy indeed. They have opened up my grandchild at the hospital, hi, hi, hi . . ."

"Eno due, due due . . . I did not know. May God go with you . . ."

"Thank you, Yaa."

"Oh, the world?"

"It's her grandchild. The only daughter of her only son. Do you remember Kojo Amisa who went to Soja and fell in the great war, overseas?"

"Yes, it's his daughter . . ."

". . . Oh, poo, pity."

"Kobina, run to the street, tell Draba Anan to wait for Nana Otua."

". . . Draba Anan, Draba, my mother says I must come and tell you to wait for Nana Otua."

"And where is she?"

"There she comes."

"Oh, just look at how she hops like a bird . . . does she think we are going to be here all day? And anyway we are full already . . ."

"Oh, you drivers! No respect for anybody . . ."

"What have drivers done?"

"And do you think it shows respect when you speak in this way? It is only that things have not gone right but she is old enough, at least, to be your mother . . ."

"But what have I said? I have not insulted her. I only think that only youth must be permitted to see Cape Coast, the town of the Dear and the Expensive . . ."

"And do you think she is going on a peaceful journey? Her only granddaughter, child of her only son, has been opened up and her baby removed from her womb."

Oh . . . God.

Oh . . .

Oh . . .

Oh . . .

Poo, pity.

"Me . . . poo, pity. I am right about our modern wives. I always say they are useless compared with our mothers."

"You drivers!"

"Now what have your modern wives done?"

"Aren't I right what I always say about them? You go and watch them in the big towns. All so thin and dry as sticks—you can literally blow them away with your breath. No decent flesh anywhere. Wooden chairs groan when they meet with their hard exteriors."

"Oh you drivers . . ."

"But of course all drivers . . ."

"What have I done? Don't all my male passengers agree with me? These modern girls . . . Now here is one who cannot even have a baby in a decent way. But must have the baby removed from her stomach. Tchiaa!"

"What . . ."

"Here is the old woman."

"Whose grandchild . . . ?"

"Yes."

"Oh, Nana, I hear you are coming to Cape Coast with us."

"Yes, my master."

"We nearly left you behind but we heard it was you and that it is a heavy journey you are making."

"Yes, my master . . . thank you, my master."

"Push up, please . . . push up. Won't you push up? Why do you all sit looking at me with such eyes as if I was a block of wood? It is not that there is nowhere to push up to. Five fat women should go on that seat, but look at you! And our old grandmother here is none too plump herself . . . Nana if they won't push, come to the front seat with me."

". . . Hei, scholar, go to the back."

". . . And do not scowl on me. I know your sort too well. Something tells me you do not have any job at all. As for that suit you are wearing and looking so grand in, you hired or borrowed it . . ."

"Oh you drivers!"

Oh you drivers . . .

—The scholar who read this telegram thing said it was made

about three days ago . . . Three days . . . Oh God—that is too long ago. Have they buried her . . . where? or did they cut her up . . . Oh I should not think about it . . . or something will happen to me. Eleven or twelve . . . Efua Panyin, Okuma, Kwame Gyasi, and who else? It is so long ago. I cannot even count them now . . . But they should have left me here. Sometimes . . . ah, I hate this nausea. But it is this smell of petrol. Now I have remembered I never could travel neatly in a lorry. I always was so sick. But now I hope at least that will not happen. These young people will think it is because I am old and they will laugh . . . At least if I knew the child of my child was alive, it would have been good. And the little things she sent me . . . Sometimes some people like Mensima and Nkansa make me feel as if I had been a barren woman instead of only a one whom death took away . . .

—I will give her that set of earrings, bracelet, and chain which Odwumfo Ata made for me. It is the most beautiful and the most expensive thing I have . . . It does not hurt me to think that I am going to die very soon and have them and their children gloating over my things. After all, what did they swallow my children for? It does not hurt me at all. If I had been someone else, I would have given them all away before I died. But it does not matter. They can share their own curse. Now, that is the end of me and my roots . . . Eternal death has worked like a warrior rat, with diabolical sense of duty, to gnaw at my bottom. Everything is finished now. The vacant lot is swept and the scraps of old sugar cane pulp, dry sticks, and bunches of hair burnt . . . how it reeks the smoke! . . .

"Oh, Nana do not weep . . ."

"Is the old woman weeping?"

"If the only child of your only child died, wouldn't you weep?"

"Why do you ask me? Did I know her grandchild is dead?"

"Where have you been, not in this lorry? Where were you when we were discussing . . ."

"I do not go putting my mouth in other people's affairs . . ."

"So what?"

"So go and die . . ."

"Hei, hci, it is prohibited to quarrel in my lorry."

"Draba, here is me, sitting quiet, and this lady of muscles and bones being cheeky to me . . ."

"Look, I can beat you . . ."

"Beat me . . . beat me . . . let's see."

"Hei, you are not civilized, eh?"

"Keep quiet and let us think, both of you, or I will put you down . . ."

"Nana, do not weep. There is God above."

"Thank you my master."

"But we are in Cape Coast already."

—Meewuo! My God, hold me tight or something will happen to me.

"My master, I will come down here."

"Oh Nana. I thought you said you are going to the hospital . . . We are not there yet."

"I am saying maybe I will get down here and ask my way around."

"Nana, you do not know these people, eh? They are very impudent here. Sit down, I will take you there."

"Are you going there, my master?"

"No, but I will take you there."

"Ah, my master, your old mother thanks you. Do not shed a tear when you hear of my death . . . My master, your old mother thanks you."

—I hear there is somewhere where they keep corpses until their owners claim them . . . if she has been buried, I must find her husband . . . Esi Amfoa, what did I come to do under this sky . . . I have buried all my children and now I am going to bury my grandchild!

"Nana we are there."

"Is this the hospital?"

"Yes, Nana. What is your child's name?"

"Esi Amfoa. Her father named her after me."

"Do you know her English name?"

"No, my master."

"What shall we do? . . ."

". . . Er, lady, we are looking for somebody."

"You are looking for somebody and can you read? If you

cannot you must ask somebody what the rules in the hospital are. You can only come and visit people at three o'clock."

"Lady, please. She was my only grandchild . . ."

"Who? And anyway, it is none of our business . . ."

"Oh, Nana, you must be patient . . . and not cry . . ."

"Old woman, why are you crying, it is not allowed here. No one must make any noise here!"

"My lady, I am sorry but she was all I had."

"Who? . . . Oh, are you the old woman who is looking for somebody?"

"Yes."

"Who is he?"

"She was my granddaughter—the only child of my son."

"I mean, what was her name?"

"Esi Amfoa."

"Esi Amfoa . . . Esi Amfoa. I am very sorry, we do not have anyone whom they call like that."

"Is that it?"

"Nana, I told you they may know only her English name here."

"My master, what shall we do then?"

"What is she ill with?"

"She came here to have a child . . . And they say, they opened her stomach and removed the baby . . ."

"Oh . . . oh, I see."

—My lord, hold me tight so that nothing will happen to me now.

"I see. It is the Caesarean case . . ."

"Nurse, you know her?"

—And when I take her back, Anona Ebusuato will say that I did not wait for them to come with me . . .

"Yes. Are you her brother?"

"No. I am only the driver who brought the old woman."

"Did she bring all her clan?"

"No. She came alone."

—Strange thing for a villager to do.

—I hope they have not cut her up already.

"Did she bring a whole bag full of cassava and plantain and kenkey?"

"No. She has only her little bundle."

"Follow me. But you must not make any noise. This is not the hour for coming here . . ."

"My master, does she know her?"

"Yes."

—I hear it is very cold where they put them . . .

It was feeding time for new babies. When old Esi Amfoa saw her young granddaughter Esi, the latter was all neat and nice. White sheets and all. She did not see the beautiful stitches under the sheets. "This woman is a tough bundle," Dr. Gyamfi had declared after the identical twins had been removed, the last stitches had been threaded off and Mary Koomson, alias Esi Amfoa, had come to.

The old woman somersaulted into the room and lay groaning, not screaming, by the bed. For was not her last pot broken?

—So they lay them in state even in hospitals and not always cut them up for instruction?

The Nursing Sister was furious. Young Esi Amfoa spoke.

And this time old Esi Amfoa wept loud and hard. Wept all her tears.

Scrappy nurse-under-training Jessy Treeson, second generation Cape Coaster, said, "As for these villagers," and giggled.

Draba Anan looked hard at Jessy Treeson, her starched uniform, apron, and cap . . . and then dismissed them all . . . "Such a cassava stick . . . but maybe I will break my tongue if I licked at her buttocks . . ." he thought . . .

And by the bed the old woman was trying hard to rise and look at the pot which had refused to get broken.

Ghana

ON THE OUTSKIRTS OF
THE CITY

RUSMAN SUTIASUMARGA

MY PAINS WERE quite strong. Saubari, my husband, had gone to fetch the *dukun*.*

This was not the first time I had given birth. I had two children already (this one would make three); but for some reason I approached this birth with anxiety.

It was the thought of the *dukun* that bothered me.

Some people said that it was better not to use a *dukun* if you were not used to doing so. But there were others who said that there was no difference between a *dukun* and a midwife attached to a hospital. An experienced *dukun* was sometimes more competent than a trained midwife.

I understood.

And it was possible that the latter view was correct. It was possible . . . The chief difference between the two kinds of practitioners was simply in the matter of cleanliness.

Would Mak† Dukun be able to maintain cleanliness?

She had already come to the house three times. Once to get acquainted, and twice to massage my belly. She was not really very old. She had a small, neat figure, her manners were good, and her speech was pleasing. But despite all that, she was still a *dukun*, a village *dukun* who could not be compared, for instance, to Mrs. M., the midwife at the Maternity Hospital in B.,

---

* A village curer treating illness with traditional remedies or by magical means; here, such a curer specializing in midwifery. The translation "midwife" would be appropriate, except that in the story the *dukun* is contrasted with the midwives trained in Western medical concepts and techniques who are attached to hospitals and perform many of the functions of obstetricians.

† "Mother," a respectful title for women.

who had tended me when I had my first baby, or to Miss S., the midwife in P., who also had once taken care of me. Mak Dukun was still just Mak Dukun, a village *dukun* . . . who also as it happened had a special habit: when she arrived, before coming and talking to me she never failed to poke her head behind the door to deposit her betel quid, which she left off chewing during the time she was with me; when she had said good-bye to me, she would retrieve it.

Little things like this are perhaps not significant, and I don't want to make too much of it, but I am not pretending when I say that this habit of hers often raised a question in my mind: "Won't Mak Dukun forget to wash her hands when she is going to receive my baby?"

From Mak Dukun I naturally did not hope for hands gloved in rubber, but I felt that it was not too much to expect clean-washed hands.

But, oh, perhaps this was simply a groundless worry. Mak Dukun was an experienced *dukun*, and she had a good reputation in our village.

There was no alternative.

Saubari himself had wanted it.

Suddenly a protest rose in my heart. Did Saubari really want it? I mean, wholeheartedly?

He had said, "Just this once, Ati, we'll see what it's like to use a *dukun*."

When Saubari talks, he often uses veiled language. Luckily I have become skilled at catching his meaning: I understood at once that when he said, "We'll see what it's like," he really meant "We are compelled."

Our village was well outside the city area. If I insisted on having a trained midwife come out, it would cost too much. And, oh, it wasn't only that. I myself had once gone to a maternity hospital to ask how much it would cost to have a midwife come to the village, and I told them where I lived. One of them replied that the fee would be such and such, and they would come only during daylight; they wouldn't come at night, she said, because they were afraid of—and here she gestured with a movement of her hand near her throat . . . Good Lord, was that what they thought about the village people? That was going too far!

My rambling thoughts jumped to events of long ago. In 'forty-one Saubari had not yet begun to work. We were still being supported by our parents. His first job was during the Japanese period, in a government office. He stayed there on into the period after the establishment of the republican government. During the disturbances in the city, I left in the evacuation, just myself and the children. Saubari continued to hang on in the city. When the interior was attacked, I returned to the city, but now we were completely destitute. Someone else was occupying our old house. Saubari had been unable to hold onto it; apparently bribed with "key money," the owner had taken it back on the pretext that he wanted to use it himself. Since then we have been forced to live on the outskirts of the city. And up to now Saubari has not been working—I mean, he has not wanted to return to his former office.

My pains grew more severe. My back was on fire. I tried to shift to a more comfortable position. But the bed slats, of which I was usually no longer even aware, now seemed to stab me, to shatter my bones.

I whimpered. And I began to feel rebellious again: "Are those hard boards what my baby is going to lie on?"

The clock in the house of a neighbor across the road (a neighbor whose acquaintance we had never made) struck nine times. And Saubari had still not come. My anxiety increased. "What will happen if Mak Dukun isn't home?"

I had often heard about women who had given birth without difficulty before the *dukun* or the midwife had time to get there. Yes, maybe so, if they had lots of people taking care of them, relatives, for example; but what if it should happen in a situation such as my present one? God . . . it's not that I do not have faith . . .

I squeezed my eyes shut. Silently I prayed to Him not to let it happen like that.

I don't know whether I dropped off to sleep or not, but when I opened my eyes, the first thing I saw was Mak Saudah, who lived in the house behind ours, already standing beside my bed, stroking my forehead.

"I just got home," she said. "I came right over. I found
nobody here, the door unlocked—what would happen if a robber
came along?"

"Oh, don't worry about it, Mak; we don't have anything here,"
I replied impulsively.

Then she reproached me for not having sent word to her that
my pains had begun.

"If I had known," she said, "I wouldn't have gone out ped-
dling. Don't be like that; if you have any trouble you must let
me know."

As she spoke she never stopped stroking my hair back, like a
mother caressing a daughter whom she loved very much.

Mak Saudah was not a relative, nor even an old acquaintance;
why was she nevertheless being so kind to me? My thoughts
then went on. Perhaps in human existence there really is a quality
of goodness, embodied in a few women such as Mak Saudah, and
in a few men such as . . . Saubari. But why are the lives of people
who possess such a quality so difficult? Mak Saudah was a hard-
working woman, pure-hearted, who was always helping others
with no thought of payment, yet she lived in poverty; she toiled
all day long for her livelihood, yet what she earned was inadequate.

And Saubari?

I give my husband, Saubari, his due. Actually I myself do not
perceive what Saubari's goodness consists of, but Mak Saudah
often said that in a hundred husbands you wouldn't find one
like Saubari. Often I smiled when I listened to Mak Saudah: a
village woman, uneducated but upright, her words frequently
amused me, yet they also contained truth. She said about Saubari
that he was a husband of a sort hard to find; I did not have to
keep thinking of ways to flatter him. I myself felt it: Saubari
really was patient, never angry even when I flew out at him; or,
if he was forced to show anger, he accompanied it with good
advice, and never uttered words that hurt a person's feelings.
Toward his wife and children he always appeared loving . . . Yes,
I have to admit it, and as a wife must naturally be proud, and
yet . . . I don't know why it is—perhaps because of my own in-
sensitivity, or because Saubari's excellence in those respects ac-

tually made it seem less essential to him to excel in other respects
—but the fact is that my present opinion, after much experience,
is that these fine qualities of Saubari's are not sufficient to guar-
antee the stability of a family.

Mak Saudah asked about Saubari, and I told her that he was
fetching the *dukun.*

"In that case, let me go get ready the water and the other
things she'll need."

I nodded.

"Your children were sleeping restlessly, so I covered them
up."

"Thank God for your help!" I said.

Mak Saudah left. My thoughts drifted to my children: Toto's
body just goes on shrinking. He is thin and his color is dark.
Only his eyes are large and round. But he seems unaware of it
himself. He is always cheerful. As a matter of fact, Toto is an
adaptable child. Tini is just the opposite; although her body has
not shown any change, she is dreadfully demanding. If she
wants something, she won't be put off; if her wishes are not
complied with, she does nothing all day except scold and cry. It
seems as though Toto takes after his father, while Tini has inherited my temperament. A child who won't accept her fate!

I heard Saubari's voice outside. I felt relieved.

Mak Dukun came in. She began to feel my belly; her hand
was cool, it felt soothing for a moment. I thought, Mak Dukun
has just washed her hands.

She adjusted the way I was lying, and asked various questions,
to which I replied with moans.

The clock sounded again; I counted ten strokes. I was strongly
aware of the stillness all around. Outside it appeared to be calm
and peaceful. It was only in my room that people were nervous
and restless. Through the glass tile directly over my bed I could
see the clear blue sky. I knew that there was a bright moon that
night, and it happened not to be raining. I thanked God and felt
that my wish had been granted: I had hoped that when I gave
birth it would be on a moonlit night without rain. Usually a
single shower is enough to turn my village to mud, and often
we were flooded for days; in which case perhaps Mak Dukun

would be reluctant to come, and, oh, what a pity it would be for . . . Saubari. Meanwhile my thoughts continued to wander freely, recalling my distant family, my mother in the interior; was she thinking of me?

Mak Saudah returned, saying that everything necessary was ready. I took hold of her hand, indicating to her that I wanted her to come close to me. Oh, why was I so anxious all of a sudden?

I moaned again.

Moaning sometimes lessened the pain somewhat, and letting my thoughts wander sometimes relieved my anxiety for a moment.

But not permanently. Suddenly, worse pains came. I sighed. It was hard to breathe. Sweat bathed my whole body. I was unbearably hot, feverish. Perhaps because the room was so small.

In this state I felt Mak Saudah's hand steadily mopping my face with a cloth, while her mouth moved, reciting some prayer or other.

Mak Dukun appeared to be restless.

In truth I had never before had such a hard time. On the previous occasions things had for the most part gone easily and smoothly. Perhaps it was because I was rundown. During my previous confinements I had followed a regular schedule of eating purée made from the peas called *katjang idjo* and other nourishing foods, but this time I had almost never had such food.

The clock struck once; another half-hour had gone by.

Suddenly a strong pang gripped me. My hands groped for something to hold on to. On one side I grasped Mak Saudah's hand, and on the other I held onto the iron bedstead near my head. I gripped it tightly, very tightly, as though trying to squeeze it to bits. In truth I longed to crush it . . . Meanwhile I pulled together all my strength, I tried to bear down with all my force, but . . . evidently it was not yet time.

Everything was still for a moment.

Everyone went back to waiting.

I was exhausted. I felt incapable of moving even a hand.

I heard Mak Saudah whispering, "Try to bear it, my dear, try to bear it! Pray to God."

I really was praying, beseeching His mercy, so that the pain would be lessened and the baby would come out quickly. Meanwhile I had a vision of Saubari's face, because he was usually the one who was always advising me to rely upon God. Was he staying calm? Wasn't he nervous? Or anxious? And was he praying to God for my safety? I moaned loudly, as thought I intended Saubari to hear it. No! No! Why should I want him to hear it? Saubari was not used to hearing moans. Before, when he had visited me in the hospital, I had usually been cleaned up and neatly clothed in my bed. No, I didn't want Saubari to hear my moans.

But . . . this time, I don't know.

The contractions began again. Worse than before. I got ready again. My mouth went on with its moaning, but my body again mustered its strength, and I willed that it had to be, it had to be this time . . .

Once more I strained, I contracted my body, I held my breath; once more I concentrated my will, it had to, it had to, it had to come out . . . Otherwise? . . .

I began to see spots before my eyes.

I had the sensation of soaring away. I don't know where. But I could still hear sounds fading in and out: Mak Dukun's voice giving orders, the creaking of the bed . . . and very faintly the neighbor's clock, striking I don't know how many times . . . then everything disappeared . . .

The first thing that slipped into my mind was the feeling that I was still lying down; and the first sound that I heard slipping into my ear was the loud, infuriated wail of a baby . . . Then one after another I heard increasingly clear sounds; I felt that my wits were collected again, but I did not yet dare to open my eyes. Mak Dukun's voice said, "No wonder it was a hard delivery! He looks as though he's going to be a real he-man . . ." She said this in a joking tone, and in a voice that showed pleasure. Pleasure at being released from concern and anxiety.

Then a voice outside—Saubari, talking to somebody or other, apparently replying to a question: "At exactly eleven o'clock . . ."

I thought, eleven o'clock, a boy, is he all right? Am I all right? I longed to open my eyes at once, but I still did not dare to. All sorts of doubts worried me: Isn't there anything wrong with him? I remembered the suffering I had experienced during the time that I was carrying him.

I tried opening my eyes slowly: there he was, lying near my left leg, and . . . oh God!—quickly I closed my eyes again, prolonging that one quick glance in my mind. No, there wasn't anything wrong with him. He was handsome, with a straight, regular nose like his father's . . . his hair was black and thick, and it was true he was a boy. A feeling of happiness and pride momentarily enveloped my soul—but the reason I had quickly closed my eyes again was that I was startled: he, my baby, was still lying there, crying—Mak Dukun had not paid any attention to him yet. I didn't know what it was Mak Dukun was giving first attention to: the navel cord was still attached, and all around was bloody filth . . . My God, I couldn't stand it. Never, never before had I seen anything like that . . .

Suddenly I heard Mak Dukun's voice calling Saubari.

I still kept my eyes squeezed shut, but I could sense that Saubari was at the door, and I called out—I don't know whether aloud, or only in my heart, I don't remember any more, but I felt, I felt that I half-screamed, "Saubari, look, your son! Everything's going to be all right, isn't it? . . . I myself . . . felt this pain, there's no way to describe it!"

Indonesia

SONG OF LAWINO

OKOT P'BITEK

Husband, now you despise me
Now you treat me with spite
And say I have inherited the stupidity of my aunt;
Son of the Chief,
Now you compare me
With the rubbish in the rubbish pit,
You say you no longer want me
Because I am like the things left behind
In the deserted homestead.
You insult me
You laugh at me
You say I do not know the letter A
Because I have not been to school
And I have not been baptized.

You compare me with a little dog,
A puppy.

My friend, agemate of my brother,
Take care,
Take care of your tongue,
Be careful what your lips say.

First take a deep look, brother,
You are now a man
You are not a dead fruit!
To behave like a child does not befit you!

Listen Ocol, you are the son of a Chief,
Leave foolish behavior to little children,
It is not right that you should be laughed at in a song!
Songs about you should be songs of praise!

Stop despising people
As if you were a little foolish man,
Stop treating me like saltless ash*
Become barren of insults and stupidity;
Who has ever uprooted the pumpkin? . . .

I was made chief of girls
Because I was lively,
I was bright,
I was not clumsy or untidy
I was not dull,
I was not heavy and slow.

I did not grow up a fool
I am not cold
I am not shy
My skin is smooth
It still shines smoothly in the moonlight.

When Ocol was wooing me
My breasts were erect.
And they shook
As I walked briskly,
And as I walked
I threw my long neck
This way and that way
Like the flower of the *lyonno* lily
Waving in a gentle breeze.

---

* Salt is extracted from the ash of certain plants, and also from the
ash of the dung of domestic animals. The ash is put in a container with
small holes in its bottom, water is then poured on it, and the salty water is
collected in another container placed below. The useless saltless ash is then
thrown on the pathway and people tread on it.

And my brothers called me *Nya-Dyang*
For my breasts shook
And beckoned the cattle,
And they sang silently:

> *Father prepare the kraal,*
> *Father prepare the kraal,*
> *The cattle are coming.*

I was the Leader of the girls
And my name blew
Like a horn
Among the Payira.
And I played on my bow harp
And praised my love.

Ocol, my husband,
My friend,
What are you talking?
You saw me when I was young.
In my mother's house
This man crawled on the floor!

The son of the Bull wept
For me with tears,
Like a hungry child
Whose mother has stayed long
In the simsim field!

Every night he came
To my father's homestead,
He never missed one night
Even after he had been beaten
By my brothers.

You loved my giraffe-tail bangles,
My father bought them for me
From the Hills in the East.

The roof of my mother's house
Was beautifully laced
With elephant grass;
My father built it
With the skill of the Acoli.

You admired my sister's
Colorful ten-stringed lion beads;
My mother threaded them
And arranged them with care.

You trembled
When you saw the tattoos
On my breasts
And the tattoos below my belly button;
And you were very fond
Of the gap in my teeth!

My man, what are you talking?
My clansmen, I ask you:
What has become of my husband?
Is he suffering from boils?
Is it ripe now?
Should they open it
So that the pus may flow out?

I was chief of youths
Because of my good manners,
Because my waist was soft.
I sang sweetly
When I was grinding millet
Or on the way to the well,
Nobody's voice was sweeter than mine!
And in the arena
I sang the solos
Loud and clear
Like the *ogilo* bird
At sunset.

Now, Ocol says
I am a mere dog,
A puppy,
A little puppy
Suffering from skin diseases.

Ocol says
He does not love me any more
Because I cannot play the guitar
And I do not like their stupid dance,
Because I despise the songs
They play at the ballroom dance
And I do not follow the steps of foreign songs
On the gramophone records.
And I cannot tune the radio
Because I do not hear
Swahili or Luganda.

What is all this?

My husband refuses
To listen to me,
He refuses to give me a chance.
My husband has blocked up my path completely.
He has put up a roadblock
But has not told me why.
He just shouts
Like houseflies
Settling on top of excrement
When disturbed!

My husband says
He no longer wants a woman
With a gap in her teeth,
He is in love
With a woman
Whose teeth fill her mouth completely
Like the teeth of war captives and slaves. . . .

The beautiful woman
With whom I share my husband
Smears black shoe polish
On her hair
To blacken it
And to make it shine,
She washes her hair
With black ink;

But the thick undergrowth
Rejects the shoe polish
And the ink
And it remains untouched
Yellowish, grayish
Like the hair of the gray monkey.

There is much water
In my husband's house
Cold water and hot water.
You twist a crosslike handle
And water gushes out
Hot and steaming
Like the urine
Of the elephant.

You twist another crosslike handle;
It is cold water,
Clean like the cooling fresh waters
From the streams
Of Lututuru hills.

But the woman
With whom I share my husband
Does not wash her head;
The head of the beautiful one
Smells like rats
That have fallen into the fireplace.

And she uses
Powerful perfumes
To overcome the strange smells,
As they treat a pregnant coffin!
And the different smells
Wrestle with one another
And the smell of the shoe polish
Mingles with them.

Clementine has many headkerchiefs,
Beautiful headkerchiefs of many colors.
She ties one on her head
And it covers up
The rot inside;

She ties the knot
On her forehead
And arranges the edges
With much care
So that it covers
Her ears
As well as the bold forehead
That jumps sparks
When lightning has splashed,
And hurls back sunlight
More powerfully than a mirror!

Sometimes she wears
The hair of some dead woman
Of some white woman
Who died long ago
And she goes with it
To the dance!
What witchcraft!

Shamelessly, she dances
Holding the shoulder of my husband,
The hair of a dead woman
On her head

The body of the dead woman
Decaying in the tomb!

One night
The ghost of the dead woman
Pulled away her hair
From the head of the wizard
And the beautiful one
Fell down
And shook with shame
She shook
As if the angry ghost
Of the white woman
Had entered her head.

Ocol, my friend,
Look at my skin
It is smooth and black.
And my boy friend
Who plays the *nanga*
Sings praises to it.

I am proud of the hair
With which I was born
And as no white woman
Wishes to do her hair
Like mine,
Because she is proud
Of the hair with which she was born,
I have no wish
To look like a white woman.

No leopard
Would change into a hyena,
And the crested crane
Would hate to be changed
Into the bold-headed,
Dung-eating vulture,

The long-necked and graceful giraffe
Cannot become a monkey.

Let no one
Uproot the pumpkin. . . .

My husband says
I am useless
Because I waste time,
He quarrels
Because, he says,
I am never punctual.
He says
He has no time to waste.
He tells me
Time is money.

Ocol does not chat
With me,
He never jokes
With anybody,
He says
He has no time
To sit around the evening fire.

When my husband
Is reading a new book
Or when he is
Sitting in his sofa,
His face covered up
Completely with the big newspaper
So that he looks
Like a corpse,
Like a lone corpse
In the tomb,

He is so silent!
His mouth begins
To decay!

If a child cries
Or has a cough
Ocol storms like a buffalo,
He throws things
At the child;
He says
He does not want
To hear noises,
That children's cries
And coughs disturb him!

Is this not the talk
Of a witch?
What music is sweeter
Than the cries of children?

A homestead in which
The cries of children
Are not heard,
Where the short little songs
Are not repeated endlessly,
Where the brief sobs
And brotherly accusations
And false denials
Are not heard!

A homestead where
Children's excreta is not
Scattered all over the swept compound
And around the granaries,

Where all the pots and earthen dishes
Are safe
Because there are no
Silly ones to break them,
No clumsy hands
Trying hard to please mother
And breaking half-gourds,

Who but a witch
Would like to live
In a homestead
Where all the grownups
Are so clean after the rains,
Because there are no
Muddy fat kids
To fall on their bosoms
After dancing in the rains
And playing in the mud?

At the lineage shrine
The prayers are for childbirth!
At the *ogodo* dance
The woman who struts
And dances proudly,
That is the mother of many,
That is the fortunate one;
And she dances
And looks at her own shadow.

Time has become
My husband's master
It is my husband's husband.
My husband runs from place to place
Like a small boy,
He rushes without dignity.

And when visitors have arrived
My husband's face darkens,
He never asks you in,
And for greeting
He says
"What can I do for you?"

I do not know
How to keep the white man's time.

My mother taught me
The way of the Acoli
And nobody should
Shout at me
Because I know
The customs of our people!
When the baby cries
Let him suck milk
From the breast.
There is no fixed time
For breast feeding.

When the baby cries
It may be he is ill;
The first medicine for a child
Is the breast.
Give him milk
And he will stop crying,
And if he is ill
Let him suck the breast
While the medicine man
Is being called
From the beer party.

Children in our homestead
Do not sleep at fixed times:
When sleep comes
Into their heads
They sleep,
When sleep leaves their heads
They wake up.

When a child is dirty
Give him a wash,
You do not first look at the sun!
When there is no water
In the house
You cannot wash the child
Even if it is time
For his bath!

Listen,
My husband,
In the wisdom of the Acoli
Time is not stupidly split up
Into seconds and minutes,

It does not flow
Like beer in a pot
That is sucked
Until it is finished.

It does not resemble
A loaf of millet bread
Surrounded by hungry youths
From a hunt;
It does not get finished
Like vegetables in the dish.

A lazy youth is rebuked,
A lazy girl is slapped,
A lazy wife is beaten,
A lazy man is laughed at
Not because they waste time
But because they only destroy
And do not produce. . . .

My husband has read much,
He has read extensively and deeply,
He has read among white men
And he is clever like white men

And the reading
Has killed my man,
In the ways of his people
He has become
A stump.

He abuses all things Acoli,
He says

The ways of black people
Are black
Because his eyeballs have exploded,
And he wears dark glasses.

My husband's house
Is a dark forest of books.
Some stand there
Tall and huge
Like the *tido* tree

Some are old
Their barks are peeling off
And they smell strongly.
Some are thin and soft.

The backs of some books
Are hard like the rocky stem of the *poi* tree,
Some are green
Others red as blood
Some books are black and oily,
Their backs shine like
The dangerous *ororo* snake
Coiled on a treetop.

Some have pictures on their backs,
Dead faces of witch-looking men and women,
Unshaven, bold, fat-stomached
Bony-cheeked, angry revengeful-looking people,
Pictures of men and women
Who died long ago. . . .

If you stay
In my husband's house long,
The ghosts of the dead men
That people this dark forest,
The ghosts of the many white men
And white women
That scream whenever you touch any book,

The deadly vengeance ghosts
Of the writers
Will capture your head,
And like my husband
You will become
A walking corpse.

My husband's ears are numb,
He hears the crackling sounds
Of the gums within the holes of his ears
And thinks this is the music
Of his people;
He cannot hear
The insults of foreigners
Who say
The songs of black men are rubbish!

Listen, my husband,
Hear my cry!
You may not know this
You may not feel so,
But you behave like
A dog of the white man!

A good dog pleases its master,
It barks at night
And hunts in the salt lick
It chases away wild cats
That come to steal the chickens!
And when the master calls
It folds its tail between the legs.

The dogs of white men
Are well trained
And they understand English!

When the master is eating
They lie by the door
And keep guard
While waiting for leftovers.

But oh! Ocol
You are my master and husband,
You are the father of these children
You are a man,
You are you!

Do you not feel ashamed
Behaving like another man's dog
Before your own wife and children?

My husband, Ocol
You are a Prince
Of an ancient chiefdom,
Look,
There in the middle of the homestead
Stands your grandfather's Shrine,

Your grandfather was a Bull among men
And although he died long ago
His name still blows like a horn,
His name is still heard
Throughout the land.

When he died
Your father proudly
Built him that Shrine!
A true son of his father
He carried out all the duties
Of a first-born son.

He himself was a great chief
Well beloved by his people.
At the *otole* dance
He was right in the middle
Completely surrounded by his host
Like the termite queen mother,
But you could spot him
By his huge headgear
Waving like a field of flowering sugar cane.

In battle he fought at the front
Fierce like a wounded buffalo-girl,
When his men struck the enemy
The heaven shook from its base;

Has the Fire produced Ash?
Has the Bull died without a Head?
Aaa! A certain man
Has no millet field,
He lives on borrowed foods.

He borrows the clothes he wears
And the ideas in his head
And his actions and behavior
Are to please somebody else.
Like a woman trying to please her husband!
My husband has become a woman! . . .

And, son of the Bull
When you are completely cured
When you have gained your full strength
Go to the shrine of your fathers,
Prepare a feast,
Give blood to your ancestors,
Give them beer, meat and millet bread,

Let the elders
Spit blessing on you
Let them intercede for you
And pray to the ancestors
Who sleep in their tombs
Face upward.

Beg forgiveness from them
And ask them to give you
A new spear
A new spear with a sharp and hard point.
A spear that will crack the rock.

Ask for a spear that you will trust
One that does not bend easily
Like the earthworm.
Ask them to restore your manhood!
For I am sick
Of sharing a bed with a woman!

Ask them to forgive
Your past stupidity,
Pray that the setting sun
May take away all your shyness
Deceit, childish pride, and sharp tongue!

For when you insulted me,
Saying
I was a mere village girl,
You were insulting your grandfathers
And grandmothers, your father and mother!
When you compared me
With the silly *ojuu* insects
That sit on the beer pot,
You were abusing your entire people.
You were saying
The customs of your people
Are like the useless things
Left in the old homestead.

When you took the ax
And threatened to cut the *Okango*
That grows on the ancestral shrine
You were threatening
To cut yourself loose,
To be tossed by the winds
This way and that way
Like the dead dry leaves
Of the *olam* tree
In the dry season.

When you have recovered properly,
Go to your old mother

And ask forgiveness from her;
Let her spit blessing in your hands;
And rub the saliva
On your chest
And on your forehead!

And I as your first wife,
Mother of your first-born,
Mother of your son and daughter,
I have only one request.

I do not ask for money
Although I have need of it,
I do not ask for meat,
I can live on green vegetables
For a while yet.
Buy clothes for the woman
With whom I share you,
Buy beads for her, and perfume;
And shoes and necklaces, and earrings!

When you have gained your full strength
I have only one request,
And all I ask is
That you remove the roadblock
From my path.

Here is my bow harp
Let me sing greetings to you,
Let me play for you one song only
Let me play and sing
The song of my youth:

> *She has taken the road to Nimule*
> *She will come back tomorrow*
> *His eyes are fixed on the road*
> *Saying, Bring Alyeka to me*
> *That I may see her*
> *The daughter of the Bull*

Has stayed away too long
His eyes are fixed on the road

All I ask
Is that you give me one chance,
Let me praise you
Son of the Chief!

Tie ankle bells on my legs
Bring *lacucuku* rattles
And tie them on my legs,
Call the *nanga* players
And let them play
And let them sing,

Let me dance before you,
My love,
Let me show you
The wealth in your house,
Ocol my husband,
Son of the Bull,
Let no one uproot the Pumpkin.

SONG OF OCOL

OKOT P'BITEK

. . . I see an Old Homestead
In the valley below
Huts, granaries . . .
All in ruins;

I see a large Pumpkin
Rotting

A thousand beetles
In it;
We will plough up
All the valley,
Make compost of the Pumpkins
And the other native vegetables,
The fence dividing
Family holdings
Will be torn down,
We will uproot
The trees demarcating
The land of clan from clan,

We will obliterate
Tribal boundaries
And throttle native tongues
To dumb death. . . .

To hell
With your Pumpkins
And your Old Homesteads,
To hell
With the husks
Of old traditions
And meaningless customs,

We will smash
The taboos
One by one,
Explode the basis
Of every superstition,
We will uproot
Every sacred tree
And demolish every ancestral shrine.

We will not just
Breach the wall
Of your mud hut
To let in the air,

Do you think
We plan merely
To bring light
Into the hut?

We will set it ablaze
Let fire consume it all
This liar of backwardness;

We will uproot granaries
Break up the cooking pots
And water pots,
We'll grind
The grinding stones
To powder;

That obsolete toy
With which you scratch the soil
And the other rusty toys
In the hut,

The dried fish
Riddled with cockroaches,
The piece of carcass
Hung above the cooking place
Black with soot . . .

We'll make a big heap
Of all the rubbish
From the hut
And set the heap
Aflame. . . .

We will arrest
All the village poets
Musicians and tribal dancers,
Put in detention
Folk-story tellers
And myth makers,

The sustainers of
Village morality;

We'll disband
The nest of court historians
Glorifiers of the past,
We will ban
The stupid village anthem of
    "Backwards ever
    Forwards never."

To the gallows
With all the Professors
Of Anthropology
And teachers of African History,
A bonfire
We'll make of their works,
We'll destroy all the anthologies
Of African literature
And close down
All the schools
Of African Studies.

Where is Aimé Césaire?
Where Léopold Senghor?
Arrest Janheinz Jahn
And Father Placide Temples,
Put in detention
All the preachers
Of Negritude;

The balloon of
The African Personality
Exploded long ago,
DuBois is dead
We will erect
No memorial for him;

Why should I care
Who built the citadel
Of Zimbabwe?
Of what relevance is it
Whether black men
Architected the Pyramid?

Smash all these mirrors
That I may not see
The blackness of the past
From which I came
Reflected in them. . . .

Sister
Woman of Acoliland
Throw down that pot
With its water,
Let it break into pieces
Let the water cool
The thirsty earth;

It is taboo
To throw down water pots
With water in them,
But taboos must be broken,
Taboos are chains
Around the neck,
Chains of slavery;

Shatter that pot,
Shatter taboos, customs,
Traditions . . .

Listen not
To the song of the poet
The blind musician
Plays for his bread,
The bread owners
Are your slavers;

Listen
My sister from Ankole
And you from Ruanda
And Burundi,

Here's a hammer,
Smash those pots
Of rotten milk
Burst open the door
Come forth into daylight. . . .

Woman of Africa
Sweeper
Smearing floors and walls
With cow dung and black soil,
Cook, *ayah,* the baby tied on your back,
Vomiting,
Washer of dishes,
Planting, weeding, harvesting,
Storekeeper, builder,
Runner of errands,
Cart, lorry,
Donkey . . .

Woman of Africa
What are you not?

In *buibui*
Your face is covered
In black cloth
Like a bat's leather wing,
Harem
Private collection
Of tasty flesh,

Do you hear the bell
Of the leading cow?
The dust you see
Is not caused by a hurricane,

It's the herds
Of the Jo-Lango;

We will destroy
All these *shenzi* cattle
The root of their savagery,
The cause of their misery
And death; . . .

Woman
I see cups of tears
Streaming down your cheeks,
Your body shaking
With anger and despair
Like a mother
Sitting by her dead son;

Let them raise the alarm,
Sound the war drums
And blow the war horns,
Let the women make ululations,
Call all the tribesmen
And all the tribeswomen,
Let them gather together
For the last time;

Let them put ash
On their heads
And on their bodies
Let the women cry aloud
And beat their chests with stones,
Let them throw themselves
On the ground
And roll in the dust
And tear their hair
In mourning!

Let the men
Polish their weapons

And arm themselves with spears,
Shields, bows, arrows
And battle axes,
Let them wear ostrich feathers
On their heads
And swishes
On their arms,

Let them blow their horns
And their wooden trumpets,
Let the youths
Perform the mock fight
And the women shout
The praise names of their men
And of their clans
And of the clans of their husbands;

Let the drummers
Play the rhythms

Of the funeral dance,
And let the people sing and dance
And celebrate the passing of
The Old Homestead!

Weep long,
For the village world
That you know
And love so well,
Is gone,
Swept away
By the fierce fires
Of progress and civilization!

That walk to the well
Before sunrise,
The cool bath in the stream,
The gathering of the family
Around the evening fire . . .

That shady evengreen *byeyo* tree
Under which I first met you
And told you
I wanted you,
Do you remember
The song of the *ogilo* bird
And the chorus
Of the gray monkeys
In the trees nearby?

Let the people drink
Kwete beer and *waragi,*
Say Good-bye
For you will never
Hunt together again,
Nor dance the war dance
Or the *bwola* dance . . .

Bid farewell
To your ancestral spirits
Fleeing from the demolished Homestead,
With their backs to you
They can no longer hear
Your prayers,
Waste no more chicken or goat or sheep
As sacrifices to them,
They are gone with the wind,
Blown away with the smoke
Of the burnt Homestead!
Stop crying
You woman,
Do you think those tears
Can quench the flames
Of civilization?

Uganda

WHO CARES?

SANTHA RAMA RAU

THE ONLY THING, really, that Anand and I had in common
was that both of us had been to college in America. Not that
we saw much of each other during those four years abroad—
he was studying business management or some such thing in
Boston and I was taking the usual liberal arts course at Wellesley,
and on the rare occasions we met, we hadn't much to say—but
when we got back to Bombay, the sense of dislocation we shared
was a bond. In our parents' generation that whole malaise was
covered by the comprehensive phrase "England-returned," which
held good even if you had been studying in Munich or Edin-
burgh, both popular with Indian students in those days. The
term was used as a qualification (for jobs and marriages) and
as an explanation of the familiar problems of readjustment.
Even after the war, in a particular kind of newspaper, you could
find, in the personal columns, advertisements like this: "Wanted:
young, fair, educated girl, high caste essential, for England-
returned boy. Send photograph." The point is that she would
have to prove herself—or rather, her family would have to
demonstrate her desirability—but "England-returned" would tell
her just about everything she needed to know about the boy:
that his family was rich enough to send him abroad for his
education, that his chances for a government job or a good job
in business were better than most, that his wife could probably
expect an unorthodox household in which she might be asked
to serve meat at meals, entertain foreigners, speak English,
and even have liquor on the premises. She would also know that
it would be a "good" (desirable, that is) marriage.

"England-returned," like that other much-quoted phrase, "Failed B.A.," was the kind of Indianism that used to amuse the British very much when it turned up on a job application. To Indians, naturally, it had a serious and precise meaning. Even "Failed B.A.," after all, meant to us not that a young man had flunked one examination, but that he had been through all the years of school and college that led to a degree—an important consideration in a country where illiteracy is the norm and education a luxury.

In the course of a generation that became increasingly sensitive to ridicule, those useful phrases had fallen out of fashion, and by the time Anand and I returned to Bombay we had to find our own descriptions for our uneasy state. We usually picked rather fancy ones, about how our ideas were too advanced for Bombay, or how enterprise could never flourish in India within the deadly grip of the family system, or we made ill-digested psychological comments on the effects of acceptance as a way of life. What we meant, of course, was that we were suffering from the England-returned blues. Mine was a milder case than Anand's, partly because my parents were "liberal"—not orthodox Hindus, that is—and, after fifteen years of wandering about the world in the diplomatic service, were prepared to accept with equanimity and even a certain doubtful approval the idea of my getting a job on a magazine in Bombay. Partly, things were easier for me because I had been through the worst of my re-adjustments six years before, when I had returned from ten years in English boarding schools.

Anand's England-returned misery was more virulent, because his family was orthodox, his mother spoke no English and distrusted foreign ways, he had been educated entirely in Bombay until he had gone to America for postgraduate courses, and, worst of all, his father, an impressively successful contractor in Bombay, insisted that Anand, as the only son, enter the family business and work under the supervision not only of the father but of various uncles.

Our families lived on the same street, not more than half a dozen houses from each other, but led very different lives. Among the members of our generation, however, the differences were fading, and Anand and I belonged to the same set, although we had never particularly liked each other. It was a moment of boredom, of feeling at a loose end, and a fragmentary reminder that both of us had been in America that brought Anand and me together in Bombay.

It was during the monsoon, I remember, and the rain had pelted down all morning. About noon it cleared up, and I decided to spend my lunch hour shopping instead of having something sent up to eat at my desk. I started down the street toward Flora Fountain, the hideous monument that is the center of downtown Bombay, and had gone about halfway when I realized I had guessed wrong about the weather. The rain began, ominously gentle at first, then quickly changing into a typical monsoon downpour. I ducked into the first doorway I saw, and ran slap into Anand, a rather short, slender young man, dressed with a certain nattiness. It was the building in which his father's firm had its offices, and Anand stood there staring glumly at the streaming street and scurrying pedestrians. We greeted each other with reserve. Neither was in the mood for a cheery exchange of news. We continued to gaze at the rain, at the tangle of traffic, the wet and shiny cars moving slowly through the dirty water on the road.

At last, with an obvious effort and without much interest, Anand said, "And what are you up to these days?"

"I *was* going to go shopping," I said coolly, "but I don't see how I can, in this."

"Damn rain," he muttered. I could hardly hear him over the sound of the water rushing along the gutters.

I said, "Mm," and, as a return of politeness, added, "And you? What are you doing?"

"Heaven knows," he said, with a world of depression in his voice. "Working, I suppose." After another long pause, he said, "Well, look, since you can't shop and I can't get to the garage for my car, suppose we nip around the corner for a bite of lunch."

"Okay," I said, not knowing quite how to refuse.

Anand looked full at me for the first time and began to smile. " 'Okay,' " he repeated. "Haven't heard *that* in some time."

We raced recklessly down the street, splashing through

puddles and dodging people's umbrellas, until we arrived, soaked and laughing, at the nearest restaurant. It was no more than a snack bar, really, with a counter and stools on one side of the small room and a few tables on the other. We stood between them, breathless, mopping our faces ineffectually with hand-kerchiefs and slicking back wet hair, still laughing with the silly exhilaration such moments produce. We decided to sit at a table, because Anand said the hard little cakes with pink icing, neatly piled on the counter, looked too unappetizing to be faced all through lunch.

Our explosive entrance had made the other customers turn to stare; but as we settled down at our table, the four or five young men at the counter—clerks, probably, from nearby offices, self-effacing and pathetically tidy in their white drill trousers and white shirts (the inescapable look of Indian clerks)—turned their attention back to their cups of milky coffee and their curry puffs. The Sikhs at the next table, brightly turbaned and ex-pansive of manner, resumed their cheerful conversation. The two Anglo-Indian typists in flowered dresses returned to their whispers and giggles and soda pop.

When the waiter brought us the menu, we discovered that the restaurant was called the Laxmi and Gold Medal Café. This sent Anand into a fresh spasm of laughter, and while we waited for our sandwiches and coffee, he entertained himself by invent-ing equally unlikely combinations for restaurant names—the Venus and Sun Yat-sen Coffee shoppe, the Cadillac and Red Devil Ice-Cream Parlor, and so on—not very clever, but by that time we were in a good mood and prepared to be amused by almost anything.

At some point, I remember, one of us said, "Well, how do you *really* feel about Bombay?" and the other replied, "Let's face it. Bombay *is* utter hell," and we were launched on the first of our interminable conversations about ourselves, our surroundings, our families, our gloomy predictions for the future. We had a lovely time.

Before we left, Anand had taken down the number of my office telephone, and only a couple of days later he called to invite me to lunch again. "I'll make up for the horrors of the

Laxmi and Gold Medal," he said. "We'll go to the Taj, which is at least air-conditioned, even if it isn't the Pavillon."

He had reserved a table by the windows in the dining room of the Taj Mahal Hotel, where we could sit and look out over the gray, forbidding water of the harbor and watch the massed monsoon clouds above the scattered islands. Cool against the steamy rain outside, we drank a bottle of wine, ate the local *pâté de foie gras,* and felt sorry for ourselves.

Anand said, "I can't think why my father bothered to send me to America, since he doesn't seem interested in anything I learned there."

"Oh, I know, I know," I said, longing to talk about my own concerns.

"Can you believe it, the whole business is run *exactly* the way it was fifty years ago?"

"Of course I can. I mean, take the magazine—"

"I mean, everything done by vague verbal arrangements. Nothing properly filed and accounted for. And such enormous reliance on pull, and influence, and knowing someone in the government who will arrange licenses and import permits and whatever."

"For a consideration, naturally?"

"Or for old friendship or past favors exchanged or—"

"Well, it's a miracle to me that we ever get an issue of the magazine out, considering that none of the typesetters speaks English, and they have to make up the forms in a language they don't know, mirrorwise and by hand."

"Oh, it's all hopelessly behind the times."

"You can see that what we really need is an enormous staff of proofreaders and only a *tiny* editorial—"

"But at least you don't have to deal with the family as well. The amount of deadwood in the form of aged great-uncles, dim-witted second cousins, who *have* to be employed!"

"Can't you suggest they be pensioned off?"

"Don't think I haven't. My father just smiles and says I'll settle down soon. Oh, what's the use?"

Our discussions nearly always ended with one or the other of us saying, with exaggerated weariness, "Well, so it goes.

Back to the salt mines now, I suppose?" I never added that I enjoyed my job.

That day we didn't realize until we were on the point of leaving the Taj how many people were lunching in the big dining room whom we knew or who knew one or the other of our families. On our way out, we smiled and nodded to a number of people and stopped at several tables to exchange greetings. With rising irritation, both of us were aware of the speculative glances, the carefully unexpressed curiosity behind the pleasant formalities of speech. Anand and I sauntered in silence down the wide, shallow staircase of the hotel. I think he was trying to seem unconcerned.

It was only when we reached the road that he exploded into angry speech. "Damn them," he said. "The prying old cats! What business is it of theirs, anyway?"

"It was the wine," I suggested. "Even people who have been abroad a lot don't drink wine at lunchtime."

"So? What's it to them?"

"Well, Dissolute Foreign Ways, and besides—"

"And besides, they have nothing to do but gossip."

"That, of course, but besides, you're what they call a catch, so it's only natural that they wonder."

Anand frowned as we crossed the road to where his car was parked against the sea wall. He opened the door for me and then climbed in behind the steering wheel. He didn't start the car for a moment or two, but sat with his hands on the wheel and his head turned away from me, looking at the threatening light of the early afternoon, which would darken into rain any minute. I thought he was about to tell me something— about a disappointment or a love affair—but instead, he clenched his fingers suddenly and said, "Well, the devil with them. Let them talk, if they have nothing better to do."

"Yes. Anyway, who cares?" I said, hoping it didn't sound as though *I* did.

He smiled at me. "That's the spirit. We'll show them."

We lunched at the Taj several times after that, but on each occasion a bit more defiantly, a bit more conscious of the appraising looks, always knowing we were the only "unattacheds" lunching together. The others were businessmen, or married couples doing duty entertaining, which, for some reason, they couldn't do at home, or ladies in groups, or foreigners.

As we stood inside the doors of the dining room, Anand would pause for a second, and then grip my elbow and say something like, "Well, come along. Let's strike a blow for freedom," or, "Throw away the blindfold. I'll face the firing squad like a man." He didn't deceive me—or, I suppose, anyone else.

Bombay is a big city—something over two million people— but in its life it is more like a conglomeration of villages. In our set, for instance, everyone knew everyone else at least by sight. At any of the hotels or restaurants we normally went to we were certain to meet a friend, a relative, an acquaintance. We all went to the same sort of party, belonged to the same clubs. People knew even each other's cars, and a quick glance at a row of parked cars would tell you that Mrs. Something was shopping for jewelry for her daughter's wedding, or that Mr. Something-else was attending a Willingdon Club committee meeting. So, of course, everyone knew that Anand and I lunched together a couple of times a week, and certainly our families must have been told we had been seen together.

My parents never mentioned the matter to me, though there was a certain wariness in their manner whenever Anand's name came up in conversation. (It's a sad moment, really, when parents first become a bit frightened of their child.) Privately, they must have put up with a good deal of questioning and comment from friends and relatives. Even to me people would sometimes say, "Can you come to a party on Saturday? Anand will be there." If Anand's mother ever lectured him on getting talked about, he evidently didn't think it worth repeating. Of them all, I daresay she was the most troubled, being orthodox, wanting a good, conservative marriage for her only son, being bewildered by what must have appeared to her—it seems astonishing in retrospect—as sophistication.

Occasionally Anand would take me home to tea after our offices had closed. I think he did this out of an unadmitted consideration for his mother, to set her mind at rest about the company he was keeping, to show her that I was not a Fast Girl even if I did work on a magazine. I don't know how much I reassured her, with my short hair and lipstick, no *tika* in the middle of my forehead. But she always greeted me politely, bringing her hands together in a *namaskar*, and gave me canny looks when she thought I wasn't noticing. We couldn't even speak to each other, since we came from different communities and she spoke only Gujarati, while my language was Hindi. She would always wait with us in the drawing room until one of the servants brought the tea; then she would lift her comfortable figure out of her chair, nod to me, and leave us alone. We were always conscious of her presence in the next room beyond the curtained archway, and every now and then we would hear her teacup clink on the saucer. Our conversation, even if she didn't understand it, was bound to be pretty stilted.

Perhaps it was this silent pressure, perhaps it was only a sort of restlessness that made Anand and me leave the usual haunts of our set and look for more obscure restaurants for our lunch dates. Liberal as we considered ourselves, we still couldn't help being affected by the knowing curiosity. There's no point in denying it (predictably, I always *did* deny it to Anand); I was concerned about public opinion. I suppose I was beginning to lose my England-returned brashness and intractability. I was not, however, prepared to stop meeting Anand for lunch. I liked him and waited with some impatience for his telephone calls, the rather pleasant voice saying things like "Hello? Is this the career girl?" (This was one of Anand's favorite phrases of defiance—a career girl was still something of a peculiarity in Bombay in those days. If you came from a respectable family that could support you, you weren't supposed to work for money. Social work would have been all right, but not something as shady as journalism.) Sometimes he would say, "This is underground agent 507. Are you a fellow resistance fighter?" or, "Am I speaking to Miss Emancipation?"

In any case, I would laugh and say, "Yes," and he would suggest that we try some Chinese food, or eat dry curried chicken at a certain Irani shop, or, if it was one of the steamy, rainless days near the end of the monsoon, go to Chowpatty beach and eat odds and ends of the delicious, highly spiced mixtures the vendors there concoct. By tacit agreement, he no longer picked me up at the office. Instead, we either met at the corner taxi rank (leaving Anand's car parked in the alley behind his office building) or arrived separately at our rendezvous.

Once, when we were driving to Colaba, the southernmost point of the island, Anand suddenly leaned forward and asked the taxi driver to stop. On an otherwise uninspired-looking street, lined with dingy middle-class houses, he had seen a sign that said "Joe's Place." Anand was entranced, and certainly the sign did look exotic among the bungalows and hibiscus. Joe's Place—named by some homesick American soldier, who had found his way there during the war—quickly became our favorite restaurant. We felt it was our discovery, for one thing, and then it had a Goan cook, which meant that, unlike at some of the other Indian restaurants, you could order beef. Most Hindus will not eat beef, cook it, or allow it on the premises; it is, as a result, the cheapest meat in Bombay. We ate a lot of beef at Joe's Place, and I often thought that Anand, at home in the evening, probably got rather a kick out of imagining how horrified his mother would be if she knew he had a rare steak inside him.

The proprietor, whom Anand insisted on calling Joe, even though he was a fat and jolly Indian, soon got used to seeing us almost every other day. We couldn't imagine how he made any money, since there never seemed to be anyone there besides Anand and me. Joe waited on table, so there weren't even waiters. Anand said that it was probably a front for black market activities and that you could expect anything of a man who ran a Joe's Place in Bombay. More likely, the real, prosaic reason was that most of Joe's business was in cooking meals to send out.

We came to feel so much at home at Joe's that we bought him a checkered tablecloth, to lend the place a bit of class, and he would spread it ceremoniously over the corner table, invariably pointing out that it had been laundered since our last meal. We kept a bottle of gin at Joe's and taught him to make fresh-lime gimlets with it, so that we could have a cocktail before lunch. He hadn't a license to sell liquor, so he always shook our cocktails in an opaque bottle labeled Stone Ginger, in case anyone came in. He probably watered the gin; but we didn't much care, because it was the idea that pleased us.

We would sit at our table between the windows, glancing out occasionally at the patch of straggly garden, the jasmine bush, the desultory traffic, and talk. How we talked! On and on and on. Sometimes it was "In the States, did you ever—" or "Do you remember—" kind of talk. Sometimes it was about incidents at home or in our offices. We talked a lot about Them—a flexible term, including any relatives or friends we considered old-fashioned, interfering, lacking in understanding. We often discussed Their iniquities, and many of our conversations began, "Do you know what They've gone and done *now?*" All through the sticky postmonsoon months, into the cooler, brilliant days of early winter, we talked. It seems a miracle to me now that we could have found so much to say about the details of our reasonably pedestrian lives.

If we'd been a bit older or more observant, we would certainly have known that this state of affairs couldn't last much longer. I was dimly aware that every day of life in Bombay relaxed our antagonism a tiny bit and blurred the outlines of our American years. However, I never guessed what Anand's family's counterattack to his England-returned discontent would be. Anand's mother was a direct, uncomplicated woman, and in her view there was one obvious and effective way to cure the whole disease without waiting for the slower methods of time.

It was at Joe's Place that Anand announced the arrival of Janaki. I had got there early, I remember, and was sitting at our table when Anand came in. He always had a certain tension in his walk, but that day it seemed more pronounced. He held his narrow shoulders stiffly and carried an air of trouble, so I asked him at once whether anything was the matter.

"Matter?" he asked sharply, as though it were an archaic word. "Why should anything be the matter?"

"Well, I don't know. You just look funny."

"Well, I don't feel funny," he said, deliberately misunderstanding.

Joe brought him his gimlet and inquired rather despairingly if we wanted steak *again*.

Anand waved a hand at him impatiently and said, "Later. We'll decide later." Then he looked at me in silence, with a portentous frown. At last he said, "Do you *know* what They've gone and done *now*? They've invited a cousin—a *distant* cousin —to stay."

This didn't seem to me any great disaster. Cousins, invited or not, were eternally coming to visit. Any relatives had the right to turn up whenever it was convenient for them and stay as long as they liked. His announcement came as an anticlimax; but since he did seem so distressed, I asked carefully, "And I suppose you'll be expected to fit him into the firm in some capacity?"

"Her," Anand said. "It's a girl."

"A *girl?* Is *she* going to work in the business?" This was really catacylsmic news.

"Oh, of *course* not. Can't you see what They're up to?"

"Well, no, I can't."

"Don't you *see?*" he said, looking helpless before such stupidity. "They're trying to arrange a marriage for me."

I could think of nothing to say except an unconvincing "Surely not."

He went on without paying any attention. "I dare say They think They're being subtle. Throwing us together, you know, so that my incomprehensible, *foreign*—" he emphasized the word bitterly—"preference for making up my own mind about these things will not be offended. We are to grow imperceptibly fond of each other. Oh, I see the whole plot."

"You must be imagining it all."

"She arrived last night. They didn't even tell me she was coming."

"But people are forever dropping in."

"I know. But she was *invited*. She told me so."

"Poor Anand." I was sorry for him, and angry on his behalf. There had never been any romantic exchanges between Anand and me, so the girl didn't represent any personal threat; but I honestly thought that a matter of principle was involved and that one should stand by the principle. We had so often agreed that the system of arranged marriages was the ultimate insult to one's rights as a human being, the final, insupportable interference of domineering families. I tried to think of something comforting to say, but could only produce, feebly, "Well, all you have to do is sit it out."

"And watch her doing little chores around the house? Making herself quietly indispensable?" He added with a sour smile, "As the years roll by. Do you suppose we will grow old gracefully together?"

"Oh, don't be such a fool," I said, laughing. "She'll have to go, sooner or later."

"But will I live that long?" He seemed to be cheering up.

"It's rather unfair to the poor thing," I said, thinking for the first time of the girl. "I mean, if they've got her hopes up."

"Now, don't start sympathizing with *her*. The only way to finish the thing once and for all—to make my position clear —is to marry someone else immediately. I suppose you wouldn't consider marrying me, would you?"

"Heavens, no," I said, startled. "I don't think you need to be as drastic as that."

"Well, perhaps not. We'll see."

At last I thought to ask, "What's she called?"

"Janaki."

"Pretty name."

"It makes me vomit."

I could hardly wait for our next lunch date, and when we met a couple of days later at Joe's Place I started questioning Anand eagerly. "Well, how are things? How are you making out with Janaki?"

Anand seemed remote, a bit bored with the subject. "Joe!" he called. "More ice, for Pete's sake. Gimlets aren't supposed to be *mulled*." He tapped his fingers on the table in a familiar, nervous movement. "He'll never learn," he said resignedly. Then, after a pause, "Janaki? Oh, she's all right, I suppose. A minor pest."

"Is she being *terribly* sweet to you?"

"Oh, you know. I will say this for her, she manages to be pretty unobtrusive."

"Oh." I was obscurely disappointed.

"It's just knowing she's always *there* that's so infuriating."

"It would drive me crazy."

In a voice that was suddenly cross, he said, "She's so *womanly*."

"Hovers about, you mean?"

"Not that so much, but I can see her *hoping* I'll eat a good dinner or have had a good day at the office, or some damn thing."

"It sounds rather flattering."

"I dare say that's the strategy. It's pathetic, really, how little They know me if They think she's the sort of girl I'd want to marry."

"What sort of girl *would* you want to marry?"

"Heaven knows," Anand said in a hopeless voice. "Someone quite different, anyway. I knew one once."

"Was there a girl in America?" I asked with interest.

"Isn't there always a girl in America? A sort of tradition. In our fathers' time, it used to be the daughter of the landlady somewhere in Earl's Court. Usually blonde, always accommodating."

"And yours?"

"Accommodating. But several cuts above the landlady's daughter. She was a senior in college. And she had quite a nice family, if you can stand families, rather timid, but determined to believe that a Good Home Environment was a girl's best protection. I don't think they would have raised many objections if we'd got married."

"Why didn't you marry her, then?"

"Oh, I don't know. Do those things work? I really don't know."

"I expect your parents would have raised the devil."

"Before—if I'd told them. Not after. By then the particular alchemy that turns a girl into a daughter-in-law would have done its work. That was really the trouble. I couldn't see her being an Indian daughter in-law living in a Bombay family— and what a mess that would have made. Hurt feelings and recriminations and disappointment all around. I'm not sentimental about her," he said earnestly, as if it were an important point. "I mean, I know she wasn't particularly good-looking or anything, but I had a separate identity in her mind. I wasn't just somebody's son, or someone to marry, or someone with good business connections."

"And all that is what you are to Janaki?"

"I suppose so. What else could I be?"

As we left Joe's Place after lunch, he said, "I think you'd better come to tea to meet her. Would you like to?"

"I was hoping you'd ask me."

"Okay, then. Tomorrow?"

Full of excitement, the next day, I met Anand after work and drove home with him. "Is your mother going to be cross about your asking me?"

"Why should she be cross? You've been to tea with us before."

"But that was different."

"I can't see why," he said, refusing to accept the situation.

"Oh, don't be so dense," I said, thinking, Poor girl, it's going to be very frustrating for her if he insists on treating her as a casual cousin come for a holiday. "Does your mother tactfully leave you alone with her for tea?"

"Never. The two of them chatter about domestic details. It's really very boring."

To me it was far from boring. For one thing, Anand's mother was far more cordial to me than she had been on previous visits, and I wondered whether she could already be so sure of the success of her plan that I was no longer a danger. And then there was the suspense of waiting to see what Janaki would be like.

She came in with the servant who carried the tea tray, holding back the curtain of the dining room archway so that he could manage more easily. A plump, graceful girl with a very pretty face and a tentative, vulnerable smile, which she seemed ready to cancel at once if you weren't going to smile with her. I saw, instantly, that she was any mother-in-law's ideal—quiet, obedient, helpful. Her hair was drawn back into the conventional knot at the nape of her neck; she had a *tika* on her forehead, wore no make-up except for the faintest touch of lipstick, and even that, I decided, was probably a new experiment for her, a concession to Anand's Westernized tastes.

She spoke mostly to Anand's mother, in Gujarati, and I noticed that she had already assumed some of the duties of a hostess. She poured the tea and asked, in clear, lilting English, whether

I took milk and sugar, handed around the plates of Indian savories and sweets.

After the first mouthful, I remarked formally, "This is delicious."

Anand's mother caught the tone, even if she didn't understand the words, and said something in Gujarati to Anand.

He translated, without much interest, "Janaki made them."

Janaki, in embarrassment, wiped her mouth on her napkin with the thorough gesture that someone unused to wearing lipstick makes, and then gazed in surprise and alarm at the pink smear on the linen. She saw me watching and gave me one of her diffident smiles.

I quickly said the first thing that came into my head, "How clever you are. I wish I could cook."

"It is very easy to learn," she replied.

"There never seems to be any time for it."

Entirely without sarcasm or envy she said, "That is true for someone like you who leads such a busy and interesting life."

I felt ashamed of myself, for no reason I could quite put my finger on.

We continued to talk banalities, and Janaki kept up her end admirably, managing to seem interested in the most ordinary comments and still keeping a watchful eye out to see that cups and plates were filled. The conversation gradually fell entirely to Janaki and me, because Anand retreated into a sulky silence. I remember thinking that one couldn't really blame him. It must have been maddening to have to face this sweet and vapid politeness every day after work. At last he jumped up, said abruptly that he had some papers to go through and left the room. I left soon after.

Janaki saw me to the front door and, with an unexpected spontaneity, put her hand on my arm. "Please come to tea again," she said. "I mean, if you are not too occupied. I should so much like it. I have no friends in Bombay."

"I'd be delighted, and you must come to tea with me."

"Oh, no, thank you very much. Perhaps later on, but I must learn the ways of this house first. You see that, don't you?"

I walked home, wondering at her mixture of nervousness and

confidence, at the fact that she already felt certain she had a permanent place in that house.

At our next lunch date, it was Anand who asked the eager questions. "Well? What did you think of her?"

And I replied noncommittally, "She seemed very pleasant."

"Quite the little housewife, do you mean?"

"No. Sweet and anxious to please, I meant."

"You sound like my mother. She says, 'A good-natured girl. You should count yourself fortunate.' I suppose she asked you to be her friend?"

"How did you know?"

"She's not as stupid as she looks. She said the same to me. 'Will you not allow us to be friendly, Anand?' " He attempted a saccharin, unconvincing falsetto. He frowned. "The thin end of the wedge, don't you see? It would be funny if it weren't so sad."

"Well, at least she's very good-looking," I said defensively.

"She's too fat."

"I think it rather suits her."

"A strong point in her favor, my mother says, to make up for my puniness." Anand was sensitive about his height. He said, in a touchy voice, daring one to sympathize with him, "Eugenically very sound. Strong, healthy girl like Janaki married to a weakling like me, and we have a chance of strong, healthy children that take after her. The children, you see, are the whole point of this stratagem. I'm an only son and must produce some. My mother has a rather simple approach to these things."

"You must admit," I said rather uncomfortably, "that she'd make a very good mother."

"Not a doubt in the world. She's a natural for the part of the Great Earth Mother. But I rather resent being viewed in such an agricultural light."

In the weeks that followed, Janaki dominated our conversation at lunchtime, and I had tea with them quite frequently. Sometimes, if Anand was kept late at his office or had to attend a board meeting, Janaki and I would have tea alone, and she would ask hundreds of questions about America, trying, I thought, to build up a picture of Anand's life there and the background that seemed to influence him so much. She claimed to be uniformly enthusiastic about everything American, and for me it was rather fun, because it made me feel so superior in experience. Once she asked me to teach her to dance, and I was unexpectedly disconcerted. There was something very refreshing about her lack of Westernization, and I didn't want to see her lose it.

"I will if you really want me to, but—"

"Anand likes dancing, doesn't he?"

"Yes, but wouldn't it be better if he taught you himself, after you—I mean, when he—what I mean is, a little later on?"

"You think that would be best?" She meant, of course, the best way of handling Anand.

"Yes, I do," I said, meaning, "You don't want to seem too eager."

"Very well." She nodded, accepting my opinion as final. On this level of unspoken frankness we understood each other perfectly.

She would question me, sometimes openly and sometimes indirectly, about Anand's tastes and preferences. We had a long session, I remember, about her looks. Should she wear make-up? Should she cut her hair? What about her clothes? I told her she was fine the way she was, but she insisted, "Has he *never* said anything? He must have made *some* remark?"

"Well," I said reluctantly, "he did once mention that he thought you were just a fraction on the chubby side."

Without a trace of rancor, Janaki said, "I will quickly become thin."

"Heavens! Don't take the remark so seriously."

"It is nothing," Janaki assured me. "One need only avoid rice and *ghi*." She did, too. I noticed the difference in a couple of weeks.

When Anand was there, the atmosphere was much more strained. From the frigid politeness of his early days with Janaki, his manner gradually changed to irritation, which expressed itself in angry silence and later in a kind of undercover teasing sometimes laced with malice. For instance, he would greet her with something like, "What have you been up to today? Hemstitching the sheets? Crocheting for the hope chest?" and Janaki would look puzzled and smile, as though she had missed the point of a clever joke. Actually, she was a beautiful needlewoman and did a good deal of exquisitely neat embroidery on all kinds of things—antimacassars, doilies, face towels—infallibly choosing hideous designs of women, in enormous crinolines, watering the flowers in an English garden, or bunches of roses with ribbons streaming from them. Once Janaki answered Anand's inquiry quite seriously with an account of her day, the household jobs she had done, the women who had called on his mother in the morning and had been served coffee, and even produced the embroidery she had been working on.

"Wonderfully appropriate for India, don't you think?" Anand remarked to me with rather labored irony.

"I think it's lovely," I said unconvincingly.

Janaki seemed unruffled. "Men do not appreciate embroidery," she said quietly.

Anand leaned back in his chair, stared at the ceiling, and gave an exaggerated sigh.

One couldn't help disliking him in this role of tormentor. The fact was, of course, that, in Anand's phrase, *I* was getting imperceptibly fonder of Janaki as his impatience with her grew more overt. There was, to me, both gallantry and an appealing innocence in her undaunted conviction that everything would turn out all right. What I didn't recognize was the solid realism behind her attitude. I started to suspect the calculation in her nature one day when Anand had been particularly difficult. He had insisted on talking about books she hadn't read and, with apparent courtesy, addressing remarks to her he knew she couldn't answer.

Janaki said nothing for a long time and then admitted, with a becoming lack of pretension, "I'm afraid I read only the stories in the *Illustrated Weekly*. But, Anand, if you would bring me some books you think good, I would read them."

"I'll see if I can find the time," he replied in a surly voice.

When Janaki showed me to the door that evening, I said in considerable exasperation, "Why do you put up with it? He needn't be so disagreeable when he talks to you."

"It is natural that there should be difficulties at first. After his life in America, there are bound to be resentments here."

"Well, I think you are altogether too forbearing. I wouldn't stand it for a second." Privately, I had begun to think she must, after all, be stupid.

Then Janaki said, "What would you do?"

"Leave, of course. Go back." And at that moment I realized what she meant. Go back to what? To another betrothal arranged by her elders? Learning to please some other man? Here, at least, she liked her future mother-in-law.

"And besides," she said, "I know that really he is kind."

In the end, Janaki turned out to be the wisest of us all, and I have often thought how lucky it was that she didn't follow my advice then. Not that Anand capitulated all at once, or that one extraordinary morning he suddenly saw her with new eyes, or anything like that. He remained irritable and carping; but gradually he became enmeshed in that most satisfactory of roles, a reluctant Pygmalion.

I noticed it first one day when he finished his lunch rather hurriedly and said, as we were going back to our offices, "That girl's conversation is driving me nuts. I think I really had better buy her some books. As long as I'm stuck with her company," he added awkwardly.

We parted at the bookshop, and in later conversations I learned that Janaki was doing her homework with diligence and pleasure.

From then on things moved fairly rapidly. I began to anticipate Anand's frequent suggestions that we spend part of the lunch hour shopping—usually rather ungraciously expressed: "We've got to get that girl into some less provincial-looking saris." "That girl listens to nothing but film music. I really must get her some decent classical stuff. What do you suggest as a beginning? Kesarbai? Subbaluxmi?"

"No Western music?" I asked pointedly.

"She wouldn't understand it," Anand replied.

All the same, at home he continued to be offhand or overbearing with her. She remained calm and accepting, a willing pupil who knew that her stupidity was a great trial to her teacher. Still, there wasn't a doubt in my mind about the change of attitude going on in Anand. I wanted a lived-happily-ever-after conclusion for Janaki; but mostly I was certain that the Pygmalion story could have only one ending, whatever the minor variations might be.

Anand's parents were evidently equally confident of the out-come, for one day at tea he announced, with an exuberance no amount of careful casualness could disguise, that his father was going to send him to New York on a business trip. He was pleased, he insisted, largely because it meant that at last he was to be trusted with some real responsibility.

I said, "And it will be such wonderful fun to be back in America."

"Oh, yes. That, too, naturally. But I don't know how much time I'll have for the bright lights and parties." He had moved so smoothly into the correct businessman's viewpoint that I wanted to laugh.

We were absorbed in discussing the details of the trip, and besides, by then Janaki had become such an accepted—and pleas-ing—part of the scenery of the house that we assumed she was listening with her usual attention and, as always, trying to fit in with Anand's mood.

So it came as quite a shock when she suddenly spoke in a flat, decisive voice. "I, too, am leaving. I am going back to my home." Dead silence for a moment. "Tomorrow," she said.

"But *why*—" I began.

"It is my decision," she said, and wouldn't look at either of us.

Anand didn't say anything, just stood up, all his bright, im-portant planning gone, and walked out of the room. We waited to hear his study door slam.

Then my affection for Janaki (and, of course, curiosity) made me ask, "But why *now*, just when things are going so well?"

"It was your advice, don't you remember?"

"But things were different then."

"Yes." She nodded as though we both recognized some partic-ular truth.

At the time I thought she believed herself defeated. I was surprised and concerned that what seemed so plain to me should remain obscure to her. "Listen," I said cautiously, "don't you see that he—that in spite of everything, he has fallen in love with you?"

I don't know quite what I had expected her response to be—
a radiant smile, perhaps, or even a sense of triumph. I hadn't
expected her to glare at me as though I were an enemy and say,
"Oh, love. I don't want him to *love* me. I want him to marry me."

"It's different for him," I said, as persuasively as I could. "For
him it is important."

She looked at me shrewdly, making up her mind about something. "You are sure?" she asked.

"Absolutely sure."

Her voice was hard and impatient. "Love, what books you
read, whether you like music, your 'taste'—whatever that may
mean. As if all that has anything to do with marriage."

"Well," I said ineffectually.

How can one make the idea of romantic love attractive to
someone who wants only a home, a husband, and children? Even
if nothing could be done about that, I thought I knew the reason
for her sudden despair. The renewing of Anand's American experiences must have seemed to her an overwhelming menace. I
tried to reassure her, reminded her that Anand would be gone
only a matter of weeks, that he would miss her, that America
would look quite different to him now, that he had changed a
lot in the past year—more than a year, actually.

But she wouldn't listen, and she kept repeating, "I must pack
my things and leave the house tomorrow."

I thought, Poor Janaki. I can see that the tedious business of
starting all over again on the unraveling of Anand's England-
returned tangles might well seem to be too much to face. It didn't
occur to me that I might equally have thought, Clever Janaki,
the only one of us who knows exactly what she wants. Leave the
house? She would have slit her throat first.

When I think of it, I can't help wondering at the extent of
my naïveté then. The fact is that women—or perhaps I mean
just the women of a certain kind of world, Janaki's world—have
inherited, through bitter centuries, a ruthless sense of self-pres-
ervation. It still seems to me ghastly that they should need it; but
it would be silly to deny that, in most places on earth, they still
do. That cool, subtle determination to find her security and hang
on to it, that all's-fair attitude—not in love, which she discounted,

but in war, for it *was* war, the gaining or losing of a kingdom—
was really no more than the world deserved from Janaki. As in
war, victory, conquest, success, call it what you will, was the only
virtue. And, of course, the really absurd thing was that nobody
would have been more appalled than Janaki if you had called her
a feminist.

As it was, I heard with anxiety Anand on the phone the next
day, saying, "Let's lunch. I want to talk to you. Joe's Place? One
o'clock?"

I was certain that Janaki had gone home, with only the indig-
nities of a few new clothes and a lot of tiresome talk to remember.

As soon as I saw him, I knew I was wrong. He had the con-
ventionally sheepish look that makes the announcing of good news
quite pointless. He said, "An eventful evening, wasn't it?"

"Yes, it was, rather."

Then there was a long pause while he looked embarrassed and
I could think of no way to help him out. At last he said, all in a
rush, "Look, this is going to seem ridiculous. I mean—well, Janaki and I are going to be married."

"You couldn't do a more sensible thing," I said, much relieved.

He looked startled. "Sensible? Perhaps it seems that way to
you. Actually, we're in love with each other."

"With *each other?*" I echoed incredulously, and regretted it
immediately.

"I knew it would seem peculiar to you. I daresay you've thought
I hated her all this time." He smiled at me in a rather superior
way. "I thought so myself for a while. And Janaki, as you well
imagine, had every reason to think so. And I must say it certainly
took a lot of courage on her part. I mean, when you think—"

"You'd better start at the beginning," I said, suddenly feeling
depressed.

"Okay. I heard you leave yesterday, and then I heard Janaki
come into the hall—you know that timid way she has of walking
—and stand outside my study door. I was in quite a state; but
I daresay that I wouldn't have done anything about anything if
she hadn't—I mean, if someone hadn't taken the initiative."

"Yes," I said, knowing what was coming but unable to shake
off my gloom. "She came to explain why she was going home."

"She said—you see, she isn't the passive, orthodox girl you think—she told me that quite against her plans or anything she'd expected, she'd—I know this will seem silly—but she'd fallen in love with me."

"I see. And that accounted for her behavior. Trying all the time to please you, I mean."

"Well, yes. Then I realized that—"

"All your resentment and bad manners were just that—" I wanted to hurry him through the story.

"Well, yes."

"Well, yes," I repeated, and couldn't look at him. We were silent for a while. "Well, congratulations," I said uneasily.

"It's funny, isn't it," he said in a confident voice, "that Their plans should have worked out—but so differently. I don't suppose They'll ever understand."

"It wouldn't be worth trying to explain."

"Heavens, no. Look, I'm taking Janaki out to lunch tomorrow. Will you join us?"

"Oh, no, surely—"

"She asked particularly that you come. She likes you very much, you know, and besides, she doesn't feel quite comfortable going out without a chaperon."

"In *that* case—" I said, with a nastiness lost on Anand. And all the time I was thinking, Have we all been made use of? A sympathetic mother-in-law, a man you can flatter, a gullible friend from whom you can learn background and fighting conditions, with whom you can check tactics and their effects. Now that she has won, she must have nothing but contempt for all of us. But simultaneously I was wondering, Is she, after all, really in love? It was a state she didn't know how to cope with, and she could hope only to use the weapon she knew, an ability to please or try to please. Why should she, or how could she, tell me all that herself—a realm of which she was so unsure, which was so far out of her experience?

Now that I have met so many Janakis of the world, I think I know which explanation was right.

"So we'll meet," Anand was saying, "at the Taj, if that's all right with you?"

He had reserved a table by the windows. Janaki was a bit late, to be sure—she explained breathlessly—that we would be there before her, because it would have been agony to sit alone.

We ordered from the Indian menu, and Anand said, with only a fleeting, questioning glance at me, "No wine, I think. There really isn't any wine at all that goes with Indian food, is there?"

India

ORDER OF THE
WHITE PAULOWNIA

Tokuda Shūsei

SHE HAD no great expectations. All she hoped was that she would attain a degree of economic security befitting her modest station in life and, when she got married, an average amount of conjugal happiness. Unlike her younger sisters, who had all succeeded in finding jobs with good prospects, she was in the dismal position of having to get married in order to live. Worse still, the years were passing rapidly as she wavered and soon she would be too old to make a satisfactory marriage.

At the moment she was working as cashier in a cheap restaurant on the Ginza. The waitresses were all about the same age as her youngest sister and they vividly brought home to Kanako the fact that she herself had already passed the prime of her youth. It had been different in the hosiery factory where she had worked before.

She often thought about that factory. It specialized in the manufacture of *tabi*.* Unfortunately the owner had started to run after women. As a result he had neglected his factory and business had fallen off badly. Just then he had died. His widow was a clever woman. Rising to the occasion, she had taken charge of the management herself. Gradually the factory had been restored to its former prosperity and Kanako had again found it a pleasure to work there.

Everything had been all right until another factory girl, who was her best friend, had a terrible accident. She had been washing her long hair and as she stood near one of the machines a few

* Japanese-style socks.

strands were caught in the cogwheel. An instant later her hair was being pulled into the machine with a fearful swishing sound. Everyone rushed up to her and someone managed to stop the machine. But it was too late. Just like a piece of lawn that has been torn out of the earth, her hair had been dragged out by its roots and nothing was left but a bleeding scalp. It had of course been the girl's fault, yet Kanako could not help being tormented by the wretched fate of her friend. The awful groaning of the machinery now made her unbearably nervous and the factory, once so enjoyable, began to strike her as gloomy and oppressive. The owner was generally considered solicitous about her workers; but Kanako now regarded her as a monster and could not bear to look at her. Her friend had returned to her home in the country immediately after the accident. Kanako did not know the details, but she understood that the amount of compensation the girl received from the factory as a result of ruining her entire life had been nothing short of derisory. Yet even this, she was told, was more than the girl would have received from most other employers. Whatever the truth of the matter might be, Kanako no longer felt like setting foot in the factory.

During the following year she lived at home and helped her mother with the housework. Kanako's mother was a fierce, dauntless woman who had been brought up in the hinterland and who after many long years had still not been softened by city ways. She was a stubborn old realist and when she was not preparing for the morrow she was making sure that not a grain of today's rice was being wasted. Even when Kanako sat down to do her sewing she felt her mother's eagle eyes on her and she could not relax for a moment.

In the end the atmosphere in the house became unbearable and Kanako went to Shitaya where her elder sister ran a little teashop. There she was able to help in the kitchen and with the clothes and the bedding. When it came to waiting on customers in the shop, however, Kanako was too heavy and sluggish by nature to be of much use. Not that she did not try. The relative gaiety of her sister's life filled her with envy and she did her her best to mix with the male customers. Yet she was not sufficiently self-confident about her looks or her manners. She tried copying the other waitresses by powdering her face and curling her hair, but it all struck her as rather pointless. As soon as she began to make herself amiable, she felt that she was in some way betraying her own nature.

"Your eyes are just like Madam's," the girls in the shop used to tell Kanako. "You've got a nice round face and lovely white skin like hers, too." She could not help smiling at these compliments; yet she was well aware that, much as she might resemble her sister in some ways, she had none of the elder girl's attraction. Never once was Kanako flattered into believing that she possessed any real charm. Her face was always slightly crooked as though she were about to cry; it reminded one of Chōjirō, the actor.

One of the waitresses in the teashop had formerly been a dancer and she told Kanako about the easy life in the dance halls. Kanako decided to take some lessons, but at her first visit to a dance hall she was thoroughly disillusioned. She could not bear the idea of being dragged round the floor in the arms of one man after another, all complete strangers.

Kanako was afraid that if she continued her present life she might succumb to temptation. She was therefore glad to accept the job as a cashier in a Ginza restaurant that one of her sister's patrons, a wool draper, mentioned to her. Here at least she was safe. But it was no easy job to stand by the cash register all day and late into the night.

Meanwhile marriage plans were being discussed. A couple who came from the same village as Kanako's mother called separately on her parents with the suggestion that she should marry Sōichi, the father's son by his first wife. Originally it had been intended that she should be the bride of Sōichi's stepbrother, Shinichi (who was the wife's son from her first marriage), and negotiations had gone on for some time between Kanako's parents and Shinichi's mother. Shinichi was a fairly pleasant young man. He often used to call at Kanako's house with a bundle of clothes for repair and he would sit for hours discussing horses with her father, who was a great racing fan. Kanako came to know him quite well. Shinichi's position as a shopkeeper was entirely to her taste and she grew used to the idea that in due course she would become his wife.

Then in the middle of it all Shinichi's stepfather, Wasao,

proposed to Kanako's parents that she should instead marry his own son, Sōichi, who was three years younger than the step-brother. Her parents made no objection. At first Kanako felt that she was somehow acting wrongly toward Shinichi, but since he did not seem to care particularly, she silently resigned herself to the new arrangement and exchanged the traditional betrothal cups with Sōichi, about whom she knew next to nothing.

Sōichi, who worked in a large clock factory where his father was a foreman, had recently come back from military service in Manchuria. Before entering the army, he had fallen in with a set of bad companions who were employed in the same factory under his father's superintendence. Through their influence he had started gambling and had also visited bars and brothels. It was with the aim of having his son settle down that Wasao arranged for him to be married immediately on his return from Manchuria. There was no pressing need for his wife's son, Shinichi, to get married and Wasao had therefore substituted Sōichi as Kanako's bridegroom.

After the marriage the young couple moved into Wasao's house. The father gave them the second story, one six-mat room and one three-mat room.* For himself, his wife and their two daughters he reserved the six-mat room and the four-mat room on the ground floor. Despite this arrangement, Kanako soon found that the crowded house prevented her from enjoying the happiness of married life to which she had so eagerly looked forward.

The younger of the two sisters, who had just turned sixteen, had suffered from an attack of pleurisy and since her recovery had been hanging about the house doing nothing. Yoshiko, the other sister, was eighteen. She had recently started to learn sewing. After the marriage she announced that it was too crowded for her to work downstairs and she installed her sewing machine in the three-mat room on the second story. Kanako soon became accustomed to the whirring of the machine, but when Yoshiko took to spreading her bedding next to the room where she and

* All Japanese-style rooms are measured by the number of straw mats (*tatami*). A mat is about 6 ft. × 3 ft.

Sōichi slept, she really found it intolerable. She felt that strange eyes were peeping into the happy world that they shared at night, and soon she became extremely reserved with her husband.

Yoshiko, on the other hand, felt as if Kanako were an elder sister who had been added to the family and for a time she tried to make friends. It soon became clear, however, that they had little in common. Kanako, thanks to her mother's training, had an eminently practical approach, whereas Yoshiko thought of nothing but films and revues. The young girl was a great fan of Chōjirō, the film actor. Not long before, Chōjirō had made a personal appearance at the nearby Kinshi Hall. Yoshiko had pushed her way through the throng of girls and young wives who flocked from the neighborhood to admire him. When she saw that the actor was going to step into his car, she leapt out in front of the crowd and tried to approach him as he stood there in his formal crested kimono. With a frenzied look in her eyes she seized his hand and screamed out his nickname, Chōsan. There was a stir among the onlookers and they broke into loud applause. Even Chōjirō, accustomed though he was to over-enthusiastic fans, was taken aback by this and he looked at the girl in blank amazement.

When Kanako heard the story, it gave her a strange feeling. She realized that such giddy behavior was fairly frequent among the younger generation, yet it seemed odd that she should be living in the same house with so uncontrolled a girl. Every time that Kanako looked at Yoshiko's freakish features, which she had obviously inherited from her mother, she felt amused and at the same time deeply sorry for her.

In order to show her friendliness, Yoshiko said that she would make a light dress for Kanako to wear in the early spring. From then on she began pestering Kanako about the exact sort of material and pattern that she wanted. It was all the more annoying in that Kanako did not have the remotest intention of wearing the dress. She would gladly have had an extra kimono to add to her wardrobe, but Western-style clothes were utterly out of character.

Kanako's main occupations were washing and sewing. As a

rule she would spend the greater part of the day working in her room on the second story without saying a word to anyone. The cooking was the responsibility of the mother and her daughters. Kanako would have liked occasionally to prepare a meal with a variety of dishes that she could enjoy with her husband. But the household stuck strictly to the rule of having only one kind of food with the rice each day. If there were potatoes, there would be nothing but potatoes for all three meals; if they had cod, there would be nothing but slices of cod. There was never the slightest effort to combine different dishes and Kanako could not help feeling depressed as she sat down with the family to their monotonous meals. To make things even more trying, they never had vegetables. Whatever else she might have missed during her life, Kanako had always had plenty of pickles, and rice without pickles struck her as extremely insipid. Her parents' house was fairly near and she now began stopping by on her way back from the hairdresser's or the public bath. She would slip in by the back door and ask for some pickles, which she then mixed in a bowl with rice and tea and gulped down greedily. Yet the knowledge that she now belonged to another family made her ashamed of these visits and took away most of the pleasure.

Her husband liked Kanako's hair best when she did it up in a *marumagé*.* At first she used to take great trouble in arranging it and would tie the chignon with a red band. Yet gradually she became imbued with the drab, gloomy atmosphere of the household. The mood that had buoyed her up during the early months of her marriage disappeared and she no longer took any pains with her coiffure. Why make her hair beautiful when everthing else was so unlovely?

It was just at this time that Sōichi came home late one night thoroughly drunk. Earlier in the evening Kanako had sat downstairs with the younger sister and listened to records. Then she had heated the sake for her father-in-law to sip when he came back from the bathhouse. Wasao returned and said that he would wait for his son to join him at his sake, as was their habit in

* Normal old-fashioned hair style for married women.

the evenings. Time went by, but still the young man did not return. Wasao was reminded of his son's nocturnal outings in the past and the sake failed to produce its usual enlivening effect. He began to mumble some halfhearted apology on behalf of Sōichi. It made Kanako rather uncomfortable and she took the first opportunity to leave him and go upstairs. Ten o'clock passed, then eleven, and still there was no sign of Sōichi. Kanako became impatient. She emptied some old photographs out of a drawer and examined them. Then she began to rummage through some old magazines and storybooks which had been gathering dust in a cupboard. At that moment she was aware of a pungent smell of sake. Sōichi was back. Without a word he sprawled out on the floor like a refractory child and fell into a drunken sleep. This was Kanako's first experience of such behavior and she felt that in a flash she had been confronted with the true nature of men.

Some time after this incident the young couple moved into a little rented house not far from the parents' home. Wasao, who would normally have objected strongly to the change, was in no position to do so. For on a certain evening while Kanako was pouring sake for him he had made an objectionable suggestion that had utterly infuriated her.

His wife had gone out that evening to the local cinema. She had taken along the youngest daughter, but Yoshiko had stayed behind. The elder girl's mental condition had been growing steadily worse and when the time came for the cherry-blossoms she had lapsed into real lunacy. After the worst period had passed, they found that her nature had completely changed. The girl, who had formerly suffered from manic frenzy, now became extremely subdued. Occasionally she fell into fits of fearful depression, but most of the time she was reasonably calm. The genesis of Yoshiko's disorder appeared to lie in her obsession with her beloved Chōjirō. One night she had jumped out of bed, crying that Chōjirō was passing outside the window, and she had tried to rush into the street. Evidently she had been aroused by the sound of a group of factory girls walking by after a visit to the cinema; this had in some way stirred up

images of the memorable occasion when she had seized Chōjirō
by the hand. Wasao was well aware that his daughter's tendency
to madness was shared by his wife, who loved him so frenziedly,
and he felt that he was imprisoned by bonds of cause and effect
from which he could never escape. He sighed deeply and took
another sip of sake. Until that year Wasao had always observed
the strictest economy. He never made any objections, however,
when his wife used to dress up and go out shopping. She used
to get terribly lonely when he left for work and sometimes she
could not bear to stay in the house. His wife really adored him.
Even in front of the children she would nestle up amorously to
her solemn-faced husband and cause him the liveliest embarrassment. The fact that she was a couple of years older than Wasao
made her affection all the keener.

"You know, my girl," he said to Kanako, "I really love the
old woman. So long as she's alive I won't do anything to cause
her unnecessary worry. But when she's dead I'm going to find
myself someone better. After all, what's the use of sweating
away and making a pile if I can't get any pleasure out of it?
The way things are now, I come straight home from work every
day. I never set foot in a teahouse, I never go to the races or
have any real fun. I just have a bottle or two of sake, get a little
tipsy, turn out the lights and go to bed. Sometimes I feel pretty
fed up, I can tell you. There are lots of ways a man can enjoy
himself in this world if he's got a little money. Why shouldn't
I want to do the same things that Sōichi likes doing? Most men
of my age when they've made a decent position for themselves
keep a mistress or two. Now don't get the idea that I'm waiting
for the old woman to die. But sometimes I can't help feeling
that it would be a good thing if she did die fairly soon. It's not
simply that I want my freedom. Just think what would happen
if I died first! It would be terrible for my poor wife and the rest
of the family would be in a pretty bad state, too."

Wasao muttered away affectedly. He drained his cup and
handed it to Kanako.

"Here, have some sake," he said.

Kanako found it irritating enough to have to pour the sake;
to be asked to drink it was doubly annoying.

"Me?" she laughed. "How absurd!"

"Too shy to drink, eh, my girl? That's rather sweet."

He pressed the cup on her, but when she again refused he gave up and resumed his rambling monologue. "That boy of mine's an awful fool," he said, "but I still love him the best, you know. Of course, my children are all the same and there's no real reason I should love one of them more than the others. But Sōichi is the living image of my dead wife. I suppose that's why I worry about him most of all. If only you could have a child by him, my girl, I could pass on my money with a free mind. The trouble is—well, I suppose it's something you should have been told about before you got married, but it was a terribly hard thing to mention at the time. Now that you're a wife you'll understand quite easily and you'll realize it's nothing so bad. The fact is that Sōichi led too wild a life before he went into the army and as a result he can't have any children. It's not all that bad, is it? Still, it makes me rather sad that my family is going to end when Sōichi dies. Now please don't think I'm using all this as an excuse. I'd hate you to think that. But suppose you were to have a child for Sōichi. You know what I mean, girl, don't you?"

Kanako had been listening carefully to what her father-in-law had to say, but suddenly her expression changed. She jumped to her feet and ran upstairs without paying the slightest attention to Wasao's apologies. A few moments later he heard her quietly leaving the house. He did not even try to stop her.

Thus Wasao's plans for a united family life in which all the money remained secure were abruptly shattered. The young couple rented a separate house and the family was split.

Kanako was happy about the change. She thought that at last she and her husband would be able to live a life of their own. She remembered the hosiery factory, which she had not thought about for a long time. When she worked there before, she had given part of her earnings to her mother and this had been a great help for the household expenses. Why should she not help her husband by doing some work now? As soon as they were settled in the new house, she visited the proprietress of the factory and discussed the matter. It was agreed that she could very well work at home on mending the *tabi* which came out of the machine with tangled threads, tears and other imperfections.

Kanako promptly set to work and to her satisfaction found that she was earning enough to pay for their rent and their rice. So long as Sōichi handed her his monthly pay packet intact, they would have enough to pay a visit to the cinema a couple of times a month, to have a meal in the restaurant of one of the big department stores when they went shopping and even to deposit something in the postal savings account.

"I'm not going to stop you two from living apart if that's what you've decided to do," Wasao had told them when they left, "but you'll have to manage your own finances from now on. Of course if you get ill or something I'll try to help out, but you'd better not count on me too much."

Kanako determined not to ask him for money whatever happened, and she made her plans for their new budget accordingly. Everything would have been all right if Sōichi had given her his full pay as agreed. But he did so only in their first month. Toward the end of the second month Sōichi took on someone else's work in the factory and Kanako was happily looking forward to the extra money that he would be earning. When pay day came, however, Kanako found that all her household plans had been in vain. Profiting from the fact that his father no longer was watching him, Sōichi had gone back to his old habit of gambling and had succeeded in losing over half his month's pay. He came home drunk and without a word threw his pay envelope on the floor. Kanako picked it up and emptied the contents.

"Is this all?" she said, holding up two notes.

Sōichi did not answer. He merely stood there, smoothing his unkempt hair.

When they had moved into their new house, Sōichi had taken out his tool box and busied himself with putting up shelves, installing the wireless that he had brought from his father's place, and other odd jobs. Occasionally he had taken his wife to a shrine festival and they had bought themselves something at a stall—a little potted tree or a cage of singing insects. Or again, he had locked up the house and taken her out to a film. Once they had been to see some Western-style dancing at the pleasure pavilion in Sumida Park and had been so captivated by the gaiety of the event that they had not returned home till quite late in the evening.

All this came to an end now that Sōichi had fallen in with his old gambling associates. A small group would get together during the lunch break and secretly play their game behind a pile of crates in one of the factory warehouses. In the evenings they would go to some house and gamble until late at night and sometimes even until dawn. Most of them worked under Wasao. In theory the foreman was supposed to prohibit gambling by his subordinates, but in fact Wasao usually turned a blind eye to what was going on. He had got into the habit of advancing money at interest to those who could not pay their gambling debts, and this obliged him to settle Sōichi's losses out of his own pocket when his son fell hopelessly in arrears. Wasao secretly fumed at the stupidity and shiftlessness of this son who, despite his utter lack of skill, had let himself become involved with experienced gamblers. But there was nothing that he could do. As a matter of fact, he himself was far from being ignorant about the game, and he would not have minded Sōichi's gambling if only the young man had been able to win a little money from time to time—money enough, for instance, to pay for an occasional visit to a brothel. But even on those rare occasions when Sōichi did manage to win, his fellow gamblers, who were well aware that his father had saved up a good sum of money over the years, were far too shrewd to let him leave while he was ahead.

Once Sōichi stayed away from home for two whole days. Kanako waited up till late at night, repairing *tabi* that had come from the factory with imperfections. Now all their household expenses had to come out of her own earnings. The New Year's holidays were only a few days off, yet she did not even have enough money left over to buy herself a new collar for her kimono. Sōichi had started to run up debts. He had borrowed money left and right, thirty yen from one man, fifty from another, until his debts, including interest, amounted to some four hundred yen. Whatever happened, he would have to pay this sum before the end of the year. He had been cudgeling his brains about how he could extract the money from his father. The

trouble was that Wasao had deliberately entrusted the responsibility for all such matters to his wife. Sōichi found it extremely
difficult to approach his stepmother. Despite her good heart she
had a very sharp tongue, and any request for money was bound
to be met with shouts of "You stupid fool!" or "You good-for-
nothing trash!" Sōichi did not relish the prospect.

As she sat sewing her socks, Kanako remembered what her
husband had intimated a few days before. "If I don't pay back
that money," he had said, "I can't possibly go on living." He
was a rather weak-kneed fellow, to be sure, but Kanako could
not help worrying lest in a moment of desperation he might have
decided to take his life. Perhaps at that very moment he was
lying on some railway track waiting for the train to run over
him. Since his attack of appendicitis this autumn, he had become
more uncontrolled than ever. "I shan't live long anyhow," he
had blurted out, "so I might as well enjoy the short time that's
left and do just what I feel like."

Kanako was half-awake all night, listening for his footsteps
at the door. Finally dawn broke and she heard the sound of
shutters being opened in the nearby houses and of people going
out to empty their buckets. Next to her house was a large yard
where a construction company stored stones and rocks, and
behind this a small house shared by an umbrella mender and
an industrious Korean scrap peddler with a Japanese wife.
Directly on the other side of the wall was a widower with two
children. Until recently he had been a traffic policeman and he
had made a good reputation for himself. Now he was confined
to bed with tuberculosis and had been obliged to leave the
force.

Kanako noticed that the Korean scrap peddler would change
into a neat cotton kimono every evening as soon as he came
home from work and that he would then take his children out
to the public bath. It looked like a happy family. People say a
lot of unflattering things about Koreans, thought Kanako, but
Koreans can be much kinder than Japanese men. The scrap
peddler's wife often used to speak to Kanako at the back door,
and Kanako began to wonder whether this woman's marriage
to a foreigner wasn't far happier than her own.

She also began to observe the other neighbors. The tubercular policeman received regular calls from the ward physician, and various members of the neighborhood committee would also come to see him. She heard that one of his children had died of tuberculosis that winter and that the father had caught the disease from him. The other two children were no doubt doomed to catch the illness themselves in due course.

In the next house lived a woman of about fifty. After working for twenty long years as a charwoman in an oil company, she had received a retirement allowance of one thousand yen. This piece of luck had completely unhinged her and during the following year she had spent the entire sum on visits to department stores and theaters. Now she scraped along by doing various odd jobs and by using the minute wages of her fifteen-year-old stepdaughter.

Kanako had seen all these people from morning till night, but it was only now that she began to think about them. Their fates struck her as an ironic commentary on human existence. Life, it seemed to her, was a very gloomy business indeed.

Toward morning Kanako managed to doze off for a while. When she awoke Sōichi had still not returned. It occurred to her that he might have gone to her sister's teashop, and asking one of the neighbors to look after the house, she set out for Shitaya. But he was not there.

"I'm fed up with him," she told her sister. "I want to leave him and work here with you."

Her sister laughed. "It's funny," she said. "You're the one who was always talking about marriage. But look, Kanako, surely the sensible thing would be to go and talk to his parents."

"I don't want to see those people."

"Well, in that case why don't I phone Wasao at the factory for you? He certainly ought to be told about his son's debts."

As a result of the telephone call, Wasao came directly from the factory in his overalls. It was evening when he reached the teashop in Shitaya. Hearing about the debts, he instantly surmised who had lent his son the money.

"Ah well," he said, "I should have kept Sōichi living with me. I'd have stopped him from this nonsense. I'm not saying that I won't settle for him, but I don't see how I'm going to hide it from the old woman. She'll make a terrible fuss when

it comes to paying off those debts. I suppose you think I'm too
easy on my wife—letting her control the money like that. But
that's how I keep things peaceful and happy at home. Well, I'll
manage somehow. Still, it's terrible to have this idiot son of mine
fleeced of the money that I've sweated for all these years." He
sat there sunk in thought and did not touch the whisky and the
plate of cheese that they set before him.

With the help of his first wife's brother, Wasao started making discreet inquiries about his son's whereabouts. Perhaps there
was some basis for Kanako's concern. It was just possible that
Sōichi might have jumped under a passing train or thrown
himself into the crater on Ōshima Island.* Tragic as this would
be, it would not, Wasao told himself, be an unmitigated disaster:
at least it would save him from having to worry about his feck-
less son.

There was no news on the following day, but on the evening
of the twenty-eighth, just at the beginning of the New Year's
holiday, Kanako's parents sent word that Sōichi had returned.
So after three days' absence his boy was safe and sound. Wasao
hurried off to see him, bringing along the money that he had
secretly put aside.

Sōichi was in the middle of supper when his father arrived.
He had evidently been involved in a long bout of gambling.
His face was unshaved, his cheeks were pale and emaciated,
but there was a glitter in his sunken eyes.

"You're safe, my boy," said Wasao. "That's all I care about.
I don't know what I'd have done if anything had happened to
you. What do four hundred or five hundred yen matter so long
as you're all right?"

The tears streamed down his face as he seized his son's hands
in his own.

One day the following summer Kanako appeared by herself at the back entrance of her sister's teashop. Since the crisis
in December she had only been there twice, once to pay a New
Year's call, once during the cherry blossom season. On both

* The crater of Mt. Mihara, a truncated volcano on Ōshima Island
(some sixty miles southwest of Tokyo), is a popular place for suicides.

occasions she had been accompanied by her husband. The sister had assumed that Kanako's married life had improved. In view of Sōichi's character this had surprised her somewhat, but at the same time she had felt greatly relieved.

Now a glance at Kanako's dejected face made her realize that her optimism had been unjustified. She put aside her movie magazine and turned off the electric fan that had been cooling her plump body.

"What's wrong?" she said.

"Nothing . . . nothing really," answered Kanako, looking aside awkwardly. It soon turned out that she had come once again to speak to her sister about separating from Sōichi. Kanako's desire for a separation, however, was rather vague and as soon as she was confronted with her direct, efficient sister she felt that her resolution was ebbing.

After the December crisis Sōichi had made a show of controlling himself. He still did not turn over his full salary, but Kanako decided that she too should try to change her attitude and she avoided speaking about money matters. Sōichi lost no time in taking advantage of this.

One day Sōichi announced that he was being granted a decoration of the eighth rank and a war medal, together with a small pension for his overseas service. He was as delighted as a child who has received a toy saber from his parents.

"I happened to see it in a copy of the *Official Gazette* at the milk bar," he told Kanako.

Kanako was overjoyed. "That's splendid," she said. "Really splendid. Don't forget to buy me a little souvenir, will you?"

"Hmm," replied Sōichi dubiously. "I don't expect I'll have much money left over. You see, I've promised to stand all my friends a treat."

"What? Already?"

"Yes. But I'm waiting till they've given me the decoration."

A few days later Sōichi received the official notice. He went to the Military Affairs Section of the War Office and was handed a box containing the Order of the White Paulownia and the war medal. On his way home he took them around to show his acquaintances.

Two days later he invited seven of his friends for dinner. He ordered the food from a nearby restaurant and also provided a generous supply of sake. After everyone had had plenty to drink, they turned on the radio and listened to a program of popular songs. One of the group who, despite his rough appearance and raucous voice, pretended to some artistic talent was inspired to give a solo recital. Next a few of the guests sang folk songs. After a time someone complained loudly about the absence of a samisen accompaniment.

"Let's go somewhere and have a good time. What about it, Sōichi?" said one of his friends.

"Good idea," chimed in another of the guests. "Let's get some girls to play for us."

"No, better stay here," someone demurred. "The Order of the White Paulownia will start weeping if it sees us celebrating like that."

Meanwhile the sake was flowing freely and soon their supply was exhausted. Kanako was wondering whether she should go and buy some more when she noticed that a couple of the guests had stood up and were about to leave. Wasao got to his feet, stuffed his purse securely in his pocket, and hurried out. Just then Sōichi came up to her.

"Money," he whispered into her ear. "For God's sake, let me have some money!"

Kanako went to her drawer and took out the thirty-three yen that she had been planning to deposit in their postal savings account. Even as she handed the sum over to her husband, she knew that she was throwing good money away on the spur of the moment, and afterward she cursed herself for having been so spiritless.

Now as she sat in her sister's room with a bowl of sherbet in front of her, Kanako felt the hot tears welling up in her eyes.

"Of course he didn't come home that night," she said. "Three yen and a few coppers—that's all he left me with. Then a couple of days ago he told me that on his next half-holiday he was planning to go to the seaside. I haven't been away a single time all summer and I was sure that he would offer to take me along. But no, it turned out that he had arranged to go to Enoshima with some friend and that he couldn't take me. It's really more than I can stand. I even have to go to the cinema by myself now. And those thirty yen—I never dreamed he'd go and spend the whole lot."

Kanako pressed a handkerchief to her eyes.

"You're partly to blame yourself," said her sister impatiently. "You should do things in a more clearcut way."

As usual, they telephoned the factory and in the evening Wasao appeared at the teashop. He was accompanied by his brother, who was the exact image of Sōichi. It was extremely hot, but Wasao did not touch the iced coffee that was placed before him. Instead he sat there wiping his forehead and complaining of his parasitic children.

"I'm not going to try to keep you from leaving him," he said after he had been told of Sōichi's latest behavior. "All the same, my girl, you were very foolish to give him such a large sum of money. I know how a woman feels in a case like that. She hands over the money before she knows what she's doing. But that's exactly the point I'd like to advise you about. You must be a little firmer, Kanako. You must take a strong attitude with Sōichi instead of just moping. The reason he behaves badly isn't that he dislikes you but that you're too easy with him. I wish you'd give him another chance. But I'm through with him myself and I really don't have the right to ask you."

The uncle, who until then had said nothing, announced his opinion. "I strongly believe that you should go back to your husband," he said.

At this, Kanako's sister took a firmer stand.

"Yes, Kanako," she said, "you really can't continue like this. Each time something goes wrong and you're unhappy, you slip into this sort of irresponsible talk about separation. After all, marriage is a very different thing from what you find in movies and novels."

"Yes, I know it is," said Kanako. "But I can't believe it's meant to be like ours. My husband has never shown me the slightest appreciation. Never once. And now I suppose he's got someone else on the side. What a fool I've been!"

"But really, Kanako, you should listen to what everyone's

telling you. There'll always be time later on to break up the marriage if it turns out to be completely hopeless."

In the end Kanako was won over by the uncle's firm attitude and she decided to try again.

A few days later a large photograph of Kanako and her husband arrived at the teashop. Sōichi was in uniform; the Order of the White Paulownia and the war medal were neatly pinned to his chest. Kanako had her hair in a *marumagé* and was wearing a silk kimono with a splashed pattern. Behind them was a Shinto shrine sacred to the spirits of the war dead.

Japan

COTTON CANDY

DORA ALONSO

THE BUTTERFLY was dancing above the trees. It would fly down, lighting on a radiant morning-glory; gather its wings, making them vibrate with a delicious quiver, and at the same time, move its light legs over the wine colored petals. In flight again, it would land on the edge of the cotton candy machine.

Lola, fascinated, watched the yellow butterfly. At once she took in the juicy acrid smell of the cubalibre branches, which she parted with her childish hands. The butterflies were falling under the green whip, dying, astonished, and young Lola was gathering her fragile harvest to offer to her first love. Donato was ten years old; he rode a bike and whistled in a strange, compelling way because of his cleft palate. Donato, recipient of dead butterflies given by the girl in an occult rite, which not even Donato knew about. From butterfly to butterfly. Donato, Domingo, Dionisio, Daniel, Danilo, David. And more and more. Lola had her fifteenth birthday, sighing under a steady rain of winged corpses, on her hair, her hands, her budding breasts. At night the sheet that covered her was a shroud seeded with wings and a luminous powder which threatened to soar in flight, taking her up in the air to where cats meowed among angels and owls.

A growing young woman under the domination of a tyrannical mother, Lola grew wild in the quiet settlement of Minas, gathering dreams which went back to Donato when she was six. At twenty, the accumulated names shouted among bands of butterflies drove her crazy.

Every day, under the weight of a repeated and unconsummated

guilt, she wanted to go with the cats and the angels; but her hot flesh got tired just with the sewing machine pedal and the rags, which necessity made her sew. At midnight she would leave her bed to go out, like a sleepwalker, onto the patio. Hearing the buzzing of the feverish beehives, Lola burned among the honey and the gyrations, wanting to sink her teeth into the sweetness full of stings. Almost insane she would invoke the names of the telegraph operators, train conductors, rural guards, circus men, traveling salesmen, cousins, and friends whom she tirelessly loved in great secrecy.

Every week the only prostitute in town would come secretly to see the tormented seamstress; she always came very early, tired and smelling of bed and tobacco. Between them they chose attractive patterns from fashion magazines. Their relationship was established on the basis of the respect of the loose woman, who employed manners and words of an exaggerated refinement, and on feigned ignorance on Lola's part. When they finished choosing a pattern for a dress, they would exchange recipes, or talk about the existence of spirits and their apparitions, while also gossiping about weddings and baptisms. The seamstress's mother was present during the visit, taking part in the innocent gossip which smelled of cumin and bright light. And when the time came for the dress to be tried on, the eyes and nose of the virgin would seek traces of guilt in the naked flesh of her best client.

The constant tightening and loosening of dreams and realities were gradually deforming the young woman. Laden with adornment triplicated by her anxiety—necklaces, ribbons, large, gaudy earrings—showing off her small feet, she would go to dances where few men asked her to dance. An instinctive defense drove them from the ardent virgin, as a devouring and persistent fire is avoided.

The monotonous years, for her repetitions of frustrations and renewed desires, killed her grandparents and uncles, and forced her relatives to emigrate. Her lonely forty years fought then, like a dog biting its chain, and her mother agreed to move to Havana. The women would soon understand that Luyano was no better than Minas. For ten more years Lola struggled to have a man in either of two ways: "Marry me," or "I'll set you up

in a room." But her mother, going against nature, hung onto her
with equal obstinacy and drowned Lola's murmurs of necessity.

On her death, the spinster felt an alleviating remorse which
dissolved into tears. She was alone now, but it was late. Lola
would have struggled a little longer with the sewing, but her
eyes refused to go on. In order to earn a living she sold fabrics
and cosmetics door to door, but she offered such good terms that
she ended up selling lottery tickets. Her hair was gray by then,
and the wrinkles began to devour her face.

Giving reasons to herself, she became used to the circum-
stances, accepting the hard buffetings of life without suffering too
much. Her bread arrived wrapped in an Official List, and each
Saturday the voice of a child from the orphanage, or of a blind
man, who would choose the lucky number while turning the
lottery box filled with numbered balls, would announce the
winner. She ended up picking a site near the zoo, as a handy
place for buyers of single or whole sheets of lottery tickets. Kind,
smiling, with a big pocket in her skirt, she would cry out the numbers with her nasal voice. At the end of the day she would ride
the bus to Luyano, to the same shack where she had always
lived.

As removed from politics as Simon the Dwarf, she did not have
to fight in any way to get the benefits of the new epoch. She
entered through the same door that solved the economic anguish
and the unfortunate life of the humble vendors in the zoo. Lola
was given a stall, to run the cotton candy machine. For the first
time she felt secure and could look around her peacefully. The
old lady ate her bread without having to worry about the next
day.

Every morning she very politely greeted the other employees;
the hundreds of them who went hurriedly on their way to the
different businesses in the park. She was by now nothing but
wrinkles and bags, crowned with an ugly mane tarnished by a
permanent. A big woman with a thick waist and straight, fat,
pianolike legs, arms with hanging flesh, and feet that walked
twisted like a wild parrot. But in spite of herself, there was a
certain virginal aspect about her disheveled figure: a seal of
something well-kept, aging without rendering any service.

The routine work allowed her to free her secret parades, which followed her throughout her long spinsterhood, like a consuming plague. While filling the metal spoon with sugar, pouring it in the electric centrifuge and forming a great cone by curling the white threads around a stick, she would indulge in unending daydreams. Old already, she built a refuge with all that was no longer living. As others recall their memories, Lola revived phantoms and butterflies.

The large human family of the zoo took a liking to her and enjoyed embarrassing her by telling her dirty jokes. Being a good woman, she would render small services and gossip about work and events of the park.

Lola needed several years to discover the background and the different relationships of the life surrounding her. It was in the spring that she glimpsed it in its limited fullness. She didn't tell anybody, but she tuned her ears, her eyes, on trees, beasts, birds. Always in wait, with each pore like a hungry mouth.

She would go to sleep wishing it was time to go back to work. When she finished work, she would use any pretext to stay longer and go slowly through the zoo in order to look with new-born pupils at the cages.

A new existence seemed to animate the animals, and she discovered and felt love in every corner and over her head. The inexpressible, contagious atmosphere fascinated her. With the beginning of the spring cycle the beasts became beautiful like the trees and the light. And the favored season inflamed the caresses of the turtle doves and the slight blue of the aparecidos de San Diego; it brought together the claws of the eagles and the crowns of the herons.

Whistles, like darts, rent the air. The exalted tenderness preceding desire began and the old woman, with her parrot feet, was a wandering elf in its pursuit.

The music of the ring dove was heard at all hours, and of the white, red breasted dove. Hummingbirds nested in Lola's ecstatic eyes.

The zoo buzzed like the distant beehives in Minas, with the bellows of the deer, reborn in his bristling hide, lapping his timid female. In the cave, forgotten by the zoo and by the noisy avenue, the gray bear, sitting on her haunches, attracted and kissed, sucked her mate, from the forehead to the mouth, the mouth . . .

The ancient virgin of the cotton candy looked blindly for any encounter with whatever sang or roared limitless love. She would be still for long periods, scrutinizing her newly discovered feelings. In the well-kept concentration camp was born the unmatched joy of heat and mating.

Lola waded through the lukewarm preludes, searching with unsure steps for the deep water of unhampered sex. The forgotten dizziness of her youth returned with the strength of a llama, who mounts his female for a very long time, hurting her. With the lasciviousness of the chimpanzees before the monstrous flower of the female; with the modesty of the spider monkey who tantalizes the imagination. With the incredible variations of the orangutans, masters of the science of the brothel; contortionists, enjoyers, human in the art of extracting from sex its rich variations. They would roll on the ground intertwined, a ball of pleasure, distilling it, silent, surrendered. Lola, followed by the furious ghost of a mother, wanted to flee, but she would stare and stare, tense, full of anguish, her mouth metallic, her knees buckling, and her face red with shame.

Her quiet blood would grow to a high tide with the repetitions of the acts. They were weeks of communal delirium in which she went from bough to cage, from one animal to the next; to the ferocious surrenders of the coupled lions who, roaring, would tear at each other, to the crosses between tiger and lion, which gave birth to ligers and tiglons.

It was the time when the guards were afraid—of the new rhythm, the delirious fights, of the seeding.

The epoch of love transformed the hours of the spinster. Lola returned to her two-strand necklaces, to her long, glittering earrings, to her rouge; to her small, high-heeled shoes stuffed with her overflowing feet. She would pin flowers on her blouse, and use French perfumes.

During the last spring she craved a hand mirror and went to look for one in the knick-knack shops, among an extravagant scramble of dust-covered objects. The mirror was a beautiful piece of embossed silver, with cupid and fawn motifs and a beautiful glass surface. She kept it in her purse, and looked at herself covered with make-up and trinkets like a barbarian queen.

In May, after eight years of mixing the sugar threads, of sighing with the birds and the beasts, of mixing her history, her ghosts, her butterflies with the colors of the birds' plumage, and the breath of the beasts in love; one Dyonisian morning in which the four thousand inhabitants of the zoo seemed to copulate in unison, in which the feverish pupils seemed to sparkle, sexes palpitate, and the painted Egyptian touracos, which the rains discolor, were floating in nuptial flight, Lola had an encounter with the Jockey.

The Jockey found her by the food stalls, and Lola saw a young man: smooth face, his teeth intact, cured of coughs and phlegms, muscular neck without hanging skin or wrinkles. She blinked in surprise. So afraid! He said something like, "You're drunk," and she shrugged her shoulders without answering. She was looking straight at the old black man in charge of the kangaroos and the llamas, who was approaching on the other side of the path. Julián seemed to be made of light and ebony. New from head to toe, the beautiful black man.

Lola hurriedly opened her purse and her hand shook when she took the mirror out. From the polished moon surface of the mirror the girl from Minas smiled at her.

Cuba

FRAGMENT FROM A LOST DIARY

Shih Ming

May 24, windy

The heaviness of this long May day nearly suffocates me. Endless hunger, endless nausea, endless doubt and anxiety. I move from my side to my back and then to my side again. The wooden planks of the bed are harder than stone. Hard, hard. It is impossible to get any rest! It is impossible for one moment to relieve the constant throbbing pain in my body, however I turn and toss. I cannot read. Only writing—since there is no one to talk with—seems to take my mind out of itself, as small idle occupations do.

Ching's forehead has become noticeably more lined since he learned the reason of my illness. Often he stares at me with wide eyes, saying nothing. When I ask why it is he looks at me like that he answers vaguely, "Nothing, nothing. Rest and get well quickly, that's all."

Meaningless words! I know well enough how inconvenient a thing I am. What small regard the female womb has for the "historic necessities"! It is its own history and its own necessity! It is the dialectic reduced to its simplest statement. What generosity of nature to make me this gift of the "illness of the rich" at just such a time!

I can't even enjoy being heroic in bearing my personal discomfort. With the tyranny of helplessness I must drag the whole of our close-knit organization into this trouble. When conditions are critical, and the situation everywhere is hostile, the individual burden unavoidably becomes the group burden. It isn't that my own small role remains unfulfilled. It's that my incapacity causes

interruptions and irregularities for everyone. Most of all for
Ching. He has become the slave at a sickbed. He is amah, nurse,
cook, errand boy—and beggar. His work is neglected, badly done,
and he goes about his duties with an absent-mindedness born of
fatigue. This in turn means confusion in the organization, and all
because of my demands. It is so terribly important that all our
plans at this time should be unfailingly sure, so much more important than this struggling life inside of me. Ching never com-
plains of this added worry and responsibility, but I know how
greatly it weighs upon him.

Now that the 30th of May is approaching he drags himself
out every morning at six and cannot return until late at night. Out
of this precious day he must steal time for me—begging a few
coppers from friend to friend to buy the small indispensable
things for me, the invalid. I know this, and I know too how it
troubles him to be away from me. Yet, under this unendurable
sickness, I forget and quarrel with him again and again for his
negligence!

Our house is like all the rest of the *kung-yu** along Sha Tan.
Our room is the middle one of three facing south. There is no
window in it. The only opening is the door. When that is closed
no air or sunshine can stir within. The room itself is very narrow,
with space only for a bed and table and a small bench. I can
reach over to the table from my bed. That at least is a convenience.

The boy hasn't cleaned our room for several days. Probably
this is because we haven't paid the rent (four dollars a month!)
since March. The wallpaper is cracked, and a corner of it hangs
from the ceiling. Dust and cobwebs drop from it. Rats run back
and forth in the bamboo rafters. Sometimes one of them, in a
fight, tumbles down to the earthen floor. It has to lie there till
Ching returns. I myself cannot get up, however nauseating the
sight and smell of the creature may be.

Everything in the room is covered with dust, blown in through
the open door—open to anyone who wants to gape in from the
courtyard. Spiders work back and forth. I look at them, entranced,
as they crawl even up to my bed, and spin their silvery threads
in the sunlight. They are at least *alive*. They are the only com-

* A lodging-house. Many are used as dormitories for men and women
students in Peiping.

panions I have. They help me to forget the oppressive loneliness and agony of this dreary May day.

Our neighbor on the left is evidently a student at Pei Ta.* He seems to be in some way related to the landlord, and for that reason hasn't paid his rent for months. The landlord has now begun to seize his mail, however, even registered letters containing money. The student doesn't complain about it. What is money to him? His fat red face radiates peace and serenity. When he needs money he tries to beg it from the landlord. If successful he goes out with a handful of coppers, and soon returns with a bottle of *pai-kan* and a piece of roast chicken. Locking himself up inside, he proceeds to drink for the rest of the day, clucking and imitating the opera stars in a mock falsetto. When the last drop is gone he gives a loud slap on his thigh, rolls over, and is soon thunderously snoring in deep contentment. Sometimes he cannot squeeze a single cash out of his relative, but receives instead a large piece of harsh criticism or advice. On these occasions he returns to his room very depressed. "Ah! . . . Sh! . . . Ha! . . ." Is he actually planning to commit suicide? Nobody worries about it, least of all the landlord.

On the other side there is a dramatist, also a student at Pei Ta. He is often away for a whole day, for which I offer thanks. When he stays at home he practices his chosen profession, and this is very tiresome indeed. He sings like a Great Painted Face of the theater, in a froglike voice. Sometimes he attempts the lines of the Bearded Face, with his voice ranging in all dimensions. But the most unbearable of all is the sound resulting when he lifts his throat to a shrill soprano and shrieks in imitation of the female lead. One can picture him twisting his waist and swinging his hips in rhythm with the singing. He frequently asks the landlord in for a chat and "refreshments." At such times he joins the villain in cursing the other lodgers.

"Ai-ya," he exclaims, "it's time even for me to pay the rent. Only this morning I reminded myself to go to the bank, but my wasteful memory has again failed me. Look, here's the account book in my pocket. You see I really intended to go there."

This fellow looks after the house servant too. Bribing him with

* Peking National University.

a handful of peanuts he collects all the gossip he can. How much money has the rickshaw-man's wife—she in the corner on the western wing—squeezed behind her husband's back? With whom has the actress been copulating? What dress did she wear? And so on. Between them a most provoking conversation ensues, evidently to the interest and high satisfaction of both. It never occurs to him to give me any consideration. Yet when I am retching with anguish he heaves audible sighs. "How unendurable! How much better off dead." Not content with exaggerated groans to himself, he sometimes ventures to tap the thin wall and whisper through the chinks in a soft, sympathetic voice, "Madam, sister, would you bring peace to my heart by permitting me to assist you? Ah, it is bitterly painful to me, painful!"

However great my contempt of him I am helpless. I say nothing. My very silence provokes him to actual savage scolding and cursing. I am a pestilence to him! We paste up the chinks in the wall, but he slits them open again with a knife. Sweet are one's neighbors, unto whom one should do as unto oneself.

The whole courtyard is crowded with quarrelsome voices. Women curse and scold and beat. There is a droning voice somewhere forever mechanically reading the old Four Books and classical poetry. Eight different families, living in a twelve-*chien* house, and each rivaling the other to produce the loudest noise and create the greatest possible friction! The whole day long this courtyard boils and seethes, and only my damp, suffocating little room contributes nothing. Perfect Confucian harmony: *li, yi, lien, ch'ih.** I am seized alternately with chills and fever. All the time I am half-famished. The hungrier I am the more I want to vomit. But not a crumb to feed that twin torment, either the hunger or the physical need for expelling food. And all this suffering utterly without significance! That I can have actually endured it for over two months! That I should think, even now, of wanting to continue to exist only as the vessel of a chemical experiment heartlessly, inexorably formulating itself within me! And against my will!

* Propriety, righteousness, honesty, humility, the "pillars of Confucian culture," which Generalissimo Chiang Kai-shek's "New Life" Movement attempted to revive in 1934.

Am I insane to think of *that* way out? But it is obviously the solution. Still, I won't consider it again today.

May 25

Ching returned last night looking like a mask of himself. He fell on the bed almost as soon as he entered the door. He was very gaunt, terribly thin, and his dark eyes opened to show frightening depths, cavernous like wells and full of foreboding.

He looked vacantly at me, while I asked him what he had eaten. He admitted having had nothing since noon, when he had bought six dry cakes from a street vendor.

At last he pulled himself from the bed and turned to cook the little tubes of wheat rolls he had brought home with him. He lighted the tiny flame under the oil lamp on the table. When the water boiled over it he put the rolls into the pan. He did not speak until then. Going to the thin panels of the wall he pressed his ear close, listening on both sides to make certain our neighbors were asleep.

"I'm afraid we'll have to leave here soon," he whispered to me. "It's unthinkable while you're so ill; and yet . . ."

He looked questioningly at me, but I simply signaled that I wanted to hear the inner truth of it.

"It's the landlord. The rent. He kicked up another storm about it. Threatened to call in the police if we don't pay or get out."

I did not say anything. There was nothing to be said. I knew quite well that Ching had not told me the whole story. The rent problem can't have reached a crisis; it has already been at that stage for weeks. This alone wouldn't alarm him. He wouldn't at any rate speak so seriously about it were this not merely a screen hiding the real facts. I didn't question him further. No doubt he knows what is best for me to hear.

And yet to move! How? First of all money is needed, and after that my health has to be mentioned.

"Can't we stay a few days longer?" I finally asked him.

"Certainly—a few days. Only we *must* be out before May the 30th. Don't worry about it, anyway. I simply told you so that you won't be surprised when the time comes. It isn't a serious matter. I will have money very soon." He smiled a little wan smile with his mouth, but his eyes did not change at all. The effect was somehow terrifying. "It will do you good to get a change of atmosphere, eh?"

He blew out the flame and drew forth some of the boiled rolls. Sitting on the bed he helped me eat. Before we had finished half the food my stomach rebelled, and up it all came. Not only the miserable food! It seemed to me that a violent internal explosion was taking place, forcing up my very soul! My eyes felt like gates being hammered at by battering-rams inside. My whole head burned as if afire. I couldn't control myself at all. Even while my body was bathed in sweat it also felt cold, and I shook all over.

Ching wasn't suffering much less. He jumped about excitedly, in a rage because he was so helpless to ease my pain. He tried to hold me up. He rinsed my mouth and nose, and bathed my eyes. He soaked towels in the hot water and put them on my forehead. He got his four limbs mixed up trying to do everything at once.

I didn't sleep all night. I could not even keep my eyes closed. After this performance I kept thinking of that hope, and it seemed to me the only way to freedom. I must have been very delirious. I remember pinching and pressing and even sharply striking my womb. How I wanted the little creature to die! And yet at the same time my heart seemed to be protesting with all the vigor left in me, responding with a blow at *me* for every one I struck at *it*! With the conflicting instincts—the one selfish, for the preservation of my child, the other unselfish, for the preservation of my usefulness—I felt for a while that only through a double death could any solution be cleanly achieved. Traitorous thought!

And yet I love this little life! With all the pain of it, I long for the wonderful thing to happen, for a tiny human creature to spring from between my limbs bravely out into the world. I need it, just as a true poet *needs* to create a great undying work. No, more than that; for my little one shall be the instrument of Mother Nature to change nature. Of that I am certain, just as I am certain even now that it is already shaping into a—man! That little fellow, at first so helpless, so full of a need of me, curious with the curiosity of little eyes slowly opening, that little man will later on stand up and assert, with his great beauty and his great power, such fine true things about men and nature that all the authorities, all the rulers of heaven and earth, cannot but bow down to his will!

Ever since my lunar pause, ever since the first quivering in my womb, my heart has been unspeakably shaken with the wonder of this knowledge. My throat has ached to proclaim it to the whole world. Despite his purity and his splendor, it would actually be upon me that this young man would bestow his first smile! It would be me whom he would call mother! Ah, yes, all that I've thought about, and known the joy and the power and the longing of it!

Where is the woman strong enough alone not to dream such dreams? No, there is not one, and certainly not I. Not one—and yet perhaps many, thousands, millions of us together! Cannot the essential spirit of motherhood, strengthened in the unity of many women, reject its selfish little individual rights? Can't we become for once *conscious* in travail, dedicate that priceless fertility to the nourishment of a vast physiological act of Mother Nature herself, enlarging her womb in our own time with a new *kind* of man?

I believe we can. Yet turning an abstract philosophy into a poisoned needle to thrust into my own womb, that is a different thing! I am full of the distress of mental and physical torment as these emotions battle ceaselessly. Still, I am determined. I am awake at last, after years of bovine slumber. I am more fully awake than when I first made up my mind to join the Revolution. Only when the beat of life is lifted to this pitch, this fury, and this danger, only when destiny (here in my case it is but a wayward sperm carrying its implacable microscopic chromosomes, but nevertheless it is a form of destiny!) poses the choice between irreconcilable desires at a given moment, only when a human being feels the necessity of ignoring personal feeling in the decision taken—only then can one talk of a revolutionary awakening!

Well, all that is to say that for the pauperized millions to bear children in society as at present disorganized is simply to increase the number of those living in hopeless misery. Every child thrust from the womb of a sick, underfed, unattended mother just so much further degrades the disinherited. For the child of poverty there lies ahead nothing but hunger, insults, ignorance, abuse, bitterness, and no hint of the spiritual exaltation that divides men from beasts of the jungle. For us the problem of new life is the problem of life as we know it now, ourselves, and this we cannot conscionably impose upon the unborn.

And yet I still fondly amuse myself with maternal fancies! I still now and then dream of freeing my own life by projecting another one into the world!

Ching will meet a Korean friend today. With the help of this fellow I may bring my plan to a practical conclusion. I told Ching to seek out this man. It never occurred to me that he would be shocked, and his curious stare and his silence dismayed me. He just stood still for a while, with his hands thrust deep in his pockets. Then he turned his head, and ground out, in a decisive tone, "Abortion! It isn't to be thought of! It's impossible."

"Abortion, on the contrary, is the only way. It is settled!"

He turned and looked at me with a strange look, as if he had been struck. He sat down on the bed and took my hands in his. His expressive eyes spoke half of compassion, half of remonstrance. I began to explain to him how I had reached the decision.

"We cannot," he broke in, and covered my mouth with his hands. Lowering his lips to my ear he whispered, "I understand, dear. I know everything you feel, but later on you will regret it. And it is dangerous, by such means . . ." He shook his head and for a while said nothing. I felt suddenly sick and lay back, silent too.

After a long while he whispered again, "However great the pain—two kinds of pain, I understand—it isn't so serious as this step. You do not know how dangerous it is—dangerous first for Li, and then it is an attack on your very life. Besides we haven't time. We must move . . ." He choked and did not finish. We both sat staring at each other, profoundly miserable.

Just then we heard a scratching sound on one of the walls. Ching looked meaningfully at the slit cut open between the paneling, and then got up, gently stroking my arm.

May 26

Can Ching actually not have returned once during the entire night? Do I deserve to be forsaken? What have I done that I must lie here in torn anguish, helpless, uncomforted, hungry, with

nothing to break the horrible monotony of these surroundings—
that old broken washstand, the stained wrappings of food, stale
spinach, and the ceiling webbed with the spider's spinnings, somehow making the room seem like a place where only discarded
things should be?

Laid away like this, a dead one, is it possible for me to feel
the same sense of value, to believe in my own significance as a
social being, as I do when living with the working masses?

Ordinarily, even when busiest, Ching never fails to get back
some time during the night. What can have happened?

I waited last night, as usual, for the sound of his footsteps. I
kept my eyes on the door steadily after the landlord's clock struck
eleven. I heard every sound it made after that: half-past eleven,
twelve, half-past twelve, and then just as regularly one, half-past,
two, half-past, three, and so on till after dawn. Every boom of the
clock deepened my own anxiety; and, as sometimes happens to
one, I became intensely aware of the irredeemable loss of each of
those hours, aware of time actively destroying me.

It was quite unnecessary for me to torture my mind worrying
about ordinary accidents, such as Ching being struck by a motor-
car, or falling dead from exhaustion, or being bitten by a mad
dog. And yet I did so. I even hoped that it was something like
that. I invented several highly improbable situations to account
for his absence. I refused to think about that most dreadful—and
yet most likely—possibility.

Just now I would welcome even the arrival of some spies or
gendarmes. I cannot stand the suspense any longer. Even to know
that he is in police hands is better than this hovering dread, this
awful uncertainty! It seems to me that I cannot breathe for another
hour! What the devil is going to happen to me? It is perhaps
preferable even to be in jail than to be an abandoned lump lying
lifelessly here . . .

Later

Lao* Li has been here and has brought news of Ching! It is, of
course, as I feared.

* Here "Lao" is not part of the name, but an honorific. Literally "Old,"
though Li is still young.

His thick brows were locked under his broad forehead, and I knew before he spoke what had happened. He came in, nodded his head in greeting, and simply said, "En!"

"What is it?"

"Ching has been arrested."

May 27

I won't die! I thought of it last night, the easiest way being simply to languish in the *kung-yu*, where nobody would lift a rice bowl to save my life. But I won't die. Lao Li gave me some encouragement. He advised me to move to his house, where his wife, a doctor, can help me. This good news, now that Ching has already lost his freedom, is perhaps the only thing that made me want to live.

Li helped me to move. I am lying now in a bed placed in one of their two small rooms, which they rent from a Korean landlord. He is a sympathetic fellow, and lives in the other part of the house himself.

Lao Li's Korean wife seems to me rather quaint in appearance, with a gray-tinted yellow face, grayish-brown eyes (very narrow), and thick lips. She is quite fat, a distinct contrast to the sharp, straight architecture of her husband's body. She has not been long in China, and has to dig for words to express herself, and often, failing to find them, she fills in the blanks with an embarrassed smile.

She was very moved when I told her what I wanted. At first she was speechless, and only shook her head violently. Then from her little eyes tears began to sprinkle her piteous face, and she jumped up impetuously and came to my bed. She held me close to her fat breasts while she shook with convulsive sobs. Almost hysterically she cried, "No, no, no! You shall not!" Her obviously deep emotion rather surprised me.

Lao Li pulled her up gently and spoke to her in Korean. I couldn't understand. She kept sobbing, as pathetically as if she were a small orphan girl. Gradually she grew quiet, under her husband's persuasion, and at last came to say that she would help me.

There is only one bed in the rooms, and last night Li and his wife had to sleep on stools set before me. During the evening Li *tai-tai* told me something of her life.

She is now thirty-nine years of age, but she has no children. She has, however, constantly longed for a son, but each time this desire seemed about to be fulfilled she was frustrated.

Li *tai-tai*'s family were Christians and furious when she married her revolutionary husband. They disowned her. What annoyed them particularly was that, after they had spent so much money educating her and getting her medical degree, she had turned it to the service of such a worthless cause. They refused to extend to her even a copper of help.

Lao Li, extremely busy in revolutionary work, rarely had any money. Often he was compelled to go into hiding for weeks or even months, leaving his wife alone. Each time she was with child it happened that Lao Li was in danger, and she had to suffer the shock, worry, and nervous tension of this knowledge as well as being left with inadequate funds for either proper care or nourishment. Seven times she lost her unborn child!

Seven! Is it possible for a woman to go through this horror seven times? Women and revolution! What tragic, unsung epics of courage lie silent in the world's history!

At the time of his wife's eighth pregnancy Lao Li, in desperation, arranged to get leave for a while, borrowed some money, and took her to the seashore. He provided her with such material comforts as he could and bent every effort toward protecting her against disturbance. The result was that at last her son was born. It grew into a beautiful, healthy child, and by the time it was seven months old delighted its parents by long and fascinating conversations carried on by the changing expressions of its face and by its adorable infant chucklings and babblings. Needless to say, the parents were enchanted with their precious possession.

At this time both Lao Li and his wife were suddenly arrested and thrown into prison, their baby with them. Ten days of that is sufficient to kill any child. Theirs died.

As the unfortunate woman talked on she wept freely. Her husband, sitting beside her, patted her gently and spoke to her in the most compassionate way. He was evidently glad that she

had taken this chance to give expression to the repressed misery
burning within her. Hardly less moved himself, he even reminded
her of details she had forgotten, and helped provide her inadequate Chinese with words and phrases whenever she paused.

This morning I took an enormous capsule, administered
by Dr. Li. She promises that one of these is sufficient to abort a
fetus one month old, and three are enough to expel one gone
three months. Three days after taking this medicine one can
hope for the best.

Afternoon

The stormy May wind, carrying down tons of Gobi dust, seems
to set fire to your eyes and nose and throat. It is enough in itself
to make most people a little ill. Now, as it howls outside, and the
fine yellow silt drifts in and covers everything, I take a savage
delight in describing my own feelings! Perhaps it will be instruc-
tive to read later on . . .

Well, then, I feel exactly as if there were dozens of repulsive
hairy worms crawling back and forth in all my joints! It seems
to me that if these worms managed to get out they would take
with them the basic tincture of my life-blood! Ugh!

Later

I just saw Ching being tortured! An old man with red, blinking
eyes bent over him, holding a huge kettle with a tiny spout, out
of which he poured "pepper water" into Ching's nose. "Among
means for the regeneration of mankind," old red-eyes quoted
Confucius, "those made with great demonstrations are of least
importance."

Ching struggled to free himself, and let out blood-curdling
groans. He tried to turn his face, but that tore his lips on the
rope binding him across the mouth to the floor. The water poured
from his nose, his mouth, and his eyes. Several times he fainted.
The torturers revived him by turning him over and emptying him
of water.

More than forty kettles had been poured into him!

Now and then the torture would cease while Ching was cross-examined. All the time I stood by, helplessly watching his agony. It seemed that already I had been shoved in front of him, and whipped on my bare back. They had demanded that I ask him to talk, to tell his address. It seemed also that my lips had already been burned by incense because I had refused to speak.

Apparently Ching did not recognize me. It may be that he could not see. His face was mottled with red, blue, purple, and greenish bruises. Blood clung to his hair. He looked dumbly at me without any comprehension in his eyes at all.

Since they already had me in custody, what was the object of torturing Ching for this information? Had he another address that they wanted? Having changed him into a different creature, why did they continue with this bestial abuse? Did they hope to break his spirit by making him admit that he was under arrest? I did not understand it. I wanted to scream. They came toward me, tore off my jacket, and prepared to whip my back and breasts in front of him. Then I did scream.

Opening my eyes I looked into the face of Li *tai-tai*, who had her arms around me. She held her narrow eyes close to mine, and they were as wide open as she could get them, full of fright and astonishment. "What is it?" she demanded. "What?"

The tortures of which I had dreamed were exactly like those used on Y. and P. But the significance of Ching's refusal to divulge his address? What was it? Obviously it betrayed my anxiety that Ching, thinking me still helpless in the *kung-yu*, was submitting to some ghastly inquisition rather than give the KMT his address.

May 28, windy

Windy indeed!

As the wind rises my fever rises, and as it dies I am shaken with chills. All the paper panes in the windows have been burst open by the storm. The wind screams like a woman, like a woman in torture and travail. It shows its torn face through the window —but am I still delirious?

Because of my fever Dr. Li refused to give me another capsule today. I pleaded with her. I insisted. Now that this is begun I want it finished quickly. I am impatient to get into the world again, to carry on Ching's work and my own. Then, too, I cannot waste any more of the Lis' energy or money than is absolutely necessary—on this useless, pointless enterprise.

I swallowed two of those great cylindrical pills at once!

Midnight

Shao Feng just ran in breathlessly. His face lengthened when he saw me here. He had come to warn the Lis to move immediately. At the same time he wanted his wounds dressed by Dr. Li.

The day before yesterday Shao Feng was carrying some things on a bicycle. As he was going along Pei Ho Yen another bicycle suddenly dashed against him. A spy jumped out, grabbed him, and yelled as loudly as possible for the police. Shao Feng succeeded in tripping the man over the rickshaw, and escaped by running down small lanes, jumping some walls, and crossing several low roofs. He tore his left arm, and it was swollen with neglect and covered with ugly dark blood. Dr. Li dressed his wound, and he left immediately, giving an anxious glance at me.

"Move at once!" What mockery to me lying here, a helpless burden, endangering the lives of my friends! Tomorrow is May 30th,* day of awakening for China, day on which the masses everywhere rise up to show their growing strength and unity. Tomorrow over the whole nation resolute young men and women will march forth, defiantly, and some of them will be killed—and from their deaths new strength will arise. But I—weighed down by a stone! Women and revolution—strange pair!

Today they will spare no search to get our people imprisoned before the demonstration . . . The Lis are talking together in Korean. I want to tell them that they must go, that I don't want them here with me, that they must leave me! But on my lips there is only a silent scream which will tell them that suddenly my womb feels as though pierced with ten thousand hot needles. I want to keep on writing this, to hide that scream which will

---

* May 30, 1925, was the day on which foreign police in Shanghai killed many students and workers in a demonstration, an incident which inflamed the whole nation to anger.

betray me . . . My whole flesh itches and stings and burns. My entire body pulses as if with anchored lightning. Everything around me is poisonous, sickening. There is that hot stone ready to burst from within me at any moment—and another ready to burst from my head.

[Here the diary ends.]

China

PART III

THREE TIMES A HUNDRED DOZEN MOONS

Over—
the time of cowardly murmuring
Over—the game
of base tactics

yesterday
a woman groaned
groaned for hours
without help
without care
lying bewildered
in a lake of blood

yesterday the wall of the Prison cracked
from its mouth
emerged bitter sobs
yesterday the severity of its look
changed into sympathy
for she who suffered

yesterday the ceiling all laughing
became indignant with anger
yesterday
from its murderous face
came tears
for she who moaned

yesterday in an unexpected calm
a hurricane passed through the Prison
above the patient
it passed in a refreshing breeze
and in the night of suffering
it reached the forehead pale with anguish

yesterday
things showed compassion
but
yesterday

the Citadel laughed
drank and feasted

in a delirium of champagne
the glasses tinkled
in an uproar of debauchery
the men brawled
under the power of the alcohol
everything swayed
the music resounded
the whisky sparkled

and the *colons*
and their women
all danced
and played
obscenely
in the most beautiful house in the city

and meanwhile

the black woman moaned
from her altered voice
only desperate sighs
emerged
her body
writhing in agony
lay upon the hard ground

yesterday the suffering intensified
yesterday desperately
the woman shrieked
without help
without care

yesterday
last night
in the black night
in the night of suffering
of pain and exhaustion
a baby came into the world
all black
and its first cradle
was the beaten floor
of a Prison
(*excerpt*)

—*N. B. Damz, Dahomey*
Translated by Nancy Milton and Naomi Katz.

THE IVORY COMB

NGUYEN SANG

IN THE BATH of dim moonlight, the hut lay hidden in the heart of the Plain of Reeds, among a thinly grown mangrove belt washed by the rising water. A liaison post on a communication artery, it was small but crowded with people. As we had to wait for our turn to leave, we now lay relaxing, now sat cross-legged on a plank bed with a sense of confinement. To while away our time we chose to tell stories. I shall never forget an aged comrade, a very talented storyteller. His smuts—Resistance smuts, too— made us die laughing. To begin, he always summoned a smile and then looked rather funny. But that night there was something different about him. He insisted that he should talk, but when all agreed he remained silent for quite a while. He bent his head a little, sat very still, and looked out into the immensity of the water around us. We stopped joking in anticipation of something serious. Outside, a gusty wind blew and the surf broke on the mangroves. The hut jolted and rocked like a boat. Some storks stirred uneasily, others flapped their wings, fluttering in the air. The waves and the wind seemed to remind him of remote events. He strained his ears as though he was listening to a distant voice. In undertones, he began his story. Turning away from us, he looked at the horizon and the twinkling stars . . .

The story went back more than a year. Every time I remember it, I still feel aghast as if I just came out of a dream.

That day I traveled from M.G. post to D.A. post. As soon as the motorboat left the shore, all of us were eager to know who was manning it. This was not merely out of curiosity. Before our departure we were told by the head of the liaison post that we had a long and dangerous journey ahead, and that we would have to go by boat and also on foot. By water, we would be easily spotted by choppers, and by land we would easily bump into commandos. Should choppers whirl overhead, we would have to remain calm and strictly abide by the steersman's orders. That meant we would place our fate in his hand. I naturally wanted to know who he was. Darkness, however, only allowed me to notice that it was a slender young girl with a U.S.-made carbine slung on her shoulder and a scarf around her neck. Her manner was rather tidy.

I knew by hearsay that this post had a very clever liaison girl. One day, she guided the way for a cadres' group. Before crossing a river, she asked them to stop in a paddy field far from the bank. Together with her male colleague, she moved forward to probe the area. On arriving at an orchard near the river bank, she realized that she had fallen into an enemy ambush. She showed no sign of embarrassment and told her friend, "Everything is all right. Go back and bring the travelers here. I'll take the boat to the other side."

She spoke in a loud voice so that the enemy could hear her. By these words, she gave a secret signal. The liaison man paced back and quietly took the travelers across the river at another point a few kilometers away. As for her, she planted two grenades then crossed the river safely. Meanwhile, the enemy lay still in wait, hoping to make a good catch. Time wore on and nothing happened. Knowing that they had been deceived, the commandos cursed one another and returned to their base. On their way, they stumbled on the grenade trap which took several lives. Later, spicing up the story, people said that the girl had a keen sense of smell, and that she could thereby locate the enemy and differentiate between the Yanks and the puppets.

If it happened that the girl who was to man this boat was the liaison woman in question, I thought, there would be no cause for much anxiety.

"How many women are working at this post?" I asked inquisitively.

"Only two, a cook and I."

It was she, without doubt, and I was greatly relieved. Hearing her voice, I guessed her to be eighteen or twenty at the most. I came to like her and wanted to ask her a few more questions. Seeing that she was busy with the starting gear, I gave up the idea. After putting the cord around the starting disk, she stood erect and turned toward a boat nearby, saying, "I start first. All right now?"

"Hear, hear, good journey!" said the liaison men on the next boat. Sometimes they called her Sister Hai (eldest), sometimes Sister Ut (youngest). She gave some witty answers, addressing the liaison men as her little brothers. Then in a polite manner, she told us to put all important belongings in our pockets or in separate parcels to avoid losses in case we should be strafed by helicopters or ambushed by commandos.

Unlike the station master she warned us against these possible mishaps in a rather mild and lovely tone. Then she bent forward and started the motor. The boat slowly left the thick mangrove belt and dashed forward. There was a pleasant chill in the air. At her instructions, the passengers busied themselves with their luggage. As for me, nothing was more precious than my papers and traveling expenses which I always kept in my pocket. Suddenly I thought of the tiny ivory comb. So I unpacked my bag, searched it out, put it together with my papers in a pouch that I slid into my breast pocket, and carefully fastened this with a safety pin.

The little comb was the last vestige of an intimate friend of mine. Whenever I looked at it, I would feel some solicitude and a pang of regret.

It was the first days following the restoration of peace. A friend of mine and I revisited our native village. We had lived next door to each other, near an estuary of the Mekong River. We both had joined the Resistance War at the beginning of 1946 after the invasion of our home province by the French. He stood sixth in his family and was accordingly called Sau. His only daughter was then barely twelve months old. Every time his wife came to see him in the liberated areas he would urge her to take their daughter along the next time she came—something she dared not do as she had to go through the jungle. For her such a journey was no easy job. Sau, therefore, could not blame her. For eight long years he saw his daughter only in a small photograph. Now on the way home, he was stirred by indescribable fatherly feelings. The boat approached a landing place. He saw a little girl of about eight, with bobbed hair, black trousers, and a red-flowered vest, playing in the shade of a mango tree in the front yard of the house. He was sure she was his daughter. Not waiting for the boat to reach the bank, he jumped: the boat was driven back and I was almost dangling. He walked forward, then stopped and shouted, "Thu, my daughter!"

Just at that moment I was close behind him. He expected his daughter to bound toward him and fling her arms around his neck. He took a few more steps, bending forward and opening his arms, ready to hold her in a warm embrace. Startled by his call, the little girl stared at him with round eyes, looking lost and puzzled. As for him, he failed to control his emotion. Every time he was seized with a sudden emotion, the scar on his right cheek turned red and grew dreadful to look at. With such a face and his hands stretching out, he slowly moved forward, and in a trembling voice, he mumbled, "Come on, daughter! Come on!"

The little girl could not understand and blinked at me as if to ask who he was. Her face suddenly grew pale. She broke away in a run and cried, "Mother, Mother!" Her father did not move. His eyes did not leave his daughter. His face was distorted with pain and his arms dropped listlessly.

As the trip had been rather long, we had only three days left to stay at home, not enough for the girl to recognize her father. That night, she did not allow him to sleep with her mother. Showing sharp protest, she got out of bed, and standing on the ground, she pulled him out. Throughout most of the day, he did not leave, trying to comfort her. His effort proved futile. He hoped so much to hear her to utter the word "Daddy," but it did not come. When her mother told her to call him in for dinner, she retorted, "You'd better call him yourself!"

The mother exploded in fury, snatched a big chopstick, and threatened to beat her, insisting that she should obey. "Come in for dinner!" Thu simply said.

Sau sat still, playing deaf, waiting for the word "Daddy."

Thu remained in the kitchen and raised her voice, "Dinner is ready." Sau did not move. The girl turned toward her mother angrily. "I've done as I was told, but he pays no heed to my call."

Sau eyed his daughter, slightly shaking his head, and smiled. Maybe he was too sorrowful to burst into tears. After putting the pot of rice on the fire, his wife set out to buy some foodstuffs to prepare for the next meal, and told Thu to ask for Father's help if need be. The pot was boiling. The girl opened the lid and stirred the rice with a big chopstick. The pot was a bit too heavy to be lifted off the tripod to pour out the excess water in it. She then looked up at Sau. I thought that she was now at the end of her tether and that all she could do was to call her father for help. She looked around for a moment.

"The pot is boiling. Reduce the water for me, please," she said aloud.

I intervened, trying to show her how to behave. "You ought to say, 'Father, please, help reduce the water.'"

She seemed to ignore my words and went her way in a loud voice. "The pot is boiling, the rice will be overcooked."

Sau stayed motionless.

"If you spoil the rice," I threatened her, "you'll surely be beaten by Mother. Why don't you call your father for help. Just say Daddy. Try it."

As the water in the pot was now boiling over, she felt some fear, looked down and pondered. But she still held her ground. With a rag, she tried to lift the pot, but without success. She looked up again. The pot boiled faster. Hard pressed, she was near to crying. She turned her eyes toward the pot, then toward us. Her fumbling manner looked both pitiful and funny. We thought she would give up. At last, she reached for a large spoon and used it to bail out the water, while muttering something we could not hear. She was terrible indeed!

During the meal, Sau served her a lump of yellow fish egg. She set it aside in her bowl with her chopsticks, then all of a sudden, she tossed it away, scattering rice all over. Angered by her behavior, he beat her on the buttocks. "Why are you so mule-headed?" he shouted.

I expected the little girl to cry or run away. But she sat still and looked down. After a moment, she picked up the egg and put it into her bowl again. Then she stood up and quietly moved toward the riverbank. She jumped into the boat, unfastened the chain, purposely jingled it noisily, took an oar, and rowed across the river. She called on her grandmother, told her what had happened, and cried. That evening, her mother tried hard to induce her to come back home, but it was in vain. Sau was to depart the next day and his wife wanted to spend the last night with him, so she did not insist on her daughter's coming back.

The next morning, relatives came in large numbers to see Sau off. The little girl was also there with her grandmother. Sau was busy receiving everybody and seemed not to pay attention to his daughter. His wife packed his belongings. Thu stood alone in a corner, then leaned against the doorpost gazing at everybody around her father. She looked rather different now, showing no more obstinacy, no frown on her brow. Her long, upturned eyelashes, which seemed to have never flickered, made her eyes look wider. She was no longer obviously thoughtful.

At the moment of departure, only after he had said good-bye to everybody did Sau run his eyes to seek his daughter, who was standing in a corner. Obviously he would have liked to embrace her. But he simply gazed at her, lest she flee again. His look was affectionate but there was a tone of sadness in it. I noticed a flicker in the girl's eyes.

"Bye-bye," Sau uttered in a soft voice.

I thought that she would stand there motionless. Unexpectedly she shouted, "Dad . . . dy, dad . . . dy."

The scream tore up the silence and rent everybody's heart. This "Daddy" broke out after being held back for many years. Stretching out her arms, Thu sprang up and rushed toward her father with the agility of a squirrel. She clung to his neck. Her hair seemed to stand on end on her head. Pressing herself tightly against his chest, she said with a sob, "Daddy, I won't let you go. Stay with me." The father hugged his daughter, who kissed him on the cheek, on the hair, on the neck, and even on the long scar on his face.

The grandmother then told the family about what had happened the night before. Trying to find out the reason why Thu refused to recognize her father she asked her why she didn't call him "Daddy."

"No, he is not Daddy," she said, tossing over on the bed.

"How do you know? Daddy has been away from home for a long time. That is why you can't recognize him?"

"The man does not look like Daddy as I see him in the photograph."

"Still, he is your father. Perhaps he looks older now after such a long time?"

"Not because he is older. Daddy has no scar on his cheek."

So Grandmother understood everything. She explained that Daddy had been away fighting against the French and had got wounded. She related how the French committed crimes at a post at the other end of the canal. The girl listened to her in silence, tossing herself every now and then, and heaved a sigh like a grownup. The next morning, she told her grandmother to bring her home.

The daughter kept pressing herself tightly against her father's chest. Sau could not contain his emotion, but he didn't want his daughter to see him cry. He carried her with one arm and wiped his tears with the other. He kissed her hair and murmured, "Let Daddy go. I'll be back home again soon."

"No," the girl screamed. She tightened her grasp around his shoulders, clinging to him with both her arms and her legs. No one present could hold his or her tears. I could not breathe easily, and would have liked very much to tell Sau to stay on for some days more. But there were some difficulties in this. We did not know whether we would remain in the South or be regrouped to the North. We had to report to our unit, to get the order and to make the necessary preparations in case we had to go North. It was time to leave. People tried to convince the girl to let her father leave.

Sau's wife told her, "Thu, my love, let Father go. He'll return here when our country is reunified."

The grandmother touched the girl's hair with her hand and said, "My good girl, let Daddy go. Tell him to buy a comb for you."

"Buy a comb for me and bring it home, Daddy," said Thu with a sob. Then she released her grasp and dropped to her feet.

Some time later, Sau and I went to East Nam Bo and worked as cadres in a mass organization. The period between 1954 and 1959 was a dark one. The U.S.-Diem regime hunted down former members of the Resistance. We had to live in the jungle. Our life and activities there were eventful and it would take me the whole night to relate them. There were nights when we were surrounded three times by commandos sent on our heels, and days without meals when we had to eat wild leaves. But that is another story.

In the jungle at night, as we would lie on our hammocks with a piece of plastic as a roof, Sau often felt a strong remorse for having beaten his daughter. Once, during our conversation, he suddenly sat up in his hammock and said, "People here often go hunting elephants. I must see whether I can lay my hands on a piece of ivory to make a comb with for my daughter."

After that he slept on this hope. Not long afterward, as our group ran short of food, we thought of hunting wild beasts with bows and arrows—not with a rifle—as the silence of the jungle had to be kept for our security. We had not planned to hunt elephants, but by chance one came across our site. None of us showed interest in the game, but Sau decided to chase it. With a friend he hid himself in a bush, waiting for the elephant to come within reach, and they hit him right between his eyes.

I still remember that afternoon. The downpour on the jungle was just over. Drops of water shone on the leaves of the trees. I was working under my plastic roof when suddenly I heard someone shouting. I looked up and saw Sau rushing through the jungle on the trail leading to our site. He raised a piece of ivory and showed it to me. His face brightened like a child's.

Afterward he hammered a twenty-millimeter cartridge into a small saw. He was often seen working laboriously on the piece of ivory to make a comb, devoting his attention, skill, and industriousness as a jeweler does to his job. I was very interested in watching him at his work. He normally did a couple of teeth a day, and completed the whole comb, which was ten by one and a half centimeters, not very long after. On the handle of the comb, Sau painstakingly engraved these words: "With my love and best thoughts for my daughter Thu."

The comb brought relief to Sau's troubled mind although his daughter did not have the opportunity to use it. On certain nights, he was seen gazing at it, polishing it on his hair. Sau longed to see his daughter again, but an unfortunate event occurred. It was near the end of 1958, at a time when we did not yet have arms. During a raid by U.S.-puppet troops, Sau was killed by a bullet fired from an American plane which hit him in the chest. He did not have enough energy to confide his last will before he died. He could only plunge his hand into his pocket and take out the comb. Handing it over, he gazed intently at me. I lack words to describe his last look. I can only tell you that from that day on, I have often seen him in my imagination riveting his eyes on me.

"I won't fail to bring the comb to your daughter," I said in a low voice, bending my head closer to him. Upon hearing this, Sau shut his eyes forever.

I must tell you that on those dark days, clandestinity was observed not only by the living—this was conceivable—but also by the dead. Sau's grave could not be built higher than the ground as was usual, for the enemy would desecrate it, should he find it. I carved a sign into the bark of a nearby tree as a reminder.

That was the way we lived and died at that time. It was unbearable and we had to rise up in arms.

Some time later I was on a comparatively safe Resistance base. A relative called on me. I wanted to send the ivory comb to Thu but I was told that she and her mother had left for somewhere in Saigon or the Plain of Reeds. The Americans and the puppets had organized "To cong"* courses, conducted terrorist raids, and burned down the people's houses to herd them into concentration camps, and after some years the village became completely desolate.

.   .   .

* Indictment of communists.

I held the comb in my hand. The sight of it gave me much pain.

The motor of the boat went on humming. I felt an eager desire to have a close look at the face of the liaison girl who held the string of my life. The night was not dark and the starry sky was covered here and there by some hazy clouds. In the faint light I could distinguish only the girl's profile, her rather round face, and a pair of eyes with an indescribable look. These struck me and I thought I had met her somewhere before.

Suddenly, someone shouted, "A plane! A plane!"

The boat rocked because of the agitation of the passengers. Many people screamed, "Make to the bank."

"Where is the plane?"

"I see its light behind us."

"Turn toward the bank! Turn toward the bank! It's a jet coming."

The liaison girl lowered the speed of the motorboat and looked at the sky for a while.

"No, it isn't a plane. It's the light of a star."

Her calm voice brought order back on the boat. It was so gentle and sweet. Then she speeded up the engine.

Our travel on motorboat after several days' walking gave me real pleasure. However, I still felt uneasy about enemy aircraft.

The boat now entered a canal running through an open field. There were no houses at all, only some bamboo clusters in the distance. As though aware of my secret feelings, the liaison girl accelerated the speed. Water swelled at the prow and two long trails behind the boat sent waves to the banks, which caused the weeds and the roots of wild ferns to quiver.

The passengers were quietly enjoying the quick trip when the liaison girl stopped the motor and shouted, "Planes."

She steered the boat toward a bamboo bush. Another boat behind us also took shelter there. Now we heard the droning of American helicopters. I could not tell if her sense of smell was as acute as the story had it—but it was amazing that she had distinguished the droning of aircraft amidst the roaring of our motor.

The boat rocked and some passengers lost their balance. She

tried to soothe them, saying, "Keep quiet, uncles; the choppers
are still far away. Jump onto the bank to disperse and hide yourselves. If they send flares on us, stay where you are without
moving."

As she spoke, everyone but me was already on the bank. I was
about to jump out when the girl said, "Stay here, uncle. We're
only a few in the boat, don't worry."

I would not have obeyed if the advice was given by anyone
else. But her behavior had so impressed me that I remained
onboard.

The choppers came up from the other end of the canal; their
flares advanced toward us. They roared like a ship convoy and
drew nearer and nearer. For such a job, the Americans usually
used three helicopters, one lighting the way and the two others
doing the strafing.

The girl repeated her advice to me. "Camouflage yourself
carefully with leaves and sit motionless."

This was the first time I was caught by choppers' flares. When
they were aimed at me, I felt their intense light and the beating
of their blades over my head. I was afraid that the boat was too
visible. The camouflage was blown up as in a whirlwind, laying
bare the knapsacks underneath. I thought I was finished and
tucked my head between my shoulders to make myself smaller.
The girl tried to quiet me again as though she guessed my
anxiety.

"They cannot see us as we do ourselves," she said.

Her words didn't have the same effect upon me as they had
had before. An idea came to me: jump into the water. But I
restrained myself in time.

The dreadful flares became less dazzling and the roaring of
the engines died down gradually as the airplanes went away.
All became dark again. Yet I dared not move, fearing that the
enemy might come back.

"They stage a show of strength, but they can't see anything
at all. We have only to keep calm and not to move," the liaison-
agent said. Then she looked up at the field and called the passengers back to the boat. Some were wet through. They grumbled
as they changed their soiled clothes. The motor roared again.

After midnight our group landed on the bank and went by foot. We walked single file along the muddy, uneven, and slippery ditches across a rice field. We carried our sandals in our hands and groped our way step by step. Even so, every now and then we fell, one after the other. At a point near a river bank, the liaison girl ordered the group to stop and sent two scouts to reconnoiter the area.

After some twenty minutes, they met with enemy commandos. The latter did not hide themselves in the foliage along the river bank as they usually did, but laid ambush in the open field. Shots were fired from all directions and cartridges flew close overhead.

"Brother Tu, guide the group away. I'll stay here," was the order of the liaison girl. From the way she spoke, I guessed that she was a team leader. I felt a strange urge to tell her to go with us, but she had already faded away. Shells continued to fly, whistling, then dropped in the distance. We lay as close to the ditch as we could, trying not to raise our heads.

I heard a carbine shot on our left. It instantly drew all the firing toward that direction. I then realized that the liaison girl had purposely drawn the enemy's attention in her direction.

"Run away, Tu," came the order. Our group rushed forward. I was not accustomed to the firing, but did not feel afraid, all my thoughts going to the fate of the liaison girl. We ran helter-skelter across the field to the bush ahead, and from there to the river, which we crossed safely.

The firing became fiercer and fiercer. I tried to make out the girl's carbine shot, but in vain, and I grew all the more anxious.

Since we fled the commandos as swiftly as we could, we arrived at the appointed place earlier than had been arranged. It was a branch in a village. But we did not have to wait long for our new guide from D.A. post. Our group gathered in a pineapple field so damaged by toxic chemicals sprayed by the enemy, that the plants did not bear fruit. None of us was missing. Some lost their rubber sandals during the race, others their knapsacks when crossing the river. Though the oldest, I did not lose anything.

We were all very tired. The guides allowed us one night's rest. Some, not bothering to hang their hammocks, lay on the ground, using their bags as pillows, and soon began to snore. As for me

I just drowsed with a disturbed mind. I dreamt that I was on the way to my native province: many villages looked strangely different, the people had been forced to dismantle their houses and to come and live in concentration camps, which they later destroyed; gardens, too, had completely changed. I saw again all the scenes when, together with Sau, I returned to my village, and when we parted with each other forever, he is handing me the comb which I still kept with me. From time to time, I woke up and thought of those who were behind to check the pursuit of the commandos, especially of the liaison girl. "What could have happened to her and the other liaison agents?" I asked myself. Then I fell asleep from exhaustion.

I heard faint noises of footsteps, voices, and laughter. When at length I woke up, I found it was dawn. Clouds hung like a banner over the sky. People were talking livelily. The liaison girl was there wet through and with mud all over her clothes. Thus, she had joined us in time.

As I approached the group, they said good-bye to one another. I saw the liaison girl, more clearly this time. She had fought against the enemy and had just come out of a dangerous situation, but looked as though nothing serious had happened to her. Sunburned and shiny-eyed, she could not be more than twenty years old. She was so childish in appearance, with her pendant earrings. She stepped toward me. I wanted to express my admiration and gratitude. With a smile I greeted her and said, "My niece, I was very anxious about you. What is your rank by birth in your family?"

"I'm the first, uncle."

"Why do they call you Sister Ut? Is it because you are mar . . . ?"

"No," she replied without giving me time to finish my question. "I'm the first and the last born, because I'm the only child of the family."

"What's the name of your village? I think I've met you somewhere before."

"I come from Culao Gieng."

I shuddered on hearing the name of my native village. Looking in her eyes, I pressed on, "Culao Gieng of Cho Moi district, Long Chau Sa province, isn't it?"

"Yes, it is."

"What's your name?"

"Thu."

"Thu, you say?" I asked in surprise. "Your father's name is Sau and your mother's Binh, isn't it?"

She was so astonished that she didn't utter a word and stood looking at me from top to bottom. Thereupon the guides of D.A. post urged us to get ready for the departure. But I didn't mind what they said nor feel like hearing anything else.

Neither of us had come back from our surprise. She continued fixing her round eyes on me. The eyes of my niece for sure, I said to myself and asked again, "Your father's name is Sau, isn't it, my niece?"

"Yes . . . but how do you know?"

I tried to overcome my emotion and went on with a trembling voice, "I'm uncle Ba. Do you remember the day when your father left home and promised to buy a comb for you?"

She nodded lightly. "Yes, I do."

Unexpected meetings like this, as you all know, often occurred during the Resistance War. Glancing at the girl, I took the ivory comb out of my pocket.

"Your father sent you this. He made it himself."

Her eyes looked bigger in her bewildered face. She took the comb which seemed to remind her of the day when her father parted with her. The sight of all this pained me to the utmost. I knew she was extremely happy and didn't want to trouble her happiness. I felt I could lie: "Father is well; he couldn't return home and asked me to bring it to you."

She murmured, her eyelids quivering, "You're mistaken, this comb is not from my father."

I was disappointed and even anxious. I asked her, "Your father is Sau and your mother is Binh, is that right?"

"Yes, it is."

She was about to cry, tears shone in her eyes, but she contained her emotion. "If you're not mistaken, then you tell a lie," she said, "because you don't want to pain me. I know my father is dead."

Her eyes twinkled again and tears rolled down her cheeks.

"I can overcome my suffering. Don't be afraid to tell me the truth. I learned two years ago that my father was dead, then I asked my mother to let me work as a liaison agent."

She wanted to say more, but she couldn't, as the words died in her throat. She bowed her head and looked to the ground; her hair quivered. I kept silent. My comrades in the group shouted to urge me to leave. I realized that I could not stay any longer. I asked for Thu's address and briefly inquired after her mother's and relatives' health.

The joy of meeting Thu lasted but a few moments. It was high time to leave. I glanced at her and instinctively said, "Good-bye, my daughter." She murmured something I could not hear between her livid lips. From a distance I turned around and saw her following us. She stopped by a ditch. Small rice plants stirred by the wind resembled waves dashing toward her. Behind her, the coconut trees defoliated by toxic chemicals looked like gigantic fish skeletons hanging in the air. Young leaves sprang up, which, seen from afar, offered the spectacle of a forest of swords raised skyward.

Vietnam

COFFEE FOR THE ROAD

Alex La Guma

THEY WERE PAST the maize-lands and driving through the wide, low, semidesert country that sprawled out on all sides in reddish brown flats and depressions. The land, going south, was scattered with scrub and thorn bushes, like a vast unswept carpet. Far to the right, the metal vanes of a windmill pump turned wearily in the faint morning breeze, as if it had just been wakened to set reluctantly about its duty of sucking water from the miserly earth. The car hurtled along the asphalt road, its tires roaring along the black surface.

"I want another sandwich, please," Zaida said. She huddled in the blanketed space among the suitcases in the back. She was six years old and weary from the long, speeding journey, and her initial interest in the landscape had evaporated, so that now she sagged tiredly in the padded space, ignoring the parched gullies and stunted trees that whisked past.

"There's some in the tin. You can help yourself, can't you?" the woman at the wheel said, without taking her eyes off the road. "Do you want to eat some more, too, Ray?"

"Not hungry any more," the boy beside her replied. He was gazing out at the barbed-wire fence that streamed back outside the rolled-up window.

"How far's it to Cape Town, Mummy?" Zaida asked, munching a sandwich.

"We'll be there tomorrow afternoon," the woman said.

"Will Papa be waiting?"

"Of course."

"There's some sheep," the boy, Ray, said. A scattering of farm buildings went by, drab, domino-shaped structures along a brown slope.

The mother had been driving all night and she was fatigued, her eyes red, with the feeling of sand under the lids, irritating the eyeballs. They had stopped for a short while along the road the night before; parked in a gap off the road outside a small town. There had been nowhere to put up for the night: the hotels were for whites only. In fact, only whites lived in these towns and everybody else, except for the servants, lived in tumbledown mud houses in the locations beyond. Besides, they did not know anybody in this part of the country.

Dawn had brought depression, gloom, ill temper, which she tried to control in the presence of the children. After having parked on that stretch of road until after midnight, she had started out again and driven, the children asleep, through the rest of the night.

Now she had a bad headache, too, and when Zaida said, "Can I have a meatball, Mummy?" she snapped irritably. "Oh, dash it all! It's there, eat it, can't you?"

The landscape ripped by, like a film being run backward, red-brown, yellow-red, pink-red, all studded with sparse bushes and broken boulders. To the east a huge outcrop of rock strata rose abruptly from the arid earth, like a titanic wedge of purple-and-lavender-layered cake topped with chocolate-colored boulders. The car passed over a stretch of gravel road and the red dust boiled behind it like a flame-shot smoke screen. A bird, its long, ribbonlike tail streaming behind it, skimmed the brush beyond the edge of the road, flitting along as fast as the car.

"Look at that funny bird, Mummy," Ray cried, and pressed his face to the dust-filmed glass.

The mother ignored him, trying to relax behind the wheel, her feet moving unconsciously, but skillfully, on the pedals in the floor. She thought that it would have been better to have taken a train, but Billy had written that he'd need the car because he had a lot of contacts to visit. She hoped the business would be better in the Cape. Her head ached, and she drove automatically. She was determined to finish the journey as quickly as possible.

Ray said, "I want some coffee." And he reached for the thermos flask on the rack under the dashboard. Ray could take care of himself; he did not need to have little things done for him.

"Give me some, too," Zaida called from the back, among the suitcases.

"Don't be greedy," Ray said to her. "Eating, eating, eating."

"I'm not greedy. I want a drink of coffee."

"You had coffee this morning."

"I want some more."

"Greedy. Greedy."

"Children," the mother said wearily, "children, stop that arguing."

"He started first," Zaida said.

"Stop it. Stop it," the mother told her.

Ray was unscrewing the cap of the thermos. When it was off he drew the cork and looked in. "Man, there isn't any," he said. "There isn't any more coffee."

"Well, that's just too bad," the mother said.

"I want a drink," Zaida cried. "I'm thirsty, I want some coffee."

The mother said wearily, "Oh, all right. But you've got to wait. We'll get some somewhere up the road. But wait, will you?"

The sun was a coppery smear on the flat blue sky, and the countryside, scorched yellow and brown like an immense slice of toast, quivered and danced in the haze. The woman drove on, tiredly, her whole mind rattling like a stale nut. Behind the sunglasses her eyes were red-rimmed and there was a stretched look about the dark, handsome, Indian face. Her whole system felt taut and stretched like the wires of a harp, but too tight, so that a touch might snap any one of them.

The miles purred and growled and hummed past: flat country and dust-colored *koppies*, the baked clay *dongas* and low ridges of hills. A shepherd's hut, lonely as a lost soul, crouched against the shale-covered side of a flat hill; now and then a car passed theirs, headed in the opposite direction, going north, crashing by in a shrill whine of slip stream. The glare of the sun quivered and quaked as if the air was boiling.

"I want some coffee," Zaida repeated petulantly. "We didn't have no coffee."

"We'll buy some coffee," her mother told her. "We'll buy some for the road as soon as we get to a café. Stop it, now. Eat another sandwich."

"Don't want sandwich. Want coffee."

A group of crumbling huts, like scattered, broken cubes, passed them in a hollow near the road and a band of naked, dusty brown children broke from the cover of a sheep pen, dashing to the side of the road, cheering and waving at the car. Ray waved back, laughing, and then they were out of sight. The wind-scoured metal pylon of a water pump drew up and then disappeared too. Three black men trudged in single file along the roadside, looking ahead into some unknown future, wrapped in tattered, dusty blankets, oblivious of the heat, their heads shaded by the ruins of felt hats. They did not waver as the car spun past them but walked with fixed purpose.

The car slowed for a steel-slung bridge and they rumbled over the dry, rock-strewn bed of a stream. A few sheep, their fleeces black with dust, sniffed among the boulders, watched over by a man like a scarecrow.

At a distance, they passed the colored location and then the African location, hovels of clay and clapboard strewn like discolored dice along a brown slope, with tiny people and antlike dogs moving among them. On another slope the name of the town was spelled out in whitewashed boulders.

The car passed the sheds of a railway siding, with the sheep milling in corrals, then lurched over the crossing and bounced back on to the roadway. A colored man went by on a bicycle, and they drove slowly past the nondescript brown front of the Railway Hotel, a line of stores, and beyond a burnt hedge a group of white men with red, suntanned, wind-honed faces sat drinking at tables in front of another hotel with an imitation Dutch-colonial façade. There was other traffic parked along the dusty, gravel street of the little town: powdered cars and battered pickup trucks, a wagon in front of a feed store. An old colored man swept the pavement in front of a shop, his reed broom making a hissing sound, like gas escaping in spurts.

Two white youths, pink-faced and yellow-haired, dressed in khaki shirts and shorts, stared at the car, their eyes suddenly hostile at the sight of a dark woman driving its shiny newness, metal fittings factory smooth under the film of road dust. The car spun a little cloud behind it as it crept along the red gravel street.

"What's the name of this place, Mummy?" Ray asked.

"I don't know," the mother replied, tired, but glad to be able to slow down. "Just some place in the Karroo."

"What's the man doing?" Zaida asked, peering out through the window.

"Where?" Ray asked, looking about. "What man?"

"He's gone now," the little girl said. "You didn't look quickly." Then, "Will we get some coffee now?"

"I think so," the mother said. "You two behave yourselves and there'll be coffee. Don't you want a cool drink?"

"No," the boy said. "You just get thirsty again afterward."

"I want a lot of coffee with lots of sugar," Zaida said.

"All right," the mother said. "Now stop talking so much."

Up ahead, at the end of a vacant lot, stood a café. Tubular steel chairs and tables stood on the pavement outside, in front of its shaded windows. Its front was decorated with old Coca Cola signs and painted menus. A striped awning shaded the tables. In the wall facing the vacant space was a foot-square hole where non-whites were served, and a group of ragged colored and African people stood in the dust and tried to peer into it, their heads together, waiting with forced patience.

The mother drove the car up and brought it to a stop in front of the café. Inside a radio was playing and the slats of the venetian blinds in the windows were clean and dustless.

"Give me the flask," the mother said, and took the thermos bottle from the boy. She unlatched the door. "Now, you children, just sit quiet. I won't be long."

She opened the door and slid out and, standing for a moment on the pavement, felt the exquisite relief of loosened muscles. She stretched herself, enjoying the almost sensual pleasure of her straightened body. But her head still ached badly and that spoiled the momentary delight which she felt. With the feeling gone, her brain was tired again and the body once more a tight-wound spring. She straightened the creases out of the smart tan suit she was wearing but left the jacket unbuttoned. Then, carrying the thermos flask, she crossed the sidewalk, moving between the plastic-and-steel furniture into the café.

Inside, the café was cool and lined with glass cases displaying cans and packages like specimens in some futuristic museum. From somewhere at the back of the place came the smell and sound of potatoes being fried. An electric fan buzzed on a shelf and two gleaming urns, one of tea and the other of coffee, steamed against the back wall.

The only other customer was a small white boy with tow-colored hair, a face like a near-ripe apple, and a running nose. He wore a washed-out print shirt and khaki shorts, and his dusty bare feet were yellow-white and horny with cracked calluses. His pink, sticky mouth explored the surface of a lollipop while he scanned the covers of a row of outdated magazines in a wire rack.

Behind the glass counter and a trio of soda fountains a broad, heavy woman in a green smock thumbed through a little stack of accounts, ignoring the group of dark faces pressing around the square hole in the side wall. She had a round-shouldered, thick body and a reddish-complexion which looked as if her face had been sand-blasted into its component parts: hard plains of cheeks and knobbly cheek bones and a bony ridge of nose that separated twin pools of dull gray; and the mouth a bitter gash, cold and malevolent as a lizard's, a dry, chapped, and serrated pink crack.

She looked up and started to say something, then saw the color of the other woman and, for a moment, the gray pools of the eyes threatened to spill over as she gaped. The thin pink youth writhed like a worm as she sought for words.

"Can you fill this flask with coffee for me, please?" the mother asked.

The crack opened and a screech came from it, harsh as the sound of metal rubbed against stone. "Coffee? My Lord Jesus Christ!" the voice screeched. "A bedamned *coolie* girl in here!" The eyes stared in horror at the brown, tired, handsome Indian face with its smart sunglasses, and the city cut of the tan suit. "Coolies, Kaffirs, and Hottentots outside," she screamed. "Don't you bloody well know? And you talk *English*, too, eh!"

The mother stared at her, startled, and then somewhere inside her something went off, snapped like a tight-wound spring suddenly loose, jangling shrilly into action, and she cried out with disgust as her arm came up and the thermos flask hurtled at the white woman.

"Bloody white trash!" she cried. "Coolie yourself!"

The flask spun through the air and, before the woman behind the counter could ward it off, it struck her forehead above an eyebrow, bounced away, tinkling as the thin glass inside the metal cover shattered. The woman behind the counter screeched and clapped a hand to the bleeding gash over her eye, staggering back. The little boy dropped his lollipop with a yelp and dashed out. The dark faces at the square hatch gasped. The dark woman turned and stalked from the café in a rage.

She crossed the sidewalk, her brown face taut with anger and opened the door of her car furiously. The group of non-whites from the hole in the wall around the side of the building came to the edge of the vacant lot and stared at her as she slammed the door of the car and started the motor.

She drove savagely away from the place, her hands gripping the wheel tightly, so that the knuckles showed yellow through the brown skin. Then she recovered herself and relaxed wearily, slowing down, feeling tired again, through her anger. She took her time out of town while the children gazed, sensing that something was wrong.

Then Ray asked, "Isn't there any coffee, Mummy? And where's the flask?"

"No, there isn't any coffee," the mother replied. "We'll have to do without coffee, I'm afraid."

"I wanted coffee," the little girl complained.

"You be good," the mother said. "Mummy's tired. And please stop chattering."

"Did you lose the flask?" Ray asked.

"Keep quiet, keep quiet," the woman told him, and they lapsed into silence.

They drove past the edge of the town, past a dusty service station with its red pumps standing like sentinels before it. Past a man carrying a huge bundle of firewood on his head, and past the last buildings of the little town: a huddle of whitewashed cabins with chickens scrabbling in the dooryard, a sagging shearing shed with a pile of dirty bales of wool inside, and a man hanging over a fence, watching them go by.

The road speared once more into the yellow-red-brown countryside and the last green trees dwindled away. The sun danced and jiggled like a midday ghost across the expressionless earth, and the tires of the car rumbled faintly on the black asphalt. There was some traffic ahead of them but the woman did not bother to try to overtake it.

The boy broke the silence in the car by saying, "Will Papa take us for drives?"

"He will, I know," Zaida said. "I like this car better than Uncle Ike's."

"Well, *he* gave us lots of rides," Ray replied. "There goes one of those funny birds again."

"Mummy, will we get some coffee later on?" Zaida asked.

"Maybe, dear. We'll see," the mother said.

The dry and dusty landscape continued to flee past the window on either side of the car. Up ahead the sparse traffic on the road was slowing down and the mother eased her foot on the accelerator.

"Look at that hill," Ray cried. "It looks like a face."

"Is it a real face?" Zaida asked, peering out.

"Don't be silly," Ray answered. "How can it be a real face? It just *looks* like a face."

The car slowed down and the mother, thrusting her head through her window, peering forward past the car in front and saw the roadblock beyond it.

A small riot van, a Land Rover, its windows and spotlight screened with thick wire mesh, had been pulled up halfway across the road, and a dusty automobile parked opposite to it, forming a barrier with just a car's width between them. A policeman in khaki shirt, trousers, and flat cap leaned against the front fender of the automobile and held a Sten gun across his thighs. Another man in khaki sat at the wheel of the car, and a third policeman stood by the gap, directing the traffic through after examining the drivers.

The car ahead slowed down as it came up to the gap, the driver pulled up, and the policeman looked at him, stepped back, and waved him on. The car went through, revved, and rolled away.

The policeman turned toward the next car, holding up a hand, and the mother driving the car felt the sudden pounding of her heart. She braked and waited, watching the khaki-clad figure stroll the short distance toward her.

He had a young face, with the usual red-burned complexion of the land, under the shiny leather bill of the cap. He was smiling thinly but the smile did not reach his eyes which bore the hard quality of chips of granite. He wore a holstered pistol at his waist and, coming up, he turned toward the others and called, "This looks like the one."

The man with the Sten gun straightened but did not come forward. His companion inside the car just looked across at the woman.

The policeman in the road said, still smiling slightly, "Ah, we have been waiting for you. You didn't think they'd phone ahead, eh?"

The children in the car sat dead still, staring, their eyes troubled. The mother said, looking out, "What's it all about?"

"Never mind what's it all about," the policeman said to her. "*You* know what it's all about." He looked her over and nodded. "Ja, darkie girl with brown suit and sunglasses. You're under arrest."

"What's it all about?" the woman asked again. Her voice was not anxious, but she was worried about the children.

"Never mind. You'll find out," the policeman told her coldly. "One of those agitators making trouble here. Awright, listen." He peered at her with flint-hard eyes. "You turn the car around and don't try no funny business, eh? Our car will be in front and the van behind, so watch out." His voice was cold and threatening.

"Where are you taking us? I've got to get my children to Cape Town."

"I don't care about that," he said. "You make trouble here then you got to pay for it." He looked back at the police car and waved a hand. The driver of the police car started it up and backed and then turned into the road.

"You follow that car," the policeman said. "We're going back that way."

The woman said nothing but started her own car, maneuvering it until they were behind the police car.

"Now don't you try any funny tricks," the policeman said again. She stared at him and her eyes were also cold now. He went back to the riot van and climbed in. The car in front of her put on speed and she swung behind it, with the van following.

"Where are we going, Mummy?" asked Zaida.

"You be quiet and behave yourselves," the mother said, driving after the police car.

The countryside, red-brown and dusty, moved past them; the landscapes they had passed earlier now slipping the other way. The flat blue sky danced and wavered and the parched, scrub-strewn scenery stretched away around them in the yellow glare of the sun.

"I wish we had some coffee," Zaida said.

South Africa

A WOMAN'S LIFE

MARJORIE J. MBILINYI

THE DAY WAS ENDED. A myriad of colors—blue and white
uniforms and dark laughing faces—could be seen in the school-
yard. Shrill cries of farewell lifted over the crowd and reached
Thecla, who was just entering her mother's Standard IV class-
room. She was a tall, ungainly thirteen-year-old, a student in
Standard VII. Her mother's room was nearly empty now, all its
pupils dispersed. Only the elderly woman remained, bent over
notebooks on the front desk. The lines on her face were drawn
in sharp relief, her eyes weary, as she looked up toward her
daughter.

"Ah, Thecla, come help me arrange these notebooks. I've
got to take them home for marking, though whether or not I'll
get around to marking I don't know."

"Aye, Mama."

Together they began putting all the flimsy notebooks in order.

"Mama, I heard some Standard IV children complaining
today. They say your arithmetic test was too hard."

"Aha. That's what they always say. Never that Kiswahili is too
hard or history, always arithmetic." The woman laughed, happy
in any case to hear herself talked about. "What else did they
say?"

"Oh, nothing. They always say you're a good teacher and
very friendly, but you give hard tests."

Mama Thecla laughed again, then said, "We'll have to go by
the fish stalls and get some food for tonight."

"Mama, you have money for fish?"

"Yes, we got paid today. Is there *sembe* at home?"

"Yes, but Mama, let's get some coconut."

"All right, Thecla. You'll pick out the coconut while I'm getting the fish. Let's go now."

Thecla took half of the notebooks, her mother the other half. The two, mother and daughter, swung out into the street, filled now with streams of people on their way home from work and women hurrying to the nearby market for their dinner's provisions. They resembled one another, though Thecla's face was clear, fresh, a lustrous brown, and reflected the beauty now erased from her mother's face. The older woman's body was full, rounded. She walked with tired grace and knowledge. In contrast, Thecla's body was angular, bony, though equally tall. She walked self-consciously as if unsure where all the parts of her body were supposed to be.

When they reached the market Thecla darted off with her mother's nylon basket to get a coconut. Mama Thecla went on to her favorite fishmonger, a parent of one of her pupils. She was always sure of a good choice at low cost. Quite a crowd of women was gathered there, all bustling to get in the front of the line before the best fish was taken. But as soon as she was seen, the fishmonger called her over.

"Mama Thecla. *Mwalimu wangu.* How are you? What can I give you today? How is my boy doing? You know this lady? She is my boy's teacher. My boy's teacher."

All the women and some other fishmongers turned to look at Mama Thecla. Some even laughed, having heard his praise of the teacher many times before.

"Yah, Mama, what can I give you? Just speak up."

"Just give me a good big meaty fish. Only one today, Baba Athumani."

"Aye, *Mwalimu,* one big fish. Is my boy doing all right? If he doesn't behave himself just give him a good beating, that's all he needs."

"Aha, he doesn't need a beating. He's a good boy, and very quick in arithmetic."

"Hah! You hear that? Just like his father! Numbers!"

He showed Mama Thecla the very shiny fat fish he had picked out for her, then wrapped it up in a newspaper.

"How much, Baba Athumani?"

"*Mwalimu*, only five shillings for you. I can't ask for more. You're our teacher."

She pulled out five shillings from her pouch and paid him, and was about to take the package when Thecla showed up by her side. When the fishmonger saw her he beamed, "Ah, my pretty little one, you going to be a teacher like your mother, yes?"

"Yes, *mzee. Shikamuu.*"

"*Marahaba*, my child. Take this package for your mother. She is tired from the long day, eh?"

Thecla took the fish and put it together with the coconut in the basket. They bid farewell to the old man and started off for home. Their own place was not too far away. As they got closer, friends, neighbors, parents of school children greeted them. They lived in a national housing flat, one of the upstairs type. It had two bedrooms, a bathroom, a kitchen of sorts, and a big sitting room, as well as a little open porch behind the kitchen. Thecla's father was an official in the Ministry of Environments, though she never was sure exactly what work he did. But because of his position, they managed to get a big place to live. There were only five in the family, Thecla and two younger brothers. An older brother had died years before of the fever. Usually there were also cousins staying with them, but no one was around these days.

Finally they reached their place. The yard in front was dry, hard-packed earth and no grass, only bits of glass, paper, other *takataka* lying around.

"Thecla, get the key out of my basket."

"Aye, Mama."

She pulled it out from underneath the fish, gave it to her mother who opened the door.

"No sight of your brothers. Where can they be?"

The boys studied at a lower primary school nearer home.

"Don't worry. They'll come when they smell food cooking."

"All right. You start the charcoal and I'll just wash up and then clean the fish."

Thecla went out to the back porch and, while her mother scaled the fish, got the fire going in the small charcoal stove they usually used. Together they worked silently to prepare the evening meal.

Just as Thecla was dumping the *ugali* on a big round aluminum plate, the two brothers came racing in.

"Mama, Mama, we've been waiting for you. We're hungry."

Thecla and her mother glanced at each other and laughed.

"So you've been waiting so long, is it? Why don't you go and wash. *Ugali* is ready."

"*Ugali* and what?"

"Never mind 'and what.' Go wash."

Charles sniffed, then clapped his younger brother on the back and shouted "Fish!" They rushed in to wash. Thecla put aside food for her father in the kitchen near the kerosene burner. The mother spread out a mat in the sitting room and they all sat down to eat. As she ate, Thecla began to feel absolute contentment. This fish was so sweet. She glanced at her mother's face after the plates were eaten clean.

"Mama, I am so full now."

"Me, too, Mama."

"And me."

Her brothers sprang up to wash their hands and scamper off again.

"Mama, what's wrong? You don't look so happy."

Her mother's face was drawn even tighter together, her eyes dim, far away.

"Why do you look so sad?"

"Sad?" the mother said. "Sad, I'm not sad." She attempted a feeble smile, her lips half-curled up but too tightly curled, her teeth broken, yellowing. Things were for an instant very still, only faint street sounds from the bigger thoroughfare came to them, honking cars, bells, shouts, then laughter from their next door neighbors. "I'm just wondering where your father is right now. He hardly ever eats at home any more, or only late at night. He is becoming a stranger in the house."

She could now pick out individual voices from next door. Visitors must have joined them for the evening meal. They sounded very happy.

"Why doesn't Baba come home any more? We hardly ever see him."

"I don't know, dear. He's too busy, I suppose."

She glanced at her daughter, wondering how she understood, noticing how much she had grown recently.

"Mama, sometimes I'm afraid of Baba. When he starts shouting and his eyes are red. I've never told you . . . do you mind?"

"No, my dear child. I don't mind. That is just how it is. Men are like that. When you first meet they seem so kind, so gentle, so sweet. They don't stay that way."

Thecla had never heard her mother speak so candidly before. She felt encouraged to go on. "Why not? Why don't they stay like that, nice I mean?"

"I don't know. Like your father, when we were first married, what a good life! Whatever I cooked pleased him, whatever I wore pleased him. He used to rush home from work to see what I was doing. You were born soon after. He was teaching in a secondary school near home. We had our own house. Then I began teaching in a nearby primary school. We used to do our homework corrections together at night."

She sighed deeply, remembering how sweetly, how swiftly, those days passed. Her daughter waited silently.

"But then, we came to Dar es Salaam. Your father got a very good job. The boys were born here, but it wasn't the same ever again."

"But Mama, you and Baba were the same."

"We were and we were not. He's always meeting big people now. He goes to parties, travels to many places. Those big wives look me up and down, see that I don't have expensive dresses and fancy shoes and wigs and they ignore me. There is nothing to talk about. They have all their own little get-togethers, their teas, and their clubs."

"But Mama, you're a *teacher*. What are they?"

"Hah, my dear, a primary school teacher is not so great as Baba Athumani thinks. Not in the city, not in Baba's world. There I'm a nobody." She was silent for a while, thinking of the past and of now. She was tempted to tell Thecla how much she worried over the girl's future, her hopes that she would get into secondary school and somehow become one of those big ladies herself. Even so she often wondered whether their lives *were* much different from her own.

"Come, Thecla. Enough talking for now. Let's start on our homework."

The day was ended. From the inner sanctum of his office Mr. Nguvumali could hear the mad rush as Ministry workers hurried to get down the stairs, out of the building, and into the buses waiting outside before they filled up. He looked at the jumble of papers and files on his desk and sighed. So much paper work. It was impossible to keep up. And meetings, meetings . . . like the lousy one that morning. His section had been called upon a while ago to provide an outline for the Minister on the next annual plan. He had thought his subordinates would be able to handle this task well enough, and hadn't bothered much with the details, only to get a call in the morning, "The Minister wants to see what progress has been made on the plan. Meeting 10:00 A.M."

He had called his assistant: not in.

He called the adviser to their section, Mr. Johnson. "Oh, my, my, Mr. Nguvumali, so soon? Why, we're still investigating last year's results!"

"Mr. Johnson, something must be handed in at 10:00 A.M. this morning. Can't you put something together?"

"Well, well, I shall do my best, though you know these things take time. It will have to be a very rough outline. No data available, I suppose?"

"Data?"

"Yes, you know—hints as to budget plans and all that sort of thing . . ."

"N . . . no . . . not that I know of . . ."

"Well, all right, Mr. Nguvumali. I shall do my best. Don't you worry."

Blasted if Mr. Johnson hadn't kept the paper to himself and presented it personally to the Minister during the meeting. "Sorry, old chap, no time for consultation!" The Minister seemed to have been satisfied enough with the contents, but Nguvumali was sure he glanced at him severely and turned to ask the Principal Secretary who the hell this man was, head of a section, with the heavy decision-making left in the hands of a European!

And he, Mr. Zachary Nguvumali, didn't know the answer to that question either. He just couldn't get down to working on these files. As soon as one was gone through a new one cropped up. It was too much. And one wrong move, one mistake, and *he* was thrown out, not *Mr.* Johnson.

The office door opened and one of his colleagues came in. "Nguvumali, let's go man, get some refreshment."

"Hi, Omari, yeah—why not? That's what I need—a good bottle of beer."

"Right. You have your car ready?"

"Yes. Just outside. Let's go."

He glanced around with distaste at his hopeless desk, hesitated as to whether or not he should take a file home, decided not to, and left quickly, locking the door behind him. The outer office was still, quiet . . . typists' desks cleared, but the "In" trays full as usual.

"Lord, just the sight of that tray and I feel sick."

"Ha, forget it."

"Yeah, man, let's forget it. You know the new place they've opened up on Pugu Road?"

"The Star Bar?"

"Right—lets try it—drink's on the house."

"Okay."

The Star Bar had that new shine that never lasted more than a month or so . . . bright lights strung up in the trees, lots of young girls standing around—plenty of customers already arrived.

"Nguvumali, how are you? Welcome, let me buy you a drink! Mr. Omari, welcome, *bwana.*"

"Thanks. Say, what's the latest news?"

"Nothing much. Did you hear, Josaphat got indicted?"

"No! What for?"

"I don't know, something about pilfering with money, and no evidence to prove it, knowing Josaphat."

"Well, here's to Josaphat."

"Right. Here's to us."

Round after round after round. Each drink, rather than bringing calm or happiness, only increased Nguvumali's bitterness. This Mr. Johnson, who was *he* anyway? If he did not exist, I could manage all right. But now, huh, when the Minister wants someone to travel with him, who does he ask? *Mr.* Johnson. "Data," "budget plans," would I, a lowly African civil servant, have access to such high-powered material? No . . . never . . . only the *Mr. Johnsons.* Damn, damn, damn what a lousy job after all. Head of Research Section, that's a laugh. Head of nothing, and me, a know-nothing. That's what they all must think, a know-no-nothing no-nothing, that's me.

He noticed the others laughing and teasing with the girls and remembered Josaphat. Josaphat, rich Josaphat. They'll let him go. He's got big friends and lots of money. That makes more friends. Only a fellow like me, position by virtue of "merit," not power, need fear the future. If power wills, position lost.

"Lo, it is too much."

"What's the matter man? C'mon, have another beer."

"Yeah, yeah, another beer, more beer, that's what we need, more beer."

"Lo, my head hurts. I have had enough."

"C'mon man, one more."

"No more. No more. Enough . . ."

Much later that night Thecla heard her father climbing the stairs to their flat. From the sound of his footsteps she could tell he was drunk. He stopped every four or five steps, muttering unintelligibly to himself, and then proceeded another four or five steps, only to stop and rest again.

She shivered and covered herself up with her sheet and tried to lie absolutely still as if she were sound asleep. She could hear the even sounds of her two brothers' breathing. They never even woke up.

Now she could hear him fumbling to open the door with his key. She held her breath waiting. Finally she heard the door bang shut. All was quiet. Then sounds came from the kitchen, something shattered on the ground, maybe a plate. She heard him cry out, "Where is everybody?" and she ducked back under the sheet.

Where is everybody, the man thought to himself, then shouted, "Where is everybody?" Trying to fake sleep, that's what they're up to. Leaving me to fix my own dinner. This blasted stove. What's the good of hot soup with cold *ugali?* What's the good of a wife? Let me go see my wife. "My wife," he shouted. He took the food and went to his bedroom, turned on the light, sat on a chair near the bed, and ate as he watched his wife's face. He saw her eyelids flicker once, then twice—just what he'd been waiting for.

"You. You. Don't pretend to be asleep. I know you're awake. You pretend to sleep and leave me to fix my own food, you lousy woman. Get up out of bed."

By this time he had put the plate down on the table, grabbed his wife's shoulder and was trying to lift her to a sitting position. Her weight was solid, heavy, massive.

"Woman . . . do you hear me? Get up! You will listen to me."

Her eyes flickered wide open. She yawned widely, "Ahhmm, yes dear, what is it? Sorry . . . sorry . . . I was sleeping."

" 'I was sleeping.' Like hell you were. You heard me come in. Why didn't you get up and fix my food. What the hell kind of a house do you run here anyway?"

"But food was there, on the stove, all ready . . ."

"Shut up!" and he struck her on the face hard . . . once, twice, three times. She screamed.

"What's the matter with you? Let go of me!" as he began shaking her violently, gripping her shoulders to do it. She tried to wriggle out of his grasp which angered him further.

"You lousy woman, what good are you? You don't keep house. You work, you tell me . . . doing what? A teacher? What do you teach, you fool? What are *you* an expert in? Making love to your boyfriend teachers at the school? I come home and you're sleeping. Are you not my wife to greet me at the door?"

All the time he was beating, kicking her. Useless to fight back. Mama Thecla cowered on the floor, wailing.

Thecla heard her father shout "My wife" and listened as he walked from the kitchen, past her own door, and on to his bedroom. Soon the thuds of her mother's beating mingled with the cries of her weeping. She tried to disappear, to merge with her bed's soft frame until there was nothing left of herself. At the same time she strained to hear every sound and felt as if she were the one being beaten. Her stomach had tightened up in painful twists and turns. She was frightened for herself without really understanding why. But one thing she had never told her mother. Not long ago when she had just turned twelve, her father had left her mother weeping on the floor and come into her room demanding that Thecla fix his food. She had lain still, so still, then slowly turned around to face him, grabbing her sheet around her. He had stared and stared at her, suddenly cursed her, and then blundered blindly out of the room. Now she was always terrified of him when he came home like this. His eyes were mean, hostile, as if he wanted to hurt her, as if he despised her. This she could not understand, the eyes that bored into her.

The man's fury spent, he sat down on the bed, pulled off his shoes, his slacks, his shirt, stretched out on the bed, and slept almost immediately. The woman remained for a few minutes crouched on the floor weeping, licking her swollen lips, her body aching, until she heard her husband's snoring. Reassured she crept onto her side of the bed. For a long time she lay staring into the miserable night.

The next morning the mother was up very early, boiling water for tea, giving the boys some bread before they dashed off to school, boiling an egg for her husband. He was always the last member of the household to get up. They usually left for school without seeing him. Today was the same. Thecla quickly swallowed down her cup of tea, grabbed a piece of bread, and followed her mother out of the house. She was burning to ask her mother only one question. "Why? Why let him hit you that way as if you were just a worthless piece of *takataka*?" They walked quickly and only just as they neared the school did Thecla have the courage to call out to her mother, "Mama . . . Mama . . . Wait a minute. I want . . . I want to talk to you."

Mama Thecla turned to look at her daughter. Her face still swollen, her eyes dark-ringed, old-looking.

"Yes, Thecla, we must hurry."

"Mama, I heard Baba last night. I heard everything. Why do you let him do it? Why?" As she asked, she became almost furious with her mother. She was shivering in her urgency to have an answer.

"Thecla, now is not the time to discuss such things." The woman saw the urgency in her daughter's face. "Thecla, what would you have me do?"

"Leave him. We can all leave together."

"And go where, my child? Besides, he wouldn't let me take you children anyway. You are *his* children according to the law." As she spoke, her bitterness crept forth and took control of her.

"Mother, how can you give up like that? How can you say, 'Go where?' Aren't you a teacher? Do not the children and their parents greet you *Shikamuu* and does not the fish seller give you his best fish? You are a teacher, not a piece of junk for Baba to kick around. Why do you let him do it? How could he stop us all from going off? What would he care anyway? You could teach in another place."

Her fury mounted as she watched her mother's face, so resigned, patiently listening. "Mama, we can't go on this way."

"Thecla, for you, you can say, let's go. But you are still young, you don't know how it is yet. A woman without a husband is a nobody or worse. You have to explain why you are without a man in the house. And he would follow us anyway and bring you children back here. Would you rather be alone with him?"

"Why could he take us away? We can tell the police how he beats you. Then they would make him leave us with you."

"My dear, the police also beat their wives. Do they care?" She stopped talking then, thinking about Baba Athumani and her pupils, then feeling the twisted swollen muscles of her face, her body, remembering her husband's words, his scorn, his demands. She looked again at her daughter.

"Thecla, maybe for you it can be different. Maybe you won't be stuck like me, lying home late at night, waiting for some man to come home, waiting for the sound of his footsteps to know what kind of a man he will be that night. But you have to *make* it different. For me . . . I don't know."

She felt empty, helpless before her daughter's gaze.

"How do I make it different?"

The mother couldn't answer. The two stood together a moment longer, each with her own thoughts, each surveying the face of the other as if an answer could be found there.

Tanzania

RESURRECTION

RICHARD RIVE

AND STILL the people sang. And one by one, the voices joined
in and the volume rose. Tremulously at first, thin and tenuous,
and then swelling till it filled the tiny dining room, pulsated into
the two bedrooms, stacked high with hats and overcoats, and
spent itself in the kitchen where fussy housewives, dressed in
black, were making wreaths.

> Jesu, lover of my soul,
> Let me to Thy Bo–som fly . . .

A blubbery woman in the corner nearest the cheap, highly
polished chest of drawers wept hysterically. Above her head
hung a cheap reproduction of a Karroo scene. A dazzling white-
gabled farmhouse baking in the hot African sun. In the distance
the low hills—*koppies*—shimmered against a hazy blue sky. Her
bosom heaved convulsively as she refused to be placated. Her
tears proved infectious and her lips quivered, and handkerchiefs
were convulsively sought.

> Hide me, O my Saviour hide,
> Till the storm of life is past,
> Safe into the haven guide . . .

sang a small boy in a freshly laundered Eton collar who shared
a stiff Ancient and Modern hymnbook with his mother. His
voice was wiry and weak and completely dominated by the
strong soprano next to him. All the people joined in and sang.
Except Mavis. Only Mavis sat silent, glossy-eyed, staring down
at her rough, though delicately shaped, brown hands. Her eyes,
hot and red, but tearless, with a slightly contemptuous sneer

around the closed, cruel mouth. Only Mavis sat silent. Staring at her hands and noticing that the left thumbnail was scarred and broken. She refused to raise her eyes, refused to look at the coffin, at the hymnbook open and neglected in her lap. Her mouth was tightly shut, as if determined not to open, not to say a word. Tensely she sat and stared at her broken thumbnail. The room did not exist. The fat woman blubbered unnoticed. The people sang but Mavis heard nothing.

> Other refuge have I none,
> Hangs my helpless soul on Thee . . .

they began the second verse. The fat woman had sufficiently recovered to attempt to add a tremulous contralto. The boy in the Eton collar laboriously followed the line with his finger. Mavis vaguely recognized Rosie as she fussily hurried in with a tray of fresh flowers, exchanged a brief word with an overdressed woman nearest the door, and busily hurried out again. Mavis sensed things happening but saw without seeing and felt without feeling. Nothing registered, but she could feel the Old Woman's presence, could feel the room becoming her dead mother, becoming full of Ma, crowded with Ma, swirling with Ma. Ma of the gnarled hands and frightened eyes.

Those eyes that had asked questioningly, "Mavis, why do they treat me so? Please, Mavis, why do they treat me so?"

And Mavis had known the answer and had felt the anger well up inside her, till her mouth felt hot and raw. And she had spat out at the Old Woman, "Because you're colored! You're colored, Ma, but you gave birth to white children. It's your fault, Ma, all your fault . . . You gave birth to white children. White children, Ma, white children!"

Mavis felt dimly aware that the room was overcrowded, overbearingly overcrowded, hot, stuffy, crammed, overflowing. And of course, Ma. Squeezed in. Occupying a tiny place in the center. Right in the center. Pride of place in a coffin of pinewood which bore the economical legend,

Maria Loupser
1889–1961
R.I.P.

Rest in Peace. With people crowding around and sharing seats
and filling the doorway. And Ma had been that Maria Loupser
who must now rest in peace. Maria Loupser. Maria Wilhemina
Loupser. Mavis looked up quickly, to see if the plaque was
really there, then automatically shifted her gaze to her broken
nail. No one noticed her self-absorption, and the singing continued uninterruptedly:

> Other refuge have I none,
> Hangs my helpless soul on Thee . . .

Flowers. Hot, oppressive smell of flowers. Flowers, death, and
the people singing. A florid, red-faced man in the doorway singing so that his veins stood out purple against the temples. People
bustling in and out. Fussily. Coming to have a look at Ma. A
last look at Ma. To put a flower in the coffin for Ma. Then opening hymnbooks and singing a dirge for Ma. Poor deceived Ma
of the tragic eyes and twisted hands who had given birth to
white children, and Mavis. Now they raised their voices and
sang for Ma.

> Leave, ah leave me not alone,
> Still support and comfort me . . .

And it had been only a month earlier when Mavis had looked
into those bewildered eyes.

"Mavis, why do they treat me so?"

And Mavis had become angry so that her saliva had turned
hot in her mouth.

"Please, Mavis, why do they treat me so?"

And then she had driven the words into the Old Woman with
a skewer.

"Because you are old and black, and your children want you
out of the way."

And yet what Mavis wanted to add was: "They want me out
of the way too, Ma, because you made me black like you. I am
also your child, Ma. I belong to you. They want me also to stay
in the kitchen and use the back door. We must not be seen, Ma,
their friends must not see us. We embarrass them, Ma, so they
hate us. They hate us because we're black. You and me, Ma."

But she had not said so, and had only stared cruelly into the eyes of the Old Woman.

"You're no longer useful, Ma. You're a nuisance, a bloody nuisance, a bloody black nuisance. You might come out of your kitchen and shock the white scum they bring here. You're a bloody nuisance, Ma!"

But still the Old Woman could not understand, and looked helplessly at Mavis.

"But I don't want to go in the dining room. It's true, Mavis, I don't want to go in the dining room." And as she spoke the tears flooded her eyes and she whimpered like a child who had lost a toy. "It's my dining room, Mavis, it's true. It's my dining room."

And Mavis had felt a dark and hideous pleasure overwhelming her so that she screamed hysterically at the Old Woman, "You're black and your bloody children are white. Jim and Rosie and Sonny are white, white, white! And you made me. You made me black!"

Then Mavis had broken down exhausted from her self-revelation and had cried like a baby.

"Ma, why did you make me black?"

And then only had a vague understanding strayed into those milky eyes, and Ma had taken her youngest into her arms and rocked and soothed her. And crooned to her in a cracked, broken voice the songs she had sung years before she had come to Cape Town.

> Slaap, my kindjie, slaap sag,
> Onder engele vannag . . .

And the voice of the Old Woman had become stronger and more perceptive as her dull eyes saw her childhood, and the stream running through Wolfgat, and the broken-down church, and the moon rising in the direction of Solitaire.

And Ma had understood and rocked Mavis in her arms like years before. And now Ma was back in the dining room as shadows crept across the wall.

> Abide with me, fast falls the eventide . . .

Shadows creeping across the room. Shadows gray and deep. As deep as Ma's ignorance.

The darkness deepens; Lord, with me abide . . .

Shadows filtering through the drawn blind. Rosie tight-lipped and officious. Sonny. Jim who had left his white wife at home. Pointedly ignoring Mavis; speaking in hushed tones to the florid man in the doorway. Mavis, a small inconspicuous brown figure in the corner. The only other brown face in the crowded dining room besides Ma. Even the Old Woman was paler in death. Ma's friends in the kitchen. A huddled, frightened group around the stove.

"Mavis, why do they tell my friends not to visit me?"

And Mavis had shrugged her shoulders indifferently.

"Please, Mavis, why do they tell my friends not to visit me?"

And Mavis had turned on her. "Do you want Soufie with her black skin to sit in the dining room? Or Ou Kaar with his *kroeskop**? Or Eva or Leuntjie? Do you? Do you want Sonny's wife to see them? Or the white dirt Rosie picks up? Do you want to shame your children? Humiliate them? Expose their black blood?"

And the Old Woman had blubbered, "I only want my friends to visit me. They can sit in the kitchen."

And Mavis had sighed helplessly at the simplicity of the doddering Old Woman and had felt like saying, "And what of my friends, my colored friends? Must they also sit in the kitchen?"

And tears had shot into those milky eyes and the mother had looked even older. "Mavis, I want my friends to visit me, even if they sit in the kitchen. Please, Mavis, they're all I've got."

And now Ma's friends sat in the kitchen, a cowed, timid group round the fire, speaking the raw guttural Afrikaans of the Caledon District. They spoke of Ma and their childhood together. Ou Kaar and Leuntjie and Eva and Ma. Of the Caledon District, cut off from bustling Cape Town. Where the Moravian Mission Church was crumbling, and the sweet water ran past Wolfgat, and past Karwyderskraal, and lost itself near Grootkop. And the

---

* Curly headed, tufted hair.

moon rose rich and yellow from the hills behind Solitaire. And now they sat frightened and huddled around the stove, speaking of Ma. Tant Soufie in a new head scarf—*kopdoek*—and Ou Kaar conspicuous in borrowed yellow shoes, sizes too small. And Leuntjie and Eva.

And in the dining room sat Dadda's relations, singing. Dadda's friends who had ignored Ma while she had lived. Dadda's white friends and relations, and a glossy-eyed Mavis, a Mavis who scratched meaninglessly at her broken thumbnail. And now the singing rose in volume as still more people filed in.

> When other helpers fail and comforts flee,
> Help of the helpless, O abide with me . . .

they sang to the dead woman.

Mavis could have helped Ma, could have given the understanding she needed, could have protected Ma, have tried to stop the petty tyranny. But she had never tried to reason with them. Rosie, Sonny, and Jim. She had never pleaded with them, explained to them that the Old Woman was dying. Her own soul ate her up. Gnawed her inside. She was afraid of their reactions should they notice her. Preferred to play a shadow, seen but never heard. A vague entity, part of the furniture. If only they could somehow be aware of her emotions. The feelings bottled up inside her, the bubbling volcano below. She was afraid they might openly say, "Why don't you both clear out and leave us in peace, you bloody black bastards?" She could then have cleared out, should then have cleared out, sought a room in Woodstock or Salt River and forgotten her frustration. But there was Ma. There was the Old Woman. Mavis had never spoken to them, but had vented her spleen on her helpless mother.

"You sent them to a white school. You were proud of your white brats and hated me, didn't you?"

And the mother had stared with oxlike dumbness.

"You encouraged them to bring their friends to the house, to your house, and told me to stay in the kitchen. And you had a black skin yourself. You hated me, Ma, hated me! And now they've pushed you into the kitchen. There's no one to blame but you. You're the cause of all this."

And she had tormented the Old Woman who could not re-
taliate. Who could not understand. Now she sat tortured with
memories as they sang hymns for Ma.

The room assumed a sepulchral atmosphere. Shadows deepen-
ing, gray then darker. Tears, flowers, handkerchiefs, and, dominat-
ing everything, the simple, bewildered eyes of Ma, bewildered
even in death. So Mavis had covered them with two pennies, that
others might not see.

I need Thy presence every passing hour . . .

sang Dadda's eldest brother, who sat with eyes tightly shut
near the head of the coffin. He had bitterly resented Dadda's
marriage to a colored woman. Living in sin! A Loupser married
to a Hottentot! He had boasted of his refusal to greet Ma socially
while she lived, and he attended the funeral only because his
brother's wife had died. This was the second time he had been
in the dining room. The first time was Dadda's funeral. And
now this. A colored girl, his niece he believed, sitting completely
out of place and saying nothing. Annoying, most annoying.

What but Thy Grace can foil the tempter's power . . .

sang the boy in the Eton collar, whose mother had not quite
recovered from the shock that Mr. Loupser had had a colored
wife. All sang except Mavis, torturing herself with memories.

"I am going to die, Mavis," those milky eyes had told her a
week before, "I think I am going to die."

"Ask your white brats to bury you. You slaved for them."

"They are my children but they do not treat me right."

"Do you know why? Shall I tell you why?" And she had
driven home every word with an ugly ferocity. "Because they're
ashamed of you. Afraid of you, afraid the world might know of
their colored mother."

"But I did my best for them!"

"You did more than your best, you encouraged them, but you
were ashamed of me, weren't you? So now we share a room at
the back where we can't be seen. And you are going to die, and
your white children will thank God that you're out of the way."

"They are your brothers and sisters, Mavis."

"What's that you're saying?" Mavis gasped, amazed at the hypocrisy. "What's that? I hate them and I hate you. I hate you!"

And the Old Woman had whispered, "But you are my children, you are all my children. Please, Mavis, don't let me die so."

"You will die in the back room and will be buried from the kitchen."

"It's a sin, Mavis, it's a sin!"

But they had not buried her from the kitchen. They had removed the table from the dining room and had borrowed chairs from the neighbors. And now while they waited for the priest from Dadda's church, they sang hymns.

Heaven's morning breaks, and earth's vain shadows flee . . .

sang the boy in the Eton collar.

In life, in death, O Lord, abide with me.

The florid man sang loudly to end the verse. There was an expectant bustle at the door, and then the priest from Dadda's church, St. John the Divine, appeared. All now crowded into the dining room, those who were making wreaths, and Tant Soufie holding Ou Kaar's trembling hand.

"Please, Mavis, ask Father Josephs at the Mission to bury me."

"Ask your brats to fetch him themselves. See them ask a black man to bury you!"

"Please, Mavis, see that Father Josephs buries me!"

"It's not my business, you fool! You did nothing for me!"

"I am your mother, my girl," the Old Woman had sobbed, "I raised you."

"Yes, you raised me, and you taught me my place! You took me to the Mission with you, because we are too black to go to St. John's. Let them see Father Josephs for a change. Let them enter our Mission and see our God."

And Ma had not understood but whimpered, "Please, Mavis, let Father Josephs bury me."

So now the priest from Dadda's church stood at the head of

her coffin, sharp and thin, clutching his cassock with his left hand, while his right held an open prayerbook.

> I said I will take heed to my ways:
> that I offend not in my tongue.
> I will keep my mouth as it were with
> a bridle: while the ungodly is in my sight.

Mavis felt the cruel irony of the words.

> I held my tongue and spake nothing.
> I kept silent, yea even from good words
> but it was pain and grief to me . . .

The fat lady stroked her son's head and sniffed loudly.

> My heart was hot within me, and while I
> was thus musing the fire kindled, and at
> the last I spake with my tongue . . .

Mavis now stared entranced at her broken thumbnail. The words seared and, filling, dominated the room.

It was true. Rosie had consulted her about going to the Mission and asking for Father Josephs, but she had turned on her heel without a word and walked out into the streets, and walked and walked. Through the cobbled streets of older Cape Town, up beyond the Mosque in the Malay Quarter on the slopes of Signal Hill. Thinking of the dead woman in the room.

A mother married to a white man and dying in a back room. Walking the streets, the Old Woman with her, followed by the Old Woman's eyes. Eating out her soul. Let them go to the Mission and see our God. Meet Father Josephs. But they had gone for Dadda's priest who now prayed at the coffin of a broken colored woman. And the back room was empty.

"I heard a voice from heaven, Saying unto me, Write, From henceforth blessed are the dead which die in the Lord: Even so saith the Spirit; for they rest from their labors . . .

"Lord take Thy servant, Maria Wilhemina Loupser, into Thy eternal care. Grant her Thy eternal peace and understanding. Thou art our refuge and our rock. Look kindly upon her children who even in this time of trial and suffering look up to Thee for solace. Send Thy eternal blessing upon them, for they have heeded Thy commandment which is Honor thy father and thy mother, that thy days may be long. . . ."

Mavis felt hot, strangely, unbearably hot. Her saliva turned to white heat in her mouth and her head rolled drunkenly. The room was filled with her mother's presence, her mother's eyes, body, soul. Flowing into her, filling every pore, becoming one with her, becoming a living condemnation.

"Misbelievers!" she screeched hoarsely. "Liars! You killed me! You murdered me! Don't you know your God?"

South Africa

MRS. PLUM

EZEKIEL MPHALELE

MY MADAM'S NAME was Mrs. Plum. She loved dogs and Africans and said that everyone must follow the law even if it hurt. These were three big things in Madam's life.

I came to work for Mrs. Plum in Greenside, not very far from the center of Johannesburg, after leaving two white families. The first white people I worked for as a cook and laundry woman were a man and his wife in Parktown North. They drank too much and always forgot to pay me. After five months I said to myself No. I am going to leave these drunks. So that was it. That day I was as angry as a red-hot iron when it meets water. The second house I cooked and washed for had five children who were badly brought up. This was in Belgravia. Many times they called me You Black Girl and I kept quiet. Because their mother heard them and said nothing. Also I was only new from Phokeng my home, far away near Rustenburg, I wanted to learn and know the white people before I knew how far to go with the others I would work for afterwards. The thing that drove me mad and made me pack and go was a man who came to visit them often. They said he was a cousin or something like that. He came to the kitchen many times and tried to make me laugh. He patted me on the buttocks. I told the master. The man did it again and I asked the madam that very day to give me my money and let me go.

These were the first nine months after I had left Phokeng to work in Johannesburg. There were many of us girls and young women from Phokeng, from Zeerust, from Shuping, from Kosten, and many other places who came to work in the cities. So the suburbs were full of blackness. Most of us had already passed Standard VI and so we learned more English where we worked.

None of us likes to work for white farmers, because we know too much about them on the farms near our homes. They do not pay well and they are cruel people.

At Easter time so many of us went home for a long weekend to see our people and to eat chicken and sour milk and *morogo* —wild spinach. We also took home sugar and condensed milk and tea and coffee and sweets and custard powder and tinned foods.

It was a home-girl of mine, Chimane, who called me to take a job in Mrs. Plum's house, just next door to where she worked. This is the third year now. I have been quite happy with Mrs. Plum and her daughter Kate. By this I mean that my place as a servant in Greenside is not as bad as that of many others. Chimane too does not complain much. We are paid six pounds a month with free food and free servant's room. No one can ever say that they are well paid, so we go on complaining somehow. Whenever we meet on Thursday afternoons, which is time off for all of us black women in the suburbs, we talk and talk and talk: about our people at home and their letters; about their illnesses; about bad crops; about a sister who wanted a school uniform and books and school fees; about some of our madams and masters who are good, or stingy with money or food, or stupid or full of nonsense, or who kill themselves and each other, or who are dirty—and so many things I cannot count them all.

Thursday afternoons we go to town to look at the shops, to attend a women's club, to see our boy friends, to go to a movie theater some of us. We turn up smart, to show others the clothes we bought from the black men who sell dry goods to servants in the suburbs. We take a number of things and they come round every month for a bit of money until we finish paying. Then we dress the way of many white madams and girls. I think we look really smart. Sometimes we catch the eyes of a white woman looking at us and we laugh and laugh and laugh until we nearly drop on the ground because we feel good inside ourselves.

What did the girl next door call you? Mrs. Plum asked me the first day I came to her. Jane, I replied. Was there not an

African name? I said yes, Karabo. All right, Madam said. We'll call you Karabo, she said. She spoke as if she knew a name is a big thing. I knew so many whites who did not care what they called black people as long as it was all right for their tongue. This pleased me, I mean Mrs. Plum's use of *Karabo*; because the only time I heard the name was when I was at home or when my friends spoke to me. Then she showed me what to do: meals, meal times, washing, and where all the things were that I was going to use.

My daughter will be here in the evening, Madam said. She is at school. When the daughter came, she added, she would tell me some of the things she wanted me to do for her every day.

Chimane, my friend next door, had told me about the daughter Kate, how wild she seemed to be, and about Mr. Plum who had killed himself with a gun in a house down the street. They had left the house and come to this one.

Madam is a tall woman. Not slender, not fat. She moves slowly, and speaks slowly. Her face looks very wise, her forehead seems to tell me she has a strong liver: she is not afraid of anything. Her eyes are always swollen at the lower eyelids like a white person who has not slept for many many nights or like a large frog. Perhaps it is because she smokes too much, like wet wood that will not know whether to go up in flames or stop burning. She looks me straight in the eyes when she talks to me, and I know she does this with other people too. At first this made me fear her, now I am used to her. She is not a lazy woman, and she does many things outside, in the city and in the suburbs.

This was the first thing her daughter Kate told me when she came and we met. Don't mind mother, Kate told me. She said, She is sometimes mad with people for very small things. She will soon be all right and speak nicely to you again.

Kate, I like her very much, and she likes me too. She tells me many things a white woman does not tell a black servant. I mean things about what she likes and does not like, what her mother does or does not do, all these. At first I was unhappy and wanted to stop her, but now I do not mind.

Kate looks very much like her mother in the face. I think her shoulders will be just as round and strong-looking. She moves faster than Madam. I asked her why she was still at school when she was so big. She laughed. Then she tried to tell me that the school where she was was for big people, who had finished with lower school. She was learning big things about cooking and food. She can explain better, me I cannot. She came home on weekends.

Since I came to work for Mrs. Plum Kate has been teaching me plenty of cooking. I first learned from her and Madam the word *recipes*. When Kate was at the big school, Madam taught me how to read cook books. I went on very slowly at first, slower than an ox wagon. Now I know more. When Kate came home, she found I had read the recipe she left me. So we just cooked straightaway. Kate thinks I am fit to cook in a hotel. Madam thinks so too. Never never! I thought. Cooking in a hotel is like feeding oxen. No one can say thank you to you. After a few months I could cook the Sunday lunch and later I could cook specials for Madam's or Kate's guests.

Madam did not only teach me cooking. She taught me how to look after guests. She praised me when I did very very well; not like the white people I had worked for before. I do not know what runs crooked in the heads of other people. Madam also had classes in the evenings for servants to teach them how to read and write. She and two other women in Greenside taught in a church hall.

As I say, Kate tells me plenty of things about Madam. She says to me she says, My mother goes to meetings many times. I ask her I say, What for? She says to me she says, For your people. I ask her I say, My people are in Phokeng far away. They have got mouths, I say. Why does she want to say something for them? Does she know what my mother and what my father want to say? They can speak when they want to. Kate raises her shoulders and drops them and says, How can I tell you Karabo? I don't say your people—your family only. I mean all the black people in this country. I say, Oh! What do the black people want to say? Again she raises her shoulders and drops them, taking a deep breath.

I ask her I say, With whom is she in the meeting?

She says, With other people who think like her.

I ask her I say, Do you say there are people in the world who think the same things?

She nods her head.

I ask, What things?

So that a few of your people should one day be among those who rule this country, get more money for what they do for the white man, and—what did Kate say again? Yes, that Madam and those who think like her also wanted my people who have been to school to choose those who must speak for them in the—I think she said it looks like a *Kgotla* at home—who rule the villages.

I say to Kate I say, Oh I see now. I say, Tell me Kate why is madam always writing on the machine, all the time everyday nearly?

She replies she says, Oh my mother is writing books.

I ask, You mean a book like those?—pointing at the books on the shelves.

Yes, Kate says.

And she told me how Madam wrote books and other things for newspapers and she wrote for the newspapers and magazines to say things for the black people who should be treated well, be paid more money, for the black people who can read and write many things to choose those who want to speak for them.

Kate also told me she said, My mother and other women who think like her put on black belts over their shoulders when they are sad and they want to show the white government they do not like the things being done by whites to blacks. My mother and the others go and stand where the people in government are going to enter or go out of a building.

I ask her I say, Does the government and the white people listen and stop their sins? She says, No. But my mother is in another group of white people.

I ask, Do the people of the government give the women tea and cakes? Kate says, Karabo! How stupid; oh!

I say to her I say, Among my people if someone comes and stands in front of my house I tell him to come in and I give him food. You white people are wonderful. But they keep standing there and the government people do not give them anything.

She replies, You mean strange. How many times have I taught you not to say *wonderful* when you mean *strange*! Well, Kate says with a short heart and looking cross and she shouts, Well they do not stand there the whole day to ask for tea and cakes stupid. Oh dear!

Always when Madam finished to read her newspapers she gave them to me to read to help me speak and write better English. When I had read she asked me to tell her some of the things in it. In this way, I did better and better and my mind was opening and opening and I was learning and learning many things about the black people inside and outside the towns which I did not know in the least. When I found words that were too difficult or I did not understand some of the things I asked Madam. She always told me You see this, you see that, eh? with a heart that can carry on a long way. Yes, Madam writes many letters to the papers. She is always sore about the way the white police beat up black people; about the way black people who work for whites are made to sit at the Zoo Lake with their hearts hanging, because the white people say our people are making noise on Sunday afternoon when they want to rest in their houses and gardens; about many ugly things that happen when some white people meet black man on the pavement or street. So Madam writes to the papers to let others know, to ask the government to be kind to us.

In the first year Mrs. Plum wanted me to eat at table with her. It was very hard, one because I was not used to eating at table with a fork and knife, two because I heard of no other kitchen worker who was handled like this. I was afraid. Afraid of everybody, of Madam's guests if they found me doing this. Madam said I must not be silly. I must show that African servants can also eat at table. Number three, I could not eat some of the things I loved very much: mealie-meal porridge with sour milk or *morogo*, stamped mealies mixed with butter beans, sour porridge for breakfast and other things. Also, except for morning porridge, our food is nice when you eat with the hand. So nice that it does not stop in the mouth or the throat to greet anyone before it passes smoothly down.

We often had lunch together with Chimane next door and our

garden boy—Ha! I must remember never to say *boy* again when
I talk about a man. This makes me think of a day during the
first few weeks in Mrs. Plum's house. I was talking about Dick
her garden man and I said "garden boy." And she says to me she
says Stop talking about a "boy," Karabo. Now listen here, she
says, You Africans must learn to speak properly about each other.
And she says, White people won't talk kindly about you if you
look down upon each other.

I say to her I say, Madam, I learned the word from the white
people I worked for, and all the kitchen maids say "boy."

She replies she says to me, Those are white people who know
nothing, just low-class whites. I say to her I say I thought white
people know everything.

She said, You'll learn my girl and you must start in this
house, hear? She left me there thinking, my mind mixed up.

I learned. I grew up.

If any woman or girl does not know the Black Crow Club
in Bree Street, she does not know anything. I think nearly everything takes place inside and outside that house. It is just where
the dirty part of the city begins, with factories and the market.
After the market is the place where Indians and colored people
live. It is also at the Black Crow that the buses turn round and
back to the black townships. Noise, noise, noise all the time.
There are woman who sell hot sweet potatoes and fruit and monkey nuts and boiled eggs in the winter, boiled mealies and the
other things in the summer, all these on the pavements. The
streets are always full of potato and fruit skins and monkey nut
shells. There is always a strong smell of roast pork. I think
it is because of Piel's cold storage down Bree Street.

Madam said she knew the black people who work in the Black
Crow. She was happy that I was spending my afternoon on
Thursdays in such a club. You will learn sewing, knitting, she
said, and other things that you like. Do you like to dance? I
told her I said, Yes, I want to learn. She paid the two shillings
fee for me each month.

We waited on the first floor, we the ones who were learning
sewing; waiting for the teacher. We talked and laughed about

madams and masters, and their children and their dogs and
birds and whispered about our boy friends.

Sies! My madam you do not know—*mojuta od'nete*—a real
miser . . .

Jo—jo—jo! you should see our new dog. A big thing like
this. People! Big in a foolish way . . .

What! Me, I take a master's bitch by the leg, me, and throw
it away so that it keeps howling, tjwe—tjwe! ngo—wu ngo—
wu! I don't play about with them, me . . .

Shame, poor thing! God sees you, true!

They wanted me to take their dog out for a walk every afternoon and I told them I said It is not my work in other houses the
garden man does it. I just said to myself I said they can go to
the chickens. Let them bite their elbow before I take out a dog,
I am not so mad yet . . .

Hei! It is not like the child of my white people who keeps
a big white rat and you know what? He puts it on his bed when
he goes to school. And let the blankets just begin to smell of
urine and all the nonsense and they tell me to wash them. Hei,
people!

Did you hear about Rebone, people? Her madam put her out,
because her master was always tapping her buttocks with his
fingers. And yesterday the madam saw the master press Rebone
against himself . . .

Jo—jo—jo! people!

Dirty white man!

No, not dirty. The madam smells too old for him.

Hei! Go and wash your mouth with soap, this girl's mouth is
dirty . . .

Jo, Rebone, daughter of the people! We must help her to
find a job before she thinks of going back home.

The teacher came. A woman with strong legs, a strong face,
and kind eyes. She had short hair and dressed in a simple but
lovely floral frock. She stood well on her legs and hips. She had
a black mark between the two top front teeth. She smiled as if
we were her children. Our group began with games, and then
Lilian Ngoyi took us for sewing. After this she gave a brief
talk to all of us from the different classes.

I can never forget the things this woman said and how she put them to us. She told us that the time had passed for black girls and women in the suburbs to be satisfied with working, sending money to our people and going to see them once a year. We were to learn, she said, that the world would never be safe for black people until they were in the government with the power to make laws. The power should be given by the Africans who were more than the whites.

We asked her questions and she answered them with wisdom. I shall put some of them down in my own words as I remember them.

Shall we take the place of the white people in the government?

Some yes. But we shall be more than they as we are more in the country. But also the people of all colors will come together and there are good white men we can choose and there are Africans some white people will choose to be in the government.

There are good madams and masters and bad ones. Should we take the good ones for friends?

A master and a servant can never be friends. Never, so put that out of your head, will you! You are not even sure if the ones you say are good are not like that because they cannot breathe or live without the work of your hands. As long as you need their money, face them with respect. But you must know that many sad things are happening in our country and you, all of you, must always be learning, adding to what you already know, and obey us when we ask you to help us.

At other times Lilian Ngoyi told us she said, Remember your poor people at home and the way in which the whites are moving them from place to place like sheep and cattle. And at other times again she told us she said, Remember that a hand cannot wash itself, it needs another to do it.

I always thought of Madam when Lilian Ngoyi spoke. I asked myself, What would she say if she knew that I was listening to such words? Words like: A white man is looked after by his black nanny and his mother when he is a baby. When he grows up the white government looks after him, sends him to school, makes it impossible for him to suffer from the great hunger, keeps a job ready and open for him as soon as he wants to leave

school. Now Lilian Ngoyi asked she said, How many white
people can be born in a white hospital, grow up in white streets,
be clothed in lovely cotton, lie on white cushions; how many
whites can live all their lives in a fenced place away from people
of other colors and then, as men and women learn quickly the
correct ways of thinking, learn quickly to ask questions in their
minds, big questions that will throw over all the nice things of a
white man's life? How many? Very very few! For those whites
who have not begun to ask, it is too late. For those who have
begun and are joining us with both feet in our house, we can
only say Welcome!

I was learning. I was growing up. Every time I thought of
Madam, she became more and more like a dark forest which
one fears to enter, and which one will never know. But there
were several times when I thought, This woman is easy to
understand, she is like all other white women.

What else are they teaching you at the Black Crow, Karabo?

I tell her I say, nothing, Madam. I ask her I say Why does
Madam ask?

You are changing.

What does Madam mean?

Well, you are changing.

But we are always changing Madam.

And she left me standing in the kitchen. This was a few days
after I had told her that I did not want to read more than one
white paper a day. The only magazines I wanted to read, I said
to her, were those from overseas, if she had them. I told her that
white papers had pictures of white people most of the time.
They talked mostly about white people and their gardens, dogs,
weddings and parties. I asked her if she could buy me a Sunday
paper that spoke about my people. Madam bought it for me. I
did not think she would do it.

There were mornings when, after hanging the white people's
washing on the line Chimane and I stole a little time to stand
at the fence and talk. We always stood where we could be
hidden by our rooms.

Hei, Karabo, you know what? That was Chimane.

No—what? Before you start, tell me, has Timi come back to
you?

Ach, I do not care. He is still angry. But boys are fools they always come back dragging themselves on their empty bellies. Hei, you know what?

Yes?

The Thursday past I saw Moruti K.K. I laughed until I dropped on the ground. He is standing in front of the Black Crow. I believe his big stomach was crying from hunger. Now he has a small dog in his armpit, and is standing before a woman selling boiled eggs and—hei, home-girl!—tripe and intestines are boiling in a pot—oh, the smell! you could fill a hungry belly with it, the way it was good. I think Moruti K.K. is waiting for the woman to buy a boiled egg. I do not know what the woman was still doing. I am standing nearby. The dog keeps wriggling and pushing out its nose, looking at the boiling tripe. Moruti keeps patting it with his free hand, not so? Again the dog wants to spill out of Moruti's hand and it gives a few sounds through the nose. Hei man, home-girl! One two three the dog spills out to catch some of the good meat! It misses falling into the hot gravy in which the tripe is swimming I do not know how. Moruti K.K. tries to chase it. It has tumbled onto the women's eggs and potatoes and all are in the dust. She stands up and goes after K.K. She is shouting to him to pay, not so? Where am I at that time? I am nearly dead with laughter the tears are coming down so far.

I was myself holding tight on the fence so as not to fall through laughing. I held my stomach to keep back a pain in the side.

I ask her I say, Did Moruti K.K. come back to pay for the wasted food?

Yes, he paid.

The dog?

He caught it. That is a good African dog. A dog must look for its own food when it is not time for meals. Not these stupid spoiled angels the whites keep giving tea and biscuits.

Hmm.

Dick our garden man joined us, as he often did. When the story was repeated to him the man nearly rolled on the ground laughing.

He asks who is Reverend K.K.?

I say he is the owner of the Black Crow.

Oh!

We reminded each other, Chimane and I, of the round minister. He would come into the club, look at us with a smooth smile on his smooth round face. He would look at each one of us, with that smile on all the time, as if he had forgotten that it was there. Perhaps he had, because as he looked at us, almost stripping us naked with his watery shining eyes—funny—he could have been a farmer looking at his ripe corn, thinking many things.

K.K. often spoke without shame about what he called ripe girls—*matjitjana*—with good firm breasts. He said such girls were pure without any nonsense in their heads and bodies. Everybody talked a great deal about him and what they thought he must be doing in his office whenever he called in so-and-so.

The Reverend K.K. did not belong to any church. He baptized, married, and buried people for a fee, who had no church to do such things for them. They said he had been driven out of the Presbyterian Church. He had formed his own, but it did not go far. Then he later came and opened the Black Crow. He knew just how far to go with Lilian Ngoyi. She said although she used his club to teach us things that would help us in life, she could not go on if he was doing any wicked things with the girls in his office. Moruti K.K. feared her, and kept his place.

When I began to tell my story I thought I was going to tell you mostly about Mrs. Plum's two dogs. But I have been talking about people. I think Dick is right when he says What is a dog! And there are so many dogs cats and parrots in Greenside and other places that Mrs. Plum's dogs do not look special. But there was something special in the dog business in Madam's house. The way in which she loved them, maybe.

Monty is a tiny animal with long hair and small black eyes and a face nearly like that of an old woman. The other, Malan, is a bit bigger, with brown and white colors. It has small hair and looks naked by the side of the friend. They sleep in two separate baskets which stay in Madam's bedroom. They are to be washed often and brushed and sprayed and they sleep on pink linen. Monty has a pink ribbon which stays on his neck most of the time. They both carry a cover on their backs. They make me fed up when I see them in their baskets, looking fat, and as if they knew all that was going on everywhere.

It was Dick's work to look after Monty and Malan, to feed them, and to do everything for them. He did this together with garden work and cleaning of the house. He came at the beginning of this year. He just came, as if from nowhere, and Madam gave him the job as she had chased away two before him, she told me. In both those cases, she said that they could not look after Monty and Malan.

Dick had a long heart, even although he told me and Chimane that European dogs were stupid, spoiled. He said One day those white people will put earrings and toe rings and bangles on their dogs. That would be the day he would leave Mrs. Plum. For, he said, he was sure that she would want him to polish the rings and bangles with Brasso.

Although he had a long heart, Madam was still not sure of him. She often went to the dogs after a meal or after a cleaning and said to them Did Dick give you food sweethearts? Or, Did Dick wash you sweethearts? Let me see. And I could see that Dick was blowing up like a balloon with anger. These things called white people! he said to me. Talking to dogs!

I say to him I say, People talk to oxen at home do I not say so?

Yes, he says, but at home do you not know that a man speaks to an ox because he wants to make it pull the plough or the wagon or to stop or to stand still for a person to harnass it. No one simply goes to an ox looking at him with eyes far apart and speaks to it. Let me ask you, do you ever see a person where we come from take a cow and press it to his stomach or his cheek? Tell me!

And I say to Dick I say, We were talking about an ox, not a cow.

He laughed with his broad mouth until tears came out of his eyes. At a certain point I laughed aloud too.

One day when you have time, Dick says to me, he says, you

should look into Madam's bedroom when she has put a notice outside her door.

Dick, what are you saying? I ask.

I do not talk, me. I know deep inside me.

Dick was about our age, I and Chimane. So we always said *moshiman'o* when we spoke about his tricks. Because he was not too big to be a boy to us. He also said to us, *Hei, lona banyana kelona* —Hey you girls, you! His large mouth always seemed to be making ready to laugh. I think Madam did not like this. Many times she would say What is there to make you laugh here? Or in the garden she would say This is a flower and when it wants water that is not funny! Or again, If you did more work and stopped trying to water my plants with your smile you would be more useful. Even when Dick did not mean to smile. What Madam did not get tired of saying was, If I left you to look after my dogs without anyone to look after you at the same time you would drown the poor things.

Dick smiled at Mrs. Plum. Dick hurt Mrs. Plum's dogs? Then cows can fly. He was really—really afraid of white people, Dick. I think he tried very hard not to feel afraid. For he was always showing me and Chimane in private how Mrs. Plum walked, and spoke. He took two bowls and pressed them to his chest, speaking softly to them as Madam speaks to Monty and Malan. Or he sat at Madam's table and acted the way she sits when writing. Now and again he looked back over his shoulder, pulled his face long like a horse's making as if he were looking over his glasses while telling me something to do. Then he would sit on one of the armchairs, cross his legs and act the way Madam drank her tea; he held the cup he was thinking about between his thumb and the pointing finger, only letting their nails meet. And he laughed after every act. He did these things, of course, when Madam was not home. And where was I at such times? Almost flat on my stomach, laughing.

But oh how Dick trembled when Mrs. Plum scolded him! He did his house-cleaning very well. Whatever mistake he made, it was mostly with the dogs: their linen, their food. One white man came into the house one afternoon to tell Madam that Dick had been very careless when taking the dogs out for a walk. His own dog was waiting on Madam's stoop. He repeated that he had been driving down our street, and Dick had let loose Monty and Malan to cross the street. The white man made plenty of noise about this and I think wanted to let Madam know how useful he had been. He kept on saying Just one inch, *just* one inch. It was lucky I put on my brakes quick enough . . . But your boy kept on smiling—Why? Strange. My boy would only do it twice and only twice and then . . . ! His pass. The man moved his hand like one writing, to mean that he would sign his servant's pass for him to go and never come back. When he left, the white man said Come on Rusty, the boy is waiting to clean you. Dogs with names, men without, I thought.

Madam climbed on top of Dick for this, as we say.

Once one of the dogs, I don't know which—Malan or Monty —took my stocking—brandnew, you hear—and tore it with its teeth and paws. When I told Madam about it, my anger as high as my throat, she gave me money to buy another pair. It happened again. This time she said she was not going to give me money because I must also keep my stockings where the two gentlemen would not reach them. Mrs. Plum did not want us ever to say *Voetsek* when we wanted the dogs to go away. Me I said this when they came sniffing at my legs or fingers. I hate it.

In my third year in Mrs. Plum's house, many things happened, most of them all bad for her. There was trouble with Kate; Chimane had big trouble; my heart was twisted by two loves; and Monty and Malan became real dogs for a few days.

Madam had a number of suppers and parties. She invited Africans to some of them. Kate told me the reasons for some of the parties. Like her mother's books when finished, a visitor from across the seas and so on. I did not like the black people who came here to drink and eat. They spoke such difficult English like people who were full of all the books in the world. They looked at me as if I were right down there whom they thought little of—me, a black person like them.

One day I heard Kate speak to her mother. She says I don't know why you ask so many Africans to the house. A few will do at a time. She said something about the government which

I could not hear well. Madam replies she says to her You know some of them do not meet white people often, so far away in their dark houses. And she says to Kate that they do not come because they want her as a friend but they just want a drink for nothing.

I simply felt that I could not be the servant of white people and of blacks at the same time. At my home or in my room I could serve them without a feeling of shame. And now, if they were only coming to drink!

But one of the black men and his sister always came to the kitchen to talk to me. I must have looked unfriendly the first time, for Kate talked to me about it afterwards as she was in the kitchen when they came. I know that at that time I was not easy at all. I was ashamed and I felt that a white person's house was not the place for me to look happy in front of other black people while the white man looked on.

Another time it was easier. The man was alone. I shall never forget that night, as long as I live. He spoke kind words and I felt my heart grow big inside me. It caused me to tremble. There were several other visits. I knew that I loved him, I could never know what he really thought of me, I mean as a woman and he as a man. But I loved him, and I still think of him with a sore heart. Slowly I came to know the pain of it. Because he was a doctor and so full of knowledge and English I could not reach him. So I knew he could not stoop down to see me as someone who wanted him to love me.

Kate turned very wild. Mrs. Plum was very much worried. Suddenly it looked as if she were a new person, with new ways and new everything. I do not know what was wrong or right. She began to play the big gramophone aloud, as if the music were for the whole of Greenside. The music was wild and she twisted her waist all the time, with her mouth half-open. She did the same things in her room. She left the big school and every Saturday night now she went out. When I looked at her face, there was something deep and wild there on it, and when I thought she looked young she looked old, and when I thought she looked old she was young. We were both twenty-two years of age. I think that I could see the reason why her mother was so worried, why she was suffering.

Worse was to come.

They were now openly screaming at each other. They began in the sitting room and went upstairs together, speaking fast hot biting words, some of which I did not grasp. One day Madam comes to me and says You know Kate loves an African, you know the doctor who comes to supper here often. She says he loves her too and they will leave the country and marry outside. Tell me, Karabo, what do your people think of this kind of thing between a white woman and a black man? It *cannot* be right is it?

I reply and I say to her We have never seen it happen before where I come from.

That's right, Karabo, it is just madness.

Madam left. She looked like a hunted person.

These white women, I say to myself I say these white women, why do not they love their own men and leave us to love ours!

From that minute I knew that I would never want to speak to Kate. She appeared to me as a thief, as a fox that falls upon a flock of sheep at night. I hated her. To make it worse, he would never be allowed to come to the house again.

Whenever she was home there was silence between us. I no longer wanted to know anything about what she was doing, where or how.

I lay awake for hours on my bed. Lying like that, I seemed to feel parts of my body beat and throb inside me, the way I have seen big machines doing, pounding and pounding and pushing and pulling and pouring some water into one hole which came out at another end. I stretched myself so many times so as to feel tired and sleepy.

When I did sleep, my dreams were full of painful things.

One evening I made up my mind, after putting it off many times. I told my boy friend that I did not want him any longer. He looked hurt, and that hurt me too. He left.

The thought of the African doctor was still with me and it pained me to know that I should never see him again; unless I met him in the street on a Thursday afternoon. But he had a car. Even if I did meet him by luck, how could I make him see that I loved him? Ach, I do not believe he would even stop to think what kind of woman I am. Part of that winter was a time of longing and burning for me. I say part because there are always things to keep servants busy whose white people go to the sea for the winter.

To tell the truth, winter was the time for servants; not nannies, because they went with their madams so as to look after the children. Those like me stayed behind to look after the house and dogs. In winter so many families went away that the dogs remained the masters and madams. You could see them walk like white people in the streets. Silent but with plenty of power. And when you saw them you knew that they were full of more nonsense and fancies in the house.

There was so little work to do.

One week word was whispered round that a home-boy of ours was going to hold a party in his room on Saturday. I think we all took it for a joke. How could the man be so bold and stupid? The police were always driving about at night looking for black people; and if the whites next door heard the party noise— oho! But still, we were full of joy and wanted to go. As for Dick, he opened his big mouth and nearly fainted when he heard of it and that I was really going.

During the day on the big Saturday Kate came.

She seemed a little less wild. But I was not ready to talk to her. I was surprised to hear myself answer her when she said to me Mother says you do not like a marriage between a white girl and a black man, Karabo.

Then she was silent.

She says But I want to help him, Karabo.

I ask her I say You want to help him to do what?

To go higher and higher, to the top.

I knew I wanted to say so much that was boiling in my chest. I could not say it. I thought of Lilian Ngoyi at the Black Crow, what she said to us. But I was mixed up in my head and in my blood.

You still agree with my mother?

All I could say was I said to your mother I had never seen a black man and a white woman marrying, you hear me? What I think about it is my business.

I remembered that I wanted to iron my party dress and so I

left her. My mind was full of the party again and I was glad because Kate and the doctor would not worry my peace that day. And the next day the sun would shine for all of us, Kate or no Kate, doctor or no doctor.

The house where our home-boy worked was hidden from the main road by a number of trees. But although we asked a number of questions and counted many fingers of bad luck until we had no more hands for fingers, we put on our best pay-while-you-wear dresses and suits and clothes bought from boys who had stolen them, and went to our home-boy's party. We whispered all the way while we climbed up to the house. Someone who knew told us that the white people next door were away for the winter. Oh, so that is the thing! we said.

We poured into the garden through the back and stood in front of his room laughing quietly. He came from the big house behind us, and were we not struck dumb when he told us to go into the white people's house! Was he mad? We walked in with slow footsteps that seemed to be sniffing at the floor, not sure of anything. Soon we were standing and sitting all over on the nice warm cushions and the heaters were on. Our home-boy turned the lights low. I counted fifteen people inside. We saw how we loved one another's evening dress. The boys were smart too.

Our home-boy's girl friend Naomi was busy in the kitchen preparing food. He took out glasses and cold drinks—fruit juice, tomato juice, ginger beers, and so many other kinds of soft drink. It was just too nice. The tarts, the biscuits, the snacks, the cakes, woo, that was a party, I tell you. I think I ate more ginger cake than I had ever done in my life. Naomi had baked some of the things. Our home-boy came to me and said, I do not want the police to come here and have reason to arrest us, so I am not serving hot drinks, not even beer. There is no law that we cannot have parties, is there? So we can feel free. Our use of this house is the master's business. If I had asked him he would have thought me mad.

I say to him I say, You have a strong liver to do such a thing.
He laughed.
He played penny whistle music on gramophone records—

Miriam Makeba, Dorothy Masuka and other African singers and players. We danced and the party became more and more noisy and more happy. Hai, those girls Miriam and Dorothy, they can sing, I tell you! We ate more and laughed more and told more stories. In the middle of the party, our home-boy called us to listen to what he was going to say. Then he told us how he and a friend of his in Orlando collected money to bet on a horse for the July Handicap in Durban. They did this each year but lost. Now they had won two hundred pounds. We all clapped hands and cheered. Two hundred pounds woo!

You should go and sit at home and just eat time, I say to him. He laughs and says You have no understanding not one little bit.

To all of us he says Now my brothers and sisters enjoy yourselves. At home I should slaughter a goat for us to feast and thank our ancestors. But this is town life and we must thank them with tea and cake and all those sweet things. I know some people think I must be so bold that I could be midwife to a lion that is giving birth, but enjoy yourselves and have no fear.

Madam came back looking strong and fresh.

The very week she arrived the police had begun again to search servants' rooms. They were looking for what they called loafers and men without passes who they said were living with friends in the suburbs against the law. Our dog's meat boys became scarce because of the police. A boy who had a girl friend in the kitchens, as we say, always told his friends that he was coming for dog's meat when he meant he was visiting his girl. This was because we gave our boy friends part of the meat the white people bought for the dogs and us.

One night a white and a black policeman entered Mrs. Plum's yard. They said they had come to search. She says no, they cannot. They say Yes, they must do it. She answers no. They forced their way to the back, to Dick's room and mine. Mrs. Plum took the hose that was running in the front garden and quickly went round to the back. I cut across the floor to see what she was going to say to the men. They were talking to Dick, using dirty words. Mrs. Plum did not wait, she just pointed the hose at the two policemen. This seemed to surprise them. They turned round and she pointed it into their faces. Without their seeing me I went to the tap at the corner of the house and opened it more. I could see Dick, like me, was trying to keep down his laughter. They shouted and tried to wave the water away, but she kept the hose pointing at them, now moving it up and down. They turned and ran through the back gate, swearing the while.

That fixes them, Mrs. Plum said.

The next day the morning paper reported it.

They arrived in the afternoon—the two policemen—with another. They pointed out Mrs. Plum and she was led to the police station. They took her away to answer for stopping the police while were doing their work.

She came back and said she had paid bail.

At the magistrate's court, Madam was told that she had done a bad thing. She would have to pay a fine or else go to prison for fourteen days. She said she would go to jail to show that she felt she was not in the wrong.

Kate came and tried to tell her that she was doing something silly going to jail for a small thing like that. She tells Madam she says This is not even a thing to take to the high court. Pay the money. What is five pounds?

Madam went to jail.

She looked very sad when she came out. I thought of what Lilian Ngoyi often said to us: You must be ready to go to jail for the things you believe are true and for which you are taken by the police. What did Mrs. Plum really believe about me, Chimane, Dick and all the other black people? I asked myself. I did not know. But from all those things she was writing for the papers and all those meetings she was going to where white people talked about black people and the way they are treated by the government, from what those white women with black bands over their shoulders were doing standing where a white government man was going to pass, I said to myself I said This woman, hai, I do not know she seems to think very much of us black people. But why was she so sad?

Kate came back home to stay after this. She still played the big gramophone loud-loud-loud and twisted her body at her waist until I thought it was going to break. Then I saw a young white

man come often to see her. I watched them through the opening
near the hinges of the door between the kitchen and the sitting
room where they sat. I saw them kiss each other for a long long
time. I saw him lift up Kate's dress and her white-white legs
begin to tremble, and—oh I am afraid to say more, my heart was
beating hard. She called him Jim. I thought it was funny because
white people in the shops call black men Jim.

Kate had begun to play with Jim when I met a boy who loved
me and I loved. He was much stronger than the one I sent
away and I loved him more, much more. The face of the doctor
came to my mind often, but it did not hurt me so any more. I
stopped looking at Kate and her Jim through openings. We
spoke to each other, Kate and I, almost as freely as before but
not quite. She and her mother were friends again.

Hallo, Karabo, I heard Chimane call me one morning as I
was starching my apron. I answered. I went to the line to hang
it. I saw she was standing at the fence, so I knew she had something to tell me. I went to her.

Hallo!

Hallo, Chimane!

O kae?

Ke teng. Wena?

At that moment a woman came out through the back door of
the house where Chimane was working.

I have not seen that one before, I say, pointing with my head.

Chimane looked back. Oh, that one. Hei, daughter-of-the-
people, Hei, you have not seen miracles. You know this is
Madam's mother-in-law as you see her there. Did I never tell
you about her?

No, never.

White people, nonsense. You know what? That poor woman
is here now for two days. She has to cook for herself and I
cook for the family.

On the same stove?

Yes. She comes after me when I have finished.

She has her own food to cook?

Yes, Karabo. White people have no heart no sense.

What will eat them up if they share their food?

Ask me, just ask me. God! She clapped her hands to show that only God knew, and it was His business, not ours.

Chimane asks me she says, Have you heard from home?

I tell her I say, Oh daughter-of-the-people, more and more deaths. Something is finishing the people at home. My mother has written. She says they are all right, my father too and my sisters, except for the people who have died. Malebo, the one who lived alone in the house I showed you last year, a white house, he is gone. Then teacher Sedimo. He was very thin and looked sick all the time. He taught my sisters not me. His mother-in-law you remember I told you died last year—no, the year before. Mother says also there is a woman she does not think I remember because I last saw her when I was a small girl she passed away in Zeerust she was my mother's greatest friend when they were girls. She would have gone to her burial if it was not because she has swollen feet.

How are the feet?

She says they are still giving her trouble. I ask Chimane, How are your people at Nokaneng? They have not written?

She shook her head.

I could see from her eyes that her mind was on another thing and not her people at that moment.

Wait for me Chimane eh, forgive me, I have scones in the oven, eh! I will just take them out and come back, eh!

When I came back to her Chimane was wiping her eyes. They were wet.

Karabo, you know what?

E—e. I shook my head.

I am heavy with child.

Hau!

There was a moment of silence.

Who is it, Chimane?

Timi. He came back only to give me this.

But he loves you. What does he say have you told him?

I told him yesterday. We met in town.

I remembered I had not seen her at the Black Crow.

Are you sure, Chimane? You have missed a month?

She nodded her head.

Timi himself—he did not use the thing?

I only saw after he finished, that he had not.

Why? What does he say?

He tells me he says I should not worry I can be his wife.

Timi is a good boy, Chimane. How many of these boys with town ways who know too much will even say Yes it is my child?

Hai, Karabo, you are telling me other things now. Do you not see that I have not worked long enough for my people? If I marry now who will look after them when I am the only child?

Hmm. I hear your words. It is true. I tried to think of something soothing to say.

Then I say You can talk it over with Timi. You can go home and when your child is born you look after it for three months and when you are married you come to town to work and can put your money together to help the old people while they are looking after the child.

What shall we be eating all the time I am at home? It is not like those days gone past when we had land and our mother could go to the fields until the child was ready to arrive.

The light goes out in my mind and I cannot think of the right answer. How many times have I feared the same thing! Luck and the mercy of the gods that is all I live by. That is all we live by—all of us.

Listen, Karabo. I must be going to make tea for Madam. It will soon strike half-past ten.

I went back to the house. As Madam was not in yet, I threw myself on the divan in the sitting room. Malan came sniffing at my legs. I put my foot under its fat belly and shoved it up and away from me so that it cried tjunk—tjunk—tjunk as it went out. I say to it I say Go and tell your brother what I have done to you and tell him to try it and see what I will do. Tell your grandmother when she comes home too.

When I lifted my eyes he was standing in the kitchen door, Dick. He says to me he says Hau! now you have also begun to speak to dogs!

I did not reply. I just looked at him, his mouth ever stretched out like the mouth of a bag, and I passed to my room.

I sat on my bed and looked at my face in the mirror. Since the morning I had been feeling as if a black cloud were hanging over me, pressing on my head and shoulders. I do not know how long I sat there. Then I smelled madam. What was it? Where was she? After a few moments I knew what it was. My perfume and scent. I used the same cosmetics as Mrs. Plum's. I should have been used to it by now. But this morning—why did I smell Mrs. Plum like this? Then, without knowing why, I asked myself I said, Why have I been using the same cosmetics as Madam? I wanted to throw them all out. I stopped. And then I took all the things and threw them into the dustbin. I was going to buy other kinds on Thursday; finished!

I could not sit down. I went out and into the white people's house. I walked through and the smell of the house made me sick and seemed to fill up my throat. I went to the bathroom without knowing why. It was full of the smell of Madam. Dick was cleaning the bath. I stood at the door and looked at him cleaning the dirt out of the bath, dirt from Madam's body. Sies! I said aloud. To myself I said, Why cannot people wash the dirt of their own bodies out of the bath? Before Dick knew I was near I went out. Ach, I said again to myself, why should I think about it now when I have been doing their washing for so long and cleaned the bath many times when Dick was ill. I had held worse things from her body times without number . . .

I went out and stood midway between the house and my room, looking into the next yard. The three-legged gray cat next door came to the fence and our eyes met. I do not know how long we stood like that looking at each other. I was thinking, Why don't you go and look at your grandmother like that? when it turned away and mewed hopping on the three legs. Just like someone who feels pity for you.

In my room I looked into the mirror on the chest of drawers. I thought Is this Karabo this?

Thursday came, and the afternoon off. At the Black Crow I did not see Chimane. I wondered about her. In the evening I found a note under my door. It told me if Chimane was not back that evening I should know that she was at 660 3rd Avenue, Alexandra Township. I was not to tell the white people.

I asked Dick if he could not go to Alexandra with me after

I had washed the dishes. At first he was unwilling. But I said to him I said, Chimane will not believe that you refused to come with me when she sees me alone. He agreed.

On the bus Dick told me much about his younger sister whom he was helping with money to stay at school until she finished; so that she could become a nurse and a midwife. He was very fond of her, as far as I could find out. He said he prayed always that he should not lose his job, as he had done many times before, after staying a few weeks only at each job; because of this he had to borrow monies from people to pay his sister's school fees, to buy her clothes and books. He spoke of her as if she were his sweetheart. She was clever at school, pretty (she was this in the photo Dick had shown me before). She was in Orlando Township. She looked after his old people, although she was only thirteen years of age. He said to me he said Today I still owe many people because I keep losing my job. You must try to stay with Mrs. Plum, I said.

I cannot say that I had all my mind on what Dick was telling me. I was thinking of Chimane: what could she be doing? Why that note?

We found her in bed. In that terrible township where night and day are full of knives and bicycle chains and guns and the barking of hungry dogs and of people in trouble. I held my heart in my hands. She was in pain and her face, even in the candle-light, was gray. She turned her eyes at me. A fat woman was sitting in a chair. One arm rested on the other and held her chin in its palm. She had hardly opened the door for us after we had shouted our names when she was on her bench again as if there were nothing else to do.

She snorted, as if to let us know that she was going to speak. She said There is your friend. There she is my own-own niece who comes from the womb of my own sister, my sister who was make to spit out my mother's breast to give way for me. Why does she go and do such an evil thing. Ao! you young girls of today you do not know children die so fast these days that you have to thank God for sowing a seed in your womb to grow into a child. If she had let the child be born I should have looked after it or my sister would have been so happy to hold a grand-

child on her lap, but what does it help? She has allowed a
worm to cut the roots, I don't know.

Then I saw that Chimane's aunt was crying. Not once did
she mention her niece by her name, so sore her heart must have
been. Chimane only moaned.

Her aunt continued to talk, as if she was never going to stop
for breath, until her voice seemed to move behind me, not one
of the things I was thinking: trying to remember signs, however
small, that could tell me more about this moment in a dim little
room in a cruel township without street lights, near Chimane.
Then I remembered the three-legged cat, its gray-green eyes,
its miaow. What was this shadow that seemed to walk about us
but was not coming right in front of us?

I thanked the gods when Chimane came to work at the end
of the week. She still looked weak, but that shadow was no
longer there. I wondered Chimane had never told me about her
aunt before. Even now I did not ask her.

I told her I told her white people that she was ill and had
been fetched to Nokaneng by a brother. They would never try to
find out. They seldom did, these people. Give them any lie, and
it will do. For they seldom believe you whatever you say. And
how can a black person work for white people and be afraid
to tell them lies. They are always asking the questions, you are
always the one to give the answers.

Chimane told me all about it. She had gone to a woman who
did these things. Her way was to hold a sharp needle, cover the
point with the finger, and guide it into the womb. She then
fumbled in the womb until she found the egg and then pierced
it. She gave you something to ease the bleeding. But the pain,
spirits of our forefathers!

Mrs. Plum and Kate were talking about dogs one evening at
dinner. Every time I brought something to table I tried to catch
their words. Kate seemed to find it funny, because she laughed
aloud. There was a word I could not hear well which began with
sem . . . Whatever it was, it was to be for dogs. This I understood by putting a few words together. Mrs. Plum said it was
something that was common in the big cities of America, like
New York. It was also something Mrs. Plum wanted and Kate

laughed at the thought. Then later I was to hear that Monty and Malan could be sure of a nice burial.

Chimane's voice came up to me in my room the next morning, across the fence. When I come out she tells me she says Hei, child-of-my-father, here is something to tickle your ears. You know what? What? I say. She says, These white people can do things that make the gods angry. More godless people I have not seen. The madam of our house says the people of Greenside want to buy ground where they can bury their dogs. I heard them talk about it in the sitting room when I was giving them coffee last night. Hei, people, let our forefathers come and save us!

Yes, I say, I also heard the madam of our house talk about it with her daughter. I just heard it in pieces. By my mother one day these dogs will sit at table and use knife and fork. These things are to be treated like people now, like children who are never going to grow up.

Chimane sighed and she says, *Hela batho*, why do they not give me some of that money they will spend on the ground and on gravestones to buy stockings! I have nothing to put on, by my mother.

Over her shoulder I saw the cat with three legs. I pointed with my head. When Chimane looked back and saw it she said Hmm, even *they* live like kings. The mother-in-law found it on a chair and the madam said the woman should not drive it away. And there was no other chair, so the woman went to her room.

Hela!

I was going to leave when I remembered what I wanted to tell Chimane. It was that five of us had collected one pound each to lend her so that she could pay the woman of Alexandra for having done that thing for her. When Chimane's time came to receive money we collected each month and which we took in turns, she would pay us back. We were ten women and each gave two pounds at a time. So one waited ten months to receive twenty pounds. Chimane thanked us for helping her.

I went to wake up Mrs. Plum as she had asked me. She was sleeping late this morning. I was going to knock at the door when I heard strange noises in the bedroom. What is the matter with Mrs. Plum? I asked myself. Should I call her, in case she is ill? No, the noises were not those of a sick person. They were happy noises but like those a person makes in a dream, the voice full of sleep. I bent a little to peep through the keyhole. What is this? I kept asking myself. Mrs. Plum! Malan! What is she doing this one? Her arm was round Malan's belly and pressing its back against her stomach at the navel, Mrs. Plum's body in a nightdress moving in jerks like someone in fits . . . her leg rising and falling . . . Malan silent like a thing to be owned without any choice it can make to belong to another.

The gods save me! I heard myself saying, the words sounding like wind rushing out of my mouth. So this is what Dick said I would find out for myself!

No one could say where it all started; who talked about it first; whether the police wanted to make a reason for taking people without passes and people living with servants and working in town or not working at all. But the story rushed through Johannesburg that servants were going to poison the white people's dogs. Because they were too much work for us: that was the reason. We heard that letters were sent to the newspapers by white people asking the police to watch over the dogs to stop any wicked things. Some said that we the servants were not really bad, we were being made to think of doing these things by evil people in town and in the locations. Others said the police should watch out lest we poison madams and masters because black people did not know right from wrong when they were angry. We were still children at heart, others said. Mrs. Plum said that she had also written to the papers.

Then it was the police came down on the suburbs like locusts on a cornfield. There were lines and lines of men who were arrested hour by hour in the day. They liked this very much, the police. Everybody they took, everybody who was working was asked, Where's the poison eh? Where did you hide it? Who told you to poison the dogs eh? If you tell us we'll leave you to go free, you hear? and so many other things.

Dick kept saying It is wrong this thing they want to do to kill poor dogs. What have these things of God done to be killed for? Is it the dogs that make us carry passes? Is it dogs that make the laws that give us pain? People are just mad they do not

know what they want, stupid! But when white policeman spoke
to him, Dick trembled and lost his tongue and the things he
thought. He just shook his head. A few moments after they had
gone through his pockets he still held his arms stretched out, like
the man of straw who frightens away birds in a field. Only when
I hissed and gave him a sign did he drop his arms. He rushed to a
corner of the garden to go on with his work.

Mrs. Plum had put Monty and Malan in the sitting room,
next to her. She looked very much worried. She called me. She
asked me she said Karabo, you think Dick is a boy we can trust?
I did not know how to answer. I did not know whom she was
talking about when she said *we*. Then I said I do not know,
Madam. You know! she said. I looked at her. I said I do not
know what Madam thinks. She said she did not think anything,
that was why she asked. I nearly laughed because she was telling
a lie this time and not I.

At another time I should have been angry if she lied to me,
perhaps. She and I often told each other lies, as Kate and I also
did. Like when she came back from jail, after that day when she
turned a hosepipe on two policemen. She said life had been good
in jail. And yet I could see she was ashamed to have been there.
Not like our black people who are always being put in jail and
only look at it as the white man's evil game. Lilian Ngoyi often
told us this, and Mrs. Plum showed me how true those words are.
I am sure that we have kept to each other by lying to each other.

There was something in Mrs. Plum's face as she was speaking
which made me fear her and pity her at the same time. I had
seen her when she had come from prison; I had seen her when
she was shouting at Kate and the girl left the house; now there was
this thing about dog poisoning. But never had I seen her face like
this before. The eyes, the nostrils, the lips, the teeth seemed to
be full of hate, tired, fixed on doing something bad; and yet
there was something on that face that told me she wanted me on
her side.

Dick is all right madam, I found myself saying. She took
Malan and Monty in her arms and pressed them to herself,
running her hands over their heads. They looked so safe, like
a child in a mother's arm.

Mrs. Plum said All right you may go. She said Do not tell anybody what I have asked about Dick eh?

When I told Dick about it, he seemed worried.

It is nothing, I told him.

I had been thinking before that I did not stand with those who wanted to poison the dogs, Dick said. But the police have come out, I do not care what happens to the dumb things, now.

I asked him I said Would you poison them if you were told by someone to do it?

No. But I do not care, he replied.

The police came again and again. They were having a good holiday, everyone could see that. A day later Mrs. Plum told Dick to go because she would not need his work any more.

Dick was almost crying when he left. Is madam so unsure of me? he asked. I never thought a white person could fear me! And he left.

Chimane shouted from the other yard. She said, *Hei ngoana'-rona*, the Boers are fire-hot eh!

Mrs. Plum said she would hire a man after the trouble was over.

A letter came from my parents in Phokeng. In it they told me my uncle had passed away. He was my mother's brother. The letter also told me of other deaths. They said I would not remember some, I was sure to know the others. There were also names of sick people.

I went to Mrs. Plum to ask her if I could go home. She asks she says When did he die? I answer I say It is three days, madam. She says So that they have buried him? I reply Yes Madam. Why do you want to go home then? Because my uncle loved me very much madam. But what are you going to do there? To take my tears and words of grief to his grave and to my old aunt, madam. No you cannot go, Karabo. You are working for me you know? Yes, madam. I, and not your people pay you. I must go madam, that is how we do it among my people, madam. She paused. She walked into the kitchen and came out again. If you want to go, Karabo, you must lose the money for the days you will be away. Lose my pay, madam? Yes, Karabo.

The next day I went to Mrs. Plum and told her I was leaving

for Phokeng and was not coming back to her. Could she give me a letter to say that I worked for her. She did, with her lips shut tight. I could feel that something between us was burning like raw chillies. The letter simply said that I had worked for Mrs. Plum for three years. Nothing more. The memory of Dick being sent away was still an open sore in my heart.

The night before the day I left, Chimane came to see me in my room. She had her own story to tell me. Timi, her boy friend, had left her—for good. Why? Because I killed his baby. Had he not agreed that you should do it? No. Did he show he was worried when you told him you were heavy? He was worried, like me as you saw me, Karabo. Now he says if I kill one I shall eat all his children up when we are married. You think he means what he says? Yes, Karabo. He says his parents would have been very happy to know that the woman he was going to marry can make his seed grow.

Chimane was crying, softly.

I tried to speak to her, to tell her that if Timi left her just like that, he had not wanted to marry her in the first place. But I could not, no, I could not. All I could say was Do not cry, my sister, do not cry. I gave her my handkerchief.

Kate came back the morning I was leaving, from somewhere very far I cannot remember where. Her mother took no notice of what Kate said asking her to keep me, and I was not interested either.

One hour later I was on the Railway bus to Phokeng. During the early part of the journey I did not feel anything about the Greenside house I had worked in. I was not really myself, my thoughts dancing between Mrs. Plum, my uncle, my parents, and Phokeng, my home. I slept and woke up many times during the bus ride. Right through the ride I seemed to see, sometimes in sleep, sometimes between sleep and waking, a red car passing our bus, then running behind us. Each time I looked out it was not there.

Dreams came and passed. He tells me he says You have killed my seed I wanted my mother to know you are a woman in whom my seed can grow . . . Before you make the police take you to jail make sure that it is for something big you should go to jail for, otherwise you will come out with a heart and mind that will bleed inside you and poison you . . .

The bus stopped for a short while, which made me wake up.

The Black Crow, the club women . . . Hei, listen! I lie to the madam of our house and I say I had a telegram from my mother telling me she is very very sick. I show her a telegram my sister sent me as if mother were writing. So I went home for a nice weekend . . .

The laughter of the women woke me up, just in time for me to stop a line of saliva coming out over my lower lip. The bus was making plenty of dust now as it was running over part of the road they were digging up. I was sure the red car was just behind us, but it was not there when I woke.

Any one of you here who wants to be baptized or has a relative without a church who needs to be can come and see me in the office . . . A round man with a fat tummy and sharp hungry eyes, a smile that goes a long, long way . . .

The bus was going uphill, heavily and noisily.

I kick a white man's dog, me, or throw it there if it has not been told the black people's law . . . This is Mister Monty and this is Mister Malan. Now get up you lazy boys and meet Mister Kate. Hold out your hands and say hallo to him . . . Karabo, bring two glasses there . . . Wait a bit—What will you chew boys while Mister Kate and I have a drink? Nothing? Sure?

We were now going nicely on a straight tarred road and the trees rushed back. Mister Kate. What nonsense. I thought.

Look Karabo, madam's dogs are dead. What? Poison. I killed them. She drove me out of a job did she not? For nothing. Now I want her to feel she drove me out for something. I came back when you were in your room and took the things and poisoned them . . . And you know what? She has buried them in clean pink sheets in the garden. Ao, clean clean good sheets. I am going to dig them out and take one sheet do you want the other one? Yes, give me the other one I will send it to my mother . . . Hci, Karabo, see here they come. Monty and Malan. The bloody fools they do not want to stay in their hole. Go back you silly fools. Oh you do not want to move eh? Come here, now I am going to throw you in the big pool. No, Dick! No Dick! no, no! Dick!

They cannot speak do not kill things that cannot speak. Madam can speak for them she always does. No! Dick . . . !

I woke up with a jump after I had screamed Dick's name, almost hitting the window. My forehead was full of sweat. The red car also shot out of my sleep and was gone. I remembered a friend of ours who told us how she and the garden man had saved two white sheets in which their white master had buried their two dogs. They went to throw the dogs in a dam.

When I told my parents my story Father says to me he says, So long as you are in good health my child, it is good. The worker dies, work does not. There is always work. I know when I was a boy a strong sound body and a good mind were the biggest things in life. Work was always there, and the lazy man could never say there was no work. But today people see work as something bigger than everything else, bigger than health, because of money.

I reply I say, Those days are gone Papa. I must go back to the city after resting a little to look for work. I must look after you. Today people are too poor to be able to help you.

I knew when I left Greenside that I was going to return to Johannesburg to work. Money was little, but life was full and it was better than sitting in Phokeng and watching the sun rise and set. So I told Chimane to keep her eyes and ears open for a job.

I had been at Phokeng for one week when a red car arrived. Somebody was sitting in front with the driver, a white woman. At once I knew it to be that of Mrs. Plum. The man sitting beside her was showing her the way, for he pointed towards our house in front of which I was sitting. My heart missed a few beats. Both came out of the car. The white woman said "Thank you" to the man after he had spoken a few words to me.

I did not know what do and how to look at her as she spoke to me. So I looked at the piece of cloth I was sewing pictures on. There was a tired but soft smile on her face. Then I remembered that she might want to sit. I went inside to fetch a low bench for her. When I remembered it afterwards, the thought came to me that there are things I never think white people can want to do at our homes when they visit for the first time: like sitting, drinking water or entering the house. This is how I thought when the white priest came to see us. One year at Easter Kate drove me home as she was going to the north. In the same way I was at a loss what to do for a few minutes.

Then Mrs. Plum says, I have come to ask you to come back to me, Karabo. Would you like to?

I say I do not know, I must think about it first.

She says, Can you think about it today? I can sleep at the town hotel and come back tomorrow morning, and if you want to you can return with me.

I wanted her to say she was sorry to have sent me away. I did not know how to make her say it because I know white people find it too much for them to say "Sorry" to a black person. As she was not saying it, I thought of two things to make it hard for her to get me back and maybe even lose me in the end.

I say, You must ask my father first, I do not know, should I call him?

Mrs. Plum says, Yes.

I fetched both Father and Mother. They greeted her while I brought benches. Then I told them what she wanted.

Father asks mother and mother asks Father. Father asks me. I say if they agree, I will think about it and tell her the next day.

Father says, It goes by what you feel my child.

I tell Mrs. Plum I say, If you want me to think about it I must know if you will want to put my wages up from six pounds because it is too little.

She asks me, How much will you want?

Up by four pounds.

She looked down for a few moments.

And then I want two weeks at Easter and not just the weekend. I thought if she really wanted me she would want to pay for it. This would also show how sorry she was to lose me.

Mrs. Plum says, I can give you one week. You see you already have something like a rest when I am in Durban in the winter.

I tell her I say I shall think about it.

She left.

The next day she found me packed and ready to return with her. She was very much pleased and looked kinder than I had ever known her. And me, I felt sure of myself, more than I had ever done.

Mrs. Plum says to me, You will not find Monty and Malan.
Oh?

Yes, they were stolen the day after you left. The police have
not found them yet. I think they are dead myself.

I thought of Dick . . . my dream. Could he? And she . . .
did this woman come to ask me to return because she had lost
two animals she loved?

Mrs. Plum says to me she says, You know, I like your people,
Karabo, the Africans.

And Dick and Me? I wondered.

South Africa

BIOGRAPHICAL SKETCHES

LU HSUN (1881–1936), revered in China today as the literary giant of the Chinese Revolution, was, in his own time, the foremost figure of the Chinese literary revolution which raged from the overthrow of the empire in 1911 through his lifetime in the 1920s and 30s. Chou Shu-jen (the writer's real name) was born in 1881 in the city of Shaoshing into a family of scholars. He naturally received a thorough tutoring in the classics, but his father's death plunged him and his mother into poverty, and it was only through enormous struggle that she managed finally to get him into government schools. However, in spite of his training in mining and engineering and his study of medicine in Japan, he returned to his native province, Chekiang, to teach.

Following the 1911 revolution, he went to Peking, and for the fifteen years after that time, his life reflected the intense intellectual activities of the period. Having accepted a position with the Ministry of Education, he taught concurrently at three different universities. At the same time, he edited literary periodicals, translated German, Russian, and Japanese books, and became associated with the *pai-hua* (vernacular) movement. Gradually, this "brush war" of the young intellectuals came to include an attack on the whole social and political ideology of the Manchu dynasty. However, it was with the publication of the "Real Story of Ah Q" in 1921 that Lu Hsun achieved national fame and the recognized leadership of the new *pai-hua* literature.

His continued attacks in his short stories on the corruption of the government led a few years later to his forced resignation from the Ministry of Education. When, shortly after, a warrant was issued for his arrest, he left Peking for Amoy, Canton, and finally went into hiding in Shanghai. The Kuomintang massacres of thousands of Shanghai and Canton students, workers, and peasants influenced Lu Hsun in his decisive turn to the left revolutionary movement, and it was there that he remained until the end of his life in 1936. Branded by the Kuomintang as a source of especially "dangerous thought" and with many of his books banned, he was forced to live the last few years of his life in relative seclusion. Great numbers of the young intellectuals around him were imprisoned, tortured, and killed during those years, and he himself was in constant danger of arrest or assassination. It was only the great veneration in which he was held and his reputation, international as well as Chinese, which permitted him sufficient immunity to write his scathing essays and poignant and bitter short stories.

CZOE ZÔNG-HÛI (1912–   ), born in northeast Korea, is today a resident of Seoul, Korea. After her college education, she worked on a variety of magazines and newspapers. In 1956 she became Editor in Chief of *Chu-bu Saeng-hwal,* a women's monthly. In 1958, she received the Seoul city award for literature, and in 1964 the annual reward for women's literature. Her novels include *A History of Humanity, The Green Door,* and *The Endless Wandering.*

PRAMOEDNYA ANANTA TOER (1925–   ) was born in Blora, Central Java. He was active in the revolution against the Dutch (1945–1950), and it was during his imprisonment at that time that he began to write seriously. In 1950, he won a literary prize for his novel *Perburuan (Pursuit)* which was followed within the next few years by another novel, *Keluarga Gerilja (Guerrilla Family),* and a collection of short stories, *Tjerita dari Blora.* In the following decade, he continued to write socially concerned literature, including a study of overseas Chinese in Indonesia at a time when they were suffering a variety of persecutions. After the coup of 1965, in which hundreds of thousands were killed, Pramoednya was imprisoned and sent to the island of Buru, where, as far as is known, he is still held with many other political prisoners.

AN SU-GIL (1911–   ) was born in northeast Korea. After leaving Japan's Waseda University, he spent some fifteen years as a journalist for several newspapers. His early writings often depicted the scenes and lives of Korean migrant farmers in Northern Manchuria. Since the liberation of Korea from Japan in 1945, his writings have often focused on realistic descriptions of urban life and the suffering and agony of intellectuals in Korean society. From 1952 to 1965 he was a lecturer on creative writing at several leading universities and colleges in Seoul, Korea. His novels include *Windmill, The Second Youth, Buk won (The Northern Prairies).*

SUN HSI-CHEN (1906–), one of the young socially conscious writers of the 1930s in China, was born in Shaoshing, Chekiang, also the birthplace of Lu Hsun. Strongly influenced by the traditional storytellers of his locale, he began to write while still a child. As a young man, he wrote of the rural China which he knew well and of the civil war in which he grew up. The trilogy, for which he was best known at the time, was *The Field of War, War,* and *After War.* In addition, before the age of thirty, he had published six novels, a critical study of Upton Sinclair and one of Gorky, a *Life of Shelley,* a *Critique of English Literature,* and the translated *East Indian Stories.* He also wrote a textbook on Western literature and edited a book of antiwar literature.

In January 1935, during the period when Sun Hsi-chen was lecturing on Chinese and Western literature at several universities in Peking, he was among two hundred writers, artists, students, and professors arrested as part of the "thought purgation" drive led by the "Blue Jackets" of the Kuomintang. Biographical information ends at this time.

AMADOR DAGUIO (1912–) grew up in the mountain province of Northern Luzon. He began his literary career while he was studying at the University of the Philippines, with the publication of prize-winning fiction and poetry in college and national magazines. He then taught for several years in the southern islands, and it was during that time that his first volume of poetry was completed. During the years of World War II, he organized the Tacloban Theater Guild, which produced two of his plays and also published his second volume of poetry and a novel. In 1951, Daguio studied at the Stanford University Creative Writing Center, where his master's thesis was a translation of the tribal harvest songs of the Kalinga people of his native province. The story "Wedding Dance" deals with the life of the Kalingas. Upon his return to Manila, Amador Daguio studied law and has since held a number of government positions, in addition to being a university lecturer.

DORA ALONSO was born in Máximo Gómez Matanzas Province, Cuba. Her novel *Tierra Inerme* (1961) received the Casa de las Américas award and has been translated into a number of European languages. She has also published a collection of children's works, many short stories, and several plays. At present Dora Alonso is living in Cuba.

ABIOSEH NICOL (1924–) is the pen-name of one of the better-known English language writers from West Africa. Born in Sierra Leone, and educated there and in Nigeria, he later studied as well at Cambridge and London, where he received degrees in the natural sciences, medicine, and philosophy. His eminent career as an academic and medical practitioner includes numerous teaching and medical service positions in West Africa, particularly Sierra Leone.

Abioseh Nicol was awarded the Margaret Wrong Prize and Medal for literature in Africa in 1952. His poems and short stories have appeared in a number of English and American publications and have been broadcast by the BBC; two anthologies of his short stories appeared in 1965.

In 1960, Dr. Nicol was appointed Principal of Fourah Bay College; later he served as Vice-Chancellor of the entire University of Sierra Leone, and in 1968 became the Sierra Leonean Ambassador to the United Nations.

AMA ATA AIDOO (1942–) was born and educated in Ghana. She attended Wesley Girls High School and the University of Ghana at Legon, where in 1964 she received a B.A. Her first play, *The Dilemma of a Ghost*, was produced at the University of Ghana in 1964.

Miss Aidoo's poems and short stories have appeared in various African journals, including the literary journal *Okeyearne* and *Black Orpheus*, and both have been frequently anthologized in Africa, and in England and the United States. Her second play, *Anowa*, based on a story she had heard from her mother in the form of a song, was published in London in 1969, and is to be translated into Swahili and produced in East Africa. Miss Aidoo now lectures and does research, particularly concerning contemporary Ghanaian drama, in the Department of African Studies at the University of Ghana.

RUSMAN SUTIASUMARGA (1917–) was born in Subang, West Java. The area from which he comes is that of the Sundanese people, and it is with this background that much of his work is concerned. He has been active in Sundanese cultural groups and activities, and most of his published stories show a strong Sundanese flavor.

OKOT P'BITEK (1931–) was born at Gulu in Northern Uganda. Educated at Gulu High School and King's College, Budo, he later studied education at Bristol, law at Aberystwyth, and social anthropology at Oxford, where in 1963 he presented his thesis on Acoli and Lango traditional songs. In 1964 he returned to Uganda, lecturing at Makerere in the Department of Sociology.

Mr. p'Bitck's Lwo novel, *Lak Tar*, appeared in 1953, *Song of Lawino* in 1966, and *Song of Ocol* in 1970, along with many poems and articles published in East African magazines and journals. *Song of Lawino* was translated from the Acoli by the author.

Mr. p'Bitek is now Director of the West Kenya section of the Extra-Mural Department, University College, Nairobi, and in 1971 was writer in residence at the University of Iowa.

SANTHA RAMA RAU (1923–   ) was born into a distinguished Indian official family. Because of the position of her father, the diplomat Sir Benegal Rama Rau, she spent some of her childhood in England and also traveling throughout various parts of her own country. As a university student, she went to the United States, where she graduated from Wellesley College. She wrote her first book while she was there.

After her return to India, she began her journalistic career working on several Bombay magazines. She published her first book in 1945, *Home to India*. In 1947, she accompanied her father, independent India's first Ambassador to Japan, and acted as his official hostess. Her subsequent travels in the Far East provided substantial material for her many articles, short stories, and books. They include *East of Home, This is India, Remember the House* (a novel), *View to the Southeast, My Russian Journey, and Gifts of Passage.* The story "Who Cares?" is an autobiographical selection from *Gifts of Passage*.

TOKUDA SHŪSEI (1870–1943) was a leader of the strict naturalist school of Japanese literature which exercised an important influence, particularly during the period following the Russo-Japanese War (1904–1905). As a young man, he had gone directly into magazine and newspaper writing after leaving school and did not receive a university education. His first serious work, which he did not begin until his thirties, consisted mainly of romantic stories. However, it was not until he finally turned to naturalism that he won recognition with his first long novel, *The New Home* (*Shinjotai*). This was then followed by a prodigious output of novels in which he continued to develop his direct, objective naturalist approach. "Order of the White Paulownia" ("Kumsho" in Japanese) was published in 1935 when the author was sixty-five and is characteristic of his interest in portraying the struggles of the women of the lower middle class and working class in Japan's industrial cities.

SHIH MING ("Lost Name" in Chinese) is one of a number of pseudonyms used by the writer Yang Ping. She was born in 1908, one of eighteen children, into a high official's family of Hupeh Province. She first became well-known as a North China student leader when she was studying at Yenching University. She was arrested in 1930 for leading a street demonstration demanding the release of fifty student political prisoners. During the period of the early thirties, she edited two magazines, *Youth of North China* and *Red Flag of the North*. In 1933, she began to write short stories and by 1934 had published six. In line with her training in sociology, in March 1937, she published a middle school textbook called "Chinese Society and Training for Future Social Life," a historical study. During the same period, she became one of the first successful newspaperwomen in China, working on the Tientsin newspaper *Ta Kung Pao*, where she edited the leading literary supplement in the country. She studied in America at Radcliffe in the late 1940s, returning to China at the end of that decade.

NYUGEN SANG's "The Ivory Comb" appears in a collection of the same name published by the Giai Phong Publishing House, Vietnam. The author's biography was unavailable.

ALEX LA GUMA (1925–   ) was born and spent his childhood in Cape Town, South Africa. After completing high school there, he worked as a clerk, factory hand, messenger, bookkeeper, and photographer. He briefly studied painting, and then turned to writing, working for a Cape Town newspaper as reporter and columnist and at the same time writing fiction.

Mr. La Guma was one of the 156 persons accused in the 1956 South African treason trial; he was acquitted three years later. During the 1960 state of emergency, as an executive member of the Coloured People's Congress, he was detained in prison for five months; a year later he was arrested again, for his activities against the Verwoerd Republic. In 1962 he was placed under house arrest for five years, and all his statements and writings were banned throughout the Republic; during this period he was also arrested and served a period in solitary confinement.

Mr. La Guma has written many short stories, published in South Africa, western Africa, Brazil, Sweden, Finland, England, and the United States. His first novel, *Walk in the Night,* appeared in 1962; two further novels, *And a Threefold Cord* and *The Stone Country,* were published in 1964 and 1967 respectively. He and his family now live in England.

MARJORIE J. MBILINYI (1943–) was born in New York City, and spent her early years in the New York area. She attended college first at Cornell and then at Stanford, where she received an M.A. in the School of Education. In 1966 she emigrated to Tanzania, teaching at the University of Dar-es-Salaam, and becoming a Tanzanian citizen in 1968.

"A Woman's Life" is Mrs. Mbilinyi's second published story; the first, "A Child is Born," appeared in *Zuka* in 1969. In addition she has done considerable academic writing, with a major focus on the position of women in Tanzania, and a second interest in rural education. Her articles have appeared in East African, Canadian, and American journals.

Mrs. Mbilinyi is at present (1972–1973) a Research Associate at the African Studies Center at Michigan State University, on leave from her position as Lecturer in the Department of Education, University of Dar-es-Salaam. She lives in Tanzania with her husband and two young daughters.

RICHARD RIVE (1931–) was born in Cape Town, South Africa, where he attended high school, after winning a municipal scholarship. Later he qualified as a teacher at Hewat Training College, and graduated in English from the University of Cape Town. Mr. Rive's many well-known short stories have appeared in South African, American, and British journals and anthologies, and in translation into more than a dozen languages, among them Swedish, German, and Finnish. He has edited two anthologies, *Quartet* and *Modern African Prose*. A collection of his own short stories, *African Songs*, appeared in 1963, and his first novel, *Emergency*, in 1964. Mr. Rive teaches English and Latin at a high school in Cape Town.

EZEKIEL MPHALELE was born in Pretoria, South Africa, and taught high school in Johannesburg until the government dismissed him for his criticism of the African educational program. In 1957 he worked for the University of Idadan in the field of English language and literature. Since then he taught English literature at University College, Nairobi, and was visiting professor at the University of Denver, where he is now a member of the faculty of the department of English. He is best known for his short stories, of which several anthologies have appeared, including *Man Must Live* (1947), *The Living and the Dead* (1960), and *In Corner B* (1967), from which "Mrs. Plum" was taken. His full-length autobiographical work, *Down Second Avenue*, was published in 1959, *The African Image*, a book of political and literary essays, in 1962, and an autobiographical novel, *The Wanderers*, in 1971.

ABOUT THE EDITORS

NAOMI KATZ is an assistant professor of anthropology at San Francisco State University. A graduate of Stanford, she lived in Paris for two years, and then received her Ph.D. in anthropology from U.C.L.A. She is an African specialist and has published articles in the areas of folklore and Native American studies as well. She is an editor of the forthcoming *100 Years of Anthropology*.

NANCY MILTON teaches English to foreign students in the San Francisco Community College district. She is a graduate in creative writing from Stanford University with an M.A. from San Francisco State. A teacher at the Peking First Foreign Languages Institute in the People's Republic of China from 1964–1969, she is currently writing a Pantheon book with her husband, David, on the Cultural Revolution and is an editor with Franz Schurmann and David Milton of Volume IV of *The China Reader*.